Praise for
THE SECRETS SHE CARRIED

"I read Barbara Davis's debut novel, *The Secrets She Carried*, deep into the night—one minute rushing to discover how the mysteries resolved, the next slowing. . . . Adele Laveau's haunting voice and Leslie Nichols's journey toward understanding lingered long after I read the final page of this engrossing tale."

—Julie Kibler, author of *Calling Me Home*

"*The Secrets She Carried* is a beautifully crafted page-turner with many twists but a simple theme: No matter how far you run, you can't escape your past. Part contemporary women's fiction, part historical novel, the plot moves seamlessly back and forth in time to unlock family secrets that bind four generations of women. Add a mysterious death, love that defies the grave, and the legacy of redemption, and this novel has it all."

—Barbara Claypole White, author of *The Unfinished Garden*

"I was swept into Adele's heartbreaking life and her devotion to those she loved."—Susan Crandall, author of *Whistling Past the Graveyard*

Written by today's freshest new talents and selected by New American Library, NAL Accent novels touch on subjects close to a woman's heart, from friendship to family to finding our place in the world. The Conversation Guides included in each book are intended to enrich the individual reading experience, as well as encourage us to explore these topics together—because books, and life, are meant for sharing.

Visit us online at www.penguin.com.

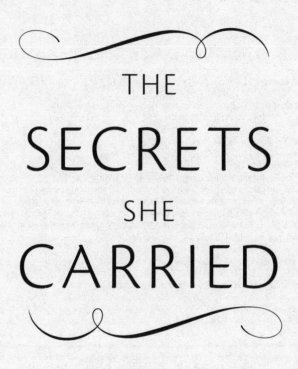

THE
SECRETS
SHE
CARRIED

BARBARA DAVIS

NAL Accent
Published by the Penguin Group
Penguin Group (USA) LLC, 375 Hudson Street,
New York, New York 10014

USA | Canada | UK | Ireland | Australia | New Zealand | India | South Africa | China
penguin.com
A Penguin Random House Company

First published by NAL Accent, an imprint of New American Library,
a division of Penguin Group (USA) LLC

First Printing, October 2013

 REGISTERED TRADEMARK—MARCA REGISTRADA

LIBRARY OF CONGRESS CATALOGING-IN-PUBLICATION DATA:

Davis, Barbara, 1961–
    The secrets she carried/Barbara Davis.
       pages cm
    ISBN 978-0-451-41877-7
       1. Homecoming—Fiction. 2. Plantations—North Carolina—Fiction. 3. Tobacco farms—North Carolina—Fiction. 4. Family secrets—Fiction. 5. North Carolina—Fiction. I. Title.
       PS3604.A95554S43 2013
       813'.6—dc23   2013017098

Printed in the United States of America
10 9 8 7 6 5 4 3 2 1

Set in Carré Noir Std
Designed by Alissa Amell

For my mother, my grandmother, and my great-grandmother: three generations of women who through their daily example taught me the true meaning of beauty, strength, and love. This book is for you—and because of you.

Acknowledgments

With a first book it's difficult to know where to begin all the thanking. So many wonderful people have been a part of this amazing journey. From the moment the first tiny seed for *The Secrets She Carried* popped into my head until the day it finally landed on the shelves, I have had more support than I can ever properly acknowledge.

However, I must begin somewhere, and there is no better place than with Tom Kelley, the love of my life and my biggest fan, for encouraging me to chase my dream, and for holding my hand every step of the way while I did. For all the brainstorming sessions, edited pages, and long drives in the country when I found myself stuck, I thank you, thank you, thank you. You are the hero I wish for all my heroines.

I would also be remiss if I did not tip my hat to fate for leading me to my amazing and tireless agent, Nalini Akolekar of Spencerhill Associates, Ltd., who believed in the book from day one, and was never too busy to walk a first-timer through the process and, more than once, to talk her back from the ledge.

Also earning a sincere thanks are my friends and writing partners from Triangle Writer's Group in Raleigh: Lisa Cameron Rosen, Matt King, Doug Simpson, Tara Lynne Groth, Susie Potter, Greg Welker, John Flanagan, and Jack De Veaux, who kindly contributed their time and ideas to the shaping of Adele's and Leslie's stories. Your support and friendship have meant more to me than you know.

Next, I must say an enormous thank-you to the entire team at Penguin, but especially to my editors, Jhanteigh Kupihea and Sandra Harding, who took four hundred pages of scribble and turned them into a book. Words cannot express how fortunate I feel to have had you in my corner.

Last, and, as they say, certainly not least, I wish to express my heartfelt thanks to every teacher I ever had and to all the teachers in our classrooms today, whose talents and dedication ensure that books will continue to be written and read. You too are my heroes.

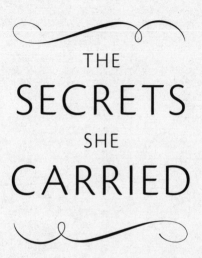

THE
SECRETS
SHE
CARRIED

Prologue

Adele

Peak Plantation, 1940

I believe it's the cold I remember most.

Yes, I still feel the cold. I still feel a lot of things. Like the deep-down shiver of my sweet little Maggie as she stands beside her daddy, stealing fingers the color of bone into his calloused brown hand, needing his warmth. But there is no warmth in him, my poor, dear Henry, and it grinds my heart to see it. Yes, I still have a heart too. Or an ache, at least, where it used to be.

Maggie clutches at the buttoned-up collar of her black wool coat, hunching her shoulders as if to hoard her heat. I want to scold her for not remembering her gloves—and Henry, too, for not looking after her. He's dressed her up, I see, put her in her yellow dress from last Easter, the one with the bow in back. Already her knees are blue with cold.

But it's not in me to be angry. The man next to Maggie hardly resembles the one I knew, and I knew Henry Gavin well. He's hollowed out now, hardly there at all, though his boots still leave prints in the earth. And he never leaves off staring at that stone. I knew right off where he was going when he cranked up that old truck, and I knew right off why. He means to tell her.

She's a beautiful child. Her face is so still and pale, like a doll's, the fine blue-white of china, and her gray eyes are wide and shimmery from the chill. My arms long to go around her, to hold her close, to keep her warm and guard her against all that may come. For a moment the pain is so raw it nearly bends me in two. You forget sometimes to steel yourself against those moments. You think it all stops, but it doesn't. You can still hurt, long after you're dead and gone.

Well, if the child must know, and it seems she must, I wish it were me doing the telling. Men don't do these things well. She's already confused. I could see it in her face when he got out of the truck and started walking, and I see it again now as she follows her daddy's eyes to the pale slab of soapstone.

It's my stone, my bones that lie beneath that mound of dark earth, all fenced in with pretty black iron. There's a gate with two doves and a shiny brass lock to keep me in my place. Too late for that, I guess. There are words inscribed there, but no dates and no name. Thank heaven, at least, for that.

The sun comes through the clouds like ice water, and the wind makes a sound like crying. Maggie's hair lifts out around her head like smoke. "It's beautiful, Daddy," is all she can think to whisper. Her voice is soft as a secret.

Henry isn't wearing a coat over his gray flannel suit, and the breeze yanks at his tie, whipping it like a flag over one shoulder. His eyes look so tired, so far away. He doesn't blink, just stares back at her with his Adam's apple bobbing against his collar. His mouth begins to churn finally, but no words come, and all at once there are no more questions in his daughter's eyes.

What can the old fool be thinking? He must see that no good can come of it. Even the child knows that. And what in God's name would the fine folk of Gavin, North Carolina, have to say if they learned he had buried his wife's maid up on his precious ridge? I don't belong here. There are places for us, separate places far off from our betters. My stone should be proof enough of that. We've already given those stiff-necks and their kind enough wood to burn.

Maggie tries again for her father's hand, but he's forgotten she's there. She steps to the stone alone and goes to her knees. Her fingers are blue as she folds them beneath her chin. It's the first time I've wanted to cry, and the first time I realize I no longer can. It doesn't seem fair when your heart still aches so. But so much isn't fair.

"It's time to go, child," Henry calls out. His voice is thick and unfamiliar, like when you wake from a dream. "I've got work to do, and your—" He stops, glances away, clears his throat. "Your mama will be wondering where you got to."

Maggie stands facing him. Her knees are stained and she scrubs at them with the heels of her hands. I'm relieved that they're going. He sees now that it's the wrong time to tell her, that it will always be the wrong time. There's no point, after all. Not anymore. But Maggie isn't ready to go. She turns back, bending to read the stone's brief inscription. Her mouth moves over the words—words so precious I feel them like a wound.

I shall but love thee better after death.

The eyes she turns to her father are shiny with tears. Her tiny shoulders rack with silent sobs. And in that moment, I see Henry change his mind.

"Maggie, I want you to listen." His voice is dry like paper as he clamps his rough brown hands on her shoulders. "There's something I—"

But she won't listen. She claps her fists over her ears, shakes her head from side to side, and her words wrench my soul. "Never say it," she whispers. "If you say it, then it's true."

For a moment Henry goes rigid, and I believe he will fall into little pieces at the child's feet. The air goes out of him suddenly, a long, slow gush of breath, a kind of caving in. It makes him smaller somehow, frail in a way I never noticed. Let it go, Henry. You must leave it where it stands. The child has asked you to.

Maggie has him by the sleeve now, tugging him against his will back to the present. "We better get back," she says, her voice strangely grown-up. "Mama's going to want to know where we've been. We'll stop up at Jackson's and get you some cigarettes. You can tell her you ran into old man Gainey or somebody."

She starts for the truck then, her cold blue fists knotted at her sides. I can tell by the tilt of her head that she's listening for footsteps, but there are no footsteps, only the low keening of her daddy's heart breaking wide open.

Chapter 1

Leslie

New York City, 2013

Leslie Nichols eyed the answering machine's cool blue pulse with fresh dread. If she'd learned anything in her thirty-seven years, it was that flashing blue lights usually meant trouble, and whatever was waiting for her on that machine would prove no exception. She knew it the same way she knew today's stack of mail meant trouble. No surprise, really. It had been that kind of year, a demoralizing charade of *let's keep in touch* lunches that never went anywhere.

It was almost hard to believe. Two years ago she'd been the hottest name in the industry, the up-and-coming diva of the luxury-lifestyle spread. Now, thanks to electronic media's blight on the magazine world, she couldn't even find a job. Print publications were quickly becoming endangered species, with new launches like *Edge*—the magazine she'd almost single-handedly put on the map—among the first to become extinct, leaving her with a stack of unpaid bills and a plummeting bank balance.

As she kicked off her shoes she gave the mail a quick shuffle—no surprises, since the senders had been thoughtful enough to stamp PAST DUE and FINAL NOTICE all over the envelopes—then held her breath and jabbed the answering machine's message button.

Leslie let her breath go when she heard the familiar voice: Gwen

Waters from the offices of Goddard and Goddard. At least she didn't owe *them* money. In fact, she wasn't even sure why they were still pestering her. Maggie's estate had nothing to do with her. There was nothing for her at Peak Plantation, just questions and ghosts, neither of which she cared to confront after thirty years of carefully preserved distance. Nothing that belonged to her, and certainly nothing she deserved.

After a year of unreturned phone calls she would have thought she'd made that much clear. But Gwen Waters was still talking, something about the window for Leslie to claim her grandmother's estate set to expire at the end of the month, about the property defaulting to another beneficiary if she didn't contact their office in the next forty-eight hours.

Leslie blinked at the machine as the message ran out. Another beneficiary? Before she could hit the button to replay the message, a new voice filled the small kitchen, deep and familiar and far less pleasant. The floor seemed to shift as it penetrated, like bourbon and smoke cutting across the distance and the latest gap of years. No explanation, no apology, just Jimmy. She didn't listen to the whole thing. She didn't have to. It was the same message he left every few years. He was about to become a free man and would need a bit of cash to finance his reentry into society. Yes, sir, he sure was looking forward to seeing his Baby Girl.

So here it was, then, the trouble she knew she'd find at the other end of that pulsing blue light: Jimmy. That she didn't want to see him made no difference. He would show up on her doorstep, unless, of course, she made it worth his while to stay away, which was the part he never said but always meant. It was how things worked between them. The last time she tried telling him no, she came home to find him on the sidewalk in front of her building with a prison haircut and an old green suitcase. She had written him a check on the spot. Only this time there wasn't any money.

The thought of Jimmy moving in brought a clammy wave of panic, the kind she'd experienced often while growing up but believed she had outgrown—or at least outdistanced. Now that distance appeared to be shrinking. Under the circumstances, it hardly seemed fair. But then, in her experience, fate was rarely fair. Time, once again, to gird her loins. Maybe her life was a huge question mark at the moment, but she'd be damned if she'd let a boozy ex-con add to the tangle, even if that ex-con *was* her father.

Staring at the stack of unpaid bills still clutched in her fist, Leslie choked back a bubble of laughter. Fate might not be fair, but it definitely had a sense of humor. Maybe there was a reason Gwen Waters called today with her time limit and threat of another beneficiary. Maybe it was to remind her that while she didn't have many options, she did have at least one.

Going back to Peak was an absurd idea, and yet the more she pondered it, the more it made perfect sense. In Gavin she'd be miserable but safe. And if Jimmy did figure out where she was, she doubted he'd have the nerve to show his face.

Still, the thought of going back made her palms go sticky. It would mean giving up her apartment, as good as an admission of defeat, but it would buy her some time. She could disappear for a while, raise some cash with the sale of the plantation. Not much probably, but enough to keep her afloat until she found a job.

Leaving the bills on the counter, she wandered into the living room and poured herself a drink, then headed for her favorite chair, a sleek red leather cube that had cost her two weeks' pay. She had grown to love New York, especially at this time of day, when the sun began to slide and the light melted like butter onto the buildings, washing the skyline like an old sepia shot. Was she really ready to walk away? To give up her swanky address and the prospect—however dim—of another six-figure salary?

The thought left her hollow, but then so did the thought of Jimmy, camped out on her doorstep. Too restless to sit, she pushed out of her chair and stepped to the window. Her knees felt like Slinkies as she stared at the cars crawling like so many ants on the street below. The vodka was doing its work. A few more and she wouldn't give a damn.

Except she had to give a damn. She had to make a decision.

Jimmy's message said a couple of weeks. That wasn't much time. Thirty years *was* a lot of time, though. Thirty years since the inquest into her mother's death. Thirty years trying to outrun demons she wasn't even sure were real. Maybe Jimmy wasn't the only reason to return to Peak, or even the best one. New York didn't offer much at the moment—no work, no love life, a handful of acquaintances she barely saw anymore. Maybe it was time to stop running and finally confront those demons—real or imagined—while Peak still belonged to her. Maybe it was simply time to go home.

Leslie felt stiff and cranky, the highway a blur of asphalt and gritty guardrail as she crossed over into North Carolina. It had taken just three days to tie up the loose ends of her life, a fact she found too depressing to examine in any depth. The truth was, aside from her apartment, which she'd managed to sublet to an old work colleague, and a designer wardrobe she had consigned to storage with the certainty that she'd never wear any of it again, there had been precious little to handle.

She still wasn't convinced that going back wasn't a huge mistake. She just hadn't been able to find enough reasons to stay. Jimmy would go to New York, but this time when he knocked on her door she wouldn't be there. There wasn't much about her father that made her laugh, but it was hard not to smirk at the thought of him being greeted by Doug Somers, with his eyebrow ring and platinum hair, or better yet, by his partner, Stephen, whose weekend tastes tended toward knockoff Vera Wang.

A sign for SR 86 suddenly loomed. Leslie jerked the wheel, waving an apology to the blaring horn behind her as she jumped three lanes of traffic. The sign at the foot of the ramp said fifty miles to Gavin. She wished it was more.

Her stomach clenched unpleasantly when she finally turned onto Gavin Boulevard, the two-lane road that cut through the heart of town. Almost nothing had changed. Here and there, pale steeples thrust themselves against the hot blue sky—Baptist, Methodist, Presbyterian, in place since time immemorial. The Gavin town hall still stood proudly, every brick and blade as it ever was, on what had once been an honest-to-God drilling green. The Mule and Tobacco Exchange still occupied the block between Meeting and Market, though a good half century had passed since it had traded either.

It took less than five minutes to cover downtown. On the way out she passed the Anytime Diner, a tarnished silver box in a half-paved parking lot, it's neon sign flickering: LAST CHANCE FOR EATS. It had been her favorite place once, a reward for good report cards and As on spelling tests. Then Jimmy had started sneaking around with Rachel Ranson, whose daddy owned the place, and no one would take her there anymore.

Goosing the pedal, she pushed through a wide curve, then flattened out on the narrow road that skirted Gavin, two lanes of pocked gray pavement that sent the late-day heat up in shiny waves. The air was full of hay and horse and fertilizer. She was getting close.

When Peak finally came into view it was unexpected somehow, like a full white moon at four in the afternoon. Leslie let the car slow to a crawl. She had expected it to be smaller, like all childhood places when you visited them as an adult. She had also expected it to be half falling down. It was neither. It was just as she remembered, lofty and bone white on its jade green hill, boasting a full complement of freshly painted porches and columns.

She parked on a patch of gravel meant for guests and sat with the car running, knuckles white against the wheel. She wasn't ready to be here. Maybe it wasn't too late to turn around and go back to New York. Maybe Doug and Stephen would let her have the spare room.

After a few moments she killed the engine and got out. The air was as thick as syrup, sticky and still and humming with tiny insects. A film of sweat beaded her upper lip as she paused in the driveway to take in old landmarks: the small cottage back in the trees, the lake where she'd learned to swim, and in the distance, the jutting shelf of land named for the great-grandfather she had never known, Henry's Ridge.

Pivoting slowly, Leslie let her eyes roam the fields, scanning row upon row of trellised vines where acres of bright leaf once stood. She hadn't expected tobacco—her grandmother had put a stop to that the day they buried her husband, a martyr to his two-pack-a-day habit. But she certainly hadn't expected grapes either. Whose idea...? Never mind. It would keep until tomorrow when she met with the attorneys. Right now all she wanted was to get through this part. Seeing the foyer and the stairs would be the worst. After that she'd be fine.

She was halfway up the walk when she realized she hadn't given a thought to how she might get in the house. It simply hadn't occurred to her. Maggie had never locked the doors. No one in Gavin did. She eyed the knocker a moment, a big brass oval with a cursive *P* carved into its heart, then realized with a small shock that the door was actually ajar.

Giving it a nudge, she stepped inside. Her eyes were slow to adjust, but gradually, shadows grew solid; a ladder-back chair, a heavy oak hall tree, a banjo clock. Her gaze slid to the foot of the stairs, to the small Turkish rug at the base of the last step. What would she find if she lifted it? Would the stain still be visible after so many years?

Leslie's throat thickened as the memory surfaced, the dark, vicious pool of her mother's blood spreading over the freshly polished floor-boards, the scissors glittering sharply between her ribs. Pressing back against the wall, she sidled toward the parlor. She wasn't ready to think about that day. Not yet.

"Hello?"

Leslie's head snapped up as if it were on marionette strings.

The disembodied voice came again, louder this time, echoing down the staircase. "Is someone there?"

There were footsteps on the landing now. He—whoever he was—stood midway down the stairs, a stepladder dangling from one shoulder. He wore jeans with one knee blown out, work boots worn dark at the toes, and a shirt that was more out than in. A repairman, Leslie guessed, probably sent by the attorneys after she called to tell them she was on her way.

"Well, well, well," he said, propping the ladder against the bannis-ter. "The prodigal granddaughter has returned at last."

Leslie blinked up at him, startled by the undisguised hostility in his voice. Before she could think of a response, he was down the stairs and standing in front of her. His eyes raked her coolly, missing nothing along the way.

"Jay Davenport," he said at last, extending a hand. Leslie shook it briefly, registering calloused fingers, nails white with caulk. She could see his face now, angled and tan, with a fresh overlay of sunburn. Pale creases fanned out from the corners of eyes the smoky amber of single-malt scotch.

"You work here, I assume?"

"Something like that," he answered without a hint of smile. "God-dard said you'd finally decided to show up."

There it was again, that snarky, undisguised antagonism. Leslie let her breath out slowly. She was too tired for a battle with a handyman, or anyone for that matter. "What is it you do around here, Mr. Dav-enport? Maggie's been gone almost a year."

The amber eyes narrowed. "You call her Maggie?"

"It was her name. And you've changed the subject."

A tiny pulse appeared along the right side of his jaw. "Your grandmother and I had an arrangement, Miss Nichols, which you'd know if you'd ever bothered to pick up a phone. I must say, your devotion is touching. It only took you a year to get here."

Leslie's mouth worked mutely as she shuffled through her deck of excuses, discarding them one by one. She deserved every word, of course, though certainly not from this stranger, whoever he might be. She would have told him so, too, if he hadn't already stalked past her and out the door.

Standing alone in the foyer, Leslie felt the silence crowding in, thick with time and memory. From somewhere in the house came the distant tick of a clock, as steady and sure as a heartbeat, unnerving somehow against the quiet. Could she do this? Live in this house with its uneasy memories? She had convinced herself it was what she needed to do, face it all head-on, stare down her guilt, sort out her questions. Now she wasn't sure.

Stepping into the parlor, she let her eyes roam the familiar, resting a moment to digest some small memory before moving on. The furniture was far from grand, a striped sofa of green and gold brocade that had once been plush but now leaned toward shabby, a pair of brocade wingbacks a bit saggy in the seat, a walnut table scattered with family photos.

The closest one was framed in heavy silver. She picked it up. She had no memory of Henry Gavin, Maggie's father and the man who'd made Peak the legend it had once been. He looked to have been in his thirties when the photograph was taken, roughhewn and handsome in a Gary Cooper sort of way, his dark suit hanging on his lean frame like someone else's skin.

Returning Henry's photo to its place, she moved on to the next, a colt-legged version of herself at five or six, preening in a swimsuit with a frilly ballerina skirt. Her mother's picture was there too, a dark-haired beauty of sixteen or so in a sundress and sandals. Seeing it beside her own took Leslie off guard. It was startling to realize just how much she resembled Amanda Nichols. How many times had she tried in vain to conjure her mother's face, when all she needed to do was look in a mirror? Her eyes slid to the portrait above the mantel. Maggie in bridal lace and the Gavin family pearls. Here too her own features were visible. Clearly, the Gavin genes ran strong.

Maggie's room, at the back of the house, was eerily unchanged. The old tester bed Leslie had napped in as a child still bloomed with pink and yellow roses. The vanity where she had played dress-up still winked with its collection of silver-topped jars. And Maggie's jewelry box. Lifting the lid, she picked through the tangle of costume pieces, looking for the pair of black velvet pouches her grandmother had always nestled near the bottom. She hadn't thought of them in years but was strangely relieved now to find them where they belonged. Breath held, she poured out the contents of the first pouch, a strand of creamy pearls, as cool and smooth as satin against her palm, a bloodred garnet winking in the heavy filigree gold clasp.

One day these will be yours. One day when I'm gone.

She had never bothered to inquire just where it was her grand-mother was going, but then children never put much stock in *one day*—perhaps because *one day* never seemed to come. Her throat burned a little as she returned the first pouch to the jewelry box and picked up the second. Its contents had always been a mystery, pre-sumably too fragile or precious for dress-up. But she was all grown up now, and there was no one to tell her no.

She worked a moment at the strings, then teased out the contents, gasping as the pale blue cameo fell into her hand. It was a beautiful piece, exquisitely carved, set in intricately woven loops of silver. But she had no recollection of Maggie ever wearing it. Lifting the cameo to her throat, she peered at her reflection in the trifold mirror and found herself startled again by her resemblance to Maggie, and to her mother.

Ghosts. Everywhere she looked—ghosts.

Chapter 2

Jay

Peak Plantation, 2013

Jay laid a second batch of bacon in the skillet, gave the potatoes a shake, then turned to take his frustrations out on a waiting bowl of eggs. He had posts to repair and the rest of the spraying to finish, and the tractor was on life support again. Instead, here he stood in Maggie's kitchen, burning daylight. Apparently, Peak's new mistress required a lesson in the differences between a working farm and a bed-and-breakfast.

But that wasn't what this morning was supposed to be about. After the mess he'd made of their initial meeting, he'd meant for breakfast to be a kind of peace offering. He had never expected her to turn up. Now that she had, he needed to make nice, despite his overwhelming desire to tell her exactly what he thought—that after all this time she had no right to her grandmother's legacy, no right to be here at all. Except she was here, and somewhere in some dark corner of his mind, he swore he heard Maggie's papery whisper.

I told you so.

Damn the Old Broad for being right after all. She'd always said Leslie would find her way home one day. Too bad it was only to collect her share of the inheritance.

Before he could work up a fresh head of steam, he heard the scuff of feet on the back stairs, followed by a whiff of something spicy and expensive. Pasting on a smile, he turned to find Leslie at the foot of the stairs, runway perfect in a white blouse and tailored black slacks, her dark hair scraped into a ponytail so tight it lifted the corners of her eyes.

She propped a hand on one hip and glared at him. "What are you doing here?"

Jay ignored the question as he filled a mug with coffee and placed it on the table beside the cream and sugar. "That's yours."

Leslie eyed it warily but finally dropped into a chair and reached for the sugar. "Thank you. Now let's try it again. What are you doing here?"

Jay divided scrambled eggs between two plates, then added bacon. "That's fairly obvious, isn't it? I'm making you breakfast."

"Why?"

"Because I thought you might be hungry. I knew there wasn't much in the house."

Her eyes were narrowed on him—startling eyes he saw now, mossy green with a blaze of bronze around the pupil. He set both plates on the table, then slid into the chair beside her. He managed a sheepish smile.

"Last night, when you came in, I was—"

"Rude?"

It was all Jay could do to keep the smile in place. "I was going to say inhospitable, but I guess rude works too."

She had been peering sideways at him over her mug. She lowered it now. "Are you always so . . . inhospitable?"

"Only when I've had a lousy day, which I had." He picked up his fork and used it to point to her plate. "Go on and eat. I put dill in the eggs. I only do that for visiting dignitaries."

Leslie shot him a look but picked up her fork, poking dubiously at her breakfast. "You seem pretty comfortable in the kitchen."

Jay shrugged. "I like to cook."

"I meant you seem pretty comfortable in *this* kitchen."

Ah, now they were getting down to it. Next would come the questions, followed by the answers she didn't want to hear, followed by God knew what. Draining his mug, he stood to retrieve the pot from the counter, as good a way as any to stall for time. The eager tap of nails alerted him that they had company, but before he had time to turn and open his mouth, Belle was already making a beeline for Leslie. He smothered a laugh as she shoved back from the table, eyes wide with alarm.

"It's a Weimaraner, Leslie, not a lion."

"I know that, but where did he come from?"

"He's a *she*, actually. And she's mine. Her name is Belle."

"As in silver bells?"

"No. As in Belle Watling from *Gone with the Wind*. Maggie named her."

Leslie stroked one of Belle's ears cautiously. "She always loved that movie."

Jay brought the pot to the table and topped off her mug. "She did. I finally broke down and bought her a copy so she could watch it whenever she wanted."

Leslie frowned but said nothing as she picked up her fork again. They ate in silence for a while, with Belle waiting nearby to scarf up the results of any mishaps. He was just beginning to think he'd sidestepped the worst of it, when Leslie pushed back her plate and turned her green eyes on him.

"So," she said, folding her arms on the edge of the table. "We've established that Maggie named your dog and that you know your way around her kitchen even better than I do. What we haven't established is why."

Jay picked up his last strip of bacon and folded it into his mouth, then stood to collect his plate and silverware. He said nothing as he carried them to the sink, content to let her wait while he peeled back his sleeves and flipped on the tap.

Leslie joined him at the sink with her plate. "Is there a reason you won't answer me?"

"There is, as a matter of fact," he said, turning off the tap and firing the sponge into the sink. "For starters, it was a stupid question. It's also one you already know the answer to, but here it is anyway. For the last five years, while you were off somewhere being important, I was right here—when she got sick, when they buried her, and every day since."

Jay wanted to regret the words but couldn't. They were true. For a moment she stood there with her plate and fistful of dirty silverware, so stunned and still he thought she might actually cry. Instead, she dumped her plate in the sink, clearly not caring that she had soaked the front of his shirt in the process.

"Why I stayed away is none of your business. Neither is why I'm back. Why you're here, however, is very much *my* business. Now, for the last time, I'd like an answer."

Jay grabbed the dish towel, making a pretense of drying himself off while he cast about for something like an answer. How much did he volunteer, and how much did he let her find out on her own? His gut told him the truth might go down more easily coming from someone else.

"Have you spoken to the lawyers?"

"Today, at one."

"And have you given any thought as to what you might do with the place?"

Leslie folded her arms. "I'm not sure how that's any of your business. I'm also not sure why my being here has pissed you off, but I am here, and I'll make my decisions when I'm good and ready."

Jay went still while the words sank in. If she decided to sell, she would blow their plans sky-high. In all his careful planning, he had never planned for this, never let himself think it could all slip through his fingers. He opened his mouth, then closed it. He simply couldn't afford to go to war with this woman. Not that he'd have much choice after she spoke to Maggie's attorney.

A string of curses issued from Young Buck Shively as Jay entered the barn, followed by a request for yet another wrench. Jay handed it off with a shake of the head. He was starting to think dynamite might be the only option for the old relic they fondly called the Beast. He'd been warned about used tractors, but buying new meant less money for other things. At the time it seemed like a no-brainer.

That was five years ago. Now it was beginning to look as though both the tractor and his luck were running out of steam. He didn't relish telling Buck the news. The man had dropped everything and dragged his family halfway across the state to be a part of this. Sooner or later, though, someone was going to ask about the BMW in the driveway, so he supposed now was as good a time as any.

He was still trying to decide how to broach the subject when Angie Shively appeared with a tray of sandwiches and apples. With a stab of relief he gave Young Buck's boot a kick. "Come on out. The little woman's here and she's got food."

Nothing made Young Buck move faster than food. Like a turtle on its back, he wriggled from beneath the tractor and stood, six feet six and as thin as a rake, with hair like a new penny and freckles so thick they could almost pass for a tan. He grinned at his wife, a moony, lopsided grin that made Jay look away. There were times when it was damned uncomfortable being around the two of them.

"So," Angie asked, eyeing the Beast as she filled two plastic cups with sweet tea, "she gonna make it 'til harvest, do you think?"

Young Buck cocked one eye and gave his chin a scratch. "At this point I'm not sure she's gonna make it 'til sundown."

Angie handed out ham and cheese sandwiches in little plastic bags, then turned her eyes to the tractor. It was the kind of look she might have given a lame horse. "Maybe it's time to do the humane thing."

Young Buck's mouth was already full. "And use what to buy a new one?"

"You know Virgil will give you whatever you need on credit," she said, swapping his empty sandwich bag for a full one. "Look, I know keeping this thing going has turned into some macho badge of honor, but harvest is six weeks out. We'll be in a fine mess if the old girl decides to give up the ghost right as the picking crew shows up."

Jay didn't say a word. She was right, of course. What she didn't know was that twenty-four hours ago, their plans had changed.

"Stop looking at me like that, Jay. I'm not asking you to flush the family goldfish. It's a tractor, for crying out loud. I know you said you didn't want to go into hock, but it wouldn't be that much. The two of you need to be out in the rows, not in here performing CPR."

Buck looked to Jay. "What do you think, boss?"

Jay kept his eyes on his sandwich as he worked it from its bag. "I think no matter what, we need to keep her breathing until we get the fruit in."

Buck nodded gravely. "I'll do what I can, but I think we may need to bring in a priest."

"Last rites?"

"Exorcism."

Jay forced himself to smile. He'd seen the flicker of concern in Angie's eyes when he said *no matter what.* The woman didn't miss a trick. "Well, if you think an exorcism will help, I'm in. Hell, at this point we've tried everything but duct tape and religion."

Buck's face fell. "Sorry, boss. Tried the duct tape this morning."

Jay grinned in earnest now. Thank God for Buck. The man was always good for a laugh, even when laughing was the last damn thing that made sense.

When the sandwiches were gone, Angie handed out the apples and collected the scraps. "I'll leave you two engineers to it, then. Try not to burn down the barn or cut off any important body parts. I'm off to ShopWay for popcorn. Sammi Lee talked me into a sleepover. Five eight-year-olds in one house—God help us all."

Jay watched Buck's eyes trail appreciatively after his wife's backside and wondered why some men hit the jackpot, while others hit the wall. "How'd you get a smart girl like that to marry you, Shively? She lose a bet or something?"

Buck pushed back a fringe of red hair and grinned. "I ask myself that almost every day. So does her daddy—every time he sees me." He paused to bite into his apple before changing the subject. "Speaking of sleepovers, I saw you had a guest yourself. Saw her pull away in her Beemer just a little bit ago—looked real nice. Maybe the lone wolf's changing his spots?"

Jay smiled tightly. Here it was, then, the moment of truth. "No, Bucko. I promise my spots are still intact. The Beemer you saw belongs to the mistress of the manor."

Buck's apple stalled midway to his mouth. "Do what?"

"Miss Scarlett has come home to Tara."

Buck's eyes widened. "No shit?"

"No shit."

Buck blinked at him. "What the hell's she been waiting for?"

Jay rifled his own half-eaten apple out the barn door and watched it wobble to a stop in the dirt. "Doesn't matter. She's headed to town right now to meet with the attorney. I think she's going to sell."

Buck went quiet. Jay knew he was calculating what the news might mean to his small family, to the arrangement that let them live rent-free in exchange for Buck's expertise as a vineyard man.

"Does she know someone?" he asked finally.

"Know someone?"

"Who wants to buy it?"

Jay shook his head. "I don't think so. We'll have some time, at least."

Buck kicked a greasy rag across the barn floor. "This is sure going to make a mess of things."

Jay gazed out at the trellised fields beyond the barn. "Yes," he said softly. "I'm afraid it is."

Chapter 3

Leslie

The office of Goddard and Goddard wasn't an office at all, but a converted three-story Queen Anne that conjured thoughts of Edgar Allan Poe and Mrs. Caswell's ninth-grade English class. The reception area, a made-over parlor, was dimly lit and reeked of stale tobacco. A woman in lumpy gray tweed looked up over enormous glasses, inquired if Leslie had an appointment, then directed her to an office at the end of a narrow hall.

The man behind the large mahogany desk was young and slender, with wheat-colored hair and pale blue eyes, too young to be an attorney, surely. He folded his hands on the blotter and smiled blandly. "Good afternoon... Ms. Nichols, is it?"

"Yes. I have an appointment with William Goddard."

"Actually, your appointment is with me. William was my grandfather. He passed away a few months back, which means you're stuck with me." He reached a hand across the desk. "Brendan Goddard."

Leslie shook his hand, then took the chair he offered. "I'm here about my grandmother's estate."

"Yes, Peak Plantation." Withdrawing a green Pendaflex file from one of the drawers, he emptied its contents onto the desk. "I'll need a few moments," he told her, pointing to a stack of storage boxes near the door. "Your file was already boxed for the move, so I haven't had a chance to review it. I must say I was surprised when you turned up out of the blue. I'm sure Mr. Davenport was as well."

Leslie wasn't in the mood to talk about Mr. Davenport. "Do you think we could proceed, Mr. Goddard?"

"Please, call me Brendan, and yes, I believe everything's in order. Generally, the reading of a will is attended by all interested parties. However, in this case, after so much time, all other parties have been apprised of your grandmother's final wishes, and all related articles of property have been disposed of." He skimmed several pages off the stack, flipping them over on the desk. "I'll be happy to cover it all, but unless you object, we can move straight to what was left to you."

Leslie nodded.

"As you probably know, Ms. Nichols, your grandmother was a woman of considerable property, real property, that is, eighty-five acres in all. There are also several houses with which you are undoubtedly familiar, various barns and outbuildings. Then there are the contents of the primary home, and a small amount of cash."

He slid a bank statement across the desk, lined up beside various deeds, surveys, and property tax assessments. It quickly blurred together with the others.

"As you can see, Ms. Nichols, the bulk of your grandmother's net worth was in the property, and her venture with Mr. Davenport."

Leslie's eyes snapped back to Goddard. "I'm sorry, did you say Mr. Davenport?"

"I assumed you knew they were partners."

"Partners?" The word caught Leslie off guard. Closing her eyes, she drew a deep breath. "Was she . . . Did she handle all this herself?"

Brendan Goddard smiled knowingly. "You're asking if your grandmother was of sound mind, as they say." He shrugged. "I never met the woman, but my grandfather never gave any indication that she wasn't. I understand why you'd wonder, though, the way she carved things up. But, Ms. Nichols, let me caution you. Contesting a will can be a nasty business."

He was leaning forward in his chair now, brows knitted. "I can see that you're upset. That's understandable. But after so long an estrangement, it might be wise to accept things as they are. In cases like these—"

Leslie was only half listening, making a mental list of questions, contemplating her next step, but finally Goddard's words penetrated.

"I'm sorry, did you just say *carved*?"

Goddard squirmed a bit in his chair. "You have spoken with Mr. Davenport, haven't you?"

"I met him last night. Why do you ask?"

"I assumed you wouldn't be very happy about . . . things."

Leslie felt the room wobble. "What . . . things? What are you saying?"

Goddard spread his hands on the desk and eyed her squarely. "I'm saying your grandmother divided her property between two beneficiaries, and one of those beneficiaries is you."

"And the other?"

"Is Mr. Davenport."

"Mr. Davenport . . . my grandmother's handyman?"

"I'm told he and your grandmother were quite close."

"And I suppose Mr. Davenport told you that?"

"Ms. Nichols, given the length of your estrangement, you can't expect—"

Leslie cut him off. "Your secretary mentioned some sort of time limit. I had a year to claim my inheritance or it would default to someone else. Might I ask who that someone is?"

"That would be Mr. Davenport, of course."

He turned the remaining paperwork around and slid it across the desk. Leslie's face went hot as she scanned the pages, scarcely able to believe what she was reading. The Big House, as well as the smaller house where she had lived with her parents, belonged to her. Jay got the cottage and deed rights to the lake. The vineyard acreage was to be divided between them. It was impossible. And yet it was all there in black and white, properly sealed and notarized. Either Maggie had been completely out of her mind, or she had a nasty sense of humor.

She pushed the papers back. "Is there something I'm supposed to sign?"

"I beg your pardon?"

"To take possession of what's mine. There are signatures required to complete these things, aren't there?"

"Well, yes, of course, but—"

"May I have a pen?"

"Ms. Nichols, we're not even close to being through. There are other documents we need to go over, so that you're clear on the details."

"I'm as clear as I need to be, Mr. Goddard. A pen, please."

He opened his mouth to protest again, then gave up with a shrug. Separating out several sheets from the stack, he scooped them into a large white envelope. "Your copy of the deed is in here, as well as the property survey. We'll need to record the transfer of deed with the county court. No liens of any kind, of course, and this year's taxes have been paid. As executor, Mr. Davenport agreed to look after your share of the property until you could be reached. I'm sure you'll find everything in order."

Executor too. Well, he had certainly maneuvered it all very neatly. Another two weeks and all of Peak would have belonged to him. No wonder he'd been so happy to see her.

Goddard was raking together the last of the papers, preparing to slide them back into their cardboard pouch, when he stopped and upended the folder, shaking a ring of keys out onto the desk. He picked them up and handed them to her.

"I have no idea what any of these go to, but they're yours—oh, and this."

Leslie stared at the old sepia photo he put into her hand and felt goose bumps rise on her arms. It was a queer shot—a solitary grave enclosed by a low iron fence, the weathered stone listing to one side as if to hear a secret. It was an amazing shot as photos went, framed by a lightning-struck oak. She flipped it over. No date, no location, nothing.

"What is this?"

"I haven't a clue, but it was in the file with your grandmother's paperwork, so I can only assume it was meant for you. You don't recognize it?"

Leslie shook her head. "Your grandfather never mentioned it?"

"Not that I recall. I suppose there could have been a mix-up while we were packing for the move. Last week I found a prenup misfiled with an adoption file. Take it. If I find out it was a mistake, I'll get in touch."

Leslie thanked him for his time, and stood.

Goddard stood, too, and walked her to the door. "Will you be staying on in Gavin, do you think?"

"Not permanently, no. I'll be here as long as it takes me to dispose of . . . things."

"I understand. My grandfather left me this place, and don't get me wrong, it was very thoughtful, but it's not exactly my style." He pointed to the grandfather clock near the door. "Take that, for instance. What am I supposed to do with something like that?"

Leslie eyed the clock, a beautiful piece of craftsmanship, and likely worth a fortune. Its cabinet was the deep rich hue of molasses, its hands and face gleaming like a Sunday choir. The time was wrong, though, as if no one had bothered to wind it since William Goddard died. Staring at the dead face and hands, she searched for something to say.

Goddard saved her by sticking out a hand. "Well, it's been a plea-sure, Ms. Nichols. I wish you luck—selling, I mean. Messy business, but the best thing for people like us."

"People like us?"

He chuckled, a cold, uncomfortable sound. "The inheritors of white elephants, I guess you'd call us; the recipients of unwanted legacies. Our grandparents left us their whole life's work, and we can't run away from it fast enough."

Leslie's heels left a trail of wounds as she crossed the smooth green lawn. She had a few questions for Mr. Davenport, and according to the paperwork, the cottage was where she was likely to find him.

She could just make it out now, tucked between the trees along the lake's eastern shore, bordered on three sides by a wall of mossy stone. In her day it was a musty shack crammed with old furniture and other assorted castoffs. Now, as she stepped from the trees, she saw that time had transformed it. Gone was the run-down shack of her memory, replaced by a quaint clapboard cottage with shiny black shutters, a white picket gate, and window boxes full of geraniums.

The front door stood open. Leslie stepped through without knock-ing. It took a moment for her eyes to adjust, but eventually she could make out her surroundings: a small parlor with a scrubbed pine floor, walls washed a soft seawater green, a smattering of simple pine furni-ture.

Something like surprise registered on Jay's face when he glanced up and saw her in the doorway. He was seated behind a battered pine desk, bare chested but for the towel draped around his neck, his hair slightly damp. He took his time closing several desk drawers, then finally met her gaze, his expression infuriatingly bland.

"Good afternoon."

Leslie wasn't in the mood for pleasantries. She crossed the room and thrust Goddard's papers at him. "You knew I'd find out about this. Why the farce?"

"There was no farce. I just thought it would sound better coming from Goddard. I assume he filled you in on all the gory details?"

Leslie mentally counted to ten before firing back. "He shouldn't have had to. As my grandmother's executor, you had an obligation to tell me the truth."

Jay looked genuinely stunned. "Obligation . . . to you? Do you really want to stand there and talk about obligations when you've just breezed into town with your hand out?"

"That's right, get all high-and-mighty. You've been hostile from the moment I showed up, but I didn't get why until I was sitting in Goddard's office. My turning up yesterday was pretty inconvenient, wasn't it?"

"Stunning is more like it."

Leslie ignored the dig. "If I had waited just two more weeks, it all would have gone to you. You can't tell me that doesn't piss you off."

Jay stood, arms rigid at his sides. "I already got more than I should have."

The response caught Leslie off guard. "Finally, something we can agree on."

"You think I swindled your grandmother out of her fortune. Is that it?"

"I think I've got a right to know how all this happened."

"You're asking if I locked her in the attic until she agreed to leave me everything."

"Goddard said you and Maggie were close. Is that true?"

Jay pulled the towel from his neck and dropped it on the chair before stepping from behind the desk. "The truth—at least the part that's any of your business—is that your grandmother and I met and hit it off. Eventually we went into business together. There was nothing sneaky about it, but I can't prove that. I had no idea about the will. She and Goddard Senior cooked that up. I was as surprised as anyone."

"I'll bet."

"I don't expect you to believe me."

"Can you see my side? I show up, and here you are, like a stray cat."

He smiled at that. "I guess I was something of a stray when I showed up."

"And Maggie just took you in?"

"Your grandmother was quite a woman, Leslie. And I'm not the only one who thought so. The whole town turned out for her funeral. It was something." He paused, locking eyes with her. "You should have been there."

Leslie winced. It was the kind of thing people said casually, about a party or a picnic, but they both knew that wasn't what he meant.

His voice was softer when he spoke again, missing some of its edge. The change was unsettling. "She never stopped waiting for you to come back, you know. To her you were still an eight-year-old in pigtails."

"I haven't been eight for a very long time."

"Maybe, but the eight-year-old was all she had."

Leslie felt her throat tighten. "Can we not talk about this?"

"You don't get it, do you? She hadn't seen or heard from you in thirty years, but she was still waiting for you to come home. You didn't, though—at least not while it mattered. So the next time you wonder why I'm hostile, you might try looking in the mirror."

Determined not to flinch, she squared her shoulders. "Goddard's papers may give you the right to half of Maggie's estate, but they don't give you the right to judge me."

She turned then and headed to the door.

"I knew her last."

The words hit her in the back, so soft that they forced her to turn around. "What?"

He closed the distance between them in a few short steps, neatly blocking her way. "You knew her first, when you were a girl. But at the end—when she needed someone—I was here. That's what gives me the right. I knew her last."

There was nothing to say to that, nothing at all. To this man she was the interloper, the grasping, illegitimate relation. And maybe he was right.

She willed herself to meet his eyes. "I'm sorry I showed up and spoiled your plans."

"That's what you think? That I want it all?" His eyes locked with hers, searching for something. After a moment he shook his head. "There isn't a shred of her in you, is there? You have her blood, even her looks, but none of her heart."

Leslie stiffened. He was a stranger to her, and a con man for all she knew. How dare he stand there and claim to know anything about her? She didn't care how long he'd been at Peak; her heart was none of his damn business. She was preparing to push past him when she remembered the photograph Goddard had given her. If he was such an expert on Maggie, then let him prove it. Fishing it out of the envelope, she handed it to him. "All right, you know so much about my grandmother. Tell me what this was doing with her papers."

Jay took the photo, studying it briefly before flipping it over. After a moment he shrugged and handed it back. "What did Goddard say about it?"

Disappointed, Leslie returned the shrug. "He didn't have a clue. His grandfather never mentioned it. For all he knows the thing was misfiled and has nothing at all to do with Maggie." She peered at the photo again. "It's strange, almost . . . familiar. Though I can't imagine what it would have to do with Maggie."

Jay let out a huff. "Could you please stop calling her that? She was your grandmother, for God's sake, not some stranger."

Leslie wanted to tell him that after thirty years Maggie was essentially a stranger. Instead, she pushed past him and out onto the stoop. "What did you call her?"

He smiled then, a genuine smile that was a little sad too. "I called her *Old Broad*."

After scrounging up a can of soup for dinner, Leslie climbed the stairs to the room that had once been her mother's, the room Maggie had always put her in when she spent the night. It felt strangely anonymous now. The walls were the same sunny shade of yellow. The old iron bed was still covered in white chenille. But the room had been carefully stripped of all traces of its former occupant, nothing personal, nothing that might evoke a memory.

Despite damp winters and blistering summers, and God only knew how many layers of old paint, she finally managed to wrestle the window open, though not without a few choice words, and eased down onto the sill. She'd spent a lot of nights in this window, lulled toward sleep by the here-then-there pulse of fireflies, the thrum and throb of night things. Now, with her eyes closed and her knees tucked up to her chin, she could almost convince herself that no time had passed, that the breeze sighing through the screen was the breeze of all those other nights. Almost.

But that girl was gone. She owned half a vineyard now, and a house full of memories, and at some point she was going to have to suck it up and begin the process of sorting through eighty years of personal effects. Without warning, William Goddard's old clock was swimming in her head along with his grandson's words, as grim as they were true. *Our grandparents left us their whole life's work, and we can't run away from it fast enough.*

In need of a diversion, Leslie slid from the sill and padded to the nightstand to retrieve the photo she had placed there. Whoever took it knew what they were doing: the use of shadow to funnel the eye, the negative space, the use of a lightning-split oak to frame the subject—all spoke of more than a weekend photographer. The lighting, though, was the remarkable thing, a single blade of sun slanting across the stone's face, so that it almost appeared to glow.

With a kind of awe, she ran a finger over the image. Something about it did feel familiar, something she could almost touch, but not. There was an inscription, a few lines etched into the stone, but they were too blanched to read. Vexed, she squinted harder, but after a few moments gave up and fell back against the spread, too exhausted to keep her eyes open. As she lay there, drifting toward sleep, she recalled her mother telling her once that every photograph told a story.

What story, then, did *this* photograph have to tell? And whose story was it?

Chapter 4

❧

Adele

August 1930

For my seventeenth birthday I'm put on the noon bus for North Carolina.

My worldly goods are stowed below, in its fume-filled belly, all neatly packed in a bright new trunk from Parson's Hardware. Mama made me three new dresses—two brown, one navy. There wasn't money for new shoes, or for a new hat either, but last night before bed I put on another layer of polish and pinned a spray of violets on my old boater. I have an address in my bag and fifty dollars pinned to my slip.

At the station Mama cries 'til her breath heaves out in great shuddering gulps. "I'm going to miss my girl," she says over and over, shaking her head like it's someone else making me go.

I don't cry.

It's the only way I know to punish her.

I don't want to go. I'm happy with things as they are: maybe not a lot to eat, and not a lot of work either, now that the country-club set has lost all their money. But we get by. Still, Mama says her girl's going to have a different life, a better life. No sewing fancy clothes for snooty ladies with high manners and low opinions of folks who make their livings with their hands. No, sir, I'm smart and I'm pretty, bright-eyed and fair skinned, with hair like smooth black glass. No reason to settle for Mama's kind of life. And when Mama makes up her mind, that's all.

I try to talk her out of it right up to the time the bus pulls into the station. I say I'll find work in the Quarter, bring home a little money. I say things will get better. She gives my arm a little jerk and shakes her head again.

"There's a path for you," she says, with her chin stuck out. "And it isn't in New Orleans. And it isn't with any of the go-nowhere boys chasing around after your skirts. There's a whole wide world out there, little girl, and you're meant for it."

"What's wrong with the world we have right now?" I ask, then look away.

I already know her answer. I've been hearing it since I was old enough to listen, and maybe even before that. I'm not going to turn out like Mama, not going to make the same mistakes, not going to throw my life away on some man who can't or won't look after me. I wish sometimes that Mama had chosen a better man when she picked my daddy. It seems he had a lot of shortcomings and that I'm always the one paying for them.

I hold my lip stiff as the bus door swings open, and ignore the sting behind my eyes.

"No looking back," Mama chokes, and gives me one last breathless squeeze. "No looking back, ever."

And then the door closes and the bus jerks away from the curb, and I'm all on my own. We haven't gone a mile and already my heart bleeds for home, and I start to think this might be the second biggest mistake Mama ever made, my daddy being the first.

I've never really believed in fairy tales—watching Mama's heart break by inches over the years has worked on me like a vaccine, so I'm not expecting a castle or happily ever after—but when I first catch sight of Gavin, North Carolina, all I can think of is getting back on that bus. How could anyone live in this place—this merciless place of scorched red earth and brown horizons, fields stripped bare as Pharaoh's Egypt, as if the God of Exodus himself had smitten the land for its sins?

There's a world out there, and I'm meant for it—Mama said so. But this can't be what she meant, this baked ground with its stubbled fields. My feet move only because I know this is just one leg of my journey. Eventually, when I've set a little money by, I'll leave and make my way to Mama's people in Chicago, finish school, and become a teacher, or maybe a nurse.

I reach the house straight from the station, wilted and hungry, my neck sticky under the collar of my new dress, my hair crushed flat as a sparrow's nest. Even my hat is a shambles, my violets lost somewhere along the way. I can hardly believe my eyes when I finally see the place, spanking white and set way up high, looking out over all that green grass. There's lots of shutters and four white columns, and a porch across the front.

I make myself go up on that front porch and bang the shiny knocker. A man answers, wearing a vest and tie. His shirt is crunchy with starch. His mouth looks starched too, while his eyes skim me from top to bottom. He tries to hide what he's thinking as he shows me into a fancy parlor with brocade curtains and a green velvet settee. He doesn't offer his name or any refreshment, and there's something in his eyes that makes me queasy as he points me toward the settee, as if he's almost sorry for me. I'm to sit quietly, he tells me in his starchy voice, and wait for the *Missus*.

The *Missus* leaves me sitting in her parlor a full twenty minutes. It's a long time to wait when you're someplace you don't want to be—someplace you don't belong. I run my eyes around the room, all glossy and spotless. There's not a speck of dust on anything except me. I fold my hands tight in my lap, careful not to touch anything. Over my head there's a paddle fan wheezing. After a while, I start to think it's going to run me crazy. I wonder what Mama is doing, if she's still crying, and if she's started supper.

My belly is empty, gnawing at my backbone, and my eyes are hard on the candy dish when Susanne Gavin finally sails in. She's thin as a fence rail, with straw-colored hair and a face like cider vinegar, trying her best to look grand for me in her filmy lavender chiffon. It flutters about her white shoulders, clings to her calves like sea-foam. It's what the ladies back home call a *to-do*—a dress not suited to the occasion. Mama would have said it wasn't her color either, that it made her look green at the gills. Her eyes fall on me as if she's afraid I might spoil the velvet on her fine settee.

I hate her on the spot.

Her hands flutter around the high round bump of her belly while she looks me over, like a pair of pale birds that don't know where to land. I congratulate her on the child because I can see she expects me to. And I hold my spine straight as a church pew because I know Mama expects me to. From the day Mama first laid eyes on me she's been planning for this, training me how to get along, how to melt in, how to be invisible. I use all of it now.

It's enough to get me the job. I expect because the other two girls who answered the ad were Negro. Missus makes it clear she'll have none of those coloreds prowling around her expensive things or around the soon-to-be heir to her precious plantation.

"We have a reputation in the town," she says, looking down her nose. "And a duty, I suppose, to set some sort of standard. Any girl working in my house has to look like she belongs."

She's looking at my shoes when she says it, at the fresh scuff marks and layers of polish. It's her way of reminding me she sees me as nothing but poor white trash. That suits me just fine.

She sits down then and crosses her legs, her thin white hands clasped over her knees, as if to keep them still. Her eyes are queer, I notice now that she's sitting close, pale as water, with tiny pupils like the prick of a pin. Her lips are curled at the corners when she leans in, as if she's about to tell me a secret.

"I suspect you know you're in the town of Gavin?" Her voice is all high-and-mighty, like the name should mean something to me.

I nod and say, "Yes, ma'am."

"Well, if you're going to work at Peak Plantation, you should know the town was named for my husband's family, back before the Revolution. And you mustn't ever forget that my husband, Henry, is a very important man."

I can see she's waiting for me to say something, but my belly's too empty to think of anything. I duck my head. That seems to satisfy her.

"Working for the Gavins is a privilege," she tells me next.

It's on the tip of my tongue to ask how many other girls have had the privilege before me, and why she had to advertise all the way down to Louisiana, but in my mind I can see Mama's face all puckered with disapproval, so I stay quiet.

The mistress of Peak Plantation frowns a little when my stomach grumbles, but it doesn't stop her from rambling on about the Big House, as she loftily calls it—that it's nearly one hundred years old, built on the highest point in the county so that it looks down on all of Gavin. I think how very much she must enjoy looking down on all of Gavin.

I know Mrs. Susanne Gavin. For years, I've watched Mama *yes, ma'am* and *no, ma'am* women just like her through a mouth full of pins—all to earn their pennies. I wonder how the rest of Gavin likes her sitting up here in her fine plantation house, surrounded by acres of tobacco and dressed for afternoon tea, while plain folks scramble to find work and put food on their tables. And I wonder what kind of man could be married to such a woman.

We talk about my duties next, my *domestic skills*, as she calls them. She seems pleased but reminds me that I am to be plain and serviceable at all times, no taking airs just because I'm in her employ and living in the finest house in the county.

And all of a sudden I understand why she wants a companion. I can see it in the pale eyes she scrapes over me. She needs someone to be better than. And that's me, with my drooping hat and wilted home-sewn dress. Next to her I'm patchwork, frayed just enough around the edges to make her superior. It may only be my gnawing belly, but the room begins to tilt and shift, like sand being sucked from under my feet. I've got one leg in the old world and one in the new.

I'm given a room at the back of the house but on the same floor as the Missus. I am to be *convenient*, near enough to see to her tiniest whim. It's a small room with papered walls and good furniture—better than I'm used to. There's also a window that lets in a nice breeze and looks out on a lake and a bit of woods. My hardware-store trunk is brought up by the man in the vest. His name is George, he tells me, still with that look on his face, as if he's just come from my funeral. There's a plate in the kitchen for me if I want it, he says, and closes the door behind him.

When he leaves I'm alone and nothing is familiar, not even the sounds coming through the screen—croaks and chirps and leaves rustling. I miss the noisy night sounds of the Quarter, men shooting dice in the alley behind the house, jazz oozing like steam from the door of the speakeasy, the pitiful wail of a saxophone on some empty corner.

I miss home. And I miss Mama.

I'm not mad anymore, just sad, and a little afraid too, I guess. But as I arrange my underwear in unfamiliar drawers, I know Mama would be pleased. I want so badly to write her, to tell her everything—that I'm safe, that I'm scared, that I want to come home. But she made me promise not to write, never to write. No looking back, ever. It's what Mama wants for me, even if I don't want it for myself. That night, as I curl into my strange bed with its crisp good sheets, I let myself cry for the first time since leaving Mama at the station.

The next morning I come awake like I've been walking in a dream, but the pillow under my head is all wrong, and the light is spilling into the room from the wrong direction. I close my eyes tight and count to ten. When I open them again I see the yellow flowers on the wallpaper and know I'm long gone from home.

My first week is hard.

After a day or two I begin to find my way, but it's a fair trial. More than once I blunder into the wrong room. Our little shotgun house in the Quarter had four doors, including the one that took you from inside to outside. I can't say how many doors are in the Big House, or how many windows, or how many porches. I expect that's why they call it the Big House—and because it sounds grand and very Old South.

It takes weeks to grasp the difference between the gallery and the foyer and the mudroom, between the sun porch and the guest porch and the reading porch, between the front parlor and the sitting parlor—and between the bedroom of Mr. Gavin and the bedroom of Mrs. Gavin, easier than the others at least, since they are situated at opposite ends of the house.

The advertisement from the *Times-Picayune* was for a lady's companion, but it doesn't take long to see I'm to be much more than that to Susanne Gavin. For my bed and board and my paltry pay I am owned body and soul, sunup to sundown and well after—hairdressing, sewing, reading aloud, pouring tea, picking out clothes, picking up clothes, dosing medicines, even handling her correspondence when she sees I have a good hand.

Susanne is something fearful, a willful child and a wicked queen all at once. She takes a kind of medicine from a brown bottle with a small dropper. Her tincture, she calls it. She takes it twice a day, ten drops in her tea in the morning, then in the afternoon another ten in some bootleg she keeps under her bed but still drinks from a teacup. One day early on I ask what it's for. She looks at me sharp and tells me it's to calm her nerves. I itch to say I don't believe it's working, but I know better, and count out the drops like she tells me.

We go into town now and then, Susanne all gussied up in her hat and white gloves, me in tow with her packages. To anyone who asks, I am her *girl*. And I am that especially to those who do *not* ask, women too busy worrying how to make a chicken stretch a full week to bother with the goings-on at Peak. For the colored women, though, she spares no breath at all, giving them a good, wide berth, as if their darkness might rub off on her milk white skin. Clear as glass she is to me, parading me and her belly under the noses of her lady friends, as if she's the first woman in the world to ever have a baby.

Yet, I see what no one else seems to, or are perhaps too polite to remark—that this baby isn't agreeing. There's no motherly glow about her, no bloom of new life in her cheeks, only a dull pallor that hangs about her, as if her light burns too low. And the more her belly burdens her, the more she presses me for pickled okra and lemon ice and back rubs, and with calls to her room in the middle of the night to brush her hair when she can't sleep. When none of these work she takes another dose of her tincture. She sleeps then and wakes up mean as anything.

She slaps me sometimes, after the tincture, calls me lazy and cracks my knuckles with her big silver hairbrush. I should care, should be hurt or angry. But I hold no fondness for her, and so I let the words glance off. Lots of girls would have left when they found out what the woman was all about. Maybe I should have too. But by then there was Henry.

Chapter 5

Three weeks pass before I lay an eye on Susanne's husband. For a while I wonder if he might not be a figment of her imagination, someone she dreamed up after taking too much of her tincture. But the baby growing in her belly is real enough, and so I guess he must be too. I can't blame him for staying gone. Susanne is either shut up in her room with a cloth over her eyes or squalling like a wet cat about something. The only time the man's even in the house is to sleep, which he does way down the hall from Susanne, which makes me wonder how that baby even got in her belly.

Then one day I'm with Susanne up in her room, pinning her hair, when I hear something rattling up the drive. I sneak a peek between the curtains. She likes them closed in the afternoons, says it keeps out the heat. I think it keeps out the air, but I keep quiet. They're her curtains.

"Someone's coming up the drive," I say when I spot a rusty-looking truck spraying gravel out behind.

Susanne shakes her head, loosening one of the curls I just pinned up. "That will be Henry," she sighs. "Master of Peak Plantation."

I pin the curl back, but I can't keep my eyes from wandering to that little slit between the curtains. The truck is parked now, with one door open, and I see a man climbing down from the seat. He's tall and rangy, wearing overalls and a plaid shirt with the sleeves pushed up. Him, I think? He's the big important man Susanne's been going on about? Climbing out of that old wreck with his knees all filthy, and a mashed-up hat on his head? I don't believe it. Then I think, Susanne would never lie about something like that.

As soon as I finish Susanne's hair, I slip down the back stairs and through the kitchen, hoping to get a closer look. I catch sight of him again from the back porch, heading into the barn with a couple colored men dressed just like him. After a while I give up on him coming out and go back inside, where Lottie's busy stirring something on the stove.

Lottie's proper name is Charlotte, although Susanne refuses to call her anything but Cook and expects me to do the same. I don't, though, when we're alone. She looks near Mama's age, looks tired like Mama too. She's big-boned and solid country, with a head of rusty hair and a voice tough as gristle. Susanne brags that she's the best cook in Gavin. I don't know if that's true, or even if it's saying anything at all. Not many folks can afford a cook these days. And the food here is different from what I'm used to back home. The corn bread and sweet potato pie are fine enough, but there isn't much flavor to the rest of it. It's all chicken and pork chops—fried, fried, fried. At least there's always plenty of it. These days, that's saying something.

Lottie's still wary of me, not sure how tight I am with the Missus, afraid I might make trouble for her. Today she pours me a glass of tea and sets a saucer down in front of me with two squares of corn bread. It's good, still warm from the oven. I wash down the first bite and think about asking if she's ever thought of throwing in some hot peppers, like Mama does. I don't, though. I don't think she'd like it.

Her back is to me; she's stirring something in a big bubbling pot.

I catch a whiff of ham hock as she drops the lid back on. "You plan on staying?" she asks, still holding her big wooden spoon.

I blink at her like she just asked to borrow a hundred dollars. I've got a job, a roof over my head. Where else would I go? Then I think of Chicago, where I'm eventually meant to end up, and of Mama's people waiting for me there. But Chicago feels a million miles away.

Lottie doesn't notice that I never answer. "Ain't really any of my business," she says in that gruff voice of hers. "And maybe I ought not to tell you, but there's been a whole passel of girls through here—girls just like you. They all leave after a while. Some don't stay a week. What about you? You gonna stick it out?"

"Have to," I say, swallowing hard. "Nowhere else to go."

"No kin to take you in?"

I shake my head, not sure if I feel bad because of the lie or because it feels true when I say it.

"Well," says Lottie, shaking some more salt into whatever it is she's cooking. "It ain't really my place to say—ain't really my business at all—and you probably don't need me to tell you, but Ms. Susanne's a handful. And she'll be getting worse if things don't go well with that belly of hers."

Lottie's eyes narrow down when she says that last part, and I can see just how badly she's itching to *make* it her business. I forget about my corn bread and lean forward in my chair. She drops down next to me at the long table, her face all screwed up with her secret.

"This one's number four," she says, squinting one eye at me. "All the rest are dead."

"Three . . . dead?" I breathe the last word out. Back home, folks would say that was some bad voodoo.

Lottie sucks at her teeth a minute, shakes her head. "Never born is more like it—lost every one."

"Oh," I say, closing my eyes at the thought of it.

"Yes, ma'am. Never had a live one yet, and it's eating her up." Lottie grunts as she hauls her stout frame out of the chair and moves back to the stove. She peeks under the pot lid, turns down the flame. "She was always an uppity thing, but nothing like she is now. I truly don't know how Mr. Henry stands it."

"For better or worse," I say, like I know something about it. "Love is supposed to be for better or worse."

Lottie gives a little snort. "No love between them two—different as pigs and chickens, and a lot less friendly. But then, what they do ain't none of my business."

I shoot a look at the door, then drop my voice. "He never goes to her room," I say with my cheeks all hot. "At night, I mean. Come to think on it, I never see them together at all."

Another snort, louder this time. "Not likely to, either. Except maybe at dinnertime. Even then they don't talk, just chew and try not to look at each other. Poor Mr. Henry..." Her voice trails off. She sucks on her teeth some more.

I press my lips together, but the words come out anyway. "As far as I can tell there's nothing poor about Mr. Henry, with all his land and his fine white house. And any man who'd marry a woman like Susanne has to be cut from the same cloth." I sound like Mama when I say it, prickly and hard, but I made up my mind about Henry Gavin long before I saw him climbing out of that rickety truck.

Lottie lays down her spoon. "It ain't like that," she says with her lips turned down, and for a minute I think she's going to cry. "He's a good man who made a bad mistake. He wasn't thinking about love when he married her, just about land, and this place. Now that's all he's got."

"You mean Peak?"

"A quarter of this land used to belong to her daddy—came to Henry when he died. He knew that woman wasn't no prize—not pretty, not sweet, and not exactly fresh at almost thirty, so he sweetened the deal to get her off his hands. Henry didn't care anything about a wife. He only took her 'cause he wanted that land and 'cause she'd been chasing him all over town for years. I guess he got tired of running."

I'm thinking of Mama now, and the man who was my daddy. He lived and died for his passions, Mama used to say—all of them except her. I'm also thinking that a man who could make a deal like that—a wedding ring for a few acres of dirt—might be exactly the kind of man Susanne deserved.

Lottie must see into my head. All of a sudden her eyes go soft. "He's a good man, Adele, got a good, big heart. His daddy died while he was in school, so he had to quit. Shame, too—he was smart, all the time reading something. But it was just him to look after his mama, and all this place too, while his friends were off at school or chasing girls. This place is all he knows. That dirt out there, that's where he lives, not this house. And those tobacco stalks are his children."

"The babies . . . he didn't want them?"

"Oh, he wanted that first one," Lottie says, wiping her forehead with the back of her hand. "Wanted the second one too, I reckon. Every man wants a boy. But after the second time with Ms. Susanne . . . well . . . I think he kind of quit hoping. She keeps trying, though, God help us all. Bound and determined to start some kind of dynasty, finally prove to folks she was good enough to marry a Gavin."

I finish my tea and corn bread, watching Lottie about her business, pulling a plate of pork chops from the ice box, mixing flour and salt and pepper in a bag while a blob of Crisco melts in a black iron skillet, and I think, she's so used to this kitchen she could probably fix supper blindfolded.

"How long have you been here, Lottie?"

"Ten years, I guess it is now. Came to cook for Mr. Henry just after his mama died. They were already married then, but Missus doesn't know the first thing about cooking."

"She isn't much on eating, either," I say. "She's so thin you can almost see through her."

"It's that stuff she takes, all them drops in her cup. It steals her appetite."

I cock an eye at her, wondering how she knows about the drops. I've never seen her outside this kitchen, and maybe the dining room, but only for as long as it takes to serve and clear away. "You know about her tincture?"

Lottie's nostrils flare like she smells something bad. "Course I know about her tincture. Who do you think gets to dose it out every time one of you girls up and leaves?" She shakes her head then and goes back to her pork chops. "I don't like to talk, though—ain't really any of my business."

A few days later I'm on my way to the kitchen when I come across Susanne in the dining room. She's wearing her pearls and that frothy lavender dress, drumming her thin fingers on the starched white tablecloth. I'm surprised to see her there. By now, Lottie generally has the plates cleared away. Henry must be late for supper.

Susanne's head snaps in my direction, her ordinarily pale face flushed with impatience. Her eyes are narrowed, her mouth already open when she realizes I am not Henry. I tuck my chin and turn to leave, but Henry is there somehow, filling up the doorway. He's as hard as a tree and planted just as firmly, as if he's grown roots to the carpet, and I wonder, as I blunder into him and stumble back, how such a big man could have come into the room so quietly.

For a minute all I can do is stare up at him, inhaling his soap and his hair tonic. He's handsome in a craggy sort of way, like a cowboy in the moving pictures, tall and lean, with a shock of dark hair slanting down over his forehead. There's a brooding look about him, like he's got a lot on his mind, but there's something else too, under all that sun-browned skin, a kind of quiet that softens up all those hard angles. Mama always said it was impolite to stare, but I can't help myself. I would never have guessed the lofty Susanne Gavin would ever marry the man standing in front of me.

Susanne's looking him up and down now, like she can't believe it either. Her eyes scrape over him slowly, as if she wants him to know she doesn't like what she sees. He's got on a clean pair of overalls, and a worn chambray shirt buttoned all the way to his Adam's apple. Her gaze lingers on his hands, tough as horn, the nails stained brown. She sighs then and waves a hand in my direction.

"This is my new girl, Henry, the one from New Orleans. Her name is Adele."

Henry nods. "Pleased to meet you, miss," he says. "We're about to have some supper. You're welcome to join us."

I don't have to look at Susanne to know what she thinks of this idea. I can feel the disgust boiling off her from across the room. Sighing, she tosses down her napkin. "It's dinner, Henry. Not supper. And Adele eats in the kitchen, with Lottie. Not with us."

Their eyes lock across the table full of silverware and china, and for a moment the quiet is so thick I think someone's going to choke on it. I try to think of something to say, something to fill up all that awful silence, but nothing comes to mind. And so I just stand there with my hands folded in front of my apron, trying not to notice that Henry seems to have shrunk a little and that Susanne's eyes keep darting in my direction.

Finally, she waves me from the room. As I turn to leave I cast one more look at Henry and feel a wash of sadness, because I realize now that for all Susanne's talk, she's ashamed of her very important husband, even in front of me—for his plain ways and plain clothes. I think about what Lottie told me, about the farmland Henry got from her daddy, and I can't help wondering if he still thinks he got a good bargain.

Chapter 6

I must go to church.

I've been at Peak nearly two months when Susanne informs me I'm to start attending services with her on Sundays. It sets a bad example, she says, that some of her help don't worship in a proper church, and asks if Lottie ever told me she's a Catholic. She says *Catholic* with her nostrils all flared, like it's something you'd catch at Maudie Raven's place back home on Decatur Street, where four dollars buys a bottle, a girl, and a room for an hour. I don't tell her I was baptized at St. Augustine's. I just iron my navy blue dress and polish up my shoes for church.

Henry is to come with us, I learn when Sunday rolls around. I've never known him to go to church before, but the tobacco is in the barns now, hung up on poles to dry in thick yellow bunches, so he's got no excuse to stay behind. He looks like a stranger in his black suit and shiny shoes. His hair is slick with tonic, and his hands won't leave off his tie, like it's a noose cinched tight around his neck. Susanne looks him over, picks something I don't see off his lapel. It's the only time I've ever seen her touch him.

We drive to town in the big black Ford. Susanne sits in front with her arms folded, breathing hard through her nose. She's angry that

Henry won't let George drive us. George always drives Susanne and me into town, maybe because she doesn't know how to drive herself, or maybe because she likes having someone drive her around.

Everyone's already inside when we arrive. I can hear the organ playing. Susanne doesn't bat an eye, just tucks her Bible under her arm and sails into the sanctuary like she's Joan of Arc, marching down to the last open pew—the one behind the deacons. It's odd to see it empty when the church is so full. Then it comes to me—no matter how full that church gets, no one's ever going to sit in that pew unless their name is Gavin. Susanne slides in, then Henry. I duck in next, careful not to kneel first, my fists balled up tight to remind me not to make the sign of the cross.

First Presbyterian isn't anything like church back home. It's all whitewash and wood, and it's small—so small you could set it right down in the middle of St. Augustine's. And like most things in Gavin—and most folks, too—it's worn. The carpet is threadbare, starting to unravel along the center aisle, the old oak pews worn to a dull shine by countless generations of Presbyterian backsides.

There's a choir up front wearing dark green robes, leading the congregation in song. I follow along the best I can from one of the thick brown hymnals. Next to me, Henry does the same. The pews are chock-full, but then Mama always did say churches fill up when pockets empty out. Most are wearing their Sunday best, dark suits and respectable dresses. But some of the children's clothes are a bit short in the sleeve, and here and there, ladies fidget to hide the tatty fingers of their not-so-white gloves. Some, though, are just plain poor. They're seated in back, mostly dark faces, but some white too, and a few shades in between, wearing whatever they had that was cleanest and least patched. They must be the folks I hear Susanne and her lady friends talk about—the folks from over the tracks.

When the plate comes around, there's a lot of shifting and clearing of throats, a lot of eyes fastened to the stained glass windows. I wonder if Susanne even notices; then I decide she couldn't, or she never would have worn that new hat with all the feathers, or all those shiny beads around her neck. It's a queer thing to be ashamed of someone who's better off than you, but I am. And I see, as he cuts his eyes in his wife's direction, that Henry is too.

Susanne wastes no time when the benediction is over. She heads for the door, leaving Henry in her wake. I hang back, watching the quiver and weave of her hat feathers up ahead, going still a moment as she pauses for a word with the preacher, then fluttering off again into a flock of ladies at the foot of the church steps.

Outside, I linger in the shade of one of the church's white pillars, fanning myself with my program. I try to be invisible like Mama taught me, but it's hard. I don't fit with the women here, all wrung of color and wearing the weight of the world on their married faces. I feel their eyes crawling over me, wondering where I came from and why I've invaded their church. I see their husbands too, trying not to gawk too long at my ankles. But there's nowhere to hide, and so I stand there, waiting for Susanne to crook her finger at me.

That's when I finally find something St. Augustine and First Presbyterian have in common. If you want to know all about a town's business, all you need to do is stand around on the church steps. That Sunday I learn all about Mary Farmer's hernia operation, and how Gladiola Vicks had to send both her girls to her sister up in Pennsylvania after Lester lost his job at the mill, and how Bobby Grayson stayed out 'til all hours of the night and came home with a black eye and a torn shirt. But it's Henry's name that makes my ears perk up.

Two men in suits stand behind the next pillar, smoking cigarettes and looking out over the crowd as it begins to thin. The larger of the two is built like a bull, thick and dark, and there's something in his face I don't like the look of, something sharp and mean.

His eyes are narrowed on Henry, watching as he crosses the lawn, shaking hands and exchanging pleasantries. "You hear Gavin's been hiring a bunch of coloreds to work out at his place?" He blows out a plume of gray smoke, spits a fleck of tobacco off his lip. "They say he's working 'em right alongside the whites, too."

His companion, a slight man in a brown suit, leans back on his heels a bit and takes a lazy pull on his cigarette. "Heard something about it," he says finally. "Didn't give it much thought, though, since it's not really any of my business."

"It's everyone's business," says the Bull. "Man's got no right giving away jobs to Negroes when there's white men hard up for work."

The man in brown gives the Bull a hard look. "Seems to me, a man's got the right to give his jobs to whoever he damn well pleases. Just like you've got a right to do what you do on your own land."

"May-be," the Bull grunts. "But I don't think there's too many who'd compare running a little shine with giving away white jobs to coloreds."

"They're family men, Porter. Not black men, not white men—family men. And Henry Gavin doesn't care what color they are. He cares how many mouths they have to feed. You're standing on the steps of a church. Do you honestly think when Christ Almighty was handing out the loaves and the fishes he turned the dark ones away?"

Porter. The Bull's name is Porter. He doesn't answer, just stalks off down the steps. I'm glad to see him go, but his name won't leave my head. It's familiar to me, though I can't recall right off where I've heard it. Then I remember the carload of boys that come around every Tuesday to bring Susanne her bootleg—brothers, I think, two half grown, and a little one who tags after the others like a puppy. I wonder if they might not be the Bull's kin, wonder too as I watch the Bull climb into an old black truck and drive away, what Susanne thinks of this business of hiring Negroes to work so close to all her fine things, and how long it'll be 'til there's trouble.

As it turns out, trouble isn't far off at all.

Tuesday is Susanne's ladies club day. The Gavin Ladies Historical Society, they call themselves, though I never hear them do much talking about history, unless it's the history of how a certain husband's been seen driving around town with his new secretary, or how a certain house is on the verge of going back to the bank, or how the silver tea service has disappeared from a certain dining room on Grover Street. It's all said with a great deal of head shaking and the woeful clucking of tongues, but there's something hard and sharp in the powdery faces of those women as they serve and digest their bits of news, gobbling it all up as greedily as they do the little frosted cakes Lottie serves on white paper doilies.

This week is Susanne's turn to play hostess, though it's me who greets them at the door. I recognize a few of the ladies from church— Sarah Harwood, whose husband is president of the bank; Betty Stillwater, who's been twice widowed and only ever wears black; and Eugenia Lane, who claims to be distant kin to James Henry Lane, who was a famous general during the Civil War. Susanne insists that this is highly unlikely since her people are from Baltimore, and as good as Yankees as far as she's concerned.

There are others too, eight more who straggle in to make an even dozen. Some smile at me and one even remembers my name, but most look right through me, and that's just fine with me. These are Susanne's friends, these sniping and vicious women who can still afford to host a luncheon now and then, whose husbands still have some semblance of income, whose gloves are still fine and white. They drink a lot of tea and eat a lot of fancy sandwiches with the crusts cut off, then tear into whatever sweets Lottie has set out on Susanne's best silver tray.

When the dessert plates are finally scraped down to the glaze, the ladies adjourn to the parlor. I top off their iced tea glasses, then pass out little lace coasters to protect Susanne's lemon-polished tabletops.

I'm about to slip from the room with the tea pitcher when I hear one of the ladies—the one who remembered my name at the door—pipe up and propose they do something for a few of the struggling families in the area, collect clothes for the children, or maybe bring by some food.

I can't help myself. I stop in my tracks, turn to look at her. I see how young she is, how her china blue eyes are soft and wide, with none of that knife-edged bitterness of the others. She's new, I think, and believes these women mean to do some good. She'll learn soon enough.

They're all looking at her now, all eleven of them. Susanne sets down her glass, her blue-white hand at her throat as if the poor woman had just suggested they invite the hogs in for tea.

"Henrietta," she says down her nose. "We are the Historical Society, not the Salvation Army. Besides, if word ever got out that we'd done for a few, we'd have the rest of them crossing the tracks in droves. The churches are there to handle that sort of thing."

But Henrietta is not dissuaded. She sits up straight in her chair, a tiny crease between her fawn-colored brows as she looks around at the circle of the Ladies Historical Society. "The churches are already stretched to breaking. If we all just pitched in a little—"

She's cut off again, this time by a woman with bobbed hair and too much rouge on her cheeks. "Good gracious, Henny, Mr. Cunningham would have a thousand fits if I told him I was going across town to deliver hand-me-downs to those people." She turns in her chair then and cuts her eyes at Susanne, her red lips turned up in a smile that's part honey, part venom. "Not every woman has a husband like Henry Gavin. Why, I hear he's the soul of Christian charity these days." She bats her eyes a time or two, then freezes that smile right on Susanne. "How proud you must be of your husband, my dear."

The quiet that falls is deafening. I can't say for sure what Mrs.

Cunningham is referring to, but when I think back to the church steps I have a pretty good idea. And I can tell by the color coming up in Susanne's cheeks that she does too—and that she doesn't like it one bit. She fiddles with her pearls a little while she collects herself; then, with her hand on her belly, she summons a brittle smile and turns it on Henrietta, as if she hasn't heard a word Mrs. Cunningham has just uttered.

"I'm afraid, my dear, that my delicate condition wouldn't allow me to participate in something like that."

There's the creak of wood and the rustle of skirts as the women all shift at once in their chairs, the rush of breaths being let out in unison, relief, and disappointment. Still, it's enough to turn the talk from Henry, which is all she wanted.

The meeting breaks up after that, but Susanne is pouty and sharp for the rest of the day, glaring out her bedroom window, gnawing on the Cunningham woman's taunt like an old bone. I do my best to steer clear of her, tiptoeing around as I hang up her clothes and tidy up her dressing table. I'm relieved when she asks me to dose out her afternoon tincture. Soon she'll drop off to sleep and I can slip away to my room. I'm sorry for Henry, though. He's due back from the Smithfield market sometime tomorrow, and I don't want to be around when he walks through the door. Nothing sits worse in Susanne's craw than humiliation.

Chapter 7

The next morning I find Susanne naked and tangled in her covers.

Her bottle of bootleg is on the floor—bone-dry—and I see that she's been at her tincture as well. She howls like a scalded cat when I try to draw back the curtains, then moans for a damp cloth for her head. When I tell her I'm going down to fetch her breakfast she turns three shades of green and sends me running for the basin.

She pretends she's just morning sick, but I know better. I've been at Peak long enough to know what Susanne Gavin's trouble is, and to know it begins and ends with the little brown bottle she keeps by her bed. She's been having me increase the drops lately, fifteen now instead of ten, and I can't help wondering, while she's sipping that terrible concoction from her pretty little teacup, if she ever thinks about the child in her belly, and if Henry knows how fast the little bottle is going down these days.

If Henry doesn't, the doctor does. Last week he had a word with the druggist about her refills. There are to be no more for two weeks, and then at only half the amount. Susanne was so incensed that she threatened to change doctors. She would have done it, too, only she's been through all the others.

For the rest of the afternoon I walk on eggshells, waiting for Henry's old truck to cough its way up the drive. When he's still not home by supper, I bring Susanne a tray. She makes me sit with her while she pushes Lottie's chicken and dumplings around her plate. I can feel the anger boiling off her like lye, waiting to spill over on whatever's nearby. When she finally pushes the tray away, I take it from her gladly, ready to be away from her and out of that stifling room. I'm almost out into the hall when I hear the truck rattle up. Susanne hears it too, and her eyes go to slits.

I hurry down to the kitchen to make myself scarce. Lottie shakes her head at the sight of Susanne's nearly full plate. She's been cooking all day, all Henry's favorites, and I can see she's not happy that even a mouthful of her chicken and dumplings has gone to waste.

"There's going to be trouble," I whisper.

Lottie pours me a glass of tea and sets down a plate in my usual place. "You mean about what that Cunningham woman said at the meeting. Yeah, I expect the Missus has been stewing on that all day."

My fork hovers on its way to my mouth. "You heard?"

She's scraping Susanne's plate off into the trash now, waiting for the dish tub to fill. "I'd have to be deaf not to hear. Nothing quiet about that woman."

I swallow my bite, wash it down with some tea. "I thought she was supposed to be Susanne's friend."

Lottie cocks her brassy head to one side and looks at me like I just said something crazy. "Ladies like that ain't got no friends; don't you know that? They only got acquaintances they're waiting to turn on. They smile and they smile, just biding their time 'til there's something to get their teeth in. Looks like it's the Missus's turn."

I chase a dumpling around my plate, too keyed up to be hungry but not wanting to put Lottie's nose out of joint. "It's because of the colored men, isn't it? That's what she meant when she said Henry was the soul of Christian charity?"

Lottie scowls over her dish tub. "Been talk for weeks now. Nothing but a handful of troublemakers stirring the pot, but they get louder every day. Most folks don't care. They're too busy trying to keep body and soul together to worry what other folks are doing. Not to mention it's Mr. Henry we're talking about. Not many in this town with a bad word to say against him, coloreds or no coloreds."

I don't say so, but I'm pretty sure Henry's wife is about to have a bad word to say, and I don't envy him one bit. My mind flashes to those church steps, to Mr. Porter and the loaves and the fishes, and all of a sudden I feel a surge of pride to be working in Henry Gavin's home. Not because he's an important man—because he's a good man.

When I'm finished with supper I slip up the back stairs, hoping to duck into my room unseen. Instead, I freeze halfway up. Susanne is standing outside her door, eyes blazing, her chin poked out like a willful child's. Henry stands at the other end of the hall, unshaven and gritty after the long drive back from Smithfield. Not a word has passed between them yet, but there's a tension crackling across all that space, like the air before a lightning storm, and I know I've blundered into the very skirmish I've been dreading all day.

I stand there clutching the banister, afraid to move a muscle. They're too busy locking eyes to notice me pressed back against the wall, halfway up and halfway down. I tell myself I should creep back down to the kitchen, wait until the storm has blown over, but when I hear Henry's voice my feet root themselves to the floor.

"Susanne, please." There's no missing the strain in his voice, like he's used to confrontations—and like he's been dreading this one. "Do you think maybe you could wait 'til I've cleaned up and had something to eat before you start in on me?"

Susanne balls her fists and stomps a bare foot on the carpet. "No, I cannot wait! And I'd appreciate it if just for once you'd think of someone besides yourself! You didn't see Celia Cunningham's face yesterday, and me sitting there having to pretend I didn't hear a word she said. This town thinks you've lost your mind, throwing good money after bad on a bunch of tramps—and colored tramps at that!"

Henry flinches, and his face goes dark. "They're working men with families to feed, Susanne. And who I hire is my business."

There's an edge to his voice, something just shy of a warning, but Susanne isn't put off. Patches of red boil up in her cheeks, down along her slender white throat, and when she finally answers it's through clenched teeth.

"Not when it's ruining my name in this town, it isn't. People are talking, and I don't just mean Celia Cunningham. They know you've taken on twice the men you did last year, and with prices way down, too. That makes you a fool—fine. I can live with being married to a fool. But what are they going to call you when they find out those coloreds are earning the same wage as white men, taking jobs that belong to whites, taking food out of white children's mouths? Way back when, your great-grandfather founded this town, Henry. You've got a duty to set some kind of a standard."

At his side, Henry's fingers curl slowly, crushing the brim of his already battered hat. "That's precisely what I am doing. And it seems to me, if I'm as God-Almighty important as you make out, I ought not to have to worry what anybody calls me—especially not the members of the Gavin Ladies Historical Society."

"Maybe you should worry about how people treat your wife!" she shrills back, so loud and sharp it makes my scalp prickle. "Instead of a bunch of those dark-skinned heathens and their brats!"

Henry's shoulders sag, as if all of a sudden he's just too tired to keep on. "I'll pay who I like, and I'll feed who I like. Colored or white, it's got nothing to do with you."

And with that, he's gone.

In the quiet I hear the lock turn on his bedroom door, as cold and final as if he had slammed it. For a moment it's only Susanne and me standing there, her with her bloodless face, me shaking like a leaf, and I know any minute she's going to see me and realize I've heard every last word. I think about losing my place, about going home to Mama, and I almost hope she does see me. But she doesn't. She only melts back into her room, banging the door shut behind her.

The blood seems to have left my legs as I make my way down the stairs. I've just entered the kitchen when I hear Susanne call for me. I close my eyes and gather my nerves, then grab one of the dark flat bottles from the back of Lottie's pantry. The Missus will be wanting a dose of her tincture.

She's sitting in the dark when I step into her room, still as death in the small square of moonlight bleeding through the window. She's stripped down to her slip now, her clothes a dark puddle on the carpet, and I see that she's pulled all the pins from her hair. It's standing out from her head like a halo of snakes. The sight of it—of her—makes me shiver.

"Ms. Susanne?" I say, soft, like I'm creeping up on something poisonous. "Do you want the light?"

When she doesn't answer, I click on the lamp. I expect to find her crying, but what I find glittering in those icy eyes has nothing to do with tears, and I know then and there that I never want Susanne Gavin holding a grudge against me.

"Go down and fetch a bottle from the pantry, Adele. I—" Her gaze falters, skittering away from mine. "I spilled the last one."

I ignore the lie and point to the bottle sitting next to the lamp. "I already brought one."

Her eyes touch mine again, a wary look that says we share a secret and if I know what's good for me it'll stay a secret. After a minute, though, they go flat and dull, as if she's somehow looking through me, and for the first time I notice her hands, darting and scratching like a pair of pale, angry birds, raising bloody welts on her wrists.

"Should I fetch Mr. Gavin? You don't look . . . well." I know, even as I say the words, that Henry's the last person she wants to see, but I have to say something—do something—before she flays herself raw.

Her eyes spark to life then, and for the moment her hands are still. "Do you know what my husband has been up to, Adele?"

The knot in my belly tightens. I don't want to hear this, don't want to hear her call Henry a fool again for making sure men can feed their children. My hands are unsteady as I splash a bit of bootleg into her pink teacup.

"Well, do you?"

The words are so sharp my head snaps up. I blink at her, trying to think what to say as I work the stopper loose from the little brown bottle and carefully, carefully, count out fifteen precious drops.

"He's been hiring colored men!" she hollers, so loud I know she means for Henry to hear her clear down the hall. "Colored men to work at Peak, when hardworking white men need jobs! It's a scandal, that's what it is, and it's going to ruin us if he keeps on."

I push the cup and saucer into her hands, praying she'll send me away now that she has what she wants. But she's not through.

"He's making a fool of me, Adele. Shaming me, and giving gossips like Celia Cunningham fat to chew in front of all my friends, and in my own house, too."

It's on the tip of my tongue to say that she should be proud of Henry for what he's doing and why he's doing it, and that any decent wife would have told Celia Cunningham so. But in my mind I see Mama shaking her head, hissing at me to hold my tongue. So I do. It's hard, though. There's a whole lot I'd like to say.

She takes a little sip from her teacup and closes her eyes as it goes down, then rattles the cup back into its saucer with a sigh. She must take my silence for sympathy, because she picks up her ranting again, like somehow since dinner we've become bosom friends.

"I'd like to know what my daddy would say if he had any idea just what kind of man he married me off to. I'll bet he'd say a man's got a duty to care what people think of him, especially when his son's about to be born. Don't you think so, Adele?"

I turn away, pretend to tidy the bed. I can't say what I think, and I can't look at her. I see her too clearly now, behind all the anger and the bootleg, too grasping and proud to care for a man who won't be tucked in, polished up, or made over. It was Peak she was chasing after all those years, and Peak that she finally married. Henry was only part of the bargain, unworthy in her eyes—of her, or Peak, or even his family name. And I see, too, that she's set all her store by the child in her belly, the son she means to bear and mold into all his father is not.

She's sipping hard from her cup now, rocking a little from side to side. I think about bringing a cloth to wipe the blood from her wrists, but I don't. Instead, I pick her dress and stockings up off the floor, then tidy up the table by her bed.

"I asked you a question, Adele. Have you nothing to say?"

I can feel her eyes boring into my back like a blade, and I turn with her bottle of tincture in my hand, tightening down the stopper and praying she's already swallowed enough to forget what I'm about to say, because suddenly the words are on my tongue and I can't stop them.

"I think Mr. Henry does a lot of good for folks, and that's something a wife should be proud of."

Her eyes go hard as stone. "You're taking up for him?"

She's fuming, but somehow I don't care. It stuns me that she cannot see the good in her husband, and that for all her fancy airs she's no better than Celia Cunningham. "I only said he does a lot of good, the kind of good they preach about on Sundays, and that not a lot of wives have that to be proud of."

"Proud?" Her eyes have gone funny, like they do after the tincture, like she expects something to spring at her from one of the corners. "I should be proud that my husband is willing to tarnish my good name over a handful of niggers?"

I go numb all over when she says it. Not what she says, but the way she says it, like it came from the deepest, blackest part of her soul. I don't mean to—or maybe I do—but I let the brown bottle slip from my hand. I don't need to look down to know it smashed. I can smell the foul stuff splattered all over the floor, all over my shoes. And if that isn't enough, the panic in Susanne's eyes is. It's her last bottle, all the more precious since the doctor cut her back.

She's on her feet now, flying across the room, and I steel myself for the crack of her hand. Instead, she collapses to her knees in all the sticky mess and broken glass, crying like it's the end of the world.

Chapter 8

Leslie

The door to Henry Gavin's study moaned in oily protest as Leslie turned the knob and pushed inside. Even now, the sound brought a guilty pang. The study, still brimming with the prized collections of her long-dead great-grandfather, had always been strictly off-limits. In fact, in the eight years she lived at Peak, she'd been allowed into the study exactly three times.

Aside from a ponderous mahogany desk and an old Victrola her grandfather had cranked up for her once, she had little memory of the room or its contents. It was why she had chosen to start here. She thought it would be easier than Maggie's room, with its drawers full of old slips and nightgowns, its nightstand littered with eyeglasses and hand creams. Now she was beginning to wonder.

Inside, all was gloomy and still, the quiet air thick with scents from another era—leather, tobacco, the musty breath of old books—as if she had breached the sanctity of some long-sealed shrine. And in a way she had. Toward the end of Henry's life the study had become his sanctuary, the place he spent his days, took his meals, and sometimes even slept, until one morning Maggie had found him slumped behind his desk. After the funeral the room had been shut up and, as far as Leslie knew, had remained so.

Now, as she drew back drapes of heavy brocade and took in her surroundings, it was easy to see why she'd been kept out as a child. This was no place for little hands. Banks of curio cabinets lined two of the walls, one wall dedicated to vintage clocks and antique pens, the other to Henry's cherished pipe collection. A third wall was lined floor to ceiling with books, heavy leather-bound editions of Cooper, Twain, and Dickens, along with other names she didn't recognize.

But it was the ornately framed oils above the fireplace that intrigued Leslie most, perhaps because their less than subtle sensuality was at such stark odds with the rest of the room. There were five in all, each hinting at some scriptural event—Delilah with her dagger, Rebecca at the well—but always the same face, haunting and honey skinned, with heavy-lidded eyes and a mouth like ready fruit.

Leslie gnawed at her thumbnail, letting her eyes move from painting to painting. It didn't fit somehow, that a man who had surrounded himself with antiques and classic literature should have a taste for racy art, but then maybe they were worth something. Standing on tiptoe, she attempted to decipher the jaunty ochre strokes at the corner of each canvas but could make nothing of them. Not that a name would matter. If they weren't van Gogh or Picasso, she was basically clueless. And these were neither, though they weren't bad. In fact, they were quite good now that she looked at them. Maybe Henry had a better eye for art than she thought. Either way, she was ready to write them off to personal taste and move on.

The massive mahogany desk was still where she remembered it, positioned at the center of the room like a stoic battleship. Leslie eased into the cracked leather chair, placing the flats of her hands on the scarred surface of the desk where the day-to-day business of Peak Plantation had been overseen and tallied. That the room was still furnished with Henry's prized possessions didn't surprise her. In his day he'd been something of a legend here in Gavin, the man who, with nothing but grit and bare hands, had created a tobacco dynasty and put a tiny town on the map.

As she glanced around the room she thought of Henry, the rawboned man in the ill-fitting suit who had collected and cherished these treasures over a lifetime. She had never known the man who smoked the pipes or wielded the pens or read the books, but somehow, just by being here, Henry Gavin had become very real.

With something like reverence, Leslie eased open the desk's center drawer, fully expecting to find it empty. Instead, she found a smattering of loose change, a pack of old playing cards, a few dusty paper clips, and a wristwatch with a missing strap, as if Henry wasn't dead at all but had only stepped away.

The rest of the drawers and compartments housed more utilitarian items: a prehistoric adding machine almost as large as a typewriter, files stuffed with receipts for things like heating oil, truck tires, and plow blades. In the final drawer she unearthed a stack of cloth-covered ledgers, Peak's accounts from the thirties. Not exactly riveting reading, but maybe the local historical society would be interested in how much bright leaf Peak yielded back in '34.

She was about to knee the drawer closed when she glimpsed what looked like a small book half-hidden behind the ledgers. It took some doing to work it free, but finally she had it—a volume of sonnets bound in dark leather. The embossing on the front cover had long since worn away, but along the spine the name Barrett Browning was thinly visible. Poetry too, then. It appeared Henry Gavin was truly a Renaissance man.

When the pages parted unexpectedly to reveal a delicate spray of dried flowers, Leslie's mouth parted in a silent O. Instinctively, her fingers sought the pale petals, paper-thin and long bled of color, trying to guess what their original hue had been—yellow, perhaps, or pink. It was impossible to say. Had they been placed between these pages for a reason, she wondered, or had the pages been chosen at random? Curious, she slid the flowers aside to read the marked passage.

> *How do I love thee? Let me count the ways.*
> *I love thee to the depth and breadth and height*
> *My soul can reach, when feeling out of sight*
> *For the ends of Being and ideal Grace.*
> *I love thee to the level of everyday's*
> *Most quiet need, by sun and candlelight.*
> *I love thee freely, as men strive for Right;*
> *I love thee purely, as they turn from Praise.*
> *I love thee with the passion put to use*
> *In my old griefs, and with my childhood's faith.*
> *I love thee with a love I seemed to lose*
> *With my lost saints,—I love thee with the breath,*
> *Smiles, tears, of all my life!—and, if God choose,*
> *I shall but love thee better after death.*

The final lines echoed in Leslie's head as she read them. She had never cared much for poetry, but something about the words of love and loss seemed to resonate deep down in her bones, and she knew as she closed the book on those faded petals that the words had not been so tenderly marked for nothing. Turning to the front cover, she found what she was looking for.

For Henry, on his birthday.

There was no signature, but the hand was almost certainly a woman's, thin and delicately slanted, more than likely belonging to Henry's wife, Susanne. Seeking confirmation, she flipped over to the back page and, instead, found a photograph.

With ginger hands, she slid it free and tipped it to the light. It was a portrait, a woman stiffly posed with a baby in her arms. She wore neat white gloves with her simple dress, and a broad-brimmed hat that left most of her face in shadow. It was impossible to guess her age or to make out anything beyond a small glimpse of mouth, except to note that she wasn't smiling. Leslie peered harder at the mottled image. Though there was no way to be sure, no writing on the back, and not enough of a face to pick out family resemblances, she knew she must be looking at her great-grandmother, Susanne, and a tiny version of Maggie.

Her grandmother couldn't have known it was here, or it would almost certainly have ended up with the others on the parlor table, rather than being left to disintegrate between the pages of an old book. Shaking her head, she studied the photo with a professional eye. It was badly deteriorated, 1920s, maybe thirties, gelatin silver, and in such bad shape that in places the image was almost completely silvered out. Worse than the chemical deterioration were the dog-eared corners and peeling edges, evidence of frequent and careless handling, and a heinous crime to any photographer worth her salt.

Leslie lingered guiltily over the photo, wondering what to do with it, though whether her guilt was professional or sentimental she couldn't say. It could probably be restored, but to what purpose? Susanne Gavin was little more than a name to her, and Maggie had ceased to be part of her life thirty years ago. She had no ties to her Gavin kin or to anything they'd left behind. Those doors had all closed long ago, rusted shut by time and distance.

In the end, she slid the photograph back into the book and returned them both to the drawer where she'd found them. Sooner or later she was going to have to pack all this up, and the photo would be safer where she found it than floating around loose somewhere.

She'd think about having it restored at some point, but right now she had other priorities.

When the doorbell rang at twenty after three, Leslie swallowed a pang of annoyance. The Gavin Yellow Pages had offered a choice of exactly three Realtors, and somehow she'd managed to choose the one who didn't own a watch. She'd set the appointment for three; showing up twenty minutes late hardly inspired confidence.

Pasting on a smile, she opened the door, squelching the urge to glance pointedly at her own watch. "Mrs. MacLean?"

Avis MacLean was nearly as round as she was tall, encased in a snug turquoise pantsuit and wearing enough jewelry to bankroll a small third-world country. She was past middle age, though precisely how far past, it was hard to say. Her skin was like saddle leather, her hair the color of unbleached cotton. When she smiled her small blue eyes all but disappeared.

"You must be Leslie," she said, poking a hand through the open door. "You don't mind if I call you Leslie, do you? I'm Avis, Avis Mac-Lean, but you just call me Avis. I hope I'm not late, though I bet I am. I thought I'd never get here. The roads are a nightmare these days with all the lane closings. I'll be late everywhere I go until they get them finished. It's like the time change. I never can get it right. Still, I manage. My, my, aren't you a pretty thing. Now, when you called this morning you said you were thinking of selling this gorgeous place."

Leslie stood blinking in the doorway until she was sure it was her turn to speak. "It's nice to meet you—and yes, Leslie's fine."

Avis gave her a glossy, coral-hued smile. "I met your grandmother once, you know," she said as she wrestled a planner from the jaws of her enormous handbag. "She was a friend of my mother's. They were involved in some group together, the Ladies Heritage Society, I think it was, something like that. I never could keep up with all her groups. I heard she'd taken to growing grapes. Your grandmother, I mean, not my mother, of course. Is my car all right where it is, do you think, or should I move it? I don't want to block the drive."

Leslie felt vaguely dizzy, like she'd been caught in a small dust storm. "It'll be fine," she said, eyeing the great white boat of a Cadillac, not so much parked as stranded in the middle of the drive, precisely where the idea to stop had obviously occurred.

"Uh . . . would you like to start with the inside?"

Avis stepped over the threshold and into the foyer. There was a clicking of bracelets as she flipped open her planner. "I'm all yours, honey. Lead the way."

She jotted notes as they moved from room to room, launching a series of rapid-fire questions. Had there been any additions, or was the whole house original? Did she know of any historic persons associated with the house, war heroes, that sort of thing? Was she aware of any structural problems? Did she know the exact year of construction or the name of the architect?

When Leslie couldn't answer a single thing, Avis patted her arm, undeterred. Such things could be researched.

Twenty minutes later the tour was over and they were back downstairs. "Well, that's the house," Leslie said to prompt her. "There's a smaller house too, out back, if you want to see it, though it's probably a wreck after sitting empty for so long. I haven't had time to check it out. So far, though, what do you think?"

There was no missing the enormous diamond on Avis's left hand as she closed her planner. "What do I think? I think it's grand. In fact it's breathtaking. But then, I don't see many houses like this gorgeous monstrosity."

"Maybe you'd be interested?" Leslie suggested, only half kidding.

Avis laughed—a hoarse, smoker's laugh. "My husband would throw me out for sure. It's an occupational hazard, you know. Last year I picked up three bargains. Then the bottom fell out."

Leslie blinked at her. "Bottom?"

"From the real estate market, I mean. Now we're like everyone else. Tapped out and sitting on a bunch of houses we can't sell. Nothing's moving."

"Nothing?"

"Haven't sold a property in eight months." Avis shook her bleachy white head. "Plenty of listings, all just sitting."

"That's not exactly what I was hoping to hear."

"I'm sure it isn't, but the recession's hit us hard here. Folks are having to leave to find work, and the banks just aren't lending, especially on rural properties."

Leslie felt a lump form in the pit of her stomach. Thus far, Avis hadn't given her a single reason to be optimistic. She was standing at the back door now, peering out at the rolling green lawn and the lake beyond.

"Lord, but it's a stunning piece of land. How much acreage did you say goes with the house?"

"I didn't, but it's about forty-five acres. The rest belongs to Maggie's former partner, who inherited it on her death, along with the cottage and lake."

"What do you call it again? The farm, I mean. I seem to remember it having a name, like Southfork in Dallas." Avis glanced back over her shoulder at Leslie. "Or maybe you don't call it that anymore since it's been split up?"

Leslie opened her mouth to answer only to find she couldn't. She'd never really thought about it, but the idea that Peak should ever be called anything *but* Peak vexed her now. Since she was selling, she supposed it really shouldn't matter one way or the other.

It shouldn't, but it did.

"Peak," she finally answered more tersely than she intended. "And yes, we still call it that."

Avis remained quiet a long time, still gazing out at the lake and the sinking sun. When Leslie couldn't stand another moment of silence, she gave her a prod. "Well, will it sell? What do you think?"

"What do I think?" Avis repeated as she turned and met Leslie's gaze squarely. "I think anyone lucky enough to inherit a place like this but wants to get rid of it has to be nutty as an outhouse rat."

Leslie forced a smile. "Maybe, but that's my plan. My life isn't here. It's in New York."

"Hard to imagine a life better than this right here, honey."

Leslie fought a sigh of frustration. "I'm in a bit of a crunch, Avis . . . if you know what I mean."

Avis's expression softened. "I think I do, honey. It's just a shame. If you'd come to me two years ago—back when things were booming—I could have gotten you a fortune. And I could have done it quick."

"And now?"

"Now I couldn't move it for half of what it's worth."

"Then you don't want the listing?"

Avis waved a jewel-covered hand. "Well, don't be ridiculous, honey. Of course I want the listing! Things won't be in the dumps forever. But you're going to have to be patient. What you've got here is an investment property, a bed-and-breakfast just waiting to happen. But there's no market for that kind of thing right now. No bank's going to touch this place until things turn around."

"How long?"

"A year. Maybe longer."

Leslie felt what was left of her hopes plummet. There were other Realtors in town—two, to be precise. But her gut told her Avis knew what she was talking about.

"If it were you, what would you do?"

Avis blinked at her a moment with her heavily made-up eyes, then let go another of her smoky laughs. "If it were me? That's easy. I'd quit moping and find a way to make a little lemonade out of this lemon." She swept her arm, encompassing the lake and hills and sky. "Take a look around, honey. You've inherited paradise."

Chapter 9

Leslie rocked slowly on the back porch, watching anvil-shaped clouds pile up over the lake, the promise of rain in their flat lavender bellies. Nothing about the day had gone according to plan. In fact, she'd accomplished exactly none of the things on her to-do list. She hadn't purged a single item from a single room, hadn't made it into town for groceries, hadn't filed a forwarding order with the post office. And she hadn't put Peak on the market.

The day's heat was finally beginning to ease, the afternoon sliding lazily toward evening. The breeze rose, sharp and moist, fragrant with green things. Leslie closed her eyes and tipped her face to it.

Paradise.

Or at least Avis MacLean thought so. And she supposed, if she took this moment—just this and nothing else—she could see it too, all sprawling lawns and antebellum charm. But she *couldn't* take just this moment; she had to take it all. All the questions she'd never asked because she was afraid to hear the answers. All the behind-the-hand whispers about what *really* happened the day her mother died. Hardly the stuff of paradise.

But Avis didn't know about those things. She promised to call in a few days, after she had done a little legwork and talked to a few folks. In the meantime she wanted Leslie to carefully consider her options before committing to something she might regret later.

Would she regret it?

Staying had certainly never been part of the plan, but then so many things lately hadn't been part of the plan. Could she actually make a life here? Turn her back on a career it had taken her more than a decade to build, and embrace the legacy of a woman she had barely known? It seemed ridiculous, and yet—

Even before she knew where she was going, Leslie was on her feet, marching down the porch steps and out across the lawn, past a cluster of weathered curing sheds, then the main barn with its ash-colored boards and rusty tin roof. It had housed a pair of tractors when she was a girl, and for one winter, a calico cat and her seven kittens. It had never occurred to her back then that it might belong to her one day. In fact, she could hardly believe it now.

Beyond the barn and a small copse of hardwoods, she could just make out the roof of the Little House, the plain two-story farmhouse where she had lived with her parents as a child. She'd been back three full days but had avoided going anywhere near the place, not ready to face the memories that awaited her in those empty rooms. Now, somehow, it was time. There were decisions to make, her future hanging in the balance. It was time to stop dithering and time to stop hiding.

As she picked her way through the trees, she envisioned empty, neglected rooms, a leaky roof, and rotting floorboards, but as the distance closed she saw that the house was in better shape than she expected—much better, in fact. The porch was freshly painted, the windows open and billowing with sheer white curtains, and along the front walk a border of pink petunias nodded in the shade. But the bigger surprise, by far, came when a little strawberry blonde burst from the screen door, tore down the front porch steps, and disappeared around the side of the house.

Astonished, Leslie could only follow. She stopped short when she reached the open gate and spotted the clothesline fluttering with pale blue sheets. There was a moment of confusion, a dizzying sense of time rewinding, smells and sounds dragging her back against her will—lemon and bleach and fresh-cut grass, the sharp snap of wet sheets on the breeze. And a dark-haired girl of about six, just home from school, playing peekaboo while her mother hung out the wash. She barely remembered that girl.

The image evaporated abruptly as Leslie noticed a woman with a halo of sun-streaked curls step from behind the sheets. She was pretty and petite, dressed in a knotted T-shirt and very skinny jeans.

"I'm Angie Shively," she said, smiling as she reached the gate. "You must be Leslie. Young Buck said you'd come."

"Young Buck?"

"That's my daddy." The girl from the front porch was beside her mother now, Jay's dog, Belle, at her side. "He's off with Uncle Jay at a meeting."

Leslie's attention shifted from daughter to mother. "Uncle . . . Jay?

Angie narrowed an eye on the girl. "All right, motormouth, can I talk now?" She turned back to Leslie with an apologetic roll of the eyes. "Sorry about that. He and Young Buck drove over to Wilkesboro to look at some equipment this afternoon, but really I think they just wanted a break from messing with that damn tractor."

The girl's head snapped up, and her pout suddenly vanished. "You said a swear! You owe me a quarter!"

Angie gave her daughter's left braid a playful tug. "Nice try, you little chiseler. You still owe me for that *ain't* in the grocery store yesterday, so the way I see it, we're even. Now, let's say hello properly. Sammi Lee, this is Daddy's new boss. Her name is Miss Nichols."

Sammi Lee cocked her head thoughtfully. "I thought Uncle Jay was Daddy's boss."

"He is, baby, and Miss Leslie is his partner. She's here to help him with the vineyard. Miss Maggie was her grandmother."

Leslie opened her mouth but didn't know what to say. She wasn't here to help with the vineyard, and she wasn't anyone's boss.

"Nice to meet you, Miss Leslie," Sammi Lee said politely. "You sure don't look like a farmer."

Leslie laughed in spite of herself. "That's because I'm not a farmer."

"Then how're you supposed to help Uncle Jay?"

Angie chose that moment to step in. "All right, Miss Priss, just you stop being so nosy. It's almost six, and past Belle's dinnertime. What would Uncle Jay say if he knew you were late?" The words were barely out of her mouth when Sammi Lee turned and tore for the house. "Only three scoops," Angie called after her. "And no more Milk-Bones!"

She was shaking her head when she turned back to Leslie. "Sorry about the third degree. She wears me out."

Leslie waved off the apology. "I'm sorry about sneaking up on you. I didn't know anyone lived here." She scanned the yard now—the deck that ran the length of the house, the picnic table and swing set—and realized how little it actually resembled the backyard of her childhood. "I used to live here."

"Maggie told me."

"You knew my grandmother?"

"I did. The woman was a force of nature." A gust of wind kicked up. Angie glanced at the sky, then her half-full basket. "Rain's coming. Do you mind? If I hurry I can get the rest up and dry before it starts to come down."

Intrigued, Leslie trailed after her to the line, plucking a handful of clothespins from the bag and feeding them to her one at a time. "I'm sorry, but did you call my eighty-year-old grandmother a force of nature?"

"No one would have guessed the Old Broad was in her eighties, at least not until right near the end." She paused, smiling sadly. "Old Broad—that's what Jay called her. She used to fuss like anything whenever he said it, but we all knew she loved it. They were a pair, those two." When the basket was empty Angie turned toward the house. "I was about to have a beer. Have one with me?"

Leslie nodded. She hated beer, but she had more questions. On the deck, she waited awkwardly in a white plastic chair until Angie emerged with an ice-filled bucket and four Bud Lights.

"Thank God that dog's a good sport," she said as she dropped into the chair beside Leslie. "I just found her dressed in half my daughter's back-to-school clothes." Twisting the cap off a beer, she handed it to Leslie, then grabbed one for herself. "So how is it being back? It must seem weird as hell after all these years." She bit her lip and threw a glance over her shoulder. "Lord, I hope Sammi Lee didn't hear that."

Leslie sipped her beer, fighting a shudder as it fizzed down her throat. "I'm guessing you two have a little game going?"

"I pay her a quarter every time she catches me swearing. She pays me every time I catch her saying *ain't*. I'm trying to teach her you can be from the country without sounding country."

"How's it working?"

Angie grinned. "She's putting me in the poorhouse. So . . . how *does* it feel to be home?"

Leslie winced at the word *home* but let it pass. "There's so much to do I don't know where to start. In fact, I haven't started at all. I've made a lot of lists, though."

"At least the place wasn't a wreck after all those months sitting empty."

She hadn't thought of it before, but now that she did she realized there hadn't been a speck of dust on anything. "Have I got you to thank for that?"

Angie chuckled. "I can barely keep up with my own house. It was Jay."

"Jay . . . Davenport?"

"He started when Maggie got sick. He'd dust or take care of the laundry, whatever needed doing. When she died he just kept on, every Monday whether it needed it or not." Tipping back her bottle, she took a long pull, then swatted at something buzzing around her head. "I guess there's still a lot to do, but at least you're finally home."

Leslie squirmed uncomfortably. Sooner or later she was going to have to say something about being back. "To tell you the truth, it doesn't feel like home at all. Everything's familiar. In fact, almost nothing has changed. It just doesn't feel like it belongs to me, or like I belong to it."

"Oh, that'll pass," Angie said, waving the remark away. "I've got a friend who moved here from Boston. She thought she'd never adjust to small-town life. Now, after less than a year, she feels like she's been here her whole life. The same thing will happen to you." Standing, she smoothed down the knees of her jeans and grabbed the bucket. "I've got to go in and start dinner. Nothing fancy, just pork chops and greens. We'd love for you to stay."

"Are you sure there's enough?"

"At this house, there's always enough. Once you meet Young Buck you'll know why. Come on, you can give me a hand."

"I'm afraid I'm not much of a cook. I do set a mean table, though."

"Great, you're hired."

Leslie followed reluctantly. It felt strange being in the same kitchen where her mother had baked muffins and helped her with her math, mostly because it bore almost no resemblance to that kitchen of her youth. Gone were the green appliances and gold-flecked Formica, replaced with clean white tile and glass-front cabinets.

"Want the nickel tour, for old times' sake?"

Leslie shook her head. "Maybe later."

For the next half hour, Angie flitted about the kitchen, seasoning and stirring and popping things into the oven, chattering about townspeople Leslie had never heard of and would probably never meet. When she poked her head around the corner and hollered for Sammi Lee to come set the table, Leslie bounced out of her chair, glad to finally be able to contribute.

Angie was bringing the last of the food to the table when Sammi Lee finally made her entrance, skidding sideways into the kitchen in a pair of fuzzy yellow socks, erupting in a fit of giggles as Belle piled into the back of her. When her mother threw her an exasperated look, she swallowed her amusement and took her place at the table. Leslie slid in beside her, holding her breath as Sammi Lee grappled with the iced tea pitcher and actually managed to fill three glasses without mishap.

Leslie had lifted her glass halfway to her lips when she felt Sammi Lee's gentle tug on her sleeve. "Grace, Miss Leslie," she whispered softly. "We gotta say grace."

Later, when the dishes were washed and put away and Sammi Lee had stomped off to take her bath, Leslie and Angie adjourned to the deck. Leslie let her head drop back against her chair, lulled by the glow of citronella candles and whatever Angie had used to lace their coffee. Night was coming fast, the air heavy with the promise of rain. In the distance, mushroomy blooms of blue-white light chased from cloud to cloud.

Beside her, Angie flipped open a box of Marlboros, slid one from the pack, and lit it. She released the first cloud of smoke on a long, ecstatic sigh, then offered the pack to Leslie.

Leslie shook her head. "I didn't picture you as a smoker."

"I'm not really," she said, setting the pack on the railing and taking another pull. "I sneak four, maybe five a day. Buck pretends not to know."

"Your husband pretends not to know you smoke?"

"Sweet, huh? I'm careful around Sammi Lee, though. I wait until she's in school or in bed." She flicked an ash over the railing. "They teach them about smoking in school now. They teach them about everything. I can't believe how much she's grown since we moved here."

Leslie saw an opening and pounced on it. "How long have you been at Peak?"

Another plume of smoke lifted into the air. "I guess it's almost five years now. We were in dire straits after the bank in Yadkin took our vineyard. If Jay hadn't turned up and made us this offer, I don't know where we'd be."

"What happened, if you don't mind me asking?"

"Drought," Angie answered flatly. "We were still in the early stages, operating on a shoestring. We couldn't afford a fancy irrigation system. Two years of no rain and we were out of business. When the bank stepped in, Buck took a job as a hand in a neighboring vineyard just to keep a roof over our heads. It was a pretty bad time."

"Until Uncle Jay rode to the rescue?"

"He's not really anyone's uncle. He turned up when we ran an ad to sell off our equipment."

"Well, that was certainly convenient."

Angie either missed the sarcasm or chose to ignore it. She flicked her Marlboro over the railing, into a nearby hedge. "He had a million questions. Didn't know the first thing about running a vineyard, but he had a dream—a great big dream—and for Buck that made him some kind of soul mate. I couldn't peel the two of them apart. Next thing I know we're hauling everything we own to someplace I've never heard of. He couldn't promise any steady money, just a roof over our heads and a piece of the action."

"He sounds like quite a salesman."

"The man's got a way with words; I'll give him that. But then you'd expect him to, I guess. Anyway, it worked. Three weeks later, here we were." Angie lit another cigarette, took a deep pull, and stared at the glowing tip. "Actually, moving here was Maggie's idea. She was smart enough to see they needed somebody with experience. And thank God, too. I don't know how much longer I could have stood Buck."

"I'm sorry about your vineyard."

Angie shrugged. "Things happen for a reason. This must be where we're supposed to be right now. And maybe when Peak starts producing we can save up enough to start over. By then, Jay won't need Buck. I've gotta give it to him. For someone who didn't know what he was doing, he's certainly brought the place a long way. It's sad Maggie couldn't live to see it. She used to talk about how Peak was a real tobacco dynasty back in the day."

"It was. Then my grandfather died of lung cancer."

Angie stubbed out the freshly lit Marlboro. "Well, I guess that explains her nagging. Do you remember him?"

"Not much. I was four, maybe five when he died. But I remember his funeral. Half of Gavin was there. After the cemetery, everybody came back to the house. But Maggie wouldn't come inside. Instead, she marched out to the fields and yanked up the first tobacco plant she came to. Then she yanked up the next one, and the next—just grabbed them and ripped them out by the roots. I could see her from the window in her good black dress, all covered in dirt. She stayed out there until it got dark, until someone went and got her. The next day she paid old man Snipes to plow it all under. She swore Peak would never grow another leaf of tobacco, and it didn't."

Angie reached for the Marlboros, then checked herself, pinning her hands between her knees instead. "She never told me that story, but it sounds like her. She loved this place so much. It was like, I don't know, the way she left her mark on the world, I guess. I think that's why Jay works so hard. He promised Maggie he'd keep it going. She'd be glad you're back home."

Leslie shifted to the edge of her seat. "I met with a real estate agent today, Angie."

Angie's shoulders, silhouetted by the candles, slumped a little. "Buck said you might. Did he have anything promising to say?"

"It's a she, but no, not really." Leslie paused to sip from her mug. "Avis is her name. A bit of a character, but she seems to know what she's talking about. I gave her the full tour, and all I found out is that the market has imploded and nothing is selling right now. She suggested I stay and turn the place into a bed-and-breakfast."

"Would that be so bad? Staying, I mean?"

"It would be . . . uncomfortable. There's just too much baggage for me here. Except—"

"Except?"

"Except there are some nice memories too, which I didn't expect— bits of jewelry and old family photos that make me think about all the women who have lived here. It's not that I'm sentimental about any of it, but just getting rid of it all seems so . . . final."

"You don't sound very sure about what you want."

Leslie sighed and slumped back in her chair. "I guess that's because I'm not. I don't know how much Maggie told you, but I had my reasons for staying away. I also had my reasons for coming back. None of which, by the way, have anything to do with getting rich, despite what Jay thinks."

"But you are thinking about selling your half?"

"Yes . . . maybe . . . I don't know. I thought it would all be cut-and-dry. Just clear the place out and put it on the market, but there's so much history here. Not mine, but my family's."

"Doesn't that make it yours too?"

"Not really. I disconnected myself from all that a long time ago. But now everywhere I look there's all this stuff—Maggie's stuff, her father's stuff—and it all used to mean something."

"Maybe it still does."

Leslie chafed at the quiet knowing in Angie's voice. "Meaning?"

"Meaning, maybe you're not as disconnected from all that *stuff* as you think. Or from Peak either. Like I said, things happen for a reason. Your grandmother left you an honest-to-God legacy here. Maybe you should take a little time before you decide to throw that away."

"You sound like Jay now."

"Sounds like you two haven't exactly hit it off."

Leslie grimaced but decided to keep her thoughts to herself.

"Look," Angie went on. "I'm not saying he doesn't come off like a jerk sometimes—he's a guy. But if he says or does something, even if it's stupid, it's because he's trying to do the right thing by a lot of folks, all at the same time. He's a good guy, Leslie, one of the few, in fact. So maybe you should give him a break and at least listen to what he has to say."

Leslie was still searching for the correct response when a jagged shaft of lightning split the sky, coupled with a sharp crack of thunder. Behind them, the kitchen light flickered.

"Mama!"

Sammi Lee's voice filtered through the screen door, high and insistent. Angie was instantly on her feet, concealing her pack of Marlboros beneath a nearby flowerpot. "I'll be right there, baby. Just sit tight with Belle until I grab the sheets off the line." She stood, smoothing down the knees of her jeans. "She's afraid of storms. Speaking of which, you'd better get back to the house before you wind up drenched."

Leslie watched another fork of lightning streak the sky. "I think you're right. Well, thanks for dinner and the, uh . . . chat."

She wasn't completely sure she meant the last part, but one thing was certain as she sprinted across the lawn in a failed attempt to beat the rain. She knew a lot more about Jay Davenport than she had when she stepped off the back porch. And not all of it was bad.

Chapter 10

Jay

Jay shielded his eyes, surveying the slopes where the sun had already burned away the morning's fringe of mist. For better or worse, it was real now, a fait accompli. Yesterday he had written a check to the now defunct Rock Ridge Winery, draining his bank account and leaving no escape hatch. They had wrangled a better price than he expected—forty grand for the stemmer, press, and tanks, another ten for the French oak barrels. A godsend to be sure at thirty cents on the dollar, but it was sobering to know that Rock Ridge was being sold off a piece at a time, and even more sobering to think that a year from now they could be in the same boat.

All that was left was to convince Leslie to come on board.

The prospect had worn a hole in his stomach on the drive home, a hole that had still been there when he woke this morning. Now, after a walk through the rows, he felt a little better. The fruit was coming in nicely; the barns and equipment should be ready in plenty of time for harvest.

There was a fresh bounce in his step as he left Block 3 and headed for Buck's place. Angie must have seen him coming. He'd barely made it onto the porch when she stepped through the screen door, a dish towel over one shoulder.

"You're up early. Come on back. Buck's still asleep, but there's coffee, or I can feed you if you're hungry."

The thought of breakfast held no appeal, but he could do with another jolt of caffeine. He followed Angie to the kitchen, where she filled a mug and pressed it into his hands.

"Buck said the trip was a success and that y'all got a great deal on the equipment."

"It was, and we did. And how did you fare back on the home front all by yourself?"

"Oh, I wasn't all by myself. Leslie came by."

Jay fought to keep his face neutral. "And what did you think of the lady of the manor?"

Angie arched one brow. "I like her—a lot, as a matter of fact."

Jay grunted into his mug.

"That attitude wouldn't have anything to do with her coming back to claim her half, would it?"

"No," he half barked. "It has to do with the fact that she waited a year to do it. She didn't give a damn about Maggie. If she did she would have been at the funeral."

"You've heard the talk about her daddy, about what folks thought when her mother died the way she did. Coming back here couldn't have been easy."

Jay set his mug on the counter more forcefully than he'd intended. "It was easy enough when she thought there was money on the table."

Angie crossed her arms, chin jutting sharply. "It took her a year to get up the nerve to even come. When my aunt Rhonda died we had cousins coming out of the woodwork the next day, and she didn't have a pot to piss in. Leslie isn't that kind of woman."

"I don't need to be told about women like Leslie, Angie. I'm well acquainted."

"I know you are," Angie said softly, and laid a hand on his arm. "Which is why I think you aren't being fair. She's not Theresa, Jay."

Jay felt the familiar grind in his belly at the mention of his ex-wife's name. "You sure don't pull any punches, do you?"

"Not when I think you're wrong, no. This is hard for her, Jay, so hard she doesn't think she can stay, and you're making it harder because she spoiled your plans. You never expected her to show up, let alone consider selling her half out from under you. Now that she has, you feel like she's taken something that belonged to you."

Jay's head snapped up. "So she *is* going to sell?"

"She's sure thinking about it—had a real estate agent here yesterday. And I can tell you, your attitude isn't exactly helping her warm to the place. If you want to make this work, you're going to have to give her a break and stop treating her as if she's stealing half *your* land."

"It's not that. It's not about her half or my half."

"Then what *is* it about?"

"It's about her waltzing back here like she was never gone, no apology, no explanation, just . . . here I am."

Angie looked faintly stunned. "Why should she owe you or anyone else an explanation? Maggie was her grandmother, no matter how long she was gone. Maggie never forgot that. Maybe you shouldn't either. She wanted her granddaughter to be happy. She wanted you to be happy too." Her voice lost some of its edge. "You could, you know."

"What?"

"Be happy."

"Let's drop it, all right?"

He was about to turn away when Angie grabbed his sleeve. "Don't be mad. We've never talked much about your old life, but I know how much you gave up, and why. At some point, though, you have to stop being mad at everything. That includes Maggie's granddaughter. She came back here to start over. So did you, so get on with it." The corners of her mouth twitched. "You're not getting any younger, you know."

Knocking on the front door felt strange after years of simply letting himself in through the mudroom, but something told him Leslie wouldn't appreciate that kind of familiarity. It had taken him the better part of the afternoon to admit that Angie was right, that in his heart Peak had already belonged to him. Every plan he'd made, every step he had taken, was based on owning *all* the grapes, calling *all* the shots. Now there were forty-plus acres of prime fruit in danger of slipping through his fingers.

If Leslie chose to sell her half of Peak, her grapes would go with it, which meant he'd have to rethink everything. Without her half it would be a year, maybe two, before they could bottle enough to open the winery's doors. The unpleasant truth was that he needed Leslie Nichols because he needed her grapes. And so far, he'd done himself no favors in that department. In the future, he was going to have to tread lightly, dust off a little of that charm he used to possess, and know when to keep his mouth shut, no matter how many of his buttons she pushed.

When his third knock still brought no response, he shifted the bottle of wine he was carrying and pushed inside. The drapes were drawn, the house murky and still. He called out as he stepped into the parlor but got no response. Then he heard the clatter of glass against glass. He followed the sound to the kitchen, where he found Leslie sorting through a collection of jars in the refrigerator, iPod on her hip, backside swaying enticingly as she crooned along to Alannah Myles's "Black Velvet."

For a moment he just stood there, vaguely guilty about playing the voyeur but not quite ready to interrupt the show. Why it surprised him to learn she could sing he had no idea. He knew nothing about her, really, except that she'd somehow managed to win over Buck's wife, which was no small feat considering Angie Shively's bullshit meter was more finely tuned than an FBI agent's. She was winding up for the big finale when he finally cleared his throat and made his presence known.

Leslie rounded on him as she yanked out her earbuds. "Don't you knock?"

"I did, as a matter of fact. You probably couldn't hear me—nice voice, by the way."

Leslie pulled the iPod from her waistband and laid it on the counter, her cheeks distinctly pinker than a moment ago. While she collected herself he took a moment to survey the chaos. Every drawer and cabinet seemed to be open, and there wasn't an inch of clear counter space to be found.

"What are you doing?"

"At the moment, I'm cleaning out the refrigerator. There must be ten jars of apple jelly in here, all of them nearly empty. And there's at least a hundred empty bread bags wadded up in these drawers, and twice as many twist ties. They're everywhere."

She paused to huff a strand of hair out of her eyes. When that didn't work she made a second attempt with her forearm. Finally, Jay stepped forward and pushed the strand off her brow, tucking it neatly behind her ear.

Leslie stepped back, murmuring an awkward thank-you. "Was there something you needed?"

"I talked to Angie this morning."

Leslie blinked at him. "And?"

"She thinks I should give you break." No words, just another long stare. Finally, he had managed to render her speechless. "Every now and then Angie Shively feels the need to kick my ass, and it seems today was one of those days."

Leslie eyed him skeptically. "Why should she care about me?"

"Because apparently you two hit it off. I'm just repeating what she said, which is that she thinks I need to give you a break."

"And what do you think?"

Time to turn on a little of that charm. "Well, I haven't completely made up my mind yet, but there's still room on my to-do list."

Leslie actually smiled. "Is that why you're here? To tell me you're considering giving me a break? And is that bottle behind your back a peace offering?"

Jay set the wine on the counter and nudged the refrigerator door closed. "Something like that. I thought it was time we had a grown-up conversation. I'm here to ask for your help."

Leslie's smile dimmed to something resembling wariness. "What kind of help?"

"I want you to taste something."

After rooting through a drawer or two he managed to locate a corkscrew, then produced a pair of wineglasses from the cabinet beside the sink. He filled both and handed Leslie a glass, waiting until she sipped before he did the same.

"It's wine," she said finally, licking the last traces from her lips.

Jay tilted his glass to the light, twirling the stem between his fingers. "It's a Chardonnay, to be precise, and it's ours—Maggie's and mine—and yours, if you want in."

He watched as she lifted her glass to the light, turning it as he had. "I thought you only grew the grapes. I didn't know you made wine. This isn't bad."

"We haven't been producing commercially. Until now we've only been able to make enough to play around with. But we're ready now. Yesterday I bought the last of what we'll need to finally produce our own label. The permits are through, the tanks and the crusher are in the barn, and the barrels are on their way. All that's left is to harvest and crush."

Leslie tucked another stray wisp of hair behind her ear. "I hate to rain on your parade, Jay, but Gavin isn't exactly wine country. I think you'd do better with some mason jars and a still made from old radiator parts. I mean, have you actually thought this through?"

Jay bit his lip, determined to ignore her snarky sense of humor. "Actually, I have thought it through, which is why I'm here talking to you. Until now, we've always sold the bulk of the harvest and turned the cash back into the vineyard. Now, finally, we're on the brink of making the next move."

"And that would be?"

"A full-fledged winery right here at Peak. Right now it's just whites—Chardonnay, Seyval, and a pretty fair Riesling—but we're really close on the reds. The only glitch is we need your grapes."

Leslie's brow scrunched, forming a small V-shaped furrow. "My grapes?"

"Half the grapes out there belong to you. That means you can sell them and pocket the cash, and there's nothing I can do about it."

"You'd still have your half."

"We'll still need to sell a portion of the yield to launch and then keep us afloat until we're on our feet. That's where your grapes come in. If we pool our yields, then sell half for working capital, we'll still have enough to bottle and launch."

"And if we don't . . . pool our yields?"

"Then I sell my grapes like I've done every year, and I'm out forty grand worth of equipment."

Leslie folded her arms and gave a low whistle. "No wonder you were miffed when I showed up. You had it all planned out."

Jay felt the air go out of the room. It wasn't exactly the response he'd been hoping for. "That's true. I did have it all planned. And I was miffed. I never expected you to show up, but you're here now, and that's how Maggie wanted it. It's your decision. You can sell your half and pocket the money. I'll set up the sale if that's what you decide."

Leslie eyed him stonily, giving nothing away. After a moment she turned back to the counter, busying herself with a damp cloth and a sticky jar of marmalade. "How much money are we talking about?"

"Not as much as you'll make down the road if you invest it back into the vineyard with me."

Leslie spun around, still holding the jar. "Have you been practicing that one, or did it just roll off your tongue?"

"Angie said you had a real estate agent here."

"I haven't signed anything."

"But you're thinking of selling and going back to New York."

Leslie shrugged. "Initially, that was the plan. Now I find myself wondering what I'd be going back to. I sublet my apartment when I left. The magazine I worked for folded almost a year ago, and the job market in my field is currently a disaster."

"Then why even consider going back?"

Leslie set the marmalade on the counter. "Because it's what I know. And because it's not here."

"Is here so bad?"

The question seemed to confuse her. She reached for her wine, taking a deep sip. "If you've been here any length of time, you've heard the rumors about my mother's death—and about my father. I was eight when it happened, but the memories are still pretty fresh. So, yes, here is a little bit bad."

Jay searched her face, noting the way her eyes never seemed to settle long in one place. There was something more, some other piece she wasn't telling him. He saw it now, as plain as a neon sign, in the rigid set of her squared shoulders, the wary tension in the angle of her jaw. How had he not seen the vulnerability before?

"It's been thirty years," he said quietly. "Maybe it's time you made some new memories. Good ones this time."

Leslie tipped her glass again, her eyes drifting beyond the kitchen window. "Do you think that's possible—to wipe the slate clean with brand-new memories? Or does that only happen in books?"

Jay cleared his throat, unsettled by her words, by the combination of cynicism and wistfulness. "I think it's what we all hope for."

She glanced up at him then, as if she'd just remembered that he was in the room, her green eyes suddenly keen. "You too?"

How had this become about him? Pretending to sip his wine, he fumbled for an answer. "I was speaking hypothetically."

"Not from experience?"

Leslie's gaze was just penetrating enough to make him squirm. "Everyone's trying to forget something, I suppose. Some have more luck than others."

Mercifully, her gaze shifted again, back beyond the window. She was quiet a long time before she finally responded. "I don't know the first thing about growing grapes or making wine."

Something like hope fluttered in Jay's belly. Had she just said she was staying?

"Buck and I can teach you that. But really, there's something else you can do for us, something besides not selling your share of Peak, that will prove far more helpful than you poking around in the vines and must vats."

Her head came around. "The *what* vats?"

Jay grinned. "You'll learn the jargon. For now, it's your marketing skills I'm after. We're going to need a logo, label designs, photos of both the crush barn and the tasting barn for our brochure, and I was thinking—since I stink at that kind of thing, and you've got a bit of experience with it—I'd like to offer you the job."

"I know absolutely nothing about wine."

"Do you know anything about marketing? About creating an image?"

"Well, yes, but—"

"Then say you'll do it, say you'll stay and be a part of this thing."

He picked up her nearly empty glass and pressed it back into her hands. "I'll tell you now, there won't be much up front. It takes a while to see a profit. But you'll have a roof over your head, and somewhere, your grandmother will be smiling at the thought of Peak in the hands of yet another Gavin woman."

Leslie closed her eyes with a groan, then pulled in a long, deep breath, holding it for what felt like an eternity. Finally, she let it out and opened her eyes. "All right. I must be out of my mind, but I'll stay. For now."

Chapter 11

Adele

Mama always says the worst sorrows come after dark.

It begins at two in the morning—a quiet rush of bloody water, a high, thin wail of despair. Too early, Susanne knows at once, much, much too early. Like the others. When the pains commence she nearly loses her mind, cursing God and raging against her body's betrayal, her eyes all queer and wrung of color. She pants like an animal, one minute howling for me to fetch Henry, vowing me to silence in the next, as if the man won't see that she's lost his child.

The horror goes on forever, hour after hour of savage, sticky anguish, of sweating and keening and writhing, all for a child who will not—who cannot—live. It's a merciless thing, I think, as I stare down at her paper white face on the pillow, to be torn apart for nothing, but sometimes life is merciless. And then, finally, it ends, with one last rush of fluid and a terrible silence.

An hour after Dr. Shaw first cracks open his satchel of instruments and vials, it's all over. He says what Susanne already knows, what we all know, that he's come too late, though sooner would have made no difference. He scoops the little thing up, silent and blue, and swaddles it in a towel. A boy, he murmurs apologetically, and hurries it away. There is a pall over the room, a blackness that is only partly to do with the child, a sense of things ending.

Henry stands at the foot of the bed, gray and stony. He can't bring himself to look at Susanne, can't bring himself to look at me either, as I strip away the bloody sheets, ruck up the cotton night-dress, and sponge the blood of his dead child from his wife's pale thighs. I try not to look at her belly, white and flaccid, empty. For more reasons than I can name, I despise her. But I never wanted this—not this.

She's quiet now, lost in the merciful haze of whatever the doctor has given her. For now at least, the thrashing and wailing are past, and Henry and I are nearly alone in that wretched room. His eyes are shiny wet, his sun-lined face so near to breaking that I can hardly bear it. There's a misery about him, a despair so complete it hangs on him like one of his old plaid shirts, and I realize with a start that his pain is my pain too, as alive and searing as if it were my own heart breaking.

My hand goes to his, curled tight on the footboard. It is not my place to touch him, to comfort him, and yet I cannot seem to stop myself. The roughness of his skin, the warmth of it against my palm, acts on me in a way I have never known. I drop my eyes and draw my hand away, wondering as I scurry back to Susanne's bloody sheets where this sudden breathless ache has come from, and how long it has been crouching within me, unseen and unbidden.

If Henry guesses what I feel, he gives no sign. He's numb, blind just now to anything but his grief, and I am relieved, at least, for that. I cannot bear the thought of his knowing. I can hardly bear to think of it myself.

For weeks, Susanne is too frail to leave her bed. She has lost too much blood—and too much hope. Her cheeks are sallow and chalky, the color of Lottie's biscuit dough, but she will take no food, only her tincture with a little of the bootleg. Dr. Shaw has increased her dosage again, to ease the pain of her empty womb, though in truth I think he has done it for Henry, to give him a little peace and spare him Susanne's rantings.

I do my best to calm her when she's in one of her moods, though at least once a day I find myself cleaning up some bit of crockery—cups, saucers, whatever is at hand to smash to the floor or hurl against the wall. She will receive no visitors, though they come in a steady stream. She will not sit by while they gloat, she tells me miserably, and of course they will gloat, happy to see her brought low yet again, denied the one thing—the only thing—she wants in all the world. They're jealous, she rails, because she has Henry and Peak, and so they're glad she cannot do and have this thing every true woman must do and have. I assure her they've come because they are her friends, to cheer her and offer condolences, but each time I say it I think of Celia Cunningham, and I know Susanne is right.

Weeks fall away like the flesh from her bones, so that by spring Susanne is only a shadow of the haughty woman who greeted me that first day in the downstairs parlor. She is older somehow, shrunken and withered, as if ten years has passed instead of ten weeks since that terrible night. Her face, never pretty, is ravaged now, by misery and too much sipping from her teacup, and so she keeps to her room, too vain to show herself for the wreck she has become.

Her moods are worse too, blank and reckless, swinging like a clock pendulum between self-pity and rage. She no longer cares for Peak and its daily workings, content to leave it all to me. And so between hair washings and letter writing, trips to the dime store, and trips to the druggist, I must now confer with Lottie about the menu for Henry's dinner, must order about the woman who comes in to clean and polish once a week, and must oversee the household accounts. When there is a squabble among the help, it is mine to solve.

When there is a choice between roasted or fried, it is mine to make. And when dinner is set out for Henry, it is mine to share.

The first time I am invited to dine with Henry, I go numb with panic and can barely summon the sense to nod my head. I feel dull and plain in my boiled white apron, but Henry pretends not to notice me chasing my carrots around my plate. It rings in my head every minute that Susanne will choose tonight to end her exile, that she will come down to find me in her place, instead of in the kitchen with Lottie where I belong, and I am torn between bolting my food to hurry the meal and pushing it away untouched.

The next night is easier. I leave my apron on the bed in my little room upstairs and slip into the chair across from Henry as if I belong, as if I were not the daughter of a French Quarter seamstress. And while Susanne pecks at the dinner I've brought up on a tray, I pass her husband the yams and the black-eyed peas, and I learn about tobacco, about priming and suckering and topping, about flue curing and the virtues of oil versus wood. I listen not because it enthralls me, but because tobacco is who and what Henry is, and because it's important to this place he loves with his whole heart.

When Lottie comes in to clear and sees me sitting in Susanne's chair, she stops dead in her tracks. Her eyes shift from me to Henry and then back again. They say nothing good can come of this. She's right, of course. How could good ever come of such a thing? Henry is fifteen years my senior, married to the woman who counts out my pay at the end of every week. But we are here now, standing on the edge of this thing that makes me want to cry and soar and sing all at once, and that is all I care for.

That night, and every night after, we share our dinner, then go into Henry's study. There is nothing improper, only Henry and me sitting among his books while he sips a bit of bourbon and enjoys his pipe. We do not speak of Susanne or the child or of that night. Henry pretends it never happened, and I let him. Still, it is there between us, this dead son, and all the ones who came before, etching quiet chinks into his armor, binding me to him.

I see him guarding his bruises, veering wide of the grief he will not share, but I have come to know every inch of his face, every line and crease, and I see behind those suede brown eyes the part of him that longs to spend its sadness, to empty itself and crumble, and I wonder if he knows how desperately I want to be there for him when he does.

Chapter 12

The book of Exodus calls me a sinner.

For surely the words *Thou shalt not covet thy neighbor's wife*, carved in stone by the hand of God, also charge that I shall not covet my neighbor's husband. But I do. I covet Henry Gavin. There. I have said it, and may God and Mama forgive me. I covet his rare sweet smile and his quiet heart, his buried wishes, his silent aches. I want them for myself. But they belong to another, to a fool who does not want them at all.

A fool, yes, but Susanne Gavin is not blind. Since that first day in the downstairs parlor when she studied my shoes with such keen distaste, I have squirmed beneath her probing eyes, prickling with dread that they might see too much. Now when they linger my legs turn to water. I'm certain they have seen through my skin, to the feelings breathing just beneath the surface, waiting to burst out of me whole and alive. Each time she looks away I'm astonished that she cannot hear the pulse and whisper of his name through my veins.

Henry. Henry. Always Henry.

The months grind past. The days are hard, too long alone in that stifling room, my spine aching with the effort to remember my place. While the sun is up Henry takes refuge in his fields. I have no such freedom. Lately, though, I am at least spared her tongue. She is numb, or nearly so, blind to anything that is not her, an untidy ghost made meek by her bourbon and her syrup. She does not leave her room, does not notice, or does not care, that I have unwittingly become, in all but name, mistress of her house, that her servants look to me now for their daily duties, and that her husband looks to me for company.

We share lunches now, Henry and I, carried down to the lake in small metal pails and eaten in the shade of the willows, where it's cool and we are shielded from Susanne's bedroom window. We do not touch, though I cannot forget that one time, when I reached out to him in his grief and felt my heart begin to beat in earnest, as if the eighteen years that came before had only been marking time. Instead, we sit carefully apart in the long, cool grass. Henry talks about tobacco or the new book he's been reading, small things of no account. I live for these times, reveling in the low, rich timbre of his voice, these few brief stolen moments when he makes me a part of his life.

There is a current that runs between us, an inescapable, yearning connection. I am drawn to him like a tide. As if it was my right. As if it was not a sin. I do not deceive myself that he can ever be mine. We are unlike, mismatched in every way that matters. There are boundaries, rules for people like him and people like me. Still, there are times, fleeting moments when he is unguarded, when I imagine in his gentle eyes a reflection of my own heart. And so long as it remains only in his eyes, I can convince myself that it's only *half* a sin.

No sooner do we finish our lunch than I begin to look toward supper and our quiet time after, when I will sit beside him in his study and listen to the slow ooze of his Carolina drawl, part tar, part honey, as he reads aloud from *Tom Sawyer* or *David Copperfield*. I love the room because it is Henry's, filled with the things he loves, his books and clocks and pipes, how it smells like him—is him. There, surrounded by these treasures, I make believe we share a life instead of only a stolen hour, and make believe I do not feel the small, harsh eyes of his wife fixed on us from the portrait above the fire.

It's only a painting, I tell myself, a few feet of canvas, a few strokes of oil, not real, not alive. Yet she is always with us over that mantel, her probing eyes cold and accusing. I pretend not to feel them. Henry pretends too.

One night, when he can no longer pretend, he lays Mark Twain aside. "It was Mama that started it all," he says, his eyes grave as he raises them to Susanne's portrait. "She wanted to see me married before she died, to know there'd be someone to look after me. Everyone in Gavin knew she was looking to find me a wife. I was too busy to care one way or the other. Then Susanne's daddy paid a call and offered all that land. At the time it seemed worth the price of a wife—even one I didn't love."

He does not love her.

Of all his words, these are the ones I hear, the ones that cause my heart to leap. Deep down, I have always known it, yet I hug the words to me like tender things, to unwrap when I am alone, to gaze upon and cherish. Who does it harm, this quiet, reckless joy? *She* has never missed his love. There is no sentiment in her, no woman's heart. She wants only his name and Peak, and those she has.

"You made your mama happy, at least," I manage to say, my heart such a tangle that I fear anything more would give me away.

Henry shakes his head and smiles, a grim twist of that full, firm mouth I've come to know so well. "Happy? No, I didn't make her happy. Susanne wasn't what my mother had in mind."

"Was there somebody else she did have in mind?"

Henry's eyes drift back to the portrait. "Anyone *but* Susanne would have been fine, I think. They were too alike. She saw through Susanne."

"But you didn't?"

"Back then all I could see was her daddy's land and all the new tobacco I could plant. We both wanted something, and for better or worse, I guess we both got it."

For better or worse.

My eyes creep to Susanne's likeness over the mantel, haughty even then in her fine white lace, and I think of Henry standing beside her at the altar, saying those words and hearing them in return. Had he meant them—even a little? Had he, in those early days, hoped for *better*, for at least some pretense of a marriage, rather than this aloof arrangement lived at opposite ends of the hall? I do not ask, but Henry answers the question as if I had.

"It went wrong from the first day," he says, his voice suddenly thick, his gaze carefully turned from mine. "We were just back from the church. Mama wasn't well and went to lie down. Susanne followed her to her room and told her she'd need to clear her things out by the end of the day, that as my wife she was entitled to the best room."

Of course she had. It was like Susanne to demand her due, proper or not.

"Mama was stunned. She'd been sleeping in that room for nearly forty years, in the bed she shared with my father until he died. And Susanne was turning her out. They went at each other like a pair of cats."

"And you were in the middle," I said softly.

"I should have been, but no. I was in my tobacco fields." His shoulders slumped then, with the kind of shame men rarely show to women, his words thick with regret. "When I heard them start up, I slipped out the back door. I didn't come in until dark. By then, Mama was hanging her clothes in one of the upstairs rooms. That's when I knew what my life would be, that for as long as they were both in this house, I'd be whittled down and pulled apart by the two of them."

My poor Henry.

He is strong in many ways, though not in ways that matter to most. He believes in the rightness of things, in honor and fairness and order. But I see in that moment that he is a man who cannot always stand in the fire. I have always known this somehow, from the first night I saw him in the dining room with Susanne. Women—strong women—overwhelm him. And so I'm determined not to overwhelm, to be, in every way I can think, different from Susanne Gavin. It is not hard. We have only our womanhood in common—and Henry.

That night I lie awake in my small room, listening to sounds that have become a part of Peak's night song and wondering how women can be so very different. I think of how we love, and where, and why. I think of Mama and the man who was my father, of the sorrow that lingers with her still, because she gave him up too late—and because she gave him up at all. And I think of the man who has seized my heart, astonished that Susanne could be made of such hard stuff.

She has no use for a husband who holds the demands of tobacco fields and curing barns above wealth and social standing. She requires a husband worthy of the mistress of Peak Plantation. But Henry is Henry, not to be tucked in, polished up, or made over. And so the future of her dynasty will rest not with Henry, but with a son, one she can mold to be all his father is not. For nine years it has been her quest. Now it seems that too is over.

The next morning Susanne calls me to her room. She tells me to draw her a bath, lay out her clothes, and put up her hair. Dr. Shaw will be paying a call to examine her and tell her how soon she can try for another child. I am stunned that she could think of it after the agony of the last time and all the times before. I wonder what Henry thinks, or if he knows, but it isn't my place to ask.

When Susanne has had her bath and dressed, she sits at her vanity, setting to work with her powders and rouges, going heavy beneath her eyes, where the shadows are deepest. She hopes the doctor will not see the wreck she has become. But there's no chance of that. She's as pale as a shade, her hair limp and bled of color, her body all sharp bones and jutting angles so that her dress hangs on her like a rag.

I keep an eye on the clock as I tidy the room, dreading Dr. Shaw's arrival. When his knock finally comes, I go down to greet him. He removes his hat and offers a smile that doesn't reach his eyes. He's brought no bag, I see. There will be no examination, then, only bad news.

Susanne rises from her dressing table and extends a pale hand as she crosses the room to meet him. Her eyes shift to me. "Leave us, Adele. I'll call for you when the doctor has finished. And close the door on your way out, please."

Susanne is already working at her buttons when Dr. Shaw suggests they sit and talk a bit. There's a flicker of fear in Susanne's eyes as they meet mine in the doorway, a moment of dark knowing. I turn away, eager to be gone when Susanne receives the news I know is coming, that her wreck of a body will not abide another pregnancy, that there will be no more babies.

I have just reached the foyer when the door to Susanne's room bangs open. "You lie!" Her words screech down the stairs, echoing in the small space at the bottom. "It's a lie! You're like all the rest. You don't want me to have a child!"

"Mrs. Gavin—"

"Get out! Get out of my house!"

The doctor's voice is louder now, no longer muffled, and I look up to find him backing out into the hall. Susanne is advancing on him, two spots of hot color blazing high on her cheeks. He stops at the head of the stairs, trying again to make her see reason. "Mrs. Gavin, surely you know there has been too much damage. While conception is still technically possible, I would be negligent if I didn't warn you that another episode like the last one could well prove fatal. Given your age and your . . . dependencies, a pregnancy is not ever likely to be . . . successful."

But Susanne isn't listening. She sends him away, fouling the air with a string of words Mama would even now wash my mouth out for using. Dr. Shaw doesn't look at me as he slips past, just sweeps his hat off the foyer table and slips out.

She calls for me then, and I go to her. Henry has disappeared into his tobacco fields, leaving me to weather Susanne's storm alone. She is at her dressing table when I enter, staring hard at her reflection.

"Am I old?" she asks without turning away from the glass. "You heard what he said, Adele—that I am too old to have a baby. Do you think I am?"

I have no earthly idea how to answer her. Instead, I reach for her tincture, startled to realize there is a part of me—an awful part—that is relieved by Dr. Shaw's news, relieved to know there will be no need for Henry to visit his wife's bed. I have seen her body; it is not beautiful, not young, yet thinking of it, of Henry doing what must be done to produce an heir, flays me raw.

I wait for the grief to tear through her, for her to dissolve into one of her sticky puddles of self-pity. I steel myself to offer the polite and proper sympathies, to splash a bit of bootleg into her teacup and dose out her tincture. But there are no tears. Instead her eyes go queer and cold in the glass.

"This is Henry's fault," she hisses. "Of course it's Henry. He's not man enough to give me a child!"

I cannot listen. I want to scream, to fly at her like a cat, to shriek what trembles on my tongue, that she has only herself to blame, that her desolate womb is a mirror of her empty heart, that she does not deserve Henry's child. But I hold my tongue. Losing my place means losing Henry. And I am too far gone for that, whatever comes.

I feel her eyes on me now, hard but unseeing. She has become a feral thing, wild-eyed and unsteady on her feet, defiance swirling about her like smoke, and for the first time I am afraid. Not of her probing eyes, but of what is in back of them, of the seething, glittering thing I am watching come to life.

"I'll show them all! That doctor, and those gloating biddies, even Henry! They think I can't produce an heir, that I'm not strong enough, not good enough. I'll prove them wrong if it kills me!"

I flinch when she says it. I cannot believe that ravaged body of hers could produce a child without killing her. And yet I know she means to try. It's a strange kind of revelation, and an uneasy one—the thought that she could die. I don't want that, I tell myself. And it wouldn't matter. Even if Henry were free, he couldn't be mine. Not in the way he's Susanne's. Not ever that way.

Chapter 13

There is no escape from the heat.

Or from the storm slowly gathering around us. Whether I speak now of Henry, of the need smoldering between us, unspoken and untouched, or of Susanne, with her frantic, reckless schemes, I cannot say. I only know in my bones that the storm is coming and that one way or another I will be caught at its center.

August is nearly over but the days ooze by like years, endless and thick with a sticky-wet heat that leaves my temper short. But it isn't only the heat that makes me cranky. From sunup 'til sundown Susanne wears me out with talk of a negro midwife from Level Grove who claims to help women have babies.

Her bedside table has become a hoard of mysterious bottles and dark vials—tonics of fennel and wild yam, a tea made from liferoot and something called squaw-weed, and a dark, sticky syrup made from berries and bark and other things I'm too squeamish to ask about—all promising to produce a healthy child, and at no small price, I'll wager.

The packages come weekly, small parcels wrapped in plain brown paper. Susanne's been paying those Level Grove boys to bring them with her bootleg because the midwife lives back up in the hills where they set up their stills, and because for a little money they'll do anything she asks and not tell a breathing soul. They may be no-account, but those boys know how to keep a secret.

None of it matters, though. Susanne is wasting her money.

I know this so-called midwife, or women like her. Back home we have them by the handful. *Traiteur*, we call them, voodoo women selling gris-gris in dark, airless shops to women desperate for love or a quickening womb. I want to tell her there are witchwomen down in the Quarter who will make her the same promise for a tenth of the money this woman is charging, my mother's kin among them. But my opinions would not be welcome, and so I keep them to myself. Still, it surpasses understanding that a woman who once held herself so high could now pin all her hopes on a colored woman and common superstition. I still shiver when I think of that awful night, so much blood, so much sadness. How, I wonder, could she ever risk another like it? Has she given no thought to what another dead child might do to Henry? These thoughts, too, I keep to myself.

She is little better than a recluse these days, a specter haunting her bedroom window, lost in the cottony haze of her tincture. Dr. Shaw gave up restricting her refills when she started phoning him at all hours, teary and panicked, claiming she was dying.

One day when her little brown bottle begins to run low, I am sent to the druggist. My heart turns a little somersault when she tells me Henry's making a trip to the hardware store and that I'll be riding with him. Aside from church, I've never been anywhere with him.

We go in the old red truck, the windows rolled down, sucking in hot red dust as we head down the drive. I've got on my good blue dress, but I've left my hat. It's too hot. Besides, no one has ever paid me any mind unless I was with Susanne. We're awkward with each other as we ride, like those early nights in the study when we would both wait for the other to finally break the silence. Like then, I sit with my hands in my lap and look straight ahead.

My handbag rests on the seat between us, Susanne's small bottle tucked inside. I wonder if Henry knows what I'm after downtown, or if he even cares. Or if he knows about Minnie Maw, and the peculiar collection of bottles beside his wife's bed. There is a part of me that wants to know but another part that would rather not think of Henry's role in Susanne's scheme to produce a child, and so I sit quietly, listening to the cough and grind of that old truck, thinking how good it is to be there beside him on those torn seats with the dust blowing in, thinking, too, that I wouldn't mind if I was never anywhere else. I'm almost disappointed when we finally pull into Meeting Street.

"Where should I drop you?"

After the silence of the ride, his voice is almost startling. I gather my bag and reach for the door handle. "This is fine," I say, though we're in front of the barber rather than the druggist. "I won't be long."

When he lays a hand on my arm I start, then steal a glance at the men loitering outside the barbershop. Henry seems not to notice. "Have you got—" He breaks off, clears his throat. "Do you have any money?"

Before I can answer, he reaches into his pocket, pulls out several neatly folded bills, and lays them on the seat next to me. I stare at them a minute, and then my cheeks go hot. He doesn't mean the money for the druggist. He means it for me. I fumble for words, but my tongue is pasted to the roof of my mouth all of a sudden, and in my head I can hear Mama lecturing me about the kinds of girls who take money from men. I turn my eyes from the neatly folded bills and reach for the door handle.

He touches my hand, but I pull away. There are too many eyes on us, curious eyes unaccustomed to seeing Henry Gavin with a young woman. But Henry doesn't notice the eyes. His gaze is fixed straight ahead, his work-roughened hands tight on the steering wheel.

"I'm sorry," he says, the words thick and awkward. "I wanted to give you . . . I wanted to show you . . ."

He doesn't finish. He doesn't have to. His eyes tell the rest, soft as they lock with mine, and in that instant the last threads of pretense unravel. My belly clenches tight, a thousand wings all taking flight at once, so that I can barely breathe.

"You have," I whisper, my throat suddenly thick. "Now, put your money away."

I'm almost dizzy as I step out of the truck and set off down the sidewalk, my eyes carefully lowered as I thread my way through the clutch of men outside the barbershop. There are five, maybe six, and I'm pretty sure I recognize two of them from church. Their heads come up one at a time over their newspapers as I pass, like bulls at a fence. Long after I've cleared the herd, I can still feel their eyes. Then I hear Henry's name and a boisterous gust of laughter.

There's nothing I want in the window of Redding's dress shop, or at least nothing I can afford, but I linger just the same, pretending to browse so I can hear what the men are saying about Henry. More nasty talk about hiring coloreds, I expect. But that's not it at all.

"Leave it to Gavin," the tallest of the bunch is saying. "To look at the man you'd swear he never had an itch in his life, and all the while he's been hiding that ripe little peach right down the hall from his wife."

There's another round of snorts and guffaws and more chatter I can barely make out, but it's enough to make my cheeks go hot and my stomach queasy.

"She'd better damn well be worth it," answers a paunchy man in a too-tight suit. His snicker makes my skin crawl. "Henry Gavin's got a lot to lose, and he'll lose it for sure if he gets caught with his hand in the fruit bowl. The girl'll get the boot, but Henry, well, he'd best watch his step is all. Can't say I blame the man, though. She's one sweet little piece, and it can't be much fun crawling under the sheets with that dried-up old scarecrow of a wife."

My mind seethes with protests to hurl back at them—that it's all a pack of foul lies, that there's nothing improper going on—but doing so would only draw attention, when all I want is to melt into the sidewalk.

Henry Gavin's got a lot to lose.

The words leave me clammy and trembling all over, so flummoxed I barely notice when the little shop bell tinkles and Celia Cunningham is suddenly standing in front of me. There's a flicker of surprise on her heavily rouged face, a quick darting of eyes beneath the brim of her clever yellow hat.

"Good afternoon . . . Adele, isn't it? Is Mrs. Gavin not with you?"

I shake my head, peering over her shoulder, praying to God the men have finished their filthy talk. I want only to be gone, to take care of my business and get home, to sit with what I've heard and decide whether to tell Henry what folks are saying about him. About us.

"I'm only in town to run an errand," I say thickly, and try to move past. But Mrs. Cunningham's feeling chatty today, or nosy, more like.

"I do hope she's well? I paid her a call a while back, you know, but she wasn't feeling well enough to see me, poor thing. Such a pity, another baby lost." She forms a pout with her bright red mouth, then arches one penciled brow. "And surely the last?"

I cannot help it; my hackles rise. I hold no ties with Susanne Gavin, nor she with me, beyond my tiny wage, but I will never forget the things Celia Cunningham said about Henry that day in the parlor. I stick out my chin and look her dead in the eye.

"I can't speak to that, ma'am. I was taught never to inquire about things that are none of my business."

She blinks at me; then her face goes all frosty. "Please tell Susanne that I asked after her."

And then she's gone, heels tapping hard and fast as she moves down the sidewalk toward the barbershop. My heart sinks when I see her grab hold of the snickering man in the too-tight suit and drag him away from his friends. Before they even reach the corner their heads are bent close, and then Celia turns to gape at me. By dinner the talk will be all over town.

Chapter 14

Leslie

Leslie felt lost as she glanced up and down Meeting Street. Nothing looked remotely familiar. The sleepy downtown she remembered was gone, made over into a kind of vintage-chic shopping district. The First National Bank housed a fitness center, Hayden's Barbershop was now a trendy boutique, and the locksmith had given way to a florist with an icy white wedding cake in the window. The newness was disturbing. Nothing had changed, and everything had. But then, after thirty years, what did she expect?

She had come on a mission, to buy clothes suitable for life in Gavin. The excursion had actually been Jay's idea. He thought she needed to work on fitting in, and while he was right—the clothes she'd brought with her were completely wrong—he could have been a little nicer about it.

"No one in Gavin's going to be impressed by your Armani suits. In fact, I'm pretty sure if you were to ask most of them, they'd agree that Armani makes a damn fine jar of spaghetti sauce."

She'd been so surprised by the remark she nearly let it pass. In the end though, she couldn't. "That's a bit harsh, don't you think?"

"No, it's fact. People around here don't care about that stuff. They don't care what you wear or what you drive. They care about who you are."

"Should I trade in the Beemer for a horse and buggy, then?"

He hadn't bothered to smile. "That's not what I meant, but you have to admit you're awfully big-city for the folks around here."

Big City.

The nickname had already stuck, and she wasn't at all sure she liked it. She'd like to believe he was only teasing, but something in his voice and in the hard, square set of his jaw when he said it made her wonder.

The familiar toll of First Presbyterian's steeple bells reminded Leslie why she'd come to town and that she didn't have much time. In two hours she was supposed to meet Jay for lunch, to go over plans for the winery and ideas about how she might contribute. It wasn't a meeting she was looking forward to. Nor was she convinced that she'd made the right decision in agreeing to stay. But she had agreed, at least for the time being, so she supposed she should get a move on.

Her heels tapped quick and sharp as she set off down the sidewalk, echoing off the neat brick shop fronts. It felt strange to walk down streets that were quiet and unhurried, where people made eye contact and smiled as they passed. In New York you just kept your head down and got where you were going. Here, no one seemed in a hurry to get anywhere, and why should they be? It was a gorgeous day, sunny and surprisingly mild after a week of crushing heat, the breeze whispering softly of summer's end. All along Meeting Street shop doors stood open, many windows already dressed for fall, tailor-made for a nice leisurely browse.

Mercifully, it didn't take long to find what she was after: boot-cut jeans, a few T-shirts, a plain denim jacket, and a pair of blue canvas Toms, all in one surprisingly trendy shop called Lulu's Closet. As she left the shop with her handful of bags, she still had an hour to kill before she was supposed to meet Jay, plenty of time to explore a few of the artsy shops that had caught her eye.

There was one in particular that looked interesting—the Poison Moon—whose windows brimmed with candles and crystals and chunky stone jewelry. She'd never gone in for all the chanting and incense, but something about the music spilling through the open door, the sound of ancient civilizations, of druids and spells, lured her inside.

Despite bare brick walls and the scuffed plank floor, there was an almost otherworldly feel to the place as she stepped inside, a melding of the earthy and the sacred—more like something she'd expect to find in the West Village than in Gavin. At the back of the shop was a kind of sitting area, a pair of pillow-strewn love seats and a low table. At the center of the table, an incense bowl gave up a wisp of silent smoke.

Leslie closed her eyes, savoring the heady scents of sandalwood and patchouli, the perfect backdrop for browsing books on herbal remedies, spell making, or tarot reading. But when she opened her eyes again, she wasn't looking at those kinds of books at all. Instead, she saw a scrubbed pine table stacked high with paperbacks, heavy, pulpy things with sentimental titles and covers to match.

Nothing about the table seemed to fit the shop, especially not the florid cardboard sign hyping the best-selling novels of J. D. Hartwell, better known in romance circles as the Master of Heartbreak. She knew the name. How could she not? There wasn't a soul on the planet who wouldn't recognize the name of the man responsible for reducing half the women in the world to tears with his soppy love stories.

Frowning, Leslie picked up one of the books and stared at the cover, a sepia shoreline marred by a single set of footprints—*Sand and Stone.* The next showed a crumpled bridal veil beside a snapshot of a flyboy and his sweetheart—*A Letter Home.* She'd heard of that one. In fact, she'd lit into an intern once for reading it at her desk.

She simply didn't understand why anyone would spend good money on something designed to make them cry when life was perfectly capable of sending you on a crying jag for free. And just what kind of sadist prided himself on a moniker like the Master of Heartbreak anyway? Flipping the book over, she searched the back cover for a photo and felt the blood drain from her face. It seemed J. D. Hartwell, the Master of Heartbreak, was living on her grandmother's farm.

She had to admit he looked every inch the part, handsome and windblown in his cable-knit sweater, perched easily on a craggy bit of rock. She scanned the bio, then the reviews beneath it, but still couldn't get her head around it. He'd obviously kept it from her on purpose. It was hardly the kind of thing you forgot to mention. But why? The question was still churning when the floor behind her groaned and a curvy blonde stepped up beside her.

"Something I can help you with?" Her smile was a bright, frosty pink, her drawl so thick it sounded put on.

"I was just . . . I was looking at these books."

"He's scrumptious, don't you think?"

Leslie opened her mouth, then closed it again. Best not to say what she was thinking at the moment.

"You have read him, haven't you?"

"No, I can't say I have."

The woman's blue eyes went wide, as if such a thing was beyond comprehension. "Why in the world not? I promise you, no one will make you cry like this guy." She grabbed another book from the table. "This one—it's called *His Kind of Girl.* It's about a woman who learns she's losing her sight. And then she meets—"

"Let me guess . . . a guy?"

"Yes! And she falls so hard for him she can't bring herself to tell him the truth. Well, of course they fall in love, and all the time he doesn't have a clue anything's wrong. Only he does! He knows the whole time that she's losing her sight but pretends not to. Oh my God, it's heartbreaking!"

Leslie was beginning to find this conversation heartbreaking. She pointed to the table. "I can't help noticing that this type of thing doesn't fit with the rest of your inventory. The owner must be quite a fan."

The bright pink smile widened. "I am," she said, offering a hand glittering with silver rings. "I'm Deanna Harper, and this is my shop."

"It's great," Leslie said. "Full of really unique things." Still, she couldn't help wondering how the Master of Heartbreak fit into Deanna Harper's merchandising scheme. "It's none of my business, but can I ask what made you stick a table of these in the middle of a new age shop? It seems so . . ."

"Out of place—yeah, I know, but I couldn't help myself. I just adore his writing. He's not one of those guys who just churns out three hundred pages a year to make a buck. He writes about real emotions. Call me a sap, but that makes me like the guy. Well, that and the fact that he's gorgeous. And even better in person than on the back of that book, if you ask me. His real name's Jay Davenport. If you're around long enough, you'll probably run into him. He lives out at Peak Plantation. Have you heard of it?"

The floor creaked as Leslie shifted her weight. "Yes, I've heard of it."

"It's a gorgeous place." Deanna's silver bangles clanked as she tidied the table. "You should drive out and take a look. It got to looking kind of run-down a few years back, but it's all fixed up again now. People used to say it was haunted. They said that back in the day a lady died—"

"I'm Leslie Nichols."

Deanna's bracelets went quiet. "Lord, aren't I the perfect dunce. I heard you were back, and here you stand while I run my mouth. So I guess you know Jay, then? Of course you do."

Leslie wasn't sure she would agree with that. She knew Jay the handyman who lived in her grandmother's cottage, Jay the cash-strapped drifter who dreamed of starting a winery, but this Jay—this best-selling author—was a stranger to her.

"He's a great guy, isn't he? Not like a celebrity at all. He hates all the fuss. In fact, I tried to get him to come in, you know, for a reading like they do, but he won't. Won't even talk about it. Hey, maybe you could get him to write something new! It's been years. Guess that's why folks let him be now. They've moved on to Nicholas Sparks. He's good too, but he's never made me cry like Jay did. And a girl needs a good cry now and then, don't you think?"

Leslie's head was too full to manage more than a distracted nod. She'd suspected him of so many things, fleecing, forgery, even outright thievery, but never of being a famous writer. It seemed that once again he'd left out a fairly important piece of the story.

"I was real sorry to hear about your grandma," Deanna said. "She was such a part of this town. Everyone loved her. We're glad you're back, though. It's been a long time."

"Yes," Leslie said, glancing at her watch. She wanted to beat Jay to Bishop's. "It was nice meeting you, Deanna, but I have to run. I'm meeting Jay for lunch."

"Well now, you don't want to be late for that, do you?"

It was obvious by her pink grin and not so subtle wink that Deanna had the wrong idea, but at the moment Leslie had bigger fish to fry. She turned toward the door, then realized she was still holding a copy of *A Letter Home*. She handed it to Deanna, who then dropped it into one of her bags with a wink.

"You can't live with the man and not have read his books."

"I don't live with him. I live *near* him."

"Sure. Right. Anyway, read that. It's my favorite. One of his really early ones, but it's one of his best. A World War Two pilot engaged to be married. Plane goes down. Oh God, you have to read it! I won't tell you any more."

Before Leslie could fish her wallet from her purse, Deanna stopped her. "No, honey, it's on me. Consider it a welcome-home present."

Leslie was already sipping a vodka tonic when Jay arrived. He was charm itself as he wove through the lunch crowd, waving to several patrons as he made his way over. He smiled as he dropped into the chair across from her.

"Looks like mission accomplished," he said, pointing to her shopping bags.

Leslie said nothing as she reached into the nearest bag, pulled out her brand-new copy of *A Letter Home*, and thumped it down on the white tablecloth.

Jay stared at it a moment before pushing it back. "Well, I see you've been to Deanna's. That is where you got it, isn't it?"

"Where I got it isn't the point, *Mr. Hartwell*," she shot back. "What is that anyway, some kind of drippy pen name you chose because you thought it would help sell books?"

"It's a family name, actually. My mother's before she and my father married. And none of that has anything to do with now."

Before Leslie could respond, a pretty brunette wearing an apron and a grin appeared over Jay's left shoulder. "Hey, stranger, nice to finally see you again."

Glancing up, Jay managed a tight smile. "Hey, Susan. How's business?"

Susan tossed her dark hair off her face and shot him a wink. "Better now that you're here. We just got the 2009 Carano Fumé Blanc in. We're pairing it with the lime-ginger shrimp you like."

"Thanks, sounds good. Bring us two."

Leslie held up her glass. "And I'll take another one of these, please." She watched Susan's retreat thoughtfully, then leaned in. "Another devoted fan?"

"She owns the place, along with her husband, Billy."

"So when were you going to tell me the truth?"

"You're suggesting I've been lying up 'til now?"

"Haven't you?"

"No."

Leslie jabbed a finger at the book lying between them on the table. "You're a best-selling writer, for crying out loud. When were you planning to bring that up? Or were you just waiting for me to find out about it like I do everything—from someone else?"

"It was a lifetime ago, Leslie."

"So now you're masquerading as a wine maker? Pretending to be flat broke?"

Jay opened his mouth but closed it again, smoldering quietly while Susan dropped off their drinks and a basket of bread. When they were alone again, he tossed down the napkin he'd been about to spread in his lap.

"I'm not pretending to be anything, Leslie. I am a wine maker. And I am flat broke—or close to it."

Leslie felt her jaw go slack. "How? Your books were everywhere—airports, drugstores, 7-Elevens, for God's sake. I threatened to fire an intern once because she was such a wreck over one of your endings that she could barely get through the day. Then she ran out and bought another one! It's like romantic crack! How could you possibly be broke?"

"I gave it away."

Vodka sloshed over the rim of Leslie's glass as she brought it down. "Gave it away?"

"Yes."

The set of his jaw told her it was true. "But . . . why?"

"So she couldn't have it."

"Who?"

"My wife. My ex-wife, that is. Theresa."

Leslie sipped her drink while she recovered. She didn't know he'd been married.

"She and my publicist were . . . involved," he said, scowling into his wine. "When I found out I didn't say a word, but suddenly I was overcome with a need to be charitable. I went to one of those groups that helps set up foundations and I started donating huge chunks of money—libraries, literacy projects, adult education programs. When it was all gone, I told her what I had done and why. Then I left."

When he looked up, his eyes were like shards of amber, brittle and clouded with old wounds. Leslie glanced away, sorry now that she had pressed him. Eventually the silence became uncomfortable.

"After the divorce you came to Gavin?"

"Not right away. I stuck around long enough to tie up the loose ends. No kids, thank God. I got the Mustang. She got the house and an alimony check that eats up most of the royalties that still trickle in." He shrugged. "Punishment for the charity business, I suppose."

Leslie offered a weak smile. "Well, at least you had the last laugh. Do you regret it now, giving all the money away, I mean?"

He took a sip of wine, then shrugged again. "All I cared about then was punishing her. Now I realize how much was my own fault."

"How is your wife's cheating your fault?"

"It just was. Or maybe fallout's a better word, but that's just semantics. I was so wrapped up in myself and my work, so drop-dead sure the world revolved around the *New York Times* best-seller list, that I forgot to take care of my life."

It was Leslie's turn to shrug. "Success doesn't come cheap. And your wife certainly benefited."

"When we got married we were like everybody else, broke but full of dreams. Then I sold my first book and the money started coming in. Everything changed. One day I looked up and I didn't know her anymore, or me either. I was too busy being important."

Leslie recognized the words. He'd thrown them up to her once. Perhaps it was time to steer the conversation to safer waters. "What about the books since the divorce? There must have been some money from them."

"There haven't been any books since the divorce."

Leslie was attempting to tear a chunk of sourdough free. She dropped it back in the basket. "None?"

"Not a word in six years. There didn't seem to be much point. My last book was, shall we say, rather coolly received by the critics, not to mention my fans. It's not easy to write about love when you've stopped believing in it. So you see, we have more in common than you think. Until the winery starts making money, we're both, as the French say, *sans le sou.*"

"I don't understand. Why bother with the winery when all you have to do is grind out another heartbreaker to get back on your feet?"

"I am back on my feet, at least in a way I give a damn about. And the last thing I want is to write another book."

Leslie shook her head as she resumed her attack on the sourdough. "I don't get it. How can you have this amazing gift and not use it?"

Jay ignored the chunk of bread she placed on his plate. "You know, you've got a pretty short memory. A minute ago my work was romantic crack. Now I have a gift? And while we're on the subject, when was the last time you used your gifts? And don't tell me about *Edge.* I'm talking about your photography. Don't look so stunned. I Googled you. I know about the write-ups and all the awards. So when was the last time you touched a camera?"

Leslie stiffened and lifted her chin. "We're talking about you."

"Not anymore we're not. You got your answers. The subject is closed."

"I'm just trying to understand."

His eyes were shuttered when they met hers, hard and unreadable. "Maybe you shouldn't ask questions you're not willing to answer yourself."

Chapter 15

At high noon the attic was stifling, the air thick with dust and discarded memories. Leslie groaned at the sight of so much junk, abandoned furniture stacked with bric-a-brac, a dizzying maze of boxes littered with papery moth corpses. It was the last place on earth she wanted to be, but Jay's words had stayed with her, awakening her at three a.m., and then again at four.

When was the last time you used your gifts?

It had been a while; years, in fact. She was only seven when she snapped her first picture, her mother beside her, her first teacher. She wasn't very good back then, but she had gotten good. Good enough to earn her way through Parsons, land a wall full of prestigious awards, and hold more than a dozen successful shows. Her mother would have been proud. But she had given it all up for *Edge*, for a title and a corner office, where she helped peddle sports cars to men with dwindling testosterone levels and hawked two-hundred-dollar cigars to big shots who probably couldn't tell the difference.

The questions were still unanswered when the alarm went off the next morning, but as she had sipped her morning coffee, her thoughts drifted to her mother's work, carefully preserved at one time in a series of leather-bound albums. What had become of them after she died? Was it possible, after all these years, that they might still be here somewhere?

And so, after an unsuccessful search of Maggie's room, she had climbed the narrow stairs to the attic. She tried not to dwell on the stacks and piles that would eventually have to be sorted through, the broken picture frames and shadeless lamp, the cartons brimming with glasses and dishes wrapped in sheets of yellowed newsprint, the pots and pans and chafing dishes, battered suitcases and disjointed umbrellas. By the look of things, most of it had been here for at least a half century. Another day or two wasn't going to make much difference.

After a cursory look through the cartons near the stairs, Leslie moved deeper into the gloomy chaos, where the castoffs were more randomly stacked and it became more difficult to navigate. She had nearly cleared a precarious jumble of old tables and chairs when she tripped over a sheet of canvas and nearly broke her neck. Dust clouded the air as she pulled back the sheet. When it settled she found herself eye to eye with the portrait of an unfamiliar bride.

The strand of pearls at the woman's throat was familiar, though, distinctive thanks to its ornate garnet clasp. They were the pearls Maggie had worn for her own bridal portrait, the pearls she had promised would one day belong to Leslie. So this was Susanne Gavin, Henry's wife, and the matriarch of three generations of Gavin woman.

Leslie tilted her head and closed one eye, searching for some scrap of recognition, but the woman might as well have been a stranger. She fell rather short of pretty, despite her lace veil and lapful of lilies, pale and sharp, with a bottomless gaze that was too chilly for comfort. It seemed the Gavin women got their dark looks from Henry's side of the family.

Finding a portrait of Maggie's mother stashed in the attic, rather than mounted in a place of honor, felt odd. But then she was in no position to judge. She'd been wondering for days what to do with some of Maggie's relics, and now here was one more. She'd deal with it later. Right now, she was here to look for her mother's albums, and she wasn't letting herself get sidetracked.

After two hours of gritty, backbreaking excavation, Leslie finally found what she was looking for, a pair of boxes tucked away in the northeast dormer, each bearing the name AMANDA LYNNE in heavy black marker. The packing tape made a sound like ripping cloth as Leslie peeled it away. Her hands trembled as she turned back the flaps and peered in at the tenderly packed bits of her mother's childhood: a once-pink tutu with sequins along the bottom, a tarnished gymnastics trophy, a faded Harvest Queen sash.

Ballerina. Gymnast. Harvest Queen.

It was hard for Leslie to imagine her mother as any of those things, let alone all of them. Since her death, Amanda Nichols had lived in her memory as the woman who read bedtime stories and made smiley faces with pancakes and bacon. But this was another Amanda, the girl she'd been before she grew up and married Jimmy, all carefully packed away in a corner of the attic.

Leslie closed up the carton of memorabilia and moved on to the next, holding her breath as she yanked back the tape and peered into the box. There they were, eight leather volumes with the year stamped in faded gold along the spine, and in surprisingly good shape from what she could see as she lifted them out, the pages brittle and brown but intact for the most part.

Laying the most recent album in her lap, she began paging through. Most were nature shots, startlingly good for someone with no formal training. Her mother definitely had an eye. They were arranged chronologically, as they'd been shot. One particular series caught her attention. It began at the mouth of a wooded track, then continued to move deeper along the sun-dappled path.

There was something uncannily pleasant about following the progress of the shots, as if she were actually walking at her mother's side as each frame was captured. But there was something else too, a niggling familiarity as she studied the play of light and shadow in each shot, a nudge toward something she couldn't quite put her finger on. And then it came, the rush of recognition so startling it set her pulse thrumming. As she turned the page, she already knew what she would find—an empty space. It would be empty because the photo that used to be there was now on her bureau, the same photo Brendan Goddard had given her in his office. And her mother had taken it.

Leslie stared at the blank space on the page, wondering what it might mean. Maggie had handed the photo over to her attorney to ensure that it found its way into her hands—her hands, not Jay's. But why? Yes, the shot was amazing, but if Maggie's intent had been to make sure she never forgot her mother, why not leave a letter instead of a mysterious photograph whose origins she had only stumbled on by accident?

Groaning, she stood and brushed the dust from the seat of her jeans. She was sticky and tired, her head swimming with questions that seemed to have no answers. She wasn't finished with this mystery by a long shot, but she needed something to drink and a little soap and water. Hoisting the carton of albums up onto her hip, she headed downstairs.

After a shower, she poured herself another glass of sweet tea and dragged the box of albums out onto the back porch. She had planned to bring *A Letter Home* down with her, to lose herself in a few chapters of mindless fiction, but she had changed her mind, deciding instead to go through the rest of her mother's albums.

Settled in a rocker at the shady end of the porch, she lifted out each volume, laying them open in her lap one at a time, leafing through page after page of her mother's work, stirring long-dead bits of memory—her mother's voice, clear and quiet, as fresh to her as yesterday.

In her lap, the photo Brendan Goddard had given her was waiting to be returned to its rightful place. But the longer she stared at the lonely grave with its nameless stone, the less she wanted to part with it. Maybe because she wanted to understand why Maggie had removed it in the first place. Or because she longed to know how her mother had stumbled onto such an amazing shot. She would never know the answer to either, of course, but she wasn't ready to put the picture away just yet.

Swatting at whatever was buzzing near her left ear, Leslie stood. While she'd been tripping down memory lane, the afternoon had slipped away and the mosquitoes had marshaled their forces. Stacking the albums in chronological order, she dragged the empty carton over with one foot, then went still as she saw the flat brown envelope lying at the bottom.

Surprised that she hadn't seen it earlier, she lifted it out. There were no markings of any kind, the back flap tucked rather than sealed. Curious, and perhaps a little wary, she was about to drop back into her rocker when another mosquito whined by and changed her mind. Tucking the envelope between her teeth, she went back to repacking the albums. Whatever it was would have to wait until she was inside, where the light was better and the mosquitoes weren't invited.

While her Lean Cuisine heated, Leslie spilled the envelope's contents onto the kitchen table. She had expected more photos, but it was only a few bits of paper: an old magazine article, a dog-eared photocopy, and a small envelope of washed-out gray paper that might once have been blue.

She frowned at the magazine article's title as she picked it up— "The Tortured Genius: Exploring the Myth of the Creative Martyr." It had been torn from the March '81 issue of the *American Journal of Visual Arts* and seemed to explore the links between creativity, addiction, and mental illness. There were plenty of examples—writers, sculptors, and painters who had struggled for their art against schizophrenia, addiction, and depression, only to die in poverty, obscurity, or both.

Some of the names were familiar: Toulouse-Lautrec, who suffered from both alcoholism and depression; van Gogh, whose epilepsy medications were now credited, at least partly, with his unique artistic style; and Sylvia Plath, who wrote brilliantly, and put her head in an oven one day while her children slept. There were other names too, names she didn't recognize, Henry Darger, Karin Boye, Jeremiah Tanner—brilliant failures, all.

Shrugging off a head full of dark images, she folded the article back in half and deposited it in the envelope, baffled as to why her mother might have been interested in such an article. Was she depressed like Lautrec? Suicidal like Plath? The question lingered as she moved on to the single photocopied page and once again found herself reading about the art world, this time in Paris's dark underbelly near the turn of the century.

Leslie ignored the microwave timer when she noticed two names that had also appeared in the journal article: Toulouse-Lautrec and Jeremiah Tanner, whose opium demon eventually leeched him of funds and friends until even his common-law wife had been forced to abandon him for the States, along with their unborn child.

Delightful.

By the time Leslie finished reading, her Swedish meatballs were cold and her head was swimming. Why her mother would have been interested in Toulouse-Lautrec and the opium dens of Montmartre, she couldn't imagine. One more thing she'd never know. The thought made her sad. So many ghosts, past lives to be sorted and disposed of—lives she was beginning to realize she knew very little about.

Hoping for something less morbid, she reached for the small gray envelope. She couldn't make out the postmark, and the address was in even worse shape, the ink strokes splotched and badly faded. The letter crackled like parchment as she teased it free. In the late-afternoon sun, the page was nearly translucent, its scratchy script a challenge to decipher.

My precious girl,

You are a woman now, a mother. And you say this man loves you. It is not what I prayed for, but then that has never made much difference for me. I only hope he will stand by you, whatever trouble comes, that he will need you more than he needs the world's opinion. I was not so lucky. Still, I know now what I did was right, though we have both suffered for that passing. You did not understand then. I pray you do now, as a mother who loves her children more than her own heart. Even now that it has all gone off the rails, I cannot regret wanting a better life for you. Know that I love you always, and carry me in your heart, as I carry you. And carry your father too, in the legacy I sent with you when I gave you up to a new and better life.

Leslie blinked at the signature, a single, illegible letter scratched at the bottom of the page. No help there. They weren't Maggie's words, though; of that she was sure. The tone was wrong, the phrasing outdated—and something else it took a moment to put her finger on. The words felt . . . careful. As if the author was afraid she might reveal too much. But to whom?

It was possible that Susanne had written it to Maggie, but then why mail it? Maggie had never lived anywhere but Peak. Besides, it felt older than that. It was more likely that Susanne's mother had written it after Maggie was born. But why would she have doubted that Henry would stand by Susanne?

Sighing, Leslie carefully folded the letter along its creases and slid it back into the small gray envelope, then eyed the carton of albums at the end of the table. It was a strange place to find an old letter. Almost as strange as finding Susanne's portrait in the attic, hidden under a sheet of dusty canvas. But then it had been a strange sort of a day.

Chapter 16

eslie stood and stretched, stiff and restless after three hours at the kitchen table with a sketch pad and her laptop. At Jay's request, she'd spent the week brainstorming ways to market the winery on their scanty budget. She had come up with some ideas: offering daily tours, wrangling all the free media they could manage, and teaming up with local inns and restaurants. They'd need a kick-ass label and brochure, as well.

She'd given that last part a bit of thought. If she designed the label and brochure herself, it would save them a fortune. And why not? If she could peddle sports cars and cigars, why not a winery? She'd been writing copy and working on a design for days and knew exactly what she wanted—the feel of antebellum lace and a sepia-washed shot of Peak standing high on its hill.

As she powered down her laptop, she tried to recall the last time she'd felt this passionate about work and realized the answer was *never*. At *Edge* she'd been driven, obsessed, even proud at times, but never passionate. A year ago she couldn't have imagined a life other than the one she'd built around success, title, and a six-figure salary. Now that life was dimming, and much faster than she expected. She found herself suddenly eager to roll up her sleeves, to make this winery a success, not for the money it might yield, but for the creative challenge of it, something she hadn't felt in years.

Just thinking about the prospect made her itch to get started. Pulling back the kitchen curtains, she peered at the sky. A little overcast, but that would probably work in her favor. She would need shots of the crush barn and the rows, and a perfect shot of the house. That's where she'd start, with the house.

But after nearly two hours she still hadn't gotten the shot she was after. The perspective was wrong. She was too close, too low, too something. Scanning the horizon, she considered and discarded several options, until her gaze settled on the sharp thrust of land known for generations as Henry's Ridge, after Maggie's father. She had ventured partway up once, when she was a girl, but had soon given up. It was hard going back then and didn't look to be any easier now. But if it meant getting the shot she wanted, she'd find a way.

Still, she hesitated at the foot of the ridge. There had been a kind of road once, a crooked clay lane that cut up through the trees, but time had had its way, whittling it to little more than a footpath. Maybe she should wait until she had better shoes, but the promise of the perfect shot beckoned.

Her legs rebelled as she started up, then pressed on until the trail became nothing but a trickle of packed red clay. At intervals she stopped to rest, attempting to shake the sense of déjà vu that moved with her as she climbed. She'd been this way just once, yet each step felt familiar, as if she'd made the trek only days ago. And then she realized she had, in the pages of her mother's album. It was here—the grave her mother had discovered and photographed all those years ago—somewhere on Henry's Ridge.

The realization came with a prickle of goose bumps, a knowing that this moment had somehow been inevitable, that for reasons she couldn't begin to grasp, Maggie had wanted her to come looking and had left the photo as a kind of treasure map. But why?

Suddenly, Leslie was covering large chunks of real estate, striding purposefully over ground strewn with pebbles and dead leaves, the Nikon thumping soundly against her ribs. By the time she reached the crest, she was drenched in sweat, a stitch nipping sharply at her side. How she'd ever make it down again she had no idea. And right now she didn't care. She had to be close—unless she was wrong about the whole thing. But no, the tree was here, overrun by years of kudzu but still here, lightning struck and split down the middle, just like in the photo. If she had her bearings right, and she was sure she did, it should be here. Only she couldn't find it anywhere. Had she been mistaken? Woods were woods, after all, and one tree did look like another. And then she saw the stone.

The years had done their best to reclaim it, the low iron fence so overrun with weeds and vines that it had nearly become part of the landscape. The top of the headstone was barely visible, crumbling and mealy with age. It bore no resemblance to her mother's photo, but then after thirty years it was hardly likely to. An eerie kind of quiet filled her head, as if her heart had suddenly stopped. Until now, her curiosity had been about the image, the art and technique of the shot itself. Now she only wanted to know who was buried in this remote place, and why.

Sadly, it seemed there was no way to get at the inscription. Efforts to locate a gate proved futile, and yanking at the tangle of vines made almost no dent in the chaos. Still, she wasn't ready to give up. It was crazy, she knew, maybe even a little macabre, but before Leslie could question her motives, she was down on her hands and knees. Now that she'd found the grave, she couldn't just leave it to the whims of nature.

She worked until her shoulders ached and her hands were raw with broken blisters, tearing at ropes of kudzu and wild grape that seemed to lead nowhere and everywhere at once, unearthing all manner of crawly things in the process. Finally, she sat back on her haunches to survey her progress. It had taken the better part of the afternoon, but she'd managed to clear a sort of path that almost reached the gate.

A low growl of thunder suddenly caught Leslie's attention. For the first time, she noticed the dark, flat-bellied clouds scudding in from the west, scented the breeze racing up the ridge's west face, sharp with coming rain. *Damn.* She hated to quit now, when she was so close. The plan had been to work until the gate was free, then come back in the morning and finish the job. She was going to have to work fast to pull that off.

But before she could reach for another vine, the sky splintered into a thousand blue-white shards, leaving a wake of crackling ozone and opening the clouds. A second fork of lightning, even closer than the last, finally got her attention. Rain was one thing; wicked bolts of random electricity were quite another. Grabbing the Nikon, she scrambled for the path. She'd gone only a few yards when the rain came in earnest, an icy deluge that soaked her to the skin in minutes. Suddenly she was running, skidding and stumbling down the soupy clay slope slick with wet leaves and shifting stones.

Between the rain and her sopping-wet hair, it was nearly impossible to grope her way down, and more than once she landed on her knees or backside, torn between protecting her camera and saving her neck. The Nikon usually won.

By the time Leslie reached the foot of the path, all she could think of was a hot bath and an even hotter cup of tea. She was exhausted and chilled to the bone, so numb she could barely keep her teeth still. She'd nearly reached the house when she heard her name over the heavy thrum of rain. She winced at the sight of Jay leaning against the door of the tractor barn. *Damn, damn, damn.* Short of being rude, though, there was no way around it. Reversing course, she headed for the barn, shaking off like a wet dog as she ducked inside.

Jay scanned her with narrowed eyes, lingering on the puddle slowly forming at her feet. "Just out for a stroll?"

Leslie opened her mouth, fully intending to tell him where she had been and what she'd found, but somehow the words stuck in her throat. The discovery was too fresh, too curious. And so she held back, like a child with a new toy, unwilling to share until the novelty had worn off.

"I was scouting shots for the brochure," she told him instead, holding up the Nikon as proof. "Before I knew it the storm blew up and I had to run for it."

Jay took the camera and set it on the workbench. "Sounds like a good way to catch pneumonia, if you ask me. Your lips are blue, and you're shaking like a leaf." Grabbing a dubious-looking towel from a nearby hook, he wrapped it around her shoulders, pulling it tight and snuggling the corners in under her chin. "Better?"

Leslie nodded, relaxing involuntarily as his hands began to move over her shoulders in long, bone-melting strokes. The rattle of rain on the roof was faintly hypnotic, the heat of Jay's body vaguely disturbing, so that soon she was aware of nothing but the smell of his soap and the sudden warmth kindling in his whisky-colored eyes.

To see it there was startling—startling, but not unpleasant. In fact, it felt a little like being drunk. Closing her eyes, she yielded to the tender assault, dimly aware of something warm and languorous stretching awake in her belly, hungry after a long, cold slumber. Would it really be such a bad thing? To let herself feel something for someone? But she already knew the answer to that. Jay wasn't some stockbroker she'd bumped into at a cocktail party. Tomorrow would come, or next week, or next month. Something would go wrong—it always did—and then they'd be stuck, tiptoeing around each other every day, trying not to make eye contact.

He was staring at her when she opened her eyes, probing for answers to the questions that hung unspoken between them. Leslie looked away first. Stepping back, she peeled off the towel. She needed to get away from him, from his warmth and his scent, before she did something they'd both regret.

"Thanks," she said, reaching for her camera. "I'm fine now."

"Did you get what you were after?"

"After?"

"The pictures you wanted for the brochure. Did you get them?"

No, she hadn't, come to think of it. The minute she'd found the grave, all thoughts of the brochure had simply evaporated. "The pictures—oh, I don't know, maybe. I won't know until I go through them. Right now, I just want to get dry. I'll see you later."

Before Jay could respond, Leslie had ducked back out into the rain and was splashing blindly across the lawn, the icy drops a relief after the close heat—and the close call—of the barn. When she finally reached the shelter of the porch, she looked back, worried that he might have followed, and wishing just a little that he had.

Four days later it was still raining.

Leslie was going stir-crazy, itching to get back to the ridge and clear a path to the stone. Instead, she'd been stuck indoors, combing through her mother's albums until she knew the order of the photographs like the back of her hand. When she grew bored with that, she had pored over the cryptic mother-daughter letter until the words were burned into her memory. And four days later, she was no closer to knowing what any of it had to do with anything.

When Angie called to suggest lunch downtown, Leslie jumped at the invitation, offering to drive, or to don flippers and a wet suit if necessary. Anything to get out of the house and away from questions that seemed only to breed more questions.

At the height of what should have been the lunch rush, Bishop's was deserted. The brass bell over the front door jangled noisily as Leslie and Angie stepped into the empty lobby. Susan Bishop looked up with a blend of surprise and relief from the stack of menus she was wiping.

"What brings you two out in this slop?"

Angie peeled out of her raincoat and hung it on the rack near the door. "I didn't care if I had to swim. I had to get out of the house. Young Buck's about to run me crazy, moaning about the rain and the threat of bunch rot setting in."

"Let's not talk about rot," Susan shot back over her shoulder as she grabbed two menus and walked them to a corner table. "I just had to toss an entire shipment of salmon. It's been like a ghost town all week. I'd tell you the specials but I didn't bother planning any."

"Actually, I think we were both going to do salads," Angie told her. "And pick us out a good bottle of Chardonnay. We're celebrating."

Susan disappeared, promising to return with bread and the requested wine.

Leslie spread her napkin in her lap and leaned in. "So what are we celebrating?"

"You. Staying. Jay told me the news yesterday. I'm glad."

Leslie made a face. "I couldn't come up with a reason not to. At least I'll have a roof over my head. Pretty pathetic, huh?"

"Sometimes that's the way it works. So what's new on the getting-settled-in front? I don't guess it's much fun sifting through all that old stuff."

Leslie thought of her recent discoveries, the letter and old photographs, articles her mother had clipped and saved for no reason she could think of. And she thought of the ridge and the stranger whose name and story she still didn't know.

"I keep finding . . . things."

"Good things?"

"Confusing things. Did you know someone was buried up on the ridge?"

Angie's expression made it clear she hadn't.

"I found it the other day, an old stone, all fenced in by itself."

Angie waited while a waitress dropped off their wine and a basket of bread. "Honey, there are graves like that all over North Carolina. You can drive down the highway and count them. Hell, I heard once that in Greenville there's a bunch in the mall parking lot."

Leslie sipped her wine, suddenly reluctant to tell Angie any more. It all seemed a little silly now, a mystery pieced together from a series of unrelated clues. Angie was right—there *were* graves all over North Carolina. She'd seen them, basking in the shade of an ancient oak or hiding in a field of corn, belonging to God knows who, erected God knows when—and every one with a story to tell.

Whether there was anyone left who knew those stories was another matter. Luckily, the arrival of lunch saved Leslie from further response. When they were alone again, she decided to steer the conversation onto a new topic.

"I know about Jay. Or maybe I should say J. D. Hartwell."

Angie put down the knife and fork she'd just picked up. "He told you?"

"No, but the sign in the Poison Moon was hard to miss."

Angie grinned as she picked up her fork again. "Deanna's quite a fan of our Jay."

"It's a weird thing to hide, don't you think?"

Angie's expression sharpened along with her tone. "He isn't hiding it. It's just not something he likes to talk about. Maggie used to pester him about writing again, but it never did any good. He's hellbent that part of his life is over."

"But he was so successful. I don't get it."

"He's stubborn, and maybe a little afraid, too. He blames himself for a lot."

"He told me. I know about his wife and the money."

Angie speared a cherry tomato but paused before popping it into her mouth. "Sounds like you two had quite a talk."

"Only to a point. He clammed up after the first few questions."

Angie nodded knowingly. "That's Jay. Get too close and he'll run every time."

"I'm not sure I blame him. I've done a bit of running myself when things got . . . uncomfortable. It's partly why I'm here."

"Then I'll tell you what I told Jay. There's a difference between running away and starting over, and only you can decide which one you're doing." She paused, leveling keen green eyes on Leslie. "Do you *know* which one you're doing?"

Leslie dropped her gaze to her plate, toying with her croutons. "I thought I did, but the longer I'm here, the less I'm sure. The day I left New York I would have bet everything I owned that I was running away. Now I don't know. I have absolutely no idea what I'm doing with the winery, but things feel right somehow."

"Jay said he asked you to handle the marketing. How's that going?"

"I've got a few ideas, small things we can handle ourselves. I should have the brochure mock-up done by the end of the week."

"Sounds like you know exactly what you're doing. I can't wait to see what you've come up with. Hey, maybe we could all get together on Friday to celebrate, go out to dinner or something."

"Dinner?"

"Sure, we could go to Colaizzi's, make it a double date."

Leslie put down her wine and eyed Angie squarely. "It wouldn't be a date, double or any other kind. It would just be a business meeting that happened to include dinner."

"Two boys, two girls, no children. Sounds like a double date to me. And would it be so bad to have a little fun, maybe wear something alluring?"

"Alluring?"

"You know, show off your legs and anything else you've got worth showing off."

"You think Jay's going to like my ideas better if I flash a little leg?"

Angie rolled her eyes. "It's not your ideas I was hoping he'd like. In case you haven't noticed, Jay isn't exactly a bad catch."

Leslie threw her a withering glance. "That might be true if I were actually looking to catch someone—which I most definitely am not. I don't think dinner's a good idea. I think it's best if we just keep things . . . professional."

"Why?"

Leslie went back to picking at her croutons. "Because we'd both be uncomfortable, and I don't want any more friction between us."

Angie lifted her glass, grinning wickedly. "You know what they say about friction, don't you? Best way to start a fire."

"Or an explosion," Leslie shot back darkly. Yet she couldn't deny the dangerous flicker in her belly whenever her thoughts strayed to the moment she and Jay had shared in the barn. Fire, indeed. "Trust me, Angie, it isn't a good idea."

Angie huffed back in her chair. "Fine, have it your way. Oh, speak of the devil, here's Deanna."

Leslie turned to see Deanna heading for their table. She wore a pink slicker and matching wellies over her jeans but still managed to look curvy and beautiful.

"Hey, you two, I just popped over for some soup. Can you believe this weather?"

"Yes, unfortunately, I can." Angie pointed to an empty chair. "Stay and eat with us."

"I wish I could, but I'm by myself today at the shop. I just wanted to say hey. If you've got time later, stop by."

Leslie held up the bottle of Chardonnay. "You can at least stay for a glass of wine."

Deanna eyed it wistfully but shook her head. "I better get back. I didn't put a sign on the door. If there's any left, bring the bottle when you come by. I'll scare us up some Dixie cups." She had almost reached the lobby when she turned and tossed Leslie one of her broad pink smiles. "If you can't get by, be sure to tell that good-looking man I said hello."

Angie grinned as she topped off Leslie's glass and then her own. "I don't suppose she was talking about Buck, do you?" When Leslie didn't respond, she let it drop. "Now, what were we talking about? Oh, yes, your legs."

"I'll thank you to leave my legs out of the conversation and to channel your matchmaking efforts elsewhere. Maybe you should focus on Deanna. God knows she's taken with the Master of Heartbreak."

"Is that jealousy I hear?"

"Just an observation," Leslie answered coolly. "Would he be interested, do you think?"

Angie shook her head. "I believe that ship would have sailed by now if it was going to. Deanna's a little . . . wide-open for Jay. Still, you never know. He's a man, and she *is* cute as a button."

Leslie's eyes slid to the door as Deanna retreated. "Yes, she is," she murmured softly into her wineglass. "Cute as a button."

Chapter 17

The next morning dawned sunny and cool, the air and earth washed clean after days of drenching rain. Leslie tipped her face to the breeze, reveling in the mingled scents of wildflowers and damp earth. But she was frustrated, too. She had stripped away the last of the vines, unearthed the fence, and breached the gate, all with one mission in mind—to reach the stone and put a name and date to this mystery. But when she had finally reached the stone late yesterday afternoon, she had found it so weathered and splotched with lichen that the inscription was indecipherable.

The disappointment stung. Somewhere along the way, through all the hours on her knees, yanking weeds and vines, curiosity had ripened into a kind of fixation, a dim but insidious awareness of nameless bones grinding to dust. But whose bones? Without an epitaph, she would never know. Then, this morning, she remembered a documentary she'd seen once on the Vietnam Veterans Memorial in D.C. and it had given her an idea.

The iron hinges wailed drily as she pushed through the gate with her paper and crayon. It was a long shot, she knew. The stone's engraving might be so far gone that she wouldn't be able to lift anything at all. Still, it was worth a try. Dropping to one knee, she pressed the sheet of white paper to the stone and started to rub, anticipation quivering in her belly as letters began to emerge, light against dark, like a photographic negative. After a few moments she sat back on her haunches and spread the tracing over her knees.

I shall but love thee better after death.

Leslie felt the air go out of her lungs as she blinked at the waxy words. They were from the book of sonnets she'd found in Henry's desk, the book she assumed had been a gift from Susanne. But Susanne was buried beside her husband in the yard at First Presbyterian, which meant this grave belonged to another woman entirely—a woman Henry had loved.

Folding the tracing carefully, she stuffed it into her shirt and scrambled back down the path, not bothering to close the door as she entered through the mudroom and hurried to the study. She'd forgotten about the photo tucked between the back pages of Barrett Browning's sonnets. Now it was all she could think of.

Extricating the small book from Henry's desk, she slid the photo free and carried it to the window, squinting hard at the mysterious woman in the wide-brimmed hat. The longer she stared at it, the more impossible it seemed that she could ever have mistaken the woman in the photo for the pale bride in the attic. The chin was too strong, the mouth too full, and the fringe of dark curls peeking from beneath the hat was completely wrong.

The implications made Leslie vaguely dizzy. If this woman wasn't Susanne—and clearly she was not—then who was she? The infant in her arms seemed to tell the story. Henry Gavin had kept a mistress, and she had borne him a child.

Lifting the book of sonnets from her lap, Leslie turned to the spray of dried flowers and began to read. The words weren't new, but they held a fresh poignancy now, an ache that seemed to twine itself around every heartbreaking line. She'd known from the first reading that the passage had been a treasured one; she just hadn't known why. Now she had her answer.

Her fingers crept to dried petals, pale and papery against the yellowed page. Had Henry picked them, or had she? And who had pressed them and placed them here for safekeeping? It seemed a woman's gesture. Had she loved Henry, then, as he loved her?

Because he had loved her.

It seemed strange to be so sure of something she couldn't possibly know, and yet she *was* sure. Henry had died in this room, had, toward the end of his life, spent all his time here, alone and deep in drink because he had never stopped mourning her. What would it be like, she wondered, to love and be loved that deeply? She wasn't ever likely to know. Nor was she ever likely to know what it was like to lose such a love.

Closing her eyes, she tried to imagine them together, Henry, tall and lean with his head of heavy dark hair, the woman dressed as she was in the photo, but her face was only a shadow. Had Susanne known? It certainly seemed that Maggie had, or had at least suspected, though it didn't explain why she'd gone to such lengths to make sure Leslie found out about the grave. Why expose her father's infidelity after so many years? And the child—what had happened to the child?

More questions, only this time they were about Henry.

Leslie let her head fall back against the chair and let her eyes roam. Sitting in Henry's chair, surrounded by his things, his pipes and books and artwork, she could almost smell his pipe tobacco in the air, the bourbon from the glass at his elbow. Finally, her eyes settled on the paintings over the mantel. The first time she saw them, they had seemed out of place, at stark odds with her image of Henry Gavin, stalwart pillar of the community. Now that image was rapidly unraveling, and given what she had discovered—an unmarked grave, a mysterious mistress, and an illegitimate child—a few racy paintings might not be as out of place as they seemed. Henry was a man, after all, presumably with a man's appetites, and yet the thought of him burying a woman in secret, with nothing but a line of poetry to mark her passing, left Leslie wondering what kind of man her great-grandfather had truly been.

Sadly, there was no one left to ask.

Chapter 18

Adele

Lies sometimes become truth.

It is late August, scorching and dusty; market time in North Carolina. Henry has been away a full week, gone to the auctions at Wilson. Without him Peak is an empty, soul-grinding place. In the evenings, when Susanne has finished with her tray and Lottie has gone home, I slip into Henry's study and sit in his chair, breathing the scent of him—leather and Pinaud talc, tobacco and bootleg bourbon.

I have never mentioned the men outside the barbershop, or the way Celia Cunningham looked back at me that day. I didn't want it on his mind while he was away at market, but he'll need to hear it when he gets back, need to know what's being whispered. Not that they'd ever have the guts to spout their pack of lies to Henry's face. They wouldn't. They'll just keep pecking at it like seed corn, until they've got it scattered all over town. And nothing on this earth would delight Celia Cunningham more than to see that their talk finds its way to Susanne, even if it means having to pay a personal call.

Meanwhile, I am certain Susanne will drive me mad. From sunup to sundown I am forced to sit with her in that airless room, with its sealed windows and drawn curtains, listening to her talk of the child she insists she will soon have, the son who will one day inherit Peak. I pray it does not happen, now or ever. For Henry's sake and for mine.

The day Henry is scheduled to return, Susanne orders me to draw a bath, telling me to be sure to add a few drops of her favorite oil to the water. I know what she's up to, but I can't allow myself to think of it. I have let myself believe—*made* myself believe—that because Henry and Susanne do not share a room, they do not share a bed. It is a silly thing to believe, a girlish thing, I know, when the memory of Susanne's swollen belly is still so vivid.

Susanne is pink and fragrant when she steps out of the bath, trailing a sickly-sweet cloud of gardenia in her wake. She makes me brush out her hair and curl it, then lay out a nightgown I have never seen her wear. Her husband is coming home, and tonight, because there is something she wants, she will play the wife.

As I slide the sheer gown over her head, I sneak a look at her wrists. The welts are still there, some scabbed over, most fresh. She is still rail thin, though she's been eating a little, for the sake of the baby, she says, as if the thing has already been done. But there is an air of decay about her, like a house that has been vacant for a very long time, and I am amazed that she could believe herself capable of bearing a child, let alone mothering one.

It is well past dark when I hear Henry's truck cough its way up the drive, and my heart begins to knock against my ribs. I take a deep breath and peer over Susanne's shoulder at my reflection. I wanted to look my best for him. Instead, I look like what I am, hired help. I'm wearing the navy blue dress that was once my best, limp as a rag now, and faded with too much washing. And I've had no time to fix my hair. It's a fright, escaping its pins and sticking damply to my neck. I only hope Henry is too weary to notice.

I breathe a sigh of relief when Susanne sends me away, but it is short-lived. I am to go down and tell Henry she is waiting. My throat goes dry when I hear the heavy clomp of his boots on the porch. And then he's through the door, dusty and stiff after the long drive back. Our fingers brush as I take his hat and smooth out the rumpled brim. Has it really been only a week that he's been gone?

"Hello, Adele."

The words are like a tonic, rough and sweet and deep. But before I can answer, Susanne's voice floats down, thin and shrill with impatience. Henry's eyes shift to the top of the stairs, and he shuffles his boots. There's no need to give him my message. He knows what is expected of him and will do his duty. I turn away, fighting the sting behind my eyes as I hear the first step groan beneath his weight.

He is with her nearly an hour.

I am in the kitchen with Lottie when he finally comes down. That he has missed me is all over his face, but he smells like her now, the cloying scent of gardenia clinging to his clothes like a poison. It is not a betrayal. How can it be when he is not mine? But it is a bitter pill to swallow.

Even Lottie can feel the tension, though it's clear she's glad to have him home. At the table she fusses over him like an old hen, heaping his plate with sweet potatoes and fried chicken, hovering at his elbow to top off his tea every time he takes a sip.

"You look tired," he says to me through a mouthful of pecan pie. "Thinner than when I left, too. Hasn't Lottie been feeding you?"

I can't seem to find my tongue. I've had a week to think of what to say. Now I choke on every bit of it. I want to tell him it's because I had no appetite for eating alone, that I was miserable while he was gone, but I don't. I don't say anything. Instead, I plead a headache and go to my room. I can feel his eyes between my shoulders as I walk out of the kitchen. I know that I've hurt him, that I am being unfair. I have no right to feel the way I do, as if something between us has died. He is Susanne's husband. It's time I remember that— time I grow up.

But by the end of the week, I catch sight of Henry out in his fields, and my resolve falters. I shouldn't go to him, but I will. I tell Lottie I'll bring his lunch pail today. She cuts her eyes at me but starts packing up the sandwiches, grumbling and sucking her teeth all the while.

Henry straightens and shoves back his hat when he sees me coming. His clothes are gritty and dark with sweat, his face flushed with the midday heat. I swallow the lump in my throat and pat my apron pocket to make sure the book of poems I have bought him is still there. Even now, with the weight of it against my hip, I still can't make up my mind to give it to him. Not because I'm prideful but because I have written his name in it. Why I would do such a foolish thing I cannot say, except that I missed him terribly.

He is smiling when I reach him, a timid smile that sits uneasily on his craggy face. It fades when I hold out the lunch pail but say nothing.

"Will you wait for me here?" His fingers brush mine, warm and coarse as a cob. "Please. I won't be long."

I wait while he stalks to the old truck and fumbles beneath the seat. He drops something into his shirt pocket, then lifts his eyes to Susanne's window. She isn't there. She has been in bed all day, still feeling last night's bourbon and this morning's dose of tincture.

When Henry returns, the face I've come to know so well is unreadable, his jaw firmly set, as if he's trying to settle an argument with himself. He takes the lunch pail from my hands and we begin to walk, moving farther and farther off, until we can barely see the house. The silence between us is cumbersome, heavy with unspoken things.

I'm startled when he halts suddenly and turns to face me. We've come to the base of the ridge, to the mouth of a rough clay track that winds its way up into the trees. I know the path well enough, though I've never taken it. The ridge belongs to Henry, his refuge from the world when disappointment and duty sit too heavily on his shoulders.

I pull in my breath as his eyes lock with mine. There is a question in their depths, an appetite that has nothing to do with the lunch I've brought, and for the first time I'm afraid—of Henry, and of myself, and of the lies those men told outside the barbershop no longer being lies. And yet, Henry is all I can see. When he holds out his hand, I take it.

By the time we reach the crest, my lungs are on fire and my hair has come free from its pins. I don't care. It's quiet at the top, wide and dizzying and glorious, the breeze sharp with grass and fresh-churned earth. Above us, the clouds sail and shred, close enough to touch. Below, the rutted fields shimmer in the August heat, stripped as bare as the first time I saw them. It's hard to remember now that I ever hated those fields.

We sit in the tall grass, sharing Henry's cheese sandwich. The trees make a patchwork of the ground, sun and shade dotted with small yellow flowers. When lunch is gone, Henry stands and hurls our apple cores into the trees; then he stoops to gather a small spray of tiny blooms and presses them into my hand. He has always been a man of few words, and I see as he reaches into his shirt pocket that he is struggling for them now.

"For you," is all he manages as he presses a small box into my hands.

Inside, in a nest of crushed black velvet, is a cameo set in delicate loops of silver, its stone the dusky blue of a storm sky. It blurs in my hand as my eyes fill with tears. I have never had anything so fine.

"It's beautiful," I whisper, thinking miserably of the small book of poems in my apron, a paltry gift compared with Henry's. "I have something for you, too." I slip the book from my pocket and put it in his hands. "It isn't much, just some poems."

When he turns it over to peer at the spine, his face softens. "It's the one we talked about—*Sonnets from the Portuguese*."

"I wrote your name in it," I confess softly. "I shouldn't have, I'm sorry. I missed you."

Before I can say another word, Henry pulls me to him, his hands caught tight in my hair. When his mouth finds mine it's like coming home, inevitable somehow. I am lost. I forget the spray of flowers crushed between our bodies, forget Barrett Browning's poems, forget everything but the raw joy of Henry's mouth on mine.

There are no eyes on us here, no portrait over the fireplace, no wife upstairs. We are alone, utterly and perfectly alone beneath an aching blue sky. His eyes ask the question again, and again I say yes. It is a pledge—one neither of us is free to make. Still, we make it. We cannot go back now. Or will not.

He smells of earth and smoke as he spreads me back onto the grass, leaving a trail of fire on my skin as he works at my buttons and straps. I shiver as his hands explore, stripped bare now to the breeze and Henry's gaze. His hands tease but take all I freely give. And then suddenly there's nothing in the world but the two of us, flesh and breath and bone, mingling beneath that blinding blue sky, a tender undoing that binds us in a way no law or preacher ever could. From this day, for better or worse, I am Henry's.

Later, I try to find some scrap of shame as I pull myself back into my dress. I cannot. There is only a raw, pulsing joy in me, a shiver at the memory of our bodies moistly fused. I think of Mama, of her heartbreak if she ever learns that I have echoed her mistake.

But then Henry's eyes are on me, warm and shining. He opens the Barrett Browning and begins to read. I lay back again in the grass, eyes closed, reveling in the deep, rusty thrum of his voice as he recites each aching line. The final words are snatched away as he reads them, lost on the wind, but not lost in my heart.

I shall but love thee better after death.

He's silent as he reaches for my small spray of flowers and closes them between the pages. For a while at least, the ridge will belong to us, and we must be content with that.

Chapter 19

Henry's child will come in the spring.

The midwife from Level Grove is being lauded as a miracle worker, the bringer of life where no life seemed possible. At last, Susanne will have her precious heir, and I must learn to live with that, learn to pretend the very thought of it does not break me into a million pieces. It is November. Beyond the windows the trees stand stripped as skeletons, grim and bony, dripping with a steady autumn rain. Susanne's room is cold, awash in watery gray light. The fire has dwindled, so I throw on some wood and take up the poker. Susanne's eyes are on me. I have grown used to them, following with vague disdain as I go about my daily work, but today they are different, sharp and feverish, skittering after me so that I hold my breath against my spine and turn away.

My gaze slides to the window, and I silently curse the rain. There will be no lunch on the ridge today. I'm about to turn away when I catch sight of Henry leaving the barn. I cannot see his face; his head is down to ward off the rain. But I would know that lanky, loose-framed stride anywhere.

I am still clutching the poker when I hear Susanne behind me. Her eyes follow mine—to Henry. Before I realize what she's about, she has snatched me by the wrist and is yanking me around to face her. I look down at her fingers, clawlike as they bite into my flesh, and see the cool metal wink of her wedding band. Her breath on my face is sickly-sweet, like the reek of spoiled peaches. I feel my breakfast scorch up into my throat. For a moment the room swims.

I am dimly aware of the poker clattering to the hearth as I fight to keep my legs beneath me. The crack of her hand against my cheek is like breaking glass, tiny shards flashing and dancing behind my eyes like flakes in a snow globe. I taste blood, the tang of iron, the sting of shame. I have always known this moment would come, that one day she would peer through my backbone, straight to the truth. There are things a woman cannot hide, especially from another woman.

Her expression is one of not astonishment, but affirmation, and I see she has suspected for some time, that she has only been waiting to be sure. And now she is, though not a single word has passed between us. Even now I say nothing. It occurs to me that I should have prepared for this moment, but what is there to say? If there is something, I am too numb to think of it.

Something—I can only call it willfulness—steals over me, a little curl of anger that flares white-hot in my head, a voice that says Susanne Gavin is not worthy of my guilt, that a woman who cannot love a man like Henry deserves to lose him to someone who can. It is not true, of course, but it is what I must hold tight to at this terrible moment.

Her face looms just inches from mine now, and I am once again startled to see the waste it has become. Her skin is like crepe, dry and slack against the bones, her cheeks as sharp as blades, splotched with flags of blood-hot color. Her mouth is pinched and pale, trembling with outrage, and for a moment I imagine Henry kissing those lips and wonder if he ever found any warmth there at all.

She draws back, strikes again. I feel the brand of her palm on my cheek. It is only for the child's sake that I do not slap her back. Instead, I meet her gaze head-on, standing straight backed against the heat of those pinpoint pupils, and I see that her anger has nothing to do with losing Henry's affection, only with knowing she has been bested. I hate her for that most of all.

"Deceitful bitch!" she shrieks. "You have taken what was mine!"

There isn't enough guile in me to deny it. I am what she says. Though, God help me, even now I would not change it. I thought there would be more time, though time for what, I cannot say. Not even time can unravel the knot we tied that day on the ridge, and now I must live with the consequences.

She grips my wrist again, squeezing until my fingers begin to tingle, and then something comes over her, a glittering, ominous quiet that makes me suck in my breath. Even her breathing is changed, deeper, slower, and for a moment it is as if she is watching a story unfold somewhere far away. I see the light flatten in her eyes, like a fire drawing down before it flares. When they refocus on me I feel the hairs on my neck prickle, and suddenly I am afraid. Not for myself, but of what she will do.

Susanne goes on staring, fixing me with an expression I cannot, at first, put a name to, and then I realize it is the nearest thing to a smile I have ever seen from her. There is something terrible in it, a calculation that makes me shrink back. Finally, she thrusts me away from her. I am dismissed to my room, where I am to remain until it is decided what will be done with me.

I blink at her, stunned, unable to put a name to the emotions warring in me, and then I realize it is a mix of relief and bewilderment that I have not been immediately dismissed, though surely she cannot mean to let me stay. I can only suppose she wishes me to remain until Henry returns from town, so she may confront her husband with the flesh-and-blood proof of his transgressions.

It sickens me to think what Henry will suffer at that moment. He will not deny it—the truth is too plain—but neither will he be proud to admit it. If I must leave Peak, and surely I must, it will be easier for him if I pack my things and go before he returns. It is on the tip of my tongue to tell her I'm free to leave when I choose, that I will not wait, but my mouth will not form the words. How can I leave without good-bye, without one final crush in Henry's arms? I go to my room to wait for Henry for the last time, but he does not come.

At dinnertime, Lottie brings me a tray. On it is a note from Susanne, curtly and unsteadily penned, a terse reminder that I am not to leave my room for any reason unless called for. When I hear Henry's truck rattle up the gravel drive, my heart batters my ribs until I can't breathe. For one outlandish moment I let myself imagine us slipping out of the house together, vanishing into the night. It is impossible, of course. I cannot ask it. And it would never occur to Henry. Peak is his duty, and so is Susanne. This can end only one way. I perch on the edge of my narrow bed and wait for his knock.

I fall asleep waiting.

The next day I hear his truck go back down the gravel. He stays gone all day. Meals arrive and are taken away untouched. There are no more notes, nothing to explain why I am still beneath Susanne Gavin's roof.

On the third day I rise while it is still dark and pack some of my things into my old leather satchel, prepared to leave as soon as the sun is up. There is nothing to stay for. I am apparently not even to have a good-bye. I cannot go home to New Orleans, not the way things are. Nor will I bring shame on Mama by heading north to her folks in Chicago. I have put a little money by and still have the fifty-dollar bill Mama pinned to my slip the day she put me on the bus. I have no idea where I will go, only that I will go today.

When a knock sounds, I hide my satchel behind the door, prepared to refuse Lottie's tray when I see a note beside the toast plate. I snatch the tray from her hands and close the door, tearing the small envelope with my teeth before I have even set the tray on the dresser. It is not Susanne's hand, but Henry's. I have been summoned to his study.

I have not left my room in three days. I take a few minutes to compose myself, to check my face in the mirror. I barely recognize myself. My eyes are puffy and red rimmed, my hair loose and wild about my face. It is not how I want him to remember me, but my brush and pins are already packed and I am too weary to dig for them.

I am acutely aware, as I leave my room and descend the stairs, that I have hardly moved in these last three days, have scarcely eaten a bite. I am stiff and off balance as I stand at the head of the stairs, disoriented by the wide-open spaces after being shut up so long. When I enter the study, Henry is in his chair, the chair where he used to read to me every evening. My eyes blur. Tears are always nearby these days.

He does not rise from his chair, only gestures for me to sit. He looks worn down, smaller and thinner than I remember him just three days ago. He does not touch me, can barely manage to meet my eyes, and I know something new has gone wrong, something more terrible than discovery, more terrible even than the good-bye that stands before us.

He means to pay me off, I think miserably, to buy my silence, because his wife knows, and because there is a child coming. I have become inconvenient. I brace myself, vowing to go quietly, and without a penny of his in my pocket. What he offers is so much worse.

"You're going to hate me for what I'm going to say, Adele."

I cannot look at him. If I do I will break apart. Instead, I lock eyes with the portrait over the mantel, Susanne, watching us still. "Henry, whatever happens, I will never hate you. I made my choice the day we went up on that ridge, and probably well before that. I knew what could happen—what *would* happen."

My voice is flat and strangely cool, masking the ache at the center of my chest. I blink back the sting of tears. How can I make him understand what I'm about to say, why I can't let him say what he's about to?

"Please don't tell me to go. I *will* go, because someone always pays for this kind of sin, and that someone has to be me. But please, Henry, let it be me who leaves." My voice breaks then, and I curse the tear that scorches its way toward my chin. I wanted to be strong. I want to be but cannot. "I don't think I could bear to hear you send me away."

He stands and takes a step toward me, then checks himself. "You don't . . . *have* to leave, Adele."

For an instant I wonder if I've taken leave of my senses. And then I look closely at his face, at the mix of emotions at play there, hope mixed with something like shame, and I know that there is more he's about to say, and that whatever it is, I'm not going to like it.

An *arrangement*, he calls it.

It is incomprehensible to me that my presence might be more desired than my absence, and by Susanne of all people. There is an heir on the way, reputations at stake. It wouldn't do to have the lady's maid deserting just now, not when Celia Cunningham was still running her mouth to anyone willing to listen. And so it seems I find myself at a strange and hideous advantage, but only if I agree to play along.

I am to be removed from Susanne's sight but kept close by, at least until the gossip dies down. It will be noised around that I've taken ill, that as a precaution I have been moved out of the house, to safeguard Susanne's delicate health. We will be able to carry on as before, Henry informs me. *Carry on*—he actually says those words.

For a moment I'm almost too stricken to speak. "How, Henry? How can you ask me to do this unnatural thing? To remain here while she—"

"I can't lose you, Adele. I won't."

"And what happens when the baby comes?"

"Nothing happens. My wife has her heir, which is all she's ever cared about. And we have each other. Susanne agreed to the bargain."

I shake my head, spilling tears down my cheeks. "Your bargain, Henry, not mine. What you're asking is a sin. Can you not see that?"

"It would be a bigger sin to throw away what we have, Adele." His voice is thick, ragged. "If you go, I lose ... everything."

The plea in his voice, in his eyes, is more than I can bear. That afternoon, Henry moves my things out of the house and into the small cottage down by the lake while George and Lottie look on with knowing eyes. I have no pride left, nothing but the horrible reality I have created for myself. And so it is time I am practical. Susanne will have her heir, and the Gavin name will be saved from scandal. I will keep a roof over my head. And I will have Henry.

Chapter 20

Jay

Jay stood beside Young Buck, poring over the plans for what would eventually become the tasting barn. It was going to take a lot of work to convert the old barn into the showplace they envisioned, not to mention most of what was left in the coffers. But if they did it right, the payoff could be big. He had been counting the days until harvest. The minute the fruit was in, they could finally get busy on the barn.

He was about to suggest a change to the bar shelves when Belle let out a gleeful yip. Leslie was hovering in the doorway. She looked good, which was surprising since her left cheek was smudged with dirt and the knees of her jeans were filthy.

He poked his pencil behind his ear and looked her up and down. "I'd ask if you came to get your hands dirty, but it looks like you already have. What have you been doing?"

Her smile was tight, tentative. "Could you come with me somewhere?"

Jay felt Young Buck's eyes slide briefly in his direction before shifting back to his plans. "That depends. Where are we going? And is there food in that bag?"

Leslie glanced down at the canvas tote she was holding. "Food? No, it's ... Can you just come with me? It's important."

Her smile had completely disappeared. Jay felt a moment of panic. Christ, what if she had decided to back out and hightail it to New York?

"Buck, I'll be back in a few. Belle, you stay here and guard the fort."

Leslie shifted the bag on her shoulder as they stepped out into the late-afternoon sunshine. "I'm sorry I interrupted you."

Jay felt himself relax. Some of the intensity had left her face.

"No biggie. We were just talking about what to do with the tasting barn. I'm leaning toward the copper top. Pricey, but it'll look great. The lumber should be here in a few weeks. Which reminds me, Virgil will be delivering a cord of wood next week. I'll show you how to build a proper fire and how to work the flue. Not much to it, but there's a right way and a wrong way."

"What makes you think I don't know the difference?"

"Let's just say I prefer not to take chances. That house survived the Civil War. I'm not about to let a Yankee burn it down now."

Leslie's eyes shot wide. "How am I a Yankee? I was born in Gavin."

"So you say, Big City, so you say. Now, how 'bout telling me where you're taking me? Or am I being kidnapped? I'm not saying I have a problem with that. I'll just need to call Buck and make sure he gives Belle her supper."

She pointed straight ahead. "We're going up there."

Jay shielded his eyes and scanned the rocky jut of land looming straight ahead. *Bloody hell.* "Why?"

"So I can show you something."

"Leslie, I've been out in the rows all day. Whatever it is, can't you just tell me about it?"

"Please?" Something flickered behind her eyes, a secret she wasn't quite ready to share. "I wasn't kidding when I said it was important."

Jay sighed. It seemed there was only one way he was going to find out what all this was about. "Lead on, then. I'm always up for a mystery."

Leslie's fingers tightened around the canvas tote. "That's good to know."

She said nothing more as she headed for the path. It was all Jay could do to keep up. While he had to grope for every foothold, she covered the trail like a Sherpa, scrambling over rock and root, popping into view now and then among the trees.

He was sweating and winded when the path finally spit him into a small clearing. For a moment he stood with his hands on his knees.

"Jesus, Big City, I never knew you were part mountain goat. Now, what is it you dragged me all the way—" He didn't finish. Instead, he straightened very slowly, stunned to find himself staring at a grave.

"I found it a week ago," Leslie told him matter-of-factly. "I take it you didn't know it was here either?"

Jay shook his head, eyes fixed on the stone as he moved toward the gate. "I was up here a few years ago. This was definitely not here."

"You don't recognize it?"

Jay turned to look at her, hands shoved deep in his pockets, his head too full of questions to respond.

"The shot I showed you," Leslie prompted. "The one I got from Goddard? My mother took it over thirty years ago, and this is the grave. It was covered with kudzu when I found it, which is probably why you didn't see it."

"What happened to the kudzu?"

Leslie pointed to a wilting pile of greenery at the edge of the trees. "I yanked it up. I couldn't stand the thought of leaving it like it was. It was just so sad. She's been here all this time with no one to look after her."

She?

Jay felt a shiver touch the back of his neck.

Leslie took a step toward him. "Don't tell me you're freaked-out."

Damn right he was freaked-out, but not for the reason she

thought. "I'm just . . . surprised; that's all. It's not exactly the kind of thing you stumble onto every day. How did you, by the way?"

"Stumble onto it, you mean? I was up here getting shots of the house. There was a tree in one corner of the photo—that one there." She paused, pointing to a lightning-ravaged oak. "The minute I saw it, I knew where I was and what I would find."

Sweet. Bloody. Jesus.

He wasn't sure what he'd expected, but it sure as hell wasn't this.

"There's no name." Her voice came to him as if from far away, a peculiar mix of tension and gloom. "No name, no date, nothing but a single line from an old poem."

Jay's thoughts began to churn. Maggie had mentioned a book that, toward the end of his life, Henry had never been without—a book of poems. He tore his eyes from the stone to look at Leslie. She was holding out a sheet of creased white paper. He took it, unfolding the sheet almost warily. It appeared to be a tracing of some sort, scratched out in black crayon.

"I couldn't read the inscription," Leslie explained as he continued to stare at the tracing. "So this morning I made a tracing. I recognized the lines as soon as I saw them." Producing a small book from her bag, she opened it and placed it in his hands.

Jay glanced down at the page, then up again. "Where did you find this?"

"Hidden in the bottom of Henry's desk. There was a picture, too, of a woman holding a baby. I think . . . I'm almost sure . . . that woman was Henry's mistress."

Jay let his breath out slowly as he closed the book and handed it back, like a balloon leaking air. He could feel Leslie's eyes between his shoulders as he pulled back the iron gate and stepped through. Bending down on one knee, he smoothed a palm over what remained of the inscription.

"Her name was Adele," he said quietly. "Adele Laveau."

Leslie took a jerky step forward, her expression incredulous. "You knew?"

"I knew her name. I didn't know she was buried up here."

"Maggie told you?"

Jay stood and brushed off his hands. "It was after she got sick. She told me about the affair and about the child—Jemmy, I think his name was. She was Susanne Gavin's maid."

For a time Leslie said nothing, her eyes downcast, still clutching the small leather book. "Why here?" she said at last. "Why is she buried up here?"

"I have no idea. I told you, I didn't know this was here. But if I were guessing, I'd say Henry wanted to keep her close. Maggie said he spent a lot of time up here."

"How did she . . . die?"

Jay stuffed his hands in his pockets and looked away. "An accident of some kind. I'm not sure what. Every time Maggie tried to talk about it, she would break down."

A crease appeared between Leslie's brows. "That doesn't sound like Maggie."

"At the end, when she knew she was . . . dying . . . your grand-mother started to talk about the past, good things mostly, about you and your mother and Peak's glory days. I think it helped take her mind off the pain. Then one day the conversation changed."

"Changed how?"

Jay turned toward the west face, scanning the shiny slick of lake below, the blue-gold horizon beyond. He didn't want to have this discussion, didn't want to resurrect those last days of Maggie's life, didn't want to remember the anguish still lurking in her eyes when they closed for the last time. Yet here he was, standing beside a grave he never knew existed, trying once again to keep nagging suspicions at bay.

So someone will finally know.

Even now, Maggie's papery whisper was never far away. They had been in her room, just back from another doctor's appointment, when she had closed her fingers over his, squeezing so tightly the web of blue veins stood out across the back of her gnarled hand. He pretended not to notice that her eyes were dimmer than they'd been the day before, dulled by pain and a new cocktail of prescriptions, but anyone who knew Maggie would have seen how tired she was, worn down by what she called *the tedious business of dying.* She was running out of fight, and in that moment they had both known it.

I must . . . tell you a story, she had rasped. *A secret I've lived with for too many years.* Her eyes had filled with tears then. She'd closed them, turning her head away on the pillow. . . . *About her.*

The hairs on the back of his neck had actually prickled. Still, he had mustered a smile, given her hand a squeeze. *Not now, Old Broad. The doctor told you to rest.*

No! The word had erupted from her pale, dry lips with an energy he hadn't known she still possessed. Then she had sagged back against her pillows. *I need . . . to tell it now. Please, I have to tell it.*

Why now, Mags? Why does it have to be now?

To this day he still couldn't say if he'd been asking Maggie or himself. He only knew he had dreaded her answer even as he had asked the question. Something in her moist, pleading eyes had warned him he might not like what he was about to hear. And he had been right.

So someone will finally know.

Overhead, the high, thin wail of a redtail pulled Jay back to the present. Tipping his head back, he watched it circle, lazily riding an updraft, its outstretched wings creamy and still against the stark blue sky.

By the time he turned back, Leslie had returned the book of poems to her bag and was stooping to gather a fistful of small yellow flowers from a nearby patch of ground. When the gate squealed open, then shut again behind him, she straightened with her makeshift bouquet, her face all business, despite the wildflowers.

"I asked you how the conversation changed. You never answered."

Jay kicked at a rock with the toe of his boot, sending it skittering toward the trees. "There was something she wanted to tell me, a secret she said she needed to tell before she died."

"Something to do with Adele?"

Jay shrugged. "I think so, but she never did tell it. She tried more than once, but every time she brought it up, she'd start to cry like her heart was breaking. I'll never know what caused her such anguish, and it will always bother me that she never made her peace with whatever it was, but I can't say I'm sorry she didn't share it with me."

Leslie looked genuinely stunned. "I don't understand. How could you not want to know?"

"Because sometimes when you care about someone there are things you just don't want to know. And because it was . . . difficult to watch."

Leslie let the wildflowers slip from her hands. "I should have been here," she said, her voice suddenly thick with emotion. "At the end, it should have been me with her."

Jay took a step closer but stopped himself before laying a hand on her arm. "I didn't tell you that to make you feel guilty."

"I know, but it did. I've been walking around for weeks now, asking myself all these questions, simple things, like why my mother would have taken an interest in a bunch of dead artists, or why my great-grandfather chose to hang five paintings of the same half-dressed woman in his study. Now there's this dead woman—Adele. And it keeps hitting me . . . there's no one to answer them, no one left who knows. I never thought I'd care, but I do, and it's too late. I came back too late." She paused, waving an arm to indicate the rolling green acres stretching beyond the ridge. "I've inherited all this, and I don't know a damn thing about the people who built it, how they lived, who they loved . . . what they regretted."

Jay had no idea how to respond. A month ago he would have

blithely reminded her that she had no one to blame but herself for those unanswered questions. But not now. She had her reasons for staying away. He didn't know what they were and probably never would, but they were enough for him.

He was silent on the trek back down. Seeing Adele Laveau's grave had rattled him more than he realized, though he supposed he could explain away its presence on the ridge if he tried. Henry would have wanted her close, to feel her nearby in the only way he could after she was gone. Even the absence of a name and date made sense. Should anyone have stumbled onto the stone, the last thing he would have wanted were questions about why his wife's maid had been buried on the ridge instead of in a proper grave in a proper cemetery. Better to be safe with one's reputation than sorry.

But what if it was something else? What if it wasn't only *his* reputation Henry had been trying to protect? What if the suspicions that had taken root in his brain more than a year ago were actually true?

Chapter 21

Leslie

Leslie came awake with a start, sitting bolt upright in bed. She'd had the dream again: Henry sitting behind his desk, Barrett Browning's poems open on his lap, a half glass of bourbon at his elbow, eyes blank and cold, fixed unseeing on the paintings over the mantel—just as Maggie had found him. She should be used to it by now, after four straight nights. But the truth was, she found the recurring dream both disturbing and baffling.

It was possible that she was romanticizing the affair between Henry and Adele, creating a grand and tragic passion from nothing but a posy of dead flowers and a few lines of poetry, but she didn't think so. Nor could she shake the niggling suspicion that the paintings were somehow part of the story, though how and where they might fit, she had no idea.

After the first night, she had been convinced the woman in the painting was Adele. It would explain Henry's fascination and his desire to spend his last days in his study. But the more she studied the face of the Rebecca, the more she knew her theory was wrong. She was no expert, but the painting's style suggested an earlier era, and there was something else that didn't fit, a brazen quality she couldn't reconcile with the primly dressed young mother in the photograph.

By the time she finished her first cup of coffee, Leslie had added another item to her to-do list. She was already heading downtown to take care of some errands. One more shouldn't throw her schedule off too much and might finally provide some answers. Forgoing her usual—and much needed—second cup, she went to the study, where she dragged a chair to the fireplace and wrestled the Rebecca from its place of honor above the mantel.

When the painting was wrapped in a sheet and carefully stowed in her car, she headed to the barn to find Jay. She would have to share her plans with him sooner or later, and if he was going to push back on her idea, she might as well know it now, before she waded in too deep.

Belle romped out of the barn to greet her, snuffling her palm like a horse after a sugar cube. Leslie bent to say hello, giggling helplessly as she tried—and failed—to fend off an assault of enthusiastic canine kisses. She didn't realize Jay was nearby until he stepped from behind one of the stainless steel holding tanks.

Wiping doggie slobber from her cheek, she stood, pretending not to notice the sinewy expanse of shoulders and chest beneath Jay's close-fitting shirt.

"So how goes it?" she asked, more brightly than intended.

Jay dragged a sleeve across his forehead. "So far, so good. Everything right on schedule."

"Schedule for what?"

"For harvest. Did you forget? The pickers will be here to harvest a week from today."

"Oh," was all she could think to say. She'd been so preoccupied with her marketing plans that she'd forgotten someone had to pick the grapes and make the wine. "Speaking of the opening—"

"Were we?"

Leslie ignored the jibe. "I have an idea I wanted to run by you."

"Shoot."

"The brochure and label designs are almost finished. I'll have the last shots tomorrow. As soon as I put them together, I'll bring you the galleys. Once you approve it, we're set to print."

"Leslie, I appreciate you wanting my input, but there's no need. I've seen enough to know I'm going to green-light whatever you say."

The casual comment brought a warm rush of pleasure. They had come a long way since those first rocky days. There was trust now, and respect, a division of labor that after only a few short weeks felt strangely seamless. And something else that made her belly go warm, and made her a little afraid too.

"Good, then, because I want us to throw a party, a kind of soft opening. We could tie it to the Harvest Festival and call it the Splash."

Jay stared at her blankly. "The Splash?"

"As in . . . a splash of wine. As in . . . making a splash. You know, a kind of, 'Here we come.'"

"And how do you propose we stretch the budget to cover that?"

Leslie stole a glance at her watch. "I, um . . . I've got a few ideas about that. Speaking of which, I need to get going. I've got a couple of appointments, but if you want to cook me dinner, I'll fill you in on the details later."

If Jay was surprised, he didn't show it. "Any requests?"

"My dinners all cook in five and a half minutes on full power. I'm in no position to be picky. Should I bring anything?"

"A bottle of wine is customary, I believe. I don't suppose you know where to get your hands on a really good Chardonnay?"

Leslie laughed, a soft, breezy sound that felt like flirting. "I'll see what I can do about the wine. See you around seven." The invitation—could you still call it an invitation if you invited yourself?—had popped out without a second thought, and now that it had she was glad.

Downtown was just beginning to stir as Leslie pulled into Meeting Street and parked along the curb in front of Randolph Estate Sales. She was glad to find the shop empty as she struggled through the door with the sheet-wrapped Rebecca.

A jangling brass bell brought a thickset man in a lumpy gray cardigan bustling from the back room. His smile was bland, his faded blue eyes comically magnified by the optical visor he wore. "Austin Randolph," he said, pumping her hand warmly, his voice thick with Carolina drawl. "You must be Miss Nichols. I believe you called about some jewelry?"

Leslie held out her wrist. "I'd like to know how much you'll give me for this."

Mr. Randolph was clearly startled by her abruptness, but after adjusting his visor, he turned his attention to her watch. "A lady's all-gold Rolex, and a fairly new one at that."

Leslie opened the clasp and slid the watch off, laying it on the glass counter. "It's two years old. I've got the original box and paperwork in the car."

Randolph picked up the watch, looking it over with a practiced eye. "Plain bezel, diamond dial . . . It's a beautiful timepiece, in excellent condition, but I'll be honest; I can't give you anywhere near what you paid. Are you quite certain you want to part with it?"

In response to Leslie's nod, he produced a jeweler's loupe from his trouser pocket and proceeded to make a more thorough inspection. When he was finally satisfied, he reached for a calculator, tapped a few buttons with the eraser of a pencil, then held it up for her to see. Leslie felt her shoulders sag but reluctantly nodded her agreement. He hadn't been kidding when he said the figure would be nowhere near what she paid, but if she was frugal, it might be enough to finance her plans for the Splash.

With the necessary papers complete and the cash counted out, Leslie inquired if there might be time to take a look at the Rebecca.

Mr. Randolph seemed only too happy to oblige. Hoisting the painting up onto the counter, he peeled back the faded floral bedsheet, adjusted his visor, and turned his attention to the canvas.

After several minutes, he tugged the visor up onto his forehead. "Are you looking to sell this piece as well?"

"I haven't decided," Leslie lied, feeling a twinge of guilt. "But I would like to know more about it. There are another four at home, all apparently painted by the same artist."

Randolph's downy gray brows lifted in surprise. "Four more, you say?" He glanced once more at the signature in the lower right-hand corner, then pulled off his visor and hung it on a nearby peg. "Art of this caliber really isn't my specialty, Miss Nichols, but if you'd allow me to, I'd like to hold on to the piece and consult with a friend of mine in the art department at UNC. I can't be certain, but I suspect it may be a rather special piece."

Leslie was disappointed at the prospect of having to wait but was intrigued by his use of the word *special*. "How long will that take, do you think?"

"It shouldn't be more than a week or two. If it's the painting you're worried about, I assure you it will be in good hands."

Leslie swallowed her disappointment; she'd been hoping for answers today. Scribbling down her number, she handed it to Mr. Randolph, thanked him for his time, and left the shop, her thoughts already shifting to her next appointment.

The *Gavin Gazette* was the last stop on her to-do list, and the most critical. She had pulled together a hasty press packet, media of the house and grounds, along with a shamelessly schmaltzy timeline of Peak's evolution from tobacco farm to winery. It was presumptuous, she knew, to suggest content to a newspaper editor, but as Jay had pointed out, harvest was around the corner and they were coming down to the wire. With advertising dollars scarce, it was starting to look like exposure was going to come down to whatever she could wrangle from the paper.

As it turned out, she had no trouble convincing Steve Whitney, the *Gazette*'s new, and somewhat wet-behind-the-ears, editor to agree to a series of local-interest pieces, culminating in a full-color spread in the *Weekender*, which would run three days before the Splash. It was more than she'd hoped for, even if she did have to flutter her lashes a bit to get it done.

Thanking him profusely, she reiterated the hope that she would see him at the Splash, then asked to be directed to the archives department. If she couldn't get instant answers about the Rebecca, maybe she could dig up something on how Adele Laveau might have died.

The archives department turned out to be a cramped and musty room at the end of the hall. A stout woman with iron gray hair and penciled-on brows informed Leslie in clipped tones that there was no research staff to assist her, but if she was willing to search on her own, she was welcome to stay until they locked up.

Leslie was glad when the woman finished her brief tutorial and left. Nothing was digitally archived, and the microfiche trays were confusing, but eventually she grasped how the information was stored. Unfortunately, with no concrete dates, there was no easy way to attack the data. All she could do was scan back editions, one at a time, in hopes that something caught her eye.

After three hours, Leslie was ready to throw in the towel. She had combed through a dozen years of minuscule print and grainy photos and had yet to run across anything remotely helpful. No surprises, no loose ends, nothing pertaining to the woman buried on the ridge or the child she had borne out of wedlock. So now what? There were hospital records she could check, and the courthouse, though in those days rural births often went unrecorded. She could visit local churches, search for a record of baptism for the boy, but it seemed unlikely that Adele would have flaunted Henry's illegitimate son in church.

Groaning, she pressed her knuckles to her lids. Perhaps it was time to admit she'd already invested more energy in this wild-goose chase than she could afford. Adele Laveau was dead and gone and had been for eighty years; nothing she learned now was going to change that. Weary and resigned, she reached to shut down the reader, then went stock-still.

MYSTERIOUS FIRE AT PEAK PLANTATION

The photo was poor, degraded after so many years, but appeared to show the foundation of a small shed heaped in ash and rubble.

January 11, 1940—An unexplained fire broke out late Thursday night in an outbuilding on Peak Plantation. Owner Henry Gavin was away from home when the fire started, but returned in time to help extinguish the blaze. The woodshed is reportedly a total loss. No injuries resulted from the fire. Wife Susanne and daughter Maggie were safely in the house when the fire occurred. At this time the cause of the blaze is unknown, but vandalism is suspected. Three local boys, Samuel, Randall, and Landis Porter, all from neighboring Level Grove, were picked up for questioning, but were later released without charges.

Leslie couldn't say why she had bothered to print the article. A shed fire might have been news in 1940, but it wasn't what she'd been looking for. As gruesome as it seemed, she'd been hoping to find some clue about the accident that had killed Adele. Instead, her big discovery had turned out to be a case of vandalism in which the only casualty was an old woodshed. Sighing, she stuffed the article into her purse and flicked off the light.

On the way home she fiddled with the radio, searching for a station that wasn't playing LeAnn Rimes or Billy Ray Cyrus and wondering why so many country singers happened to have three names. As she turned onto Gavin Boulevard she caught sight of First Presbyterian's soaring steeple, white and piercing against the bright blue sky. Without thinking, she pulled into the deserted lot, cut the engine, and got out.

Something wobbled in her chest as she stepped onto the cracked slate path. For a moment she stood staring at the church's neat white double doors, its redbrick walls and stained glass windows. Generations of Gavins had attended service in its sanctuary, sung in its pews, wed at its altar, been buried on its grounds. Suddenly, the gravity of tradition, of years and loss, was stifling. What was she doing here?

In the yard behind the church, headstones stood like rows of well-tended teeth. Leslie forced her feet off the path, navigating them like land mines as she crossed to where the dead Gavins slept. Henry's lofty granite obelisk made the family plot easy to locate, a shaft of sullen gray marble adorned with a heavy bronze plaque. Beside him, Susanne rested more modestly, her epitaph as inconspicuous as her plain granite headstone. She had gone first, six years before Henry, at only forty-seven.

Leslie's breath caught when she saw the small stone in the grass to Susanne's right, nameless and etched with a solitary date—a child lost too soon to even be named. Miscarriages and stillbirths were a fact of life in those days, but the sight of it, so tiny and final, was sobering. A few feet away, Maggie's headstone basked in the last rays of afternoon sun. It was hard to believe she'd been gone a whole year, harder still to realize thirty years had passed since she had decorated gingerbread men or carved a pumpkin with her grandmother. How could thirty years feel like yesterday?

The marker beside Maggie's was a perfect match, slate gray granite etched with crosses at the corners, belonging to the grandfather who lived in Leslie's memory not as flesh and blood, but as a blend of remembered scents—peppermint, tobacco, the faint limey tang of hair tonic.

And then there was her mother's stone, a heart-shaped slab of pink-veined marble standing alone in the shade of a nearby oak. Until that moment she had never laid eyes on it. Maggie hadn't thought it a good idea to let her attend the funeral. And then, three days later, Jimmy had taken her away. Stepping into the shade, she read the epitaph.

Amanda Lynne Nichols
April 4, 1953–October 27, 1984
Beloved daughter, devoted mother,
Cruelly stolen from those who loved her.

Stolen.

The word rocked her.

Maggie had chosen it, of course, a glaring indictment of the son-in-law she blamed for the death of her little girl. And she'd been far from alone in her suspicions. There had been an inquest, and the not-so-subtle whispers when Jimmy had failed to appear at his wife's funeral. No one knew it was because he couldn't stand up long enough to dress himself. The memory of her father—drunk and sobbing on the bathroom floor—still made Leslie shudder. But the memory came with a rush of understanding too, about what she was doing here.

She had never said good-bye.

She had carried her mother's death quietly, locking it away, burying it deep. But now, like the ridge with its abandoned stone and rusted iron gate, time had found its way in. Suddenly, she was weeping, quiet sobs that rushed up from nowhere to fill her throat, for all the lost years and all the unsaid good-byes. Until now, she hadn't understood how irrevocably linked it all was, and how inevitable. Peak was Maggie's legacy, enduring and unshakable, tying the past with the future, and somehow, she had unwittingly followed it home.

Leslie had no idea how long she lingered before finally heading back to the car. She only knew that the sun had begun to dip and she was finally cried out, emptied, and strangely at peace. She had come to say good-bye and she had, to her mother, and to Maggie, and perhaps to some part of her past.

Chapter 22

Leslie arrived for dinner fifteen minutes early, wearing black slacks and a matching turtleneck, a chilled bottle of Chardonnay in hand. The cottage door stood open. She walked through to find Jay in the kitchen, contemplating a pair of bronze-skinned fish.

The smile he flashed when he glanced up was slightly distracted, almost boyish. "I hope you like sea bass."

"Sure, I guess. As long as you promise there won't be a face on mine. Faces on my food make me queasy."

"No face, I promise," he said over the *shing-shing* of his knife against the sharpening steel. "I'm going to fillet them, then roast them with a sweet-corn and black-eye succotash."

Leslie lifted a brow in approval. "Sounds wonderful, and very southern. I'm guessing you didn't learn to cook like that in Connecticut."

"And you'd be right. Maggie and I had a standing date every Friday night. We would trade off cooking for one another. I taught her how to fry oysters and make Yankee pot roast. She taught me to make corn bread and fry okra." His hands went still over the fish, the ghost of a smile on his lips. "I never tasted okra until I met your grandmother."

"I'm glad you were here," Leslie said quietly. "I'm glad she didn't . . . I'm glad she wasn't alone."

Jay looked up then, his hands momentarily quiet. "Maybe it's time to open the wine."

Leslie cleared her throat, grateful for the change of subject. She felt like a novice as she fumbled with the bottle, an awkwardness only intensified by the surgeon-like precision with which Jay was wielding his knife. He wrote books, cooked gourmet meals, knew about wine, and wasn't afraid to get dirty. It was a daunting combination, and rather attractive, now that she thought about it. The kitchen was small and he filled it completely, lean and tan in his khakis and plain white oxford, and—she couldn't help noticing—smelling faintly, but distractingly, of sandalwood.

Pouring a glass of wine, she set it beside the cutting board, then poured one for herself, happy to have something to at least occupy her hands. She should offer to help, to peel something or chop something, but when it came to food prep, she didn't have a clue and had no wish to demonstrate her lack of skills. Thankfully, she spotted several bowls and a handful of utensils in the sink. She could at least handle a sponge.

Jay glanced up from his chopping but made no comment when she picked up the sponge and turned on the tap. They worked in companionable silence, elbow to elbow in the tiny kitchen until the fish was ready to go into the oven.

Jay set the timer, then topped off their glasses and carried them to the small café table in the corner, indicating the chair across from his. "Now, I believe you promised to tell me what you're up to. Something about a party?"

Leslie took a sip of wine, surprised at the butterfly wings suddenly fluttering in her belly. She hadn't realized until that moment just how much she wanted his approval.

"I've been kicking it around for about a week now, and I'm convinced we need to get some early buzz going, get the locals excited about what we're doing here. A soft opening timed to coincide with the Harvest Festival is just the kind of thing we need. It would be a lot of work, and on very short notice, but the payoff in exposure could be huge."

Jay narrowed one eye. "In case you haven't noticed, Big City, we're not exactly rolling in cash."

Leslie crossed her arms with a self-satisfied smile. "What if I told you it wouldn't drain the coffers by a single penny?"

"Then I guess I'd want to know how you plan to pull it off."

"By networking. I called Susan Bishop a few days ago to find out what catering would cost, and she immediately wanted in. She volunteered to kick in with food, then offered to pave the way with other locals she thinks will want to participate in exchange for the publicity."

Jay looked mildly exasperated. "Leslie, the doors aren't even open. What kind of publicity do they think they're going to get?"

Leslie smiled, a slow-spreading Cheshire grin. "The kind that comes from a full-color spread in the *Gazette*'s *Weekender*."

"A full color—" He sat up straighter, set aside his wine. "And how much is that going to cost?"

"Not a cent."

"You're telling me the paper isn't charging us for a full-color ad?"

"Not an ad, a two-page feature. We're talking pictures, history, the works. I also got them to agree to two preview pieces. The first will be about Peak's history; the second will cover the harvest."

Clearly impressed, Jay leaned back in his chair, a smile playing at the corners of his mouth. "Dare I ask how you pulled off this magic feat?"

Leslie took a leisurely sip of wine, savoring the moment. When she knew she had his full attention, she crooked a finger, drawing him closer. "I'm going to tell you something not many people know about me," she said in hushed tones. "But first, I need to know you can keep a secret."

When Jay leaned in expectantly, she met him partway across the tiny table, her voice a mere whisper. "I'm actually very charming."

Jay's face went momentarily blank, the expression followed by a burst of laughter so loud it brought Belle scrambling to see what all the fuss was about.

Leslie glowered at him, arms folded. "It wasn't supposed to be *that* funny."

Jay made a halfhearted attempt at self-control. "I just expected you to say something else; that's all."

"No, you're right. I've never been charming. When your only role models are the barflies your father brings home on Friday nights, you tend to get shortchanged in the charm department."

Jay's amusement fizzled abruptly, leaving a yawning silence in its wake. Leslie looked away, cursing herself for ruining the moment with that vivid and unsavory image of her childhood. She was relieved when the timer went off and Jay rose to serve up dinner.

Leslie stood too. "If you point me toward the silverware, I'll go ahead and set the table."

"The drawer beside the sink. And if you would, pull the salads out of the fridge."

Leslie did as she was told, adding a pair of cloth napkins she found at the back of the drawer. Jay came up behind her, holding a single candle and a disposable lighter.

"What's this?" she asked, taking them from him.

"I thought we'd do it up right. You know, celebrate your success today."

"Oh."

"Charm aside, I really would like to know how you pulled it off. Go ahead and refill the glasses and I'll be right there. Then you can tell me all your naughty tricks."

As their plates gradually emptied, Leslie fleshed out her ideas for the Splash, barely pausing in her enthusiasm to breathe between topics. She was pleasantly surprised by Jay's level of interest, as he asked questions, pointed out challenges, even suggested a few ideas of his own. She was also surprised at how good it felt to talk through her day over a simple meal in the kitchen. She'd been on her own for so long, cut off from anything remotely resembling intimacy, that she hardly knew how to include someone else in her life. It was funny how you couldn't know you'd been missing a thing until you actually found it.

Finally, Jay pushed back his plate and laid his napkin aside. "In case I haven't said it, I'm impressed, though I suppose I shouldn't be. You've got a real head for this stuff."

"Yes, well, I'm afraid I was rather shameless with Mr. Whitney."

"Used your feminine wiles to get your way, did you?"

Leslie lifted her nose with a sniff. "Certainly not."

"Then what?"

"I used cunning and guile."

Jay grinned, teeth flashing white in the soft candlelight. "Why does it sound so dangerous when you say it?"

"Not dangerous, effective. I threw my old title around, empathized with him about the trials and tribulations of underappreciated editors. He lapped it up like cream. Plus, the stuff I gave him was really good, if I do say so myself. It's hard to believe my time at *Edge* prepared me to market a winery."

"It did, though," he said, his tone suddenly thoughtful. "While my career did nothing to prepare me for this . . . or for anything, really."

"Oh, I don't know about that." Leslie reached for the bottle of Chardonnay, divvying the last of it between their glasses. "As a writer you created stories out of thin air, and that's exactly what you've done with Peak. You created a story out of thin air."

Jay met her eyes over the candle, his face all angles in the wavering light. "What a nice thing to say."

Leslie squirmed, keenly aware of the warmth fluttering in her belly. "Yeah, well, I have my moments. And while we're on the subject of your writing—"

Pushing back from the table, Jay stood, effectively cutting her off. "I'll make some coffee."

Leslie blinked up at him. What had just happened? Before she could respond, he was at the counter with the dinner plates, his spine as stiff as a two-by-four while he waited for the sink to fill.

Gathering up the silverware, she followed him to the sink. "Jay, I wasn't . . . I didn't mean to push. I just wondered if you'd ever thought of writing about Peak. Maybe not a novel, but something about its history, about the people who built it and lived here."

"About Adele and Henry, you mean?"

"Well, it's intriguing, don't you think? Forbidden love, a mysterious grave."

Jay turned off the tap and turned to face her. "Stories have to have endings, Leslie, and this one doesn't. Adele died—we don't know how. The child vanished—we don't know where. There's nothing to write."

Leslie reached into her pocket and withdrew the folded *Gazette* article. "I went to the archives at the paper today. I was hoping to find something about Adele's death. This was all I found."

Jay dried his hands on his pants before taking the article. He scanned it a moment, then glanced up. "This is about a shed fire."

"When I first ran across it, I thought it might have been the accident Maggie told you about, but it says no one was hurt. Did Maggie ever mention it?"

"Leslie, things like this go on all the time on a farm."

"It says they suspected vandalism. It mentions names."

"What difference does any of this make now? Adele is dead. You've seen her grave. Can't we just leave it there?"

"Why?"

The one-word question seemed to catch Jay off guard. Tossing the article aside, he turned back to the sink and fished a plate from the water. "Because I think you're letting this get under your skin."

"I'm just curious about what happened."

A pulse flickered along his jaw. "That's how it starts. Believe me when I tell you, you can get sucked into these things, and before you know it they're eating you up."

Leslie stifled a sigh. He was being dramatic, but he was a little bit right. She knew it too. Clearing the grave, schlepping the Rebecca downtown, combing through years of newspaper archives, all pointed to a growing fixation. She also knew she couldn't afford distractions when so much was on the line for Peak's success.

"You're right," she said, taking the dripping plate from his hand and picking up a towel. "It's not like we'll ever know. Forget I brought it up, okay?"

Jay seemed visibly relieved as he handed off another plate, then picked up the silverware Leslie had carried from the table. "What should we talk about instead?"

Instead of answering, Leslie began to giggle, the sight of him at the sink with a fistful of knives and forks prodding memories of their early days.

Jay peered at her over his shoulder. "What's so funny?"

"I was thinking about the first time you cooked for me."

"Ah yes . . . breakfast."

"And I repaid you by hurling my plate into the sink and drenching you." The corners of her mouth lifted wryly. "So much for charm."

Jay turned off the tap and faced her, his hands heavy and damp on her shoulders. "I happen to think you have a great deal of charm, Big City, in spite of your cunning."

It took all she had to stand still and meet his gaze. "And my guile?"

"Especially your guile."

His voice was like raw silk, raspy and deep, setting off little tongues of warmth just south of her navel. There was nowhere to run, no door to scurry through, and this time Leslie didn't want one. He was going to kiss her and she was going to let him—the kiss had been too long in coming. She swallowed a moan as his mouth closed over hers, deep and greedy, tasting faintly of wine. His hands were on her neck, her face, tangled in her hair, and for one mad moment she never wanted to open her eyes again, never wanted this warm, wet yielding to end.

It was Jay who pulled away first. "Should I say I'm sorry?"

Breathless and disoriented, Leslie touched her fingers to her lips. "I think I've wanted you to do that for a long time."

"You could have fooled me. That day in the barn, when I touched you—you ran away like I was some kind of masher."

"I'm sorry. I'm not good at this."

"On the contrary. I'd say you're very good at it."

"Not this. The you-and-me thing. I don't . . . let people in."

Jay reached for her then and drew her close. "Neither do I. So we'll take it slow. It doesn't have to be scary."

"It already is," Leslie breathed against the collar of his shirt.

"Yes," he murmured, his lips wing soft as they brushed hers. "I suppose it is."

Chapter 23

Jay

Jay peered at the bedside clock and swore softly; twenty after three and he was still awake, wrestling with the memory of Leslie's mouth against his, the undeniable passion that had erupted as he had pulled her tight against him. Was he crazy to think this could work? Crazy to risk a working relationship that was only just beginning to mesh for a chance at something he wasn't sure he was even ready for? The look on her face after the initial kiss—confusion and abject terror—seemed to suggest he was. And yet, she had kissed him back, and not just once.

He still wasn't sure which of them had had the presence of mind to cool things down before they passed the point of no return. He wanted to believe it was him, that in the end his chivalrous instincts had kicked in, but as he lay in the dark, still feeling the warmth of her mouth against his, he had serious doubts.

She had kissed him softly as she left, her face unreadable as she thanked him for dinner and slipped out the back door. Now, as he flipped his pillow over in search of a cool patch of pillowcase, he wondered if she was lying awake too, replaying the evening and feeling regret.

Beside him, Belle fidgeted, nudging a chilly nose into the crook of his arm in case he'd forgotten she was there and available for petting. Jay gave her an obligatory pat as he kicked off the covers and reached for the sweatshirt and jeans draped over the footboard.

In the kitchen, he stared into the fridge, debating whether a sandwich might provide a plausible distraction, but soon decided it would not. Being in the kitchen, the scene of the crime, as it were, only served to remind him of Leslie. Only now, it wasn't the kissing he was thinking of. He was thinking about the article she had handed him. A shed fire, it said. No injuries. But what if it wasn't true? What if someone *had* been hurt, and instead of being reported to the authorities, the truth had been covered up?

What if someone had died?

Jay closed his eyes, suddenly back in Maggie's room, her voice gauzy with pain and with something else he'd never let himself put a name to—guilt. Snatches of conversation were floating back, things he'd the spent the last year pretending he hadn't heard. He *had* heard them, though—talk of an accident, of a bolted door with no escape. Even then the hair on the back of his neck had prickled. Now there was proof of a fire, resurrecting the suspicions that had been niggling at him for months. What if the accident that killed Adele Laveau hadn't been an accident at all?

Please, God, let him be wrong.

In the living room, he moved to the desk, easing open the middle drawer to stare at the neat white stack of pages. After six years of not writing a word, of shuddering at the very thought, the muse had suddenly returned with a vengeance, prickling like a phantom limb, and God help him, he had yielded.

It had begun in earnest the day Leslie brought him to the ridge, the day he'd first set eyes on Adele Laveau's grave; a few late-night notes added to those he had scribbled into a notebook after Maggie's death, just to empty his head, he told himself, even when those notes began to spin themselves into fully fleshed-out pages. He'd never meant for it to go anywhere. It was just a way to clear his thoughts, to work it all out on paper, and once and for all lay his suspicions to rest.

Only it hadn't worked. No matter how many times he tried to shut Adele out, she came, nudging him awake, whispering in his ear, urging him to fill page after page. It wasn't new. Back when he was writing it had always been like this, characters so real they refused to let him sleep, fighting, loving, laughing, dying, all in full color and full sound—a lot like schizophrenia, except you got paid for being delusional.

But this was different. Adele's story wasn't a work of fiction. It was real life, so shrouded in mystery and rife with sadness that even he couldn't have invented it, a surefire best-seller if he was interested, which he absolutely was not. The bones in the Gavin closet were none of his business. And even if he decided to make them his business, what was the point of rattling them now? Of exposing truths no one wanted to know, least of all him? Maggie had taken her secret to the grave, and for that he was grateful. Whatever her sins, they were buried now and best left that way.

There was only one problem. While doing everything in his power to discourage Leslie from snooping around in Adele's death, he had been quietly and methodically committing her story to paper, a fact Leslie was likely neither to appreciate nor to understand, given her zeal for absolute honesty and his tendency to skirt the truth when the truth might prove inconvenient. It wouldn't matter that his intent had been to insulate her from some rather nasty possibilities or that he never intended to publish a single word of what he'd written. She wouldn't see it that way. He had deliberately misled her—again. Period. And the longer he waited to come clean, the worse it was going to turn out.

Shred it. Purge your hard drive. Pretend you never wrote it.

But he couldn't. As he lifted the stack of pages from the drawer,

he reveled in their weight, the heft of hard-fought words, perhaps—
no, almost certainly—the best and truest he'd ever written. Even if
he never added another word or page, which he almost certainly
would not, how could he just pretend the ones now in his hand had
never poured out of him?

And yet he knew as long as the story sat in his desk, he would
continue to struggle with his conscience and his choices: tell Leslie
about the half-written story and the real reason he couldn't bring
himself to finish it, or keep it to himself and tell her nothing at all. He
didn't care much for either option, but even in the interest of truth, it
made no sense to share his suspicions about Adele's fate when it was
highly unlikely that either of them would ever really know what happened.

He stared at the stack of pages in his hand, hesitating a moment
more before slipping them back into the drawer. How the hell had he
gotten here? Two months ago his life had been settled, his course
neatly and cleanly charted. Or so he thought. Then Leslie had shown
up, and now nothing felt safe. Not his tightly woven plans or his
carefully crafted walls, and sure as hell not his heart.

Chapter 24

Adele

For the second time in my life I wake not knowing where I am.

I open my eyes and stretch, confused when my gaze lights on familiar sheets, my travel trunk from Parson's, my robe draped neatly over the footboard. But this is not my room, not my bed. I make myself sit up and look about, blinking in confusion at the gritty walls and dusty floorboards. And then I remember where I am—and why.

I am in a narrow loft on the upper floor of the cottage, large enough only for a bed and small chest of drawers. There is a single grimy window looking out over the lake. I cross the room and drag open the sash, then perch on the peeling sill, gulping deep lungs full of muggy morning air, shaken by this new turn my life has taken. It is not shame I feel, though I feel that too, beneath all the rest, and suspect that I will feel it more keenly in the future. But just now, staring out over Peak's vast green hills and shining lake, I grapple with my new place in the world and with the realization that I am suddenly quite rudderless.

I am neither married nor single, neither free nor attached. There is no one to whom I answer, no railing to endure, no eggshells to walk upon, no Susanne just down the hall. But it is an uneasy freedom. I am no longer the green, wide-eyed child I was when I came to Peak. I am a woman grown, mistress of my own home, such as it is. But I have no work, no husband to do for, no child to see to, no friends to call upon—no earthly idea how to fill my time.

But as I make my way downstairs, I begin to see how I will at least fill part of it. The cottage has been vacant for years, bare except for a few sticks of shabby furniture and the dust clots and cobwebs choking the corners. I shudder when I enter the kitchen, grimy in the glare of a single bare bulb, skittering with eight-legged things. The stove is something ancient, coated with a film of grease so thick I'm certain the thing will catch fire the first time I try to light it. I shudder at the thought. I have never been easy with fire.

Still, I am undaunted. It is part of my penance, I suppose, and I will do what is necessary. I start in the kitchen, scaring up a broom, bucket, and scrub brush from the tiny closet I will eventually make into a pantry. When I've swept the filth out the back door, I go down on my knees and begin to scrub. My back is miserable when I finally stand up, but the scuffed oak boards are spotless—almost clean enough to satisfy Mama.

It takes a week to finish the rest, working sunup to sundown, scrubbing walls and polishing floors, cleaning years of grime from the windows, scouring soot from the rough brick hearth. When the cleaning is finished I set to work on curtains, then move on to covers for the furniture. By the time I finish, winter is nearly over. I am pleased with my little home, for a home it has become, small and spare, but enough for me.

With the cottage finished, my days are harder to fill. Henry brings surprises from time to time, practical things, mostly—magazines from the drugstore, a table radio for the parlor, novels from his study to fill the time when he cannot be with me—but the days are long and unravel too slowly.

It is planting time, and Henry is needed in the fields. When planting's done he'll be needed in the barns, preparing for harvest and drying. I cannot begrudge him this. Times are hard for the people of Gavin, hard all over if the stories in the *Gazette* are true. Money is scarce, work near impossible to find—unless you have two able hands and know my Henry. In the past year he's given work to nearly half the men in town, bringing them on in two-week shifts so that everyone earns a little something to feed their families.

I keep to the cottage now, so as not to raise eyebrows. Susanne keeps to the house, cloaked in the fog of her precious tincture. She no longer cares what Henry does, and so at the end of the day he comes to me. We are awkward with each other at first, like children playing house. Soon, though, as the weeks pass, we find a rhythm. He comes to me at the end of the day, and we share a meal in the tiny kitchen with its new checked curtains, then move to the parlor. Henry reads to me and puffs on his pipe. It feels good and right having him there beside me. But then the mantel clock strikes ten and he must kiss me good night, to return to the house and his own bed. There are times, though, when the clock strikes, that he takes my hand and leads me upstairs. He is always gone when I wake, slipping away before first light with only the dent on his pillow to show he's been there. Those are hard mornings.

We do not speak of Susanne, or only rarely so, and for that mercy I am thankful. Henry scarcely sees her now, shut up in her room with the poor girl she has hired to take my place, ticking off the days until her quest to hold Henry's child is finally achieved. The thought of it sickens me, and yet it will happen. I only wonder how I will live with it when it does.

I don't like to think about what might happen when the child arrives, that Susanne and Henry and the baby will be a family—that I might suddenly become inconvenient. I have made foolish, some would even say wicked, choices in all of this. I suppose I would say it too. But I am not a fool. I know how quickly things can change, how easily a woman in my place can be set aside. Yet in my heart, I do not believe it. And that is why, despite everything, I stay. I could have gone, left Henry behind and struck out on my own. It would have been the right thing to do, the proper thing, but by then it was too late for right, and certainly too late for proper.

Chapter 25

Henry's daughter is the apple of his eye.

She enters the world just before dawn, a squalling pink bundle with all her fingers and toes and a head full of soot black curls. She is called Margaret, after Henry's mother—Maggie for short—and from her first breath she is the sun her father revolves around, the warm, sure center of his universe. And he is hers.

From the day she begins to toddle it is clear that her heart belongs to this place, her soul so deeply rooted in the land that at times I think she has sprung from the soil itself. She is never far from Henry, spending every moment at his side, in the barns and the fields, the red-brown grit of Gavin soil worked deep under her nails, as true a son as her daddy ever wished for.

I confess I am jealous. I am a shadow now, always nearby but not quite belonging, living at the edge of their world. It is my punishment, I suppose, and my lot, to ache for things that can never be. My one—my only—satisfaction, is that there is nothing of Susanne in her, no trace of the pale, bitter woman she calls Mother.

Still, there are times, rare and precious times, when she slips away to be with me, when we play dress-up in my bedroom upstairs. We giggle together in front of the mirror as I pin up her hair, then place a hat full of feathers on her head, cocking it just so. She begs prettily to wear the Blue Lady, the cameo her father gave me the first time he brought me to the ridge. It is the only piece of jewelry I own, my most precious possession, but she knows as well as I that I can deny her nothing. It will be hers one day anyway, a pretty keepsake from the nice lady who used to live in the cottage by the lake. As I fasten it to my old blue dress, I brush her cheek with a kiss, pretending in that moment that she is my own, which she can never be in truth but will always be in my heart.

When the first day of school comes, it is me who walks with her to the end of the drive to wait for the bus. Her eyes are wide and unblinking as she stares down the misty road, her face washed pale in the chilly morning light. She's trying to be brave, clutching her lunch sack and her pencil case like a good little soldier, but her hand holds to mine like a lifeline. I do not have to look to know that Susanne is at her window. I can feel her there, boring holes in my spine. I don't care. I promise Maggie I will be here again when the bus drops her off in the afternoon, and I am.

She is six now, long limbed and pretty, with hair the color of India ink and fathomless gray eyes, like the sky before a storm. They are restless eyes, too keen for a child, and I cannot help wondering, when they settle on me, just how much she sees. How much, I wonder, will she ever truly know about her mother and father, and how will she come to know it? I think about the Celia Cunninghams of the world, women who wound for sport, and I pray with everything in me that Henry's little girl will never have to pay for her father's sins—or for mine.

Chapter 26

There is to be another child, and this one will be mine.

I don't let myself believe it at first, though I know the signs—the weepiness and wringing fatigue, the vague queasiness while I'm frying up bacon in the morning. When I lose my breakfast for the third day in a row, I'm finally certain. My heart soars at the thought of it, but I am torn, too. I wonder how Henry will take the news. We have never talked about what would happen, how we might . . . manage things. Still, I am filled with a fierce joy. I'm going to be a mother, and nothing—no threat, no guilt, no fear—will ever rob me of that.

That night, I prepare a special dinner of Henry's favorites, then put on my best dress, but he's late coming in from the fields. I fret that dinner will be spoiled, that he'll be worn-out when he finally comes, and I think maybe I should save the news. But I know I can't. Maybe it's just Mama whispering in my ear, but I need to know that he wants this child, inconvenient as it may be, that he'll be with me as I raise it, that he'll love it as he loves Maggie.

He is exhausted when he finally comes in, so tired I see he's forgotten to take off his hat when he comes looking for me in the kitchen. I remove it, smoothing my fingertips over his brow, trying to erase the creases that are part weather, part weariness.

"My poor Henry, you look so tired."

He nods, scraping back the hank of hair that's forever flopping onto his forehead. "Had a hell of a scuffle in the barn just as we were knocking off." He sighs heavily, shaking his head. "Had to let a man go. I didn't like to do it, but they know the day I take 'em on what I expect. And what I won't stand for."

I make the appropriate sounds as I put a cold glass of tea into his hand, but all the while I'm thinking that this isn't the right time to tell him my news. He's got too much on his mind already. I'll wait. Then he drops into his chair at the kitchen table and turns a tired smile on me.

"Have you got any good news for me, Adele? 'Cause I sure could use a little about now."

I blink at him, then set my own glass down on the counter. "I'm going to have a baby." And that's how I tell him—just blurt it out with no warning at all.

His face goes through all sorts of contortions while I stand there worrying the corner of my apron, his mouth opening and closing like a fish. I feel like I might start to cry, and I wish he'd just say whatever it is he's going to say, even if I'm not going to like it. But he can't seem to make any words come out, and I finally turn away, looking for something, anything, to do with my hands.

I don't hear him get up out of his chair, but suddenly he's there, his hands heavy on my shoulders, turning me into his arms, crushing me against that broad flannel chest. The smell of tobacco and male sweat rises between us, mingled with the aromas of ham and sweet potatoes. For a moment my stomach rolls, but I cling to him. When I finally find the strength to look up, there is only joy in his eyes.

The child will come in late spring, a boy, I hope, for Henry's sake. He says he doesn't care—ten fingers and ten toes is all he's hoping for—but I know better. Every man wants a son, and Henry has waited far too long for his. It would be a lie to say I didn't pray every day that this baby will be a boy, the son Susanne has never been able to give him, not to best her, but to ease the pain of all those other losses.

My belly swells as the months rush past, and at first the days are a blur. The upstairs needs papering, and the bed needs to be moved to make way for the bassinet. The child will need things too, bottles and blankets and diapers. But goods are hard to come by these days. No one's buying anything, and when they do find a few spare pennies, the store shelves are nearly bare. I can still get cloth and thread, though, and Mama made sure I was good with a needle, so at least Henry's child won't run naked.

I scare up one of Henry's old cigar boxes to make a sewing box and set my chair near the window where the light is good and I can see the leaves beginning to turn. Now and then, I let myself wonder what Maggie will think when the baby comes. I wonder if she will grow to love the child or if she will see it as a rival. She's got a good, sweet heart in her, but she has always worshipped her daddy. It will be hard, I think, for her to share him with someone else. In fact, I'm not sure she's quite keen on having to share him with me. She gets a look sometimes, when she thinks I don't see, confusion mingled with hurt, and maybe a little anger too, as if she's wishing me a thousand miles away.

As for Susanne, I do not let myself think about what her reaction will be when she finally spies my belly from her window. I keep close to the cottage most days, working the small patch of garden behind the kitchen, where I can't be seen from the house. Lottie comes by now and then to take home a handful of whatever's ready for picking and leave a bit of whatever she's been cooking.

She tries to give me news from the house, but I don't want it. I don't want to hear how crazy Susanne's been acting or how bad she looks. Instead, we talk about the town, what latest family has lost its farm, and who's been put out of work. When she comes by just before Christmas she tells me Celia Cunningham's husband got caught taking money from the bank and was likely going to jail. That last part makes me feel just a little bit good. Then I remember they have two girls, tiny things in grade school, and I feel sorry.

Spring is slow in coming, the days raw and perpetually wet. By the end of March I am miserable, tired to death of being indoors, of endlessly, endlessly waiting. But if I am restless, Henry is worse. His eyes go with me everywhere, greeting me at the end of each day with the same unspoken question. And each day my answer is the same—not yet.

I'm alone when the first pain comes, tearing me from a warm, deep sleep. I blink at the sheets, bone white in the splash of moonlight streaming through the window, and try not to panic. Beyond the dark panes there is only night sky and the cold prickle of stars. It will be hours before Henry comes, and then he'll still have to fetch the midwife. I'm not sure the child will wait.

An hour later my water lets go and I start to pray. Not the prayers of a woman full-grown, but snatches of the words Mama taught me to say when I was little, silly bits of rhyme that catch in my throat between sobs. The pains are coming harder now, and my back feels fit to break. I watch the sky, petrified as I try not to think of that awful night in Susanne's room and the look on Henry's face when his son slid into the world, silent and blue.

By the time I finally hear Henry's voice echo up the stairs, I have lost all sense of time. I don't know how he knew to come. I am only thankful to God that he has. I sob with relief when he appears in the doorway, his hair still disheveled from sleep, eyes wide with panic.

He drops to his knees beside the bed, his calloused fingers gentle as he pushes the hair back from my sticky face. "Is everything—?"

He doesn't finish. He doesn't have to. Before I can utter a word, another contraction grabs hold, turning me inside out. "Go!" I grit through my teeth. "Bring her quick."

The sky has gone a dull shade of pink when I hear Henry's truck finally rattle back up the drive. It's none too soon. I am near senseless now, my body battered and limp. I can endure no more on my own. Then comes the slow, steady tread of feet on the stairs, and when I turn my head on the pillow she is there, bulky and slightly stooped in her wool kerchief and worn cloth coat, her skin the color of polished mahogany in the dim lamplight; Minnie Maw Speights, the midwife from the hills of Level Grove who once sent her tonics to Susanne.

She wastes no time. She sets a heavy cloth bag at the foot of the bed, her jaw squarely set as she surveys the situation. Her eyes meet mine briefly as she peels out of her coat and kerchief. There is no softness there, no pity or warmth of any kind, only a calm resolve to be about her business of bringing another child into the world.

She peers under the sheets, then prods my belly with firm, practiced hands, pausing until the latest wave of agony releases me. Henry hovers behind her, wide-eyed and anxious, dwarfed somehow by her presence. She has brought a girl with her too, a stringy child about Maggie's age, all elbows and knees and great white eyes as she huddles in the corner, staring at me panting with my knees up around my ears.

"The child's coming," Minnie announces to no one in particular. "Be here right along with the sun, I expect." She turns to Henry then, tilting her wiry gray head toward the door.

"Time for you to get on out now."

Henry's boots scuff heavily, but he does not move.

"Mr. Henry," she says with her bottom lip jutting, "I've brung over two hundred babies in my time, your little girl among 'em. I reckon I can bring this one without your help."

His eyes shift to mine, anxious, helpless. I try to find a smile but can't manage it. I cannot worry about Henry now. The next wave of pain is already gathering, waiting to crash over me, to bury me.

"Go on, now," I tell him raggedly.

I'm calmer with Henry gone, though the pains are coming one on top of another now, no time to breathe, no time to prepare. I lose track of Minnie as she shuffles about the room, readying a small tray of things at the foot of the bed. I'm so tired and so sore, like my insides are all ripped to bits. If I could only sleep a little . . .

"Annie Mae Speights!"

Minnie's voice is like a whipcrack, jolting me back to something like awareness, though some small part of me understands it isn't me she's talking to.

"You come out from that corner and help Minnie Maw, now," she's saying over her shoulder. "I didn't tote you with me to stand there with your eyes closed. It's time you learned what's what."

Annie Mae does as she's told, emerging reluctantly from her corner, though she's plainly terrified, doing everything in her power not to let her eyes settle on me or on what might be going on beneath the clean white sheet tented over my knees.

"This here's Annie Mae," Minnie says, still fishing around in her bag. "Belongs to my oldest boy. I brought her along to learn. I was already helping my mama when I was her age, but Annie Mae's a little skittish. Doesn't like it when the hollerin' starts."

I feel bad for Annie Mae because I can see she'd rather be anywhere than where she is at this moment and because I know full well that the hollering is about to start.

Minnie draws a rusty-looking knife from her bag, pausing a moment to run a finger along the edge of the blade. For the first time, something like a smile crosses her lips. "Don't mean nothing, but I still do it," she says, dropping the knife beneath the bed with a clatter. "Because my mama always did it."

I muster a smile for the familiar words and lift my head weakly. "Because it cuts the pain in two?"

Minnie nods, then moves to my head, dragging me up against my pillows. "That's right, child. Now, get yourself ready. Me and you got some work to do."

Chapter 27

Leslie

Leslie dubiously eyed the mess surrounding her: sketches, legal pads, sticky notes, and newspaper clippings, all organized into haphazard piles around her laptop. It was one of the pitfalls of living alone. Because there was no one to share a meal with and no one to complain, one's kitchen table gradually morphed into a kind of makeshift desk, until one eventually found oneself eating over the sink. It hadn't gotten that bad yet, but it was certainly heading in that direction.

She could have used the desk in the study, but the truth was, she found the room and all its sad reminders a little disquieting, as if she was never quite alone. Once again, her thoughts strayed to the shed fire and the article she still couldn't bring herself to throw away. It had nothing to do with Adele, nothing to do with anything, really, and yet she couldn't shake the feeling that it did mean something. She recalled the names at the bottom of the page, Samuel, Randall, and Landis Porter—the boys the police had questioned. Were any of them still alive? And if so, would they be able to tell her anything?

It was a silly idea, she knew. They would be Maggie's age by now, or older. Still, the urge to do a little investigating was there, nudging her to abandon her work, which was something she really couldn't afford to do. To quote Jay, the harvest had been an unqualified success—no equipment issues, perfect picking weather, and an even better than expected yield. She wanted to be able to say the same about the Splash, and with less than two weeks to finalize things, she didn't have time to go on a wild-goose chase.

Forcing her brain back to the matter at hand, she picked up this morning's *Gazette*, studying the slightly grainy shot of Jay and Young Buck working the crush pad. She had been pleasantly surprised to see the harvest story had made the front page. Must have been a slow news day, not that she was complaining. It was a great piece, even better than the first, which had already generated a nice bit of buzz with the locals. She needed to send Steve Whitney a great big thanks.

She had just opened her e-mail inbox when a quick tap sounded on the mudroom door. A minute later, Angie poked her head around the corner.

"I made a double batch of lasagna last night. Thought I'd bring some by and keep you from having to cook."

"Keep me from having to microwave, you mean," Leslie shot back. "But thanks."

Angie set the plate on the counter, eyes widening as she scanned the kitchen table. "Wow, when you said you had a lot of ideas for this shindig of yours, you weren't kidding."

"I've got a whole new respect for party planners these days; I can tell you that. But at least I can focus now that the harvest is over and done." She made a face as she rubbed her backside. "Speaking of which, I can't believe I'm still sore."

"I can. A corner office doesn't exactly prepare you for picking seventy acres of grapes. You did great, though. Jay was impressed with how you pitched right in. By the way, I couldn't help noticing you two seem to be getting along better. Anything you'd like to share?"

Leslie looked away, pretending to tidy a stack of sketches. No, there wasn't anything she'd like to share. Mostly because she had no idea what, if anything, had actually started that night in Jay's kitchen. It was a handful of kisses over a sink full of dishes. And with the bustle and prep for harvest, they really hadn't seen much of each other since, and never alone. Not that either one of them seemed in any great hurry to find out what came next.

"We're taking it . . . slow," Leslie answered finally. "Whatever that means."

Angie wasted no time and pounced. "So there is something there!"

"I don't know, maybe. We kissed and it was . . ."

"Nice?"

"Amazing."

"Funny," Angie responded drily. "I could've sworn I heard the word *amazing* come out of your mouth just then. So how come you look like someone just ran over your prize pig?"

Leslie chose to ignore both the sarcasm and the humor. "Because *amazing* can get you into all kinds of trouble, and I don't know if I'm ready for a serious relationship yet."

"Yet?" Angie snorted, then leveled hard green eyes on Leslie. "I hate to break it to you, honey, but you're staring down the barrel of forty. You think you might be getting ready anytime soon?"

Leslie winced. There it was, that right-between-the-eyes honesty Angie hauled out when she wanted to get your attention. "Angie, this isn't about age, or biological clocks, or any of that. It's about whether I'm ready to open my life up to someone. Aside from you and Buck, I don't know too many people that's actually worked out for, which is why I'm not sure I see the point in starting something that's only going to end up being temporary."

"Who says it has to be temporary?"

"I do. I have some history with this."

"Leslie, most of us get it wrong the first time, but we have to keep trying."

"Why?"

"Because the alternative is being alone." She paused, bringing her tone down a notch. "Look, I'm not trying to push Jay down your throat—well, maybe a little—but it's because I don't want to see you make up your mind about forever based on a few bumps in your past. Don't close the door is all I'm saying. I'm going to leave now, before I get thrown out. Come by the house later for coffee if you have time. No sermons, I promise."

Leslie slid back into her chair, listening to the slap of Angie's flip-flops receding down the back porch steps. Her advice had been kindly meant, the words of a friend, however bluntly spoken. But it wasn't that simple. She was scared, though of what she couldn't say. She'd been in relationships before, had survived her fair share of breakups, sustained the usual nicks and bruises to her pride. So why was this so different?

It was a question she'd been asking herself for days now, though she wasn't at all sure she was ready to face the answer, that with Jay there was more than just her pride on the line, and that she might already be in too deep to walk away.

Leslie blinked at her laptop, trying to recall what she'd been about to do before Angie popped in, when she spotted the brand-new message in her inbox from Doug Somers. Her stomach clenched as she opened it, praying he and Stephen hadn't changed their minds about subletting her apartment. The last thing she needed right now was one more distraction. But the e-mail wasn't about the apartment at all.

Les—

Just an FYI—some guy came around yesterday looking for you. Claimed to be your father. Didn't tell him anything except that you had moved. Asked if I knew where. Told him no. Thought you should know. The guy looked a little worse for wear. D.

Leslie slumped back in her chair and closed her eyes, forcing herself to breathe slowly. Jimmy was out, then, in New York and apparently hot on her trail. At least she'd been given a heads-up. It was unlikely that he'd heard about Maggie's death or her inheritance. Peak might not occur to him. But if it did? She thought of the proceeds from her watch, stashed in the top drawer of her bureau, allocated for things like tent rental, lighting and decorations, and the band she'd already hired. It would get him to go away, at least for a while.

And then what? When it was gone he'd be back.

She shut down the laptop and sat very still, listening to the faint whir of the refrigerator and the steady ticktock of the kitchen clock. She had spent the first eight years of her life at Peak but had returned as a stranger. Now, somehow, while she wasn't looking, it had become her home. Not the kind of home she'd had in New York—a small, sterile space carved out of concrete and glass—but a real home, where her heart could live and breathe.

There were people in her life now, Angie and Young Buck, and a strawberry blond eight-year-old who called her Aunt Leslie. And somewhere in all of it, there was Jay. She had become part of a circle, part of the life and purpose that pulsed through Peak, and she liked it. Jimmy wasn't ruining that. Let him come if he wanted, but he wasn't staying, and he wasn't getting a cent.

For all her resolve, Leslie almost jumped out of her chair when her cell phone went off. No one ever called these days. Peering at the display, she saw that the number was local, though it wasn't one she knew. It took a moment to recognize the voice on the other end.

"Mr. Randolph?"

"Do you have a minute to talk? I've just had a call about your painting. Turns out it's a bit of a rarity."

Leslie grabbed a Diet Coke from the fridge and stepped out onto the back porch, concerns about Jimmy temporarily on the back burner. "A rarity in what way?"

"Well, for starters, it appears to have been painted by a rather obscure artist, a man by the name of Tanner, who painted in Paris between 1905 and 1915 or so."

Leslie dropped heavily into the nearest rocker. "I'm sorry, did you say Tanner?" She had seen the name before, in the articles her mother had saved about addiction and mental illness. Now here it was again, directly connected to the Rebecca.

"I did. Jeremiah Tanner was his full name. He was a minor artist in his day, had a reputation as a bit of a ne'er-do-well, but after his death in 1917, his work started to gain attention. There are six known works of merit attributed to him, and somehow your great-grandfather managed to get hold of five of them."

"Have you—? Do you have any idea—?"

"How much it's worth? No, I'm afraid I don't. It's difficult when there are no recent sales on which to base a price. I haven't given up yet, though. There's one more painting out there we haven't accounted for, and the trail ends with a man named Fornier, a gallery owner who once owned the entire collection. Apparently, he got mixed up with some unsavory political types and had to emigrate from France to avoid arrest. That was back in 'thirty-seven or 'thirty-eight. We're fairly certain he brought the paintings with him, though we believe they were liquidated not long after."

"Is there a way to know who may have bought them?"

"That's what I'm calling to tell you. The Fornier Gallery is still operating."

Leslie watched a pair of cardinals vying for the bird-feeder left-overs as she digested this bit of news. "He's still alive?"

"Good heavens, no. Claude Fornier died in 'seventy-two. His granddaughter owns the place now. I tried to get in touch with her to see if she knew the fate of the collection, but all I got was a recording that the gallery is closed for the season. I'm afraid we'll have to wait until it reopens in the spring. At any rate, we don't need the painting anymore, if you'd like to pick it up."

"Thank you, Mr. Randolph." Leslie tried to keep the frustration from her voice. Spring was an eternity away. "I'll be by in a day or two, if that's all right. In the meantime, would you mind if I tried to get in touch with Fornier's granddaughter?"

"Not at all. It's your painting. I'd be obliged, though, if you'd let me know what you find out. This will probably sound silly to you, but in my line of work, you learn that old things tend to have stories, and something tells me this one might be a doozy."

Leslie didn't think it sounded silly at all. Things *did* have stories. Photos and paintings and gravestones had stories, and like Mr. Randolph, she wanted to know what they were and why she couldn't shake the feeling that those stories were somehow connected. After jotting down the number for the Charleston gallery, she ended the call.

Two hours later she was still waiting to hear back from Ms. Fornier. She had reached the same recorded message as Mr. Randolph. The gallery was closed for the season and would reopen on March first. She hadn't bothered to leave a message. Instead, she hopped online. It had taken less than thirty minutes to locate an address and phone number for Ms. Emilie Fornier of Charleston, South Carolina. Her message was short and sweet; she would like to speak with Ms. Fornier at her earliest convenience, with regard to several paintings from her grandfather's private collection. It was presumptuous, she knew, and would probably turn out to be a huge waste of time, but it was the only lead she had. She couldn't do anything now, but when the Splash was behind her, she'd have some free time. If it was wasted, so be it. At least she would know she had tried.

She was finishing up a few e-mails the next morning when her cell went off. She immediately recognized the 843 area code. The voice on the other end was cool and brisk, opening with a series of rapid-fire questions. How had she gotten this number? Was she a collector? A dealer? Was she looking to make a purchase?

Inexplicably, Leslie found herself tongue-tied. She had tracked the woman down at home on a Sunday, and now that she was on the line, she didn't know where to begin. In the end, she decided to keep Mr. Randolph out of it, saying only that she had inherited a painting that might be the work of Jeremiah Tanner, and that since her grandfather had been a collector of Tanner's work, she hoped Ms. Fornier might be able to authenticate the piece.

It took a bit of doing, but Emilie Fornier finally agreed to view the Rebecca, scheduling an appointment at her home on the Tuesday after the Splash. Leslie felt almost giddy as she ended the call. It would only be a day trip, but she could do with a change of scenery. Maybe she'd invite Jay along. It was time they got to know each other better, time to stop all the wary circling and finally figure out what they wanted from each other.

By late afternoon she had finally screwed up the courage to actually extend the invitation. She found Jay out behind the cottage in his garden. She paused at the gate, watching him turn what was left of the herb beds. When he finally looked up, he seemed startled.

"Ah, you're just in time to help."

"With what? It looks like you're almost finished."

"With this part, yeah. But then I'm planting some winter lettuce."

"You're quite the Renaissance man." She stepped through the gate, letting it close behind her. "Have you got a minute? There's something I want to talk to you about."

"All right. I was about to get myself some tea. Can I bring you out a glass?"

Leslie nodded, though she wasn't thirsty. She wondered how Jay would react when she told him she was going all the way to Charleston on the hunch that there was a connection between Adele and the paintings in Henry's study. He'd already questioned her once, accusing her rather heatedly of letting Adele get under her skin. Well, maybe she was. But her gut told her she was on to something, and her conversation with Mr. Randolph only served to strengthen that conviction.

Jay reappeared with a glass in each hand and a bag of pretzels between his teeth. Leslie relieved him of the pretzels and one of the glasses.

"Let's sit a minute," he suggested, pointing to a shady stretch of stone wall. "My back is killing me."

Leslie dropped down beside him on the mossy stones, feeling the cool damp seep through the seat of her jeans. Jay tore into the pretzels, then offered her the bag, but she declined.

"I'm going to Charleston the Tuesday after the Splash," she said without preamble.

Jay blinked at her. "What's in Charleston?"

"An art gallery—or rather, the owner of an art gallery. Her name is Emilie Fornier."

"Does this have to do with your photography?"

"My photography?" Leslie frowned, then shook her head. "No. It's about the paintings in Henry's study. There's a woman who owns a gallery there who might be able to give me some information on them."

"You do realize Charleston is almost six hours away?"

"I do."

"And just what is it you'd drive six hours to find out?"

"I had someone look at one of the paintings—an expert. He said it was painted by a man named Jeremiah Tanner. Apparently, he only painted six pictures, which means Henry was one shy of owning the entire collection. Before that, the collection belonged to a man named

Fornier from Charleston." Leslie paused, plucking a pretzel from the bag. "Unfortunately, no one knows what happened to them after they left Fornier's hands. It's like they vanished, except five of the six are hanging in Henry's study."

Jay looked mystified. "That's it? You're going to drive all the way to South Carolina to find out why your great-grandfather had a study full of paintings? Leslie, Henry was fairly well-off, and at a time when no one trusted the banks. Maybe he saw art as a safe place to park his money."

Leslie sipped her sweet tea as she considered the idea, plausible enough given the economic climate after the crash, but something still didn't feel right. Finally, she shook her head. "No, that wasn't it. Other than Maggie's portrait in the parlor, and the one of Susanne up in the attic, there isn't another scrap of art in this house. Why these paintings? Why Tanner?"

"Why not Tanner?"

Spying a pair of finches, Leslie crushed what was left of her pretzel and tossed the crumbs, watching as they pounced on the sudden windfall. "The articles I found in the attic mention Jeremiah Tanner specifically. My mother kept them for a reason, and she kept them together with the letter, which I'm now sure belonged to Adele. She obviously believed they were connected, and so do I. I just don't know how yet. You said Maggie had a secret she wanted to tell you. She left the photo of Adele's grave with Goddard so I'd be sure to get it. There was something she wanted us to know."

Jay had been rubbing salt off a pretzel with the ball of his thumb. His hand went quiet now. "You're chasing ancient history, Leslie, about a woman who's been dead for God knows how long. I don't see what going to Charleston about a handful of paintings is going to prove."

Leslie met his eyes, chin tipped slightly. "I don't either, but I'm going. I need to know more about Tanner, and Ms. Fornier has agreed to see me. I know it's a long shot, but I'm hoping she can tell me when Henry bought the painting, and maybe even why. I came to ask if you want to go with me."

Jay's brows shot up. "You're serious about this, then?"

"Yes, I am."

She wished she could explain why this was important to her, but nothing she said would make sense. "I know you think I'm crazy to care about any of this, and you're probably right, but I used to think my family's secrets all had to do with my mother's death. Now I think there's more, something from a long time ago that has to do with Henry's mistress. And yes, with those paintings. Emilie Fornier may be the one person who can help me figure it out. I set up the appointment for the Tuesday after the Splash."

Jay said nothing, his brow furrowed in what looked like resignation.

Leslie handed him a pretzel. At least he hadn't said no. "If it's a nice day we could take the Mustang."

Chapter 28

The night of the Splash had finally arrived, a crisp October evening that might have been made to order. In the lavender dusk, the trees were alive with twinkling white lights. The mellow strains of "Carolina in My Mind" were already in the air. Leslie roamed the tents and grounds, looking for something to do, but found nothing. The tasting barn was finished, every floorboard gleaming, every wineglass polished and at the ready. The bandstand, a simple plywood dais, had been transformed with wine barrels, hay bales, and a few cleverly positioned spotlights. The tents had been raised, the food delivered. They were ready.

So why did she feel like throwing up?

She found Angie in the refreshment tent, standing over a punch bowl with a knife, a bowl of fruit, and several bottles of Seyval Blanc, a flour sack towel draped over the shoulder of her little black dress. She glanced up, then let out a soft whistle. "Wait 'til Jay gets a look at you in that dress. You look gorgeous."

Leslie smoothed her hands down the clingy sheath of cobalt blue velvet she'd found in a vintage boutique this morning and purchased on a whim. "You don't think it's too much?"

"I think it's perfect, and I like your hair up like that. But you don't look happy. What's wrong?"

Leslie made a noise that was half sigh, half groan. "I don't know. I just feel like I should be doing something."

"Honey, you've done enough. There's only the last-minute stuff left, and I can handle that. You just go breathe into a paper bag or something."

Leslie laughed, but it quickly faded. "What if no one comes?"

Angie put down her knife and wiped her hands. "Okay, you need to stop now. When you first suggested this, I thought you were crazy. But you pulled it off. This is the biggest shindig this town's ever seen, and you made it happen. Go enjoy yourself."

Leslie lingered in the doorway of the tent, gazing at the smattering of stars appearing in the eastern sky and trying to choose between looking for Jay and sneaking off with one of Angie's bottles of wine. Before she could decide, the first set of headlights peeled off the road and headed up the drive, a white Caddy the size of a small fishing vessel. That would be Avis.

Her heart clenched with relief as she watched the steady crawl of headlights moving in Peak's direction, all of them pulling off to park. In the twilight, silhouettes began to emerge, mostly in pairs, crossing the lawn to converge on the refreshment tent. Leslie smoothed her dress once more, gave her hair a quick pat, and put on her best hostess smile.

She was surprised at how quickly a few could become a crowd. Most were strangers, but there were a few familiar faces: Avis and her husband, O.W., Susan and Bobby Bishop, Virgil Snipes from the hardware store, and Deanna, who, she was inexplicably relieved to see, had brought a date.

Scanning the sea of faces, she located Jay in the doorway of the crush barn. He looked relaxed in a coat and open shirt, laughing and chatting with Bobby Bishop. She was startled when his eyes strayed to hers, as if he'd known she was there all along. She had wrestled all week with the feeling that he was purposely avoiding her, too busy to stop for lunch or even a cup of coffee. Well, he clearly wasn't avoiding her now. She warmed under his gaze, a long, lazy look that traveled the length of her and then back again.

Pleased by his obvious approval, Leslie shot him a smile, already mapping out a path through the crowd when Deanna appeared at her elbow, looking predictably gorgeous in a dress of clingy eggplant-colored silk. She introduced her date, the muscular and decidedly un-new-agey Kyle Pritchett, who, when he wasn't building houses, was a member of Gavin's volunteer fire department, then proceeded to gush about everything from the food to the twinkle lights in the trees. Leslie maintained her smile and made all the polite responses, though her eyes strayed more than once to the tasting barn. By the time Deanna ran out of steam and allowed Kyle to lead her back to the punch bowl, Jay had disappeared.

The next few hours passed in a blur of smiles and tag-team introductions, until Leslie's head began to swim and she realized she hadn't eaten since breakfast. It took some doing, but she finally managed to duck into the refreshment tent, fix a small plate of food, and grab a bottle of water. She'd had enough punch. Making her way to the small patio behind the tasting barn, she dropped onto one of the benches and slipped off her shoes. It was relatively quiet behind the barn, dark and blessedly secluded, and for a time she was content to sit with her plate untouched, reveling in the evening's success. She had no idea how many people had shown up. She only knew that she was exhausted, smiled out and talked out, and that it felt awfully good.

"Hello, stranger."

Leslie started at the sound of Jay's voice. "I didn't know anyone was out here," she said, stuffing her feet back into her shoes. "I needed a minute to catch my breath."

Jay stepped out of the shadows and dropped down on the bench beside her. "I know what you mean. I haven't been this wrung out since my last book tour."

"Was it this much fun?"

"What, book signings? Think of doing this three or four times a week, for a month or more. Every day in a different city, every night in a different motel. Alone."

"Hmm, doesn't sound very glamorous. At least when we fall into bed tonight we'll know where we are when we wake up."

Leslie cringed, grateful for the dark as the remark stretched into an awkward silence. She was still deciding whether she should clarify what had somehow come out sounding like a come-on, or simply leave it alone, when Jay took her hand.

"You did amazing tonight."

Leslie felt her cheeks color again, this time with pleasure. "Thanks. It feels good. I was terrified the whole thing would turn out to be a big old flop."

"It's anything but. People are going to be talking about this for a long time."

"I had a lot of help. You and Buck did an amazing job with the tasting barn. Angie coordinated all the food. And I'll never be able to thank Susan for all she did."

"That's true, but you're the one who worked yourself silly pulling it all together, and I'm trying to say thank you. You got us the publicity, and that's the part that's going to pay off come spring. Whitney's already talking about doing a spread for the opening."

Leslie groaned as she set aside her untouched plate. "I can't think about that yet. Right now, I just want to savor tonight. And then sleep."

There was a long stretch of quiet, both of them content to stare at the sky and listen to the muffled strains of "Desperado" drifting from the bandstand.

"Thank you," Jay said finally.

"You said that already."

"I don't mean for tonight. I mean for coming back. For staying."

"Oh, then I guess you're welcome."

His lips were featherlight on her cheek, lingering and almost shy, his fingertips soft in their wake, touching the place his mouth had just been, as if to seal the kiss. "I'd best get back to our guests. You stay and rest awhile. And eat something."

But Leslie wasn't hungry anymore. Her belly was too busy doing the two-step as Jay walked away, and she wondered as he rounded the corner and disappeared if he was taking it slow for her sake or for his own. Rising from the bench, she wandered out onto the lawn, not ready yet to plunge back into the festivities. When she had put enough distance between herself and the barn, she stopped to lean against an old maple. Away from the lights and noise, the night felt cooler. Closing her eyes, she pulled in a deep lungful of crisp, still air.

Something, a coarse whisper or whiff of cigarette smoke, made her open her eyes and glance toward the road. She smiled as she spotted a couple walking arm in arm in her direction, weaving their way back to the party from what appeared to be a romantic rendezvous. She was about to turn away, to give them their privacy, when she felt the first prickle of warning.

There was something peculiar about the couple's progress: not like lovers at all, and not really moving in the direction of the party, but straight for her. Her eyes locked on the cherry-red arc of a cigarette, the weaving that spoke of too much bourbon, and she prayed— prayed the dark shape coming toward her was only a figment of her imagination, conjured by exhaustion and too much punch. But it wasn't a dream, and it wasn't the punch. It was Jimmy.

A few steps more and he broke from the shadows. Leslie sagged against the maple's rough bark, scanning the lawn for guests. She didn't know whether to be relieved or panicked to find herself alone. She had no wish for witnesses to what she was sure was about to unfold. On the other hand, if things turned ugly, there would be no witness to that either.

He was standing in front of her now, the cigarette between his lips churning out a steady pall of blue-white smoke. Six years in prison had done nothing to soften him. He was the same bull of a man she'd grown up with, built square and low to the ground. He wore a dark wool jacket with frayed lapels, and jeans that might have belonged to someone else.

A million things crowded into her head but somehow got lost on the way to her tongue. It wasn't surprising to see Rachel Ranson at his side, though it was difficult to say just who was holding whom up. She couldn't smell the bourbon, but the signs were all there, the distant eyes and slack jaw, the less-than-steady posture. He was drunk.

Jimmy staggered closer. "What, no hug for your old man?"

"What are you doing here, Jimmy?"

"It's Daddy to you, Baby Girl. And what do you think I'm doing here? I wanted to be part of my little girl's big shindig. Must have misplaced my invite, though."

Jimmy seemed to find that amusing, laughing so hard he toppled sideways and had to make a grab for Rachel's arm. He teetered a moment, then made a show of smoothing his jacket. "I went all the way up to that Yankee hellhole looking for you. Did you know there are a couple of fairies living at your place?"

Leslie took a deep breath and held it. This wasn't happening. Despite the cool evening air, she felt the first trickle of sweat trace down her spine, heard the warning whispering in her blood. It had been twenty years since she'd had an attack. Please, God, not tonight. Not here.

"It's not my place anymore," she managed to say numbly. "I live here now, at Peak."

Jimmy's mouth twisted in something like a smile, and for a moment the old timbre was back in his voice. "That's why I'm here. I thought it was time we both came home."

The words hit Leslie like ice water. Even drunk, there was an air of resolve about him, a look that said he'd come with a purpose and meant to see it through. But if Jimmy registered her horror, he showed no sign.

"I gotta hand it to you, Baby Girl. You sure got your mama's flair for social occasions. Look at that bash, Rachel. First-class all the way. Just like her mama."

Leslie didn't want to hear him talk about her mother, didn't want to be his *Baby Girl*. She wanted to cover her ears, to run, to hide. But she couldn't do any of those things. She had to look him in the eye and stand her ground, or she would concede it forever.

"You're drunk, Jimmy, and I want you to leave."

Jimmy turned his head, coughing wetly into his hand. He was sweating profusely now, mopping his face on the sleeve of his jacket. "Not drunk...," he croaked between coughs, "sick."

"Sick?" Leslie heard the high, thin note of panic in her voice, but she no longer cared. "Oh wait, I remember now. You're powerless over alcohol. That's what they teach you to say at the meetings, isn't it?"

He was weaving visibly now. Even in the moonlight Leslie could see the oily sheen of sweat coating his cheeks and forehead. Rachel saw it too. She laid a hand on Jimmy's arm.

"Maybe we should go. You don't look so hot."

But Jimmy wasn't in the mood for advice. He glared at Rachel until she withdrew her hand, then turned his attention back to Leslie, pulling himself up to his full height. When he spoke, the words came slowly and thickly, as if the act of forming them required herculean effort. "Tough to be strong when a man can't count on his own flesh and blood. Family's all a man's got, Baby Girl."

Leslie felt a bubble of laughter catch in her throat, a sure sign that she was close to coming apart. It took everything she had to look him in the eye and keep her voice steady. "Jimmy, I want you to listen to me. You've wasted your time coming here. The free ride is over." She looked at Rachel, standing sheepishly at his side. "Take him wherever he's staying, and make sure he understands he can't come back."

Jimmy stared at her as if waiting for her words to penetrate. When they finally did, he lurched forward, his face scant inches from her own. "I'm your father, goddamn it. I haven't seen you in over six years. Not one lousy word. Now you stand there and call me Jimmy?"

For Leslie it was the tipping point. If he didn't leave—if she didn't get away—she would soon be on her knees, or worse. The world was starting to recede, growing smaller and dimmer, until all that re-mained was her father's rage-filled face. And then, through the swell of panic, Jay was coming toward them, closing the distance in long, purposeful strides.

"Go now," she hissed raggedly. "Please. I'll get you some money. Just please go." The only thing more humiliating than Jimmy airing his dirty laundry out here on the lawn was Jay standing by while he did it.

"I'll go when you ask me nice. Like a girl should ask her daddy."

Leslie blinked hard, forcing herself to focus, to hold on. She had just agreed to give him what he came for. What more did he want? And since when did he care what she called him? But there was no time to ask. Jay was beside her.

"Leslie?" He was clearly waiting for an introduction. When none came, he turned to Jimmy. "Is there something I can do for you, Mr. Nichols?"

Jimmy made an attempt to square his shoulders. "I know . . . who you are," he said, slurring thickly now. "She's my little girl, and this is none of your business."

He made a move then, an aborted lunge that landed him on his knees in the grass. Leslie was only dimly aware of Jay hauling him back to his feet, Jay's voice echoing up from the bottom of a very deep well.

"Rachel, help me get him to the car."

He touched her arm then and locked eyes with her. When he mouthed the word *go*, she didn't wait. She fled to the house, tears blur-ring her way as a thousand tiny lights began to tumble from the trees.

The sky was falling.

Chapter 29

Jay

The house was dark when Jay slipped in through the mudroom door, nothing but the steady drip of the kitchen faucet. He heard it then, a thin whimper coming from the parlor, like a child in the throes of a bad dream. He nearly tripped over her in the dark, propped against the wall, knees drawn to her chest. After fumbling with the lamp, he dropped down beside her. She was clammy and rigid, trembling all over, her eyes clenched tight.

"Leslie—what's going on?"

She had half-moons of smeared mascara beneath each eye. Groaning, she covered her face, shaking her head from side to side.

"I'm trying to understand. What did your father want?"

"What he always wants: money."

"There had to be more to it than that. When I walked up you looked like you'd just seen a ghost. Now I find you crying in the dark. What did he do to scare you?"

She surprised him by throwing her head back and laughing. "He didn't *do* anything. He didn't have to. He just had to show up." She sniffed, then hiccupped. "You asked me once if I believed what everyone else did about my mother's death."

She was looking past him now, rather than at him, her hands

pleating and unpleating the velvet of her dress. "I was there when it happened. I was playing under the stairs. They were fighting. He said he'd . . . he said he'd break her neck. Then I heard her scream. When I came out she was at the bottom of the stairs. She'd been cutting fabric for my Halloween costume. She fell on the scissors."

"Jesus. Maggie told me how she died, but not that you were there."

"She never knew. No one did. They held her body for almost two weeks before they ruled it an accident."

"Maybe it was."

"Maybe." She wiped her eyes, making an even bigger mess of her makeup. "He was too drunk to go to the funeral, but that night he came back from wherever he'd been and threw me in the back of the car. I never saw Maggie again."

Jay stood and went to the little tea cart Maggie always kept stocked with a few bottles and poured a healthy draft of vodka, then handed it to her. "Drink this."

She choked as it went down.

"There. Now let's have the rest of it. I want to help, but I can't if I don't know what's going on."

Leslie sat very still, both hands wrapped around her glass. "I told you, he wants money. He's spent the last six years in jail. Now he's out, and he wants money. That's what he was doing here. A friend told me two weeks ago that he was in New York looking for me. I don't know why I thought he wouldn't track me down. He always does."

"Always?"

"Anytime he gets out, I'm his first stop."

"Because he knows you'll give him what he wants?"

She took another pull of vodka, her eyes shiny with fresh tears. "Anytime I've tried to refuse him, he threatens to move in with me. He doesn't care anything about me; he just knows it'll get him what he wants."

Jay let his breath out very slowly, fighting the urge to break something. "Why didn't you tell me about any of this?"

Leslie shrugged, swiping her eyes with the back of her hand. "It's my problem."

"This is your house. He can't come back unless you let him. And you're not going to let him."

"It sounds so simple."

"It is simple, Leslie. You just say no." She was staring at him, her eyes heavy and dazed. "Did you ever get anything to eat?"

"My God, the party—!"

"Buck and Angie had it under control when I left."

"Did anyone—?"

"See what happened? No."

"Where did . . . what happened to my father?"

"I had Rachel take him home. Apparently, he's staying at her place."

The relief on her face was plain. He saw no reason to bring up the meeting he had scheduled for the next morning. Plenty of time to tell her about that after Jimmy left town, because one way or another, the bastard *was* leaving.

She was staring through him now, her eyes focused on nothing at all, the glass of vodka in her hand forgotten. She flinched when he touched her arm.

"Go on, drink up. It'll help you sleep."

He watched her obediently drain her glass, then hand it back, dabbing her mouth on her sleeve. The desire to pull her up into his arms was suddenly overwhelming, but now wasn't the time.

"Go on up now. I'll make sure everything's locked up."

She lingered a moment at the base of the stairs, one hand clutching the newel for support, her face pale, her eyes fathomless. "Thank you for . . . everything."

She turned then and was gone, the soft rustle of velvet receding in her wake. He waited for her door to close, counting the hours until he could look Jimmy Nichols in the eye.

Jay slid into the Anytime's last open booth, the sticky blue vinyl pocked with scars from the days when smoking was still allowed in restaurants. He would have preferred a table away from the window, where they wouldn't be seen, but this wasn't going to take long. Behind the counter, Rachel was filling a napkin dispenser, doing her best to avoid his eyes. Jimmy was already late. Jay didn't care. If the bastard no-showed he'd just drive over to Rachel's and drag him out by the scruff of the neck.

He looked over the menu, though he'd already decided on the pancakes. Even at a dump like this, the pancakes were usually safe. A waitress appeared, a stack of dirty plates in one hand, a pot of coffee in the other. Jay flipped over his cup, letting her fill it, and informed her that he was waiting for someone. She gave him a *suit yourself* shrug and shuffled back toward the kitchen.

The coffee was drinkable with enough sugar. Jay emptied a second packet into his cup, stirring absently. He glanced up when a man in a plaid flannel shirt came in, pausing to scrape his boots on the greasy welcome mat. It had been too dark last night to get a good look at Jimmy, but this man was much too tall. Getting antsy, Jay checked his watch. Then the door opened again, and he saw Rachel's spine stiffen.

The man pulling back the door couldn't be anyone *but* Jimmy Nichols, unshaven, and more than a little worse for wear in a dark green hunting jacket and sagging jeans. A cigarette fumed defiantly at the corner of his mouth.

Jay raised his coffee cup to get Jimmy's attention. For a moment their eyes clashed, and then Jimmy began walking toward him. He moved like a man used to looking over his shoulder, arms tensed at his sides, eyes constantly shifting. He slid into the booth without waiting to be invited.

On cue, the waitress appeared with her pot, flipped Jimmy's cup, and filled it. "No smoking, Jimmy, remember? I'll bring you something to put it out in. You want the special again? Eggs up?"

Jimmy nodded, hands clasped tight around his mug.

She turned to Jay. "And you?"

"I'll have the pancakes, and a little more coffee."

The waitress left and returned with a saucer, sliding it in front of Jimmy with a pointed look at the cigarette fuming between his fingers. He pushed it away, in no hurry to use it. Jay let the silence thicken while Jimmy struggled to get his cup to his lips. He'd seen more lifelike faces in a wax museum. Served the bastard right after last night, though he was surprised the man wasn't immune to hangovers.

"Why are you here, Mr. Nichols?"

Jimmy glared at him. "Your meeting. You tell me."

"I want to make sure we understand each other."

Jimmy spewed a pall of smoke and crushed out his cigarette. "You think I don't understand you, Hemingway? You think I been back a whole week and I don't know how you're all tangled up in this?"

Jay let the remark pass. "Your daughter told me what you want."

"Did she, now?"

"You've wasted your time coming back here. Leslie doesn't have a cent. And if she did, I'd make damn sure you never saw it."

Jimmy's fist crashed to the table, overturning the makeshift ashtray. "Let me tell you something, fancy boy—"

The rest of the threat never came. Jimmy closed his eyes, shoulders hunched as if the weight of his head was suddenly too much for him. The spell lasted less than a minute, but when he finally opened his eyes the anger was gone. His hands shook as he pulled a soft pack of Winstons from his jacket, then tossed it down in annoyance.

Jay looked at his watch, ready for the meeting to be over. "Mr. Nichols, let's not waste time. Leslie doesn't want you here. And I wasn't kidding about the money. She's broke."

Before Jimmy could respond, their waitress reappeared. She dropped off their plates, fished a bottle of ketchup from her apron, and left without a word. Jay picked up his knife and began buttering his pancakes, as if he actually meant to eat them.

"I didn't come for money."

Jay laid his knife across his plate. If possible, Jimmy had grown paler, sagging now in the blue vinyl booth. "If last night wasn't about money, what *was* it about?"

"I told you. I wanted to see my daughter. I've been . . . away."

"You can drop all the mystery. I know where you've been. I also know what happens every time you get out, only this time you're going to have to find another meal ticket."

Jimmy jabbed his fork at the congealing yolks on his plate, then shoved the mess away. "Davenport, you can take it to the bank when I tell you a meal ticket's the last thing I'm worried about. I just want to see my little girl. We've got business we need to get straight."

"And did that business include getting liquored up and embarrassing your daughter in front of half the town?"

Jimmy looked as if he'd been slapped. "She thinks I was drunk," he mumbled thickly. "Hell, I guess she would. I know what people think, and I know why they think it. But I wasn't drunk. It wasn't easy coming back here, you know. I had one, maybe two."

"For a man who wasn't drunk, you're nursing a hell of a hangover."

"I'm sick."

"I'm not surprised, considering what you must have put away."

"I'm sick," Jimmy repeated, and suddenly Jay knew he didn't mean hungover.

"What kind of sick?"

"The bad kind."

"How bad?"

"About as bad as it gets, I'd say."

The waitress was looming with her coffeepot. Jay waved her away. "That's why you came back."

"Yes."

Jay pushed his pancakes away, suddenly queasy. He'd just accused the man of being hungover when there was a very real possibility that he was seriously ill. There was also a very real chance that he was bullshitting, though it was hardly the kind of thing you called a man's bluff on.

"You're saying you're—"

"Dying? Yeah. Or so the prison doctors tell me."

"How long?"

Jimmy shrugged. "A year, maybe."

Jay narrowed his eyes, still not convinced. "What are you supposed to be dying from?"

Jimmy frowned into his coffee cup. "Living," he said finally. He set his cup aside and looked Jay dead in the eye. "I've done a long, awful dance, Davenport. Made a lot of mistakes. Hurt a lot of people. And now my sins have followed me home." He paused, clearing his throat with a phlegmy rumble. "And that's why I came back. There are things I have to say, before I can't say them anymore. I don't want anything from her. I just want her to listen."

"You want forgiveness."

"No," Jimmy said flatly. "I don't deserve that. But there are things I need her to know."

Jay couldn't think of a polite way to say what he was thinking, so he just came out with it. "You wouldn't be bullshitting me, would you?"

"I can't say I blame you for asking, but no, I'm not bullshitting you. I met a man in the infirmary, sicker than me. He told me when I got out I needed to mend my fences with the people I hurt. Most of them are dead now. But Leslie . . . well, maybe that's a fence I can still mend."

Jay felt his throat thicken as Jimmy's eyes sheened over. Goddamn the man. Was he supposed to just take him at his word? After last night, how could he let him anywhere near Leslie? But if it was true, did he have the right to block what might be a dying man's last chance to make things right?

"Mr. Nichols—Jimmy—it pains me to say it, but I think you're right. Leslie should know."

"But she isn't going to know."

Jay's brows shot up. "Why the hell not?"

"Because I want her to hear what I have to say as her father, not some sickly old man she has to feel sorry for. I've done a lot I'm ashamed of. Coming back to see my daughter isn't going to be one of them. I'm going to say my piece, and maybe die with a little self-respect. And no one's going to stop me."

"I'm not going to try to stop you, Jimmy. But I am going to ask you to wait."

"In case the dying thing didn't give it away, Davenport, time isn't exactly on my side."

Jay nearly smiled. "I want time to check out your story. And because if what you're saying is true, I might know someone who can help. A friend of my father's is head of Internal Medicine at Bristol Medical Center. But if I agree to help you, you're going to do what I say."

If Stephen Gates agreed to take Jimmy as a patient, and the fool managed to keep himself out of trouble, there might still be time to heal the scars between father and daughter. He didn't know if the man was telling the truth or just rewriting history, but he did know something had to give. If not, Jimmy would die with his version of the truth, and Leslie would go on living with hers. And nothing good would come of that.

Jimmy eyed him warily. "Why would you do all this for me?"

"I wouldn't do it for you. But I would do it for your daughter."

"You two an item?"

"We're business partners."

"But you love her."

Jay squirmed under his narrowed gaze. "We're friends," he said evenly. "And I'd like her life to be easy for a change, which isn't likely with you hanging around looking like you've just come off a ten-day drunk. Maybe if you cleaned up your act she'd at least listen to you. When was the last time you saw a doctor?"

"A week before I got out. Almost three months ago now."

"If I decide to help you, you're going to have to spend some time up north. I'll call my father and see if he can help me set something up."

Jimmy put a hand up, cutting him off. "I appreciate all this, but I don't have money for any fancy doctor."

"Let me worry about that. Right now you're going to tell me why you deserve a second chance with your daughter. If I'm satisfied, I'll make that call. Your end of the deal is to walk the straight and narrow and do what you're told. If you don't, I pull the plug and you kiss your chances with Leslie good-bye. In the meantime, make yourself scarce until you hear from me. And I promise you, if it turns out you are bullshitting me, I'll bury you under the grapes where they'll never find you. Do we understand each other?"

Jimmy surprised him by smiling. "You sure you don't love her?"

Chapter 30

Adele

Henry has a son.

Minnie Maw lays him across my middle, a small slippery stranger, and yet familiar somehow, part of me still, despite the midwife's neat work with her scissors, as if the cord that has bound us all these months has not been severed at all and is never likely to be. Something wells up in me then, something fierce and almost feral, as I look into those tiny unseeing eyes. His name is Jemmy, and whatever comes, he is mine.

It is all I can do to let him out of my arms when Minnie Maw takes him from me and passes him to Henry.

"A boy," she murmurs gruffly, then jerks her chin at Annie Mae, who has gone faintly green and stands cowering behind Henry. "Bring the basin, girl, and stop fooling. It's all over now but the mopping up."

Henry's eyes are wet with joy, his face shining as he stares down at the life we have made. If he cares that his son is more Laveau than Gavin, he gives no sign—there is only love on his careworn face. His Adam's apple wobbles as he glances up at me, lying spent against my pillows. His expression is a mixture of wonder and relief, and I see that he's as worn-out from worrying as I am from hollering. But that's what comes, I guess, of sitting helpless in some other room, waiting for the storm to pass.

I sleep for a while, the dense and dreamless sleep of the bone weary. When I wake, Minnie Maw is gone and Henry is dozing in a chair, one hand draped over the edge of the bassinet in case the baby stirs. I lie quiet, watching a while and reveling in the goodness of the moment. The sunlight has mellowed, leaving deep yellow patches on the floorboards, glinting where it touches the heavy stubble on Henry's chin. He has been with me all day, I realize. It is only the second time I've ever known him to miss a day's work—the other was the day Maggie was born. He has always been a good father to Maggie, and he will be a good father to our boy.

As the months skim past, it becomes plain Jemmy will not favor Henry. He is cut from my kin's cloth, a sturdy, honey-skinned boy with russet eyes and a head of curls like spun copper. It's a strange thing to look at your child and see the echo of a man you've never met, but one day while I'm peeling potatoes I look down where he's crawling around my ankles, and there it is, staring up at me, a younger version of the photograph Mama keeps on her dresser and dusts faithfully every Saturday morning. The realization knocks me back a little, because somehow I have never noticed it, and because I know the time has come to write to Mama.

It is a letter I am loath to write, but one I know I must. God knows I have waited as long as I can before finally picking up my pen, but it's time now to confess what a mess I've made of all her careful plans. Time, too, that she knows she is a grandmother. She will take little pleasure in the news, or in the life I have chosen. How can she, when the same mistakes have brought her nothing but heartache?

I wait until Henry is out in the fields to sit down with my paper and pen. I am ashamed as the words begin to spill onto the plain white page, but there are things that must be told, and so I keep my hand moving, each tear-blotched line a testament to my sins, each word a fresh wound. My belly knots as I picture her face when she reads that I am unmarried, that the man I love, and whose son I have just borne, is not free. I can only hope the news that Jemmy favors my father will somehow soften the blow. It will not atone, I know, but it might help her forgive me a little.

When the bad news is all out on the page, I beg her forgiveness and assure her that what I have done cannot be laid at her door. I tell her I am happier than I have a right to be, that I care nothing for the world's opinion so long as I have Henry's love and can hold my little patchwork family together. It will not matter, I think, as I seal the envelope and fix the stamp. She will blame herself. I could have lied, I suppose, or at least softened the news, but that has never been the way between Mama and me. She deserves to know the truth, even if it shames us both.

A week later Henry brings me a present, a small box of dark green velvet he pulls from his pocket when I've finally gotten Jemmy to sleep. I wonder if he bought it because he has sensed a change in my mood. I have become sullen and restless since mailing the letter, anxious about what Mama will say when she writes, but more afraid that she will not write at all.

I am shy about opening the box; I'm not used to presents but can see that he's eager. I hold my breath as I raise the lid, then let it out again when I catch sight of the pendant—a tiny book fashioned of silver. It is a lovely thing, bright and charming, though I have no idea why Henry has chosen it. Still, I smile as I lift it out by the chain, watching it glitter and twirl in the lamplight.

"I drove over to Level Grove to get it," he says, sidling closer to me on the settee. "It's a locket. Here, let me show you." He works at the hasp a moment with his thumbnail, then hands it back. "See? There are little pages inside for . . . family pictures."

The last words are a whisper, an apology for all he cannot give me and for all that's been taken away. I manage a nod, but my heart squeezes hard against my ribs, the ache suddenly too much to bear. When his arms go around me, I finally break, all the months and years of holding in, of pretending this half-life is somehow enough, spilling from me in great, wrenching sobs.

We have each played our part in this wicked thing, each turned our backs on decency. But I am the woman. It was my place to say no, to stay strong and not yield. Instead, I sold my soul.

Chapter 31

It's plain that Maggie blames me.

She is still too young to ask questions, though they live unasked in her sharp gray eyes whenever they settle on Jemmy. He is her rival—and he is my fault.

Henry's love for his little girl has not faltered; she has always been, and still is, the brightest part of his life. But I would be lying if I said he is not smitten with his new son. He is gone from the Big House now, for longer and longer stretches, spending two or three nights out of each week at the cottage, while Maggie is left alone in her rosebud-papered room down the hall from Susanne.

I miss her terribly. She rarely comes to the cottage now, and never when Henry is gone. And in those rare and precious times when we are all together, she makes it clear she wants no part of me, casting sullen looks in my direction while she clings to her father. It hurts me to see it, though I do my best to pretend I don't. I think of all the frigid mornings I held her hand while she waited for the bus, or the after-noons when we played dress-up, and I wonder if it can ever be like that again. I fear it cannot. I lost the affections of Henry's daughter the day I gave him a son.

By the end of summer Jemmy is toddling and Maggie has come

around. She has all but forsaken her favorite doll, preferring to dress up poor Jemmy instead, pouring out endless cups of imaginary tea or hanging on for dear life while I haul the pair of them up and down the drive in her wagon. She is leery of me still, but less sullen, and now and again, I fancy I catch a longing in her eyes when they fall on me, a sort of wistfulness for the way things used to be before Jemmy was born. I know that she has not forgiven me yet, but for now it is enough.

I adore every part of being Jemmy's mother, but there are times I find it hard to believe that one tiny boy has so altered my life. There is no longer any order to my days, only an unrelenting sense of never enough sleep, never enough quiet, and always, always, more to do. I wouldn't trade any of it for the world.

At least going into town is easier now, with Jemmy in tow. There is still always the customary knot of loiterers in front of the barber's, but they pay me less mind now. I am no longer the naïve young girl Henry dropped off in their midst all those years ago—no longer a *ripe little peach*. Now when they look at me, their eyes hold different kinds of questions, mostly about who might have fathered my boy. These are the moments I'm actually glad Jemmy looks nothing at all like his daddy.

The gossip has finally quieted. It helps that the Gavin Historical Society has disbanded and that Celia Cunningham has moved away—gone to live with her sister in Kentucky while her husband serves his time for stealing from the bank—though, if you were to ask Mama, she'd probably tell you folks are just too worn down with their own trials to care about sticking their noses in their neighbor's troubles.

Lottie comes less and less now, usually on her way home, when it's dark and she can't be seen from the house. Susanne has threatened to fire her if she catches her visiting me.

"I ain't worried, though," Lottie tells me with a grin. "Mr. Henry won't let her do that. He hired me way back when. He ain't gonna let me go just for being neighborly."

I nod my head, but I wonder. I see that deep down she does too, now that Henry takes most of his meals at the cottage. And now that Susanne's got a new girl to fetch and carry for her.

"At least you don't have to spend your days running up and down stairs now that Lyla's come to look after Susanne."

Lottie sucks her teeth, then follows it with a snort. "Shoot, that girl can barely find her way around the house yet. She ain't lazy, but she's scared of her own shadow, and slow-witted as all get-out. You should have seen her face when them boys came knocking at the back door."

I frown as I hand her a piece of sweet potato pie. "What boys?"

"The same bunch who used to bring Susanne's bootleg. She can get it legal now, but she still pays them to come over from Level Grove a couple times a week and do odd jobs, hauling trash, raking leaves, toting wood in from the shed. Never see 'em do any of it, though, just come round for their money at the end of the day. Shifty no-accounts is all they are. Wouldn't want them hanging around my place, or hanging around my girl either."

Lottie's expression makes me uncomfortable, like she's trying to say something without saying it. I wait to see if she'll say more, but she just keeps pecking away at her pie. Before I can ask her more, I hear Jemmy start to cry.

In the coming days, Lottie's words stick with me. I can't help wondering what would possess Susanne to let such trashy boys anywhere near Maggie, and I wonder if it might not be time to talk to Henry. Surely he knows a decent man or two who would be happy to have the work, though it will mean having to deal with Susanne, something he seems more and more reluctant to do these days.

I can't say I blame him. From the stories Lottie tells, Susanne is no longer in her right mind, though she is still at her window most

days. When the light is just right, I can make out her face, like a vig-
ilant ghost peering out between the curtains, pale and ravaged and
full of hate as she stares down at my boy. And then there is a day that
lodges in my memory like a bone, a day when our eyes meet through
the glass and I see something new in her expression, a brand of mal-
ice that makes me shiver, that makes me want to pick up my son and
run. And keep on running.

The next morning I'm surprised to hear a knock on the cottage
door. Lottie's the only person who ever comes calling, and she never
knocks, just sticks her head in and hollers. There's a girl standing on
the stoop when I open the door, shadow thin, with eyes round as
quarters, her mouse brown hair tied back from a face like spoiled
milk. She's wearing one of my old aprons.

"Yes?" I say, wondering what this is all about and why the girl isn't
saying a word.

She blinks slowly, like she's just come awake, then looks down,
fingers worrying the hem of her apron. "Mrs. Gavin says you're to
come up to the house."

I look back at Jemmy, finally asleep after a long, fussy morning.
"My son is asleep. What does she want?"

Her eyes are dull but faintly pleading, her mouth working sound-
lessly as she backs slowly down the stoop. For a moment I think she
might burst into tears. "The Missus says for you to come now," she
blurts, then turns to scurry back toward the house.

She leaves me to stare after her, my belly clenched tight as a fist. I
have always known this day would come, that she would seek out
fresh ways to punish me, and that when that time came it would be
my son she used against me.

Jemmy protests, mewling softly as I rouse him from his nap, his
curly head warm and heavy against my shoulder. I loathe the very
thought of taking him into that house, or anywhere near that woman,
but there is no one else to look after him. Henry has gone into town

this morning, though that's for the best, I suppose. He would not want to be nearby when Susanne and I finally bare our claws.

I pass quietly through the mudroom door and into the kitchen. Lottie glances up from a freshly plucked chicken, her small cleaver suspended in midair when she sees me standing there with Jemmy in my arms.

"Girl, what are you doing here with that boy?"

I nod toward the back stairs. "I was sent for."

Lottie heaves a gusty sigh, and the lines in her weathered face deepen. "Leave the child with me, then, when you go up."

I shake my head, tightening my grip on Jemmy until I feel him begin to squirm. I have no idea how long this encounter might last, but I do know my son won't be out of my sight so long as I am in Susanne's house.

I catch a flash of white apron in the pantry as I turn and head for the stairs, then a glimpse of stringy brown hair though the crack in the door, and I wonder how much young Lyla knows about the girl who once served in her place. But then, it is no matter. I am long past caring what most people think.

I pause at the top of the stairs, dizzied by the memories that seem to hover like ghosts, cold but not quite gone, of a child lost, and a love found, of discovery, and heartache, and such terrible shame. It's the first time I've been back since the day my things were moved out to the cottage, and I'm startled to find I have forgotten the grandeur of its rooms, its fine furnishing and wide airy spaces, and how empty and cold it always felt.

My eyes skim along the gloomy hall, lingering on Henry's door, then move on to the room that was once mine. I'm strangely glad to catch a glimpse of rosebud-covered walls and of Maggie's precious Violet, propped unseeing against a shiny bank of pink satin pillows. It helps, somehow, to think of her saying her nightly prayers, then closing her eyes beneath the same bit of roof that once sheltered me, as if, despite the sin that separates us, we are in some small way connected.

I gird myself then and hold tight to Jemmy as I move to Susanne's door and knock. I don't wait for an answer, just turn the knob and go in. The room is stifling, thick with the stench of dirty linen and unwashed flesh. The bed is unmade, the sheets rumpled and gray, half-puddled on the floor, as if Susanne has only just climbed out from between them.

She is still in her nightgown, though it is past noon, sitting at her dressing table where I used to fix her hair. Her eyes are slow to meet mine in the glass, and for a moment she seems confused, almost startled to see me standing there.

I am astonished by her reflection, by the wicked toll the years have taken since I saw her last. She is all sinew and shadow now, a specter of the woman who once looked down her nose at me in the downstairs parlor, her powderless skin like parchment, stretched tight and sallow over too-sharp cheekbones, her eyes so deep in shadow they appear mere hollows in her face.

In her lap, her hands are anxiously at work, endlessly scraping at wrists that are a ruin of white and purple scars. They go still when her eyes light on Jemmy, and I find I have to fight the urge to take a step back.

"How dare you bring your bastard here—to *my* house!"

Her voice is like venom, a rasp meant to wound. But the words miss their mark. I am beyond wounding. At least by her.

"You sent for me," I say, shifting Jemmy to my other hip. He is wide-awake now, squirming to be put down.

Susanne lurches unsteadily to her feet, grasping the edge of the dressing table for support. Before I can step away, she has reached out to touch one of Jemmy's curls, testing its coppery springiness.

She pulls back in revulsion. "The boy is . . . Henry's?"

"You know he is."

Her eyes glitter shrewdly. "He doesn't look like my husband."

"Neither does Maggie."

It is a small victory, but a victory nonetheless, to see her already pale face go paler, to see her weave her way to the bedside table and pick up her teacup with unsteady hands. The bottle of tincture is still there, alongside a half-drained bottle of bourbon. She makes use of the bourbon, splashing some into the cup, then draining it, wiping her chin on the sleeve of her nightgown. I understand now why Henry never speaks of her. It is too terrible.

"Perhaps he is . . . some other man's brat," she slurs, rattling the cup back onto the table. "And not Henry's at all."

I keep my face blank, determined to end this as quickly as possible. "Why am I here, Susanne?"

"Why?" She blinks back at me as if she's forgotten, then hooks both fists on her hips. "You're here because I want you and that bastard boy of yours gone from Peak."

"Only Henry can send me away, and he won't."

Her chin comes up a measure. "He will when he knows what you are."

I nearly laugh, but something in Susanne's eyes checks me, something shiny and sharp I don't like the look of. "You don't think, after all these years, that Henry knows everything there is to know? You chose, Susanne. You got Maggie, which is all you ever wanted from your marriage, and I got Henry."

I see at once it's the wrong thing to say. Her face is a mask of fury as she begins to advance, moving closer and closer, until I can see the tiny black specks of her pupils.

Jemmy is whimpering now, struggling to be out of my arms.

"Stay away from my son," I warn her, hearing the high, thin thread of panic in my voice.

"Then get him out of my sight!" The words are part hiss, part shriek, laced with the stench of bourbon and decay. "And that goes for Maggie too! I don't want you or that . . . that . . . *brat w*ithin a mile of here. Do you hear me?"

My mouth falls open in disbelief. "You would punish Maggie just to spite me?"

Susanne's smile spreads like an infection, slow and malicious, revealing teeth gone to ruin with neglect. "I would do anything to spite you."

"Please, Susanne, you can't do this. They're just children. They share the same blood."

In that moment her face drains of color, and she starts to tremble from head to foot. "Don't you say that! Don't you ever say that! Do you really believe people—decent people—will want anything to do with a daughter of mine if they know she's kin to that little savage?"

Jemmy begins to cry, a high, bloodcurdling wail that threatens to rattle the panes out of the windows. Susanne grabs on to the headboard, dragging her head from side to side, trying to ward off the noise. When she finally looks up, her eyes are cold and wild.

"Shut that boy up, or I will!"

I take a step back and raise my free hand, ready to strike if she moves any closer. She has frightened me before, but this time is different, as if she's finally lost her grip on her senses, as if anything might happen. She is still shrieking as I throw open the door and hurry from the room, still hurling vile things at my back as Jemmy and I flee down the stairs.

Chapter 32

I have a letter from Mama.

I hold it in my hands for a long time, afraid to know what it says, to know once and for all what she thinks of her little girl. My eyes blur when I finally open it and catch the first glimpse of Mama's thin, scratchy hand, and for a moment I swear I can almost smell her lilac talc. She has not signed it, only scratched out her initial at the bottom of the page, but the opening words are all I need.

My precious girl.

The tears come in earnest then, running down my cheeks and off my chin, dripping onto my son's soft curls as I read. There is no mistaking Mama's disappointment; it runs heavy between each line. But there is no condemnation. I am not hated, not reviled for the choices I have made. She is only worried that one day I will find myself alone, as she did so many years ago.

I read the letter several times before I tuck it away in my dresser. I will share it with Henry, but not yet. Things are tense still between us since my clash with Susanne. I should have known better than to light into him the way I did, to put him in the middle of two women and ask him to take sides, but I was too overwrought to reason it through. I was only thinking of the children, wanting to keep them from being torn apart in all of this.

But Henry wanted no part of it. I was dumbfounded—though I suppose I should not have been—when he made it clear he was not disposed to involve himself in our *women's quarrel*. He was tired after a long day, too tired to listen to me rant, I suppose, and by then I was half out of my wits. Still, I expected a stronger reaction than his weary sigh and a second splash of bourbon in his glass.

It will blow over, was all he kept saying as he drank.

But it will not blow over. It will never, ever blow over. I know his hands are full, that for part of the time at least, he must dwell in the same house as Susanne, and that all he wants while he's there is some small bit of peace, but surely he must see that it's an ill wind that's begun to blow.

It is three weeks now since Susanne called me to the house, three weeks since Jemmy's been allowed to play with Maggie. He misses her something terrible. He cannot understand why she lingers just beyond the stacked stone wall that separates the house from the cottage, her little face wistful as she watches him hover nearby while I work in the garden or hang out the wash.

It's plain that she misses him, though she's made herself some new friends too, and not ones I'm at all keen on. She's taken to running with those boys from Level Grove, the ones who pretend to do odd jobs for Susanne, and with Annie Mae Speights, Minnie Maw's granddaughter, who tags behind like a lost puppy, and who no one ever seems to pay much mind.

Lottie was right—those boys are trouble. More than once I have found my trash pail turned over, or my clothes pulled off the line and stomped in the dirt. One day I went out to the garden to find all my greens had been pulled up. And they look at me funny, always watching when I'm in the yard with Jemmy, or walking alone down by the lake. Sometimes they shout things, ugly words I can't make myself say, even now. And they do it in front of Maggie.

And then comes the day things finally come to a head. I'm walking back from the mailbox when I hear laughter coming from behind the woodshed, the kind of laughter that lets you know someone's up to something they shouldn't be. I slip quietly around back, and there they all are, Maggie and Annie Mae and the boys. The tall one is holding out a cigarette to Maggie, while a second boy is blowing smoke rings into the air. It's Annie Mae who spots me first, her eyes wide and white in her dark face. Her mouth rounds, but no sound comes out. Then she's gone, overturning the cask she's been using as a seat as she ducks around the side of the shed.

The boys turn and eye me through their greasy bangs, puffing their cigarettes bold as brass. I stare them down, hands fisted on my hips, but only one looks away. After a minute he breaks from the pack, darting off after Annie Mae. There are just the two boys then, and Maggie, whose eyes are fixed hard on the dirt.

I am astonished by the sight of her, sickened to realize all at once that no one has been looking after the child. Her hair is a filthy tangle, her feet bare, though it cannot be above fifty degrees, and I am fairly certain the grubby clothes she's wearing are the same ones she had on three days ago.

"Miss Maggie!" I bark. I wait then, until her eyes lift grudgingly to mine, glittering gray and wondering what comes next. "Go on back to the house now, before these boys get you into trouble. And before your daddy finds out what you've been up to."

Before Maggie can move a muscle, the tallest boy steps forward. He flicks his cigarette into the woodpile, then spits noisily at the ground. "Everybody knows you ain't allowed near the girl, so why don't you go back where you belong, 'fore I call Mrs. Gavin?"

I stiffen, meeting his brazen gaze blink for blink, determined not to let him see that his words have shaken me. It shames me to realize this ruffian knows about Susanne's edict, but it shames me more that he has flung it in my face in front of Maggie. He's grinning at me now, a malicious smirk that makes me long to grab him by the collar and give him a good shake.

Instead, I force myself forward, closing the space between us. When I open my mouth, my voice is strangely calm, low and steady, and deadly earnest. "If I were the two of you, I'd take myself off before Mr. Gavin hears you've been bothering his little girl. And I promise you, he will hear of it."

The boy postures a moment, balling his fists and puffing up his chest, then seems to think better of it. He spits once more, then turns and walks away without a backward glance, leaving me alone with Maggie behind the woodshed.

She stands there glaring at me with glittering eyes, her bottom lip stuck out in a pout, her little chin thrust forward. It's the only time she has ever reminded me of Susanne.

This time I don't wait for Henry to come home, or even go back to the cottage to check on Jemmy. I just march straight out to the barns, where Henry and several of his men are working to patch one of the roofs. The men go still when they see me. Several tip their hats, though it's plain they're curious about my sudden and rare appearance.

Henry is the last to notice me. He murmurs a few words to the man beside him, then climbs down the ladder and heads in my direction. His expression darkens when he sees that I'm trembling. He reaches for my arm, then catches himself and pulls back.

"What's happened?"

I'm shocked when I look at him, shocked to realize I blame him for all of this—for Maggie's bare feet and unwashed hair, for her running wild with a pack of scoundrels, for being made to feel shame by that no-account boy. But mostly, I blame him for the look on his daughter's face when I left her just now behind the woodshed.

"It's Maggie."

Henry shoves back his hat, his face suddenly anxious. "Is she hurt?"

I shake my head, so angry I hardly know where to begin.

"Then what?"

"I just caught her out behind the woodshed with those boys Susanne hired. They were teaching her to smoke."

Henry sighs, the same weary sigh he gave me the last time I tried to talk to him about Susanne. "Adele, this is hardly the time. I've got work to finish, and the sun's going down."

"Your daughter is running wild, Henry!" The words burst out of me unchecked, so shrill they ring in the chilly air. "She's got no business around boys their age, and they've no business around her. It'll lead to no good!"

"Go back to the cottage, Adele," Henry says, his voice tight with feigned patience. "We'll finish this later."

We have never quarreled, and certainly not in front of anyone. Now every hammer has gone still, every eye has fixed on us from the roof. I'm aware that I've made a spectacle of myself, of us both really, but I'm too angry to care. When I see he will say no more, I walk away and go back to the cottage to wait.

He is barely through the door when I start in, determined this time to make him hear me, if not for my sake, for Maggie's. "Henry, you have to get rid of those boys."

He walks past me into the kitchen. I trail behind, holding my tongue while he pours a glass of bourbon and takes a deep swallow. When he finally turns his eyes on me, there is something like a plea in them.

"Adele, please. Can this not wait a little?"

It's my turn to sigh now, though whether the sigh is one of guilt or frustration, I truly cannot say. "Wait for what, Henry? You're through with work. There's no one watching. So no, this cannot wait. Someone's got to look out for that girl."

He looks up from his glass then, genuinely surprised. "You don't think I look out for my daughter?"

I soften my tone then because I can see I have hurt him, and because I need him to listen to what I have to say. "I think you work hard to provide for her, Henry, but that's not the same thing as looking after her. She looked like some sort of orphan today. I'd swear on my life she hasn't had a bath in a week, or had anyone brush her hair. And she was running barefoot, for pity's sake—in October!"

"She's never been a prissy girl, Adele."

"That's not what I mean, and you know it. I don't care if the girl ever takes another bath as long as she lives, but she cannot be allowed to hang around with those awful boys."

Henry gulps a mouthful of bourbon, then scrubs a hand through his hair. "I'll tell Lyla to keep an eye on them."

I can only glare at him, incredulous that he believes a milk-faced girl would be any match for that pack of ruffians. "Not Lyla, Henry— you. You have to make them go away and stay away. You didn't see them. They mocked me, right in front of Maggie!"

"Is that what this is about? Adele, they're just boys."

"Who were teaching your little girl to smoke! God only knows what they'll be teaching her next. Do you not see what could happen?" I pause, making sure I have his attention, then say the thing I know I must say. "Or is it just easier not to see it, Henry?"

In the eight years I have known Henry Gavin, I have never roused his anger. Now I see a shadow steal across his face as he digests my words. Finally, he brings his glass down on the counter with a sharp crack.

"Jemmy is your concern, Adele. And Maggie is Susanne's. I know that isn't pleasant to hear, but it's not your place to worry about this, or to blame me for it either."

Henry's words leave me speechless, more stinging than if he'd struck me across the face. That he should fling such a thing at me, purposely wound me in order to distract from his refusal to deal with the situation and with his wife, is unthinkable. I find I have nothing to say as he stalks past me and out of the kitchen. Minutes later, as I hear the cottage door bang shut behind him, I cannot help but recall a line from Mama's letter.

I only hope he will stand by you, whatever trouble comes . . .

Chapter 33

Leslie

Leslie lifted her face to the breeze as the Mustang crested the Cooper River Bridge. Jay had dropped the top shortly after crossing over into South Carolina, and as they headed toward the coast, the spires and steeples of Charleston's historic downtown stood in sharp relief against a blue-white sky.

Jay played tour guide as they headed into downtown proper, slowing now and then to point out bits of history or architecture: the Custom House and the Old Slave Mart; the Circular Church, which boasted the town's oldest cemetery; or the columned facade of City Market. She had always heard Charleston described as charming. Now she understood why. Everything about the town seethed with a sense of antiquity and old southern charm.

"If the winery goes belly-up you can always get a job as a tour guide," she teased, as he pointed out the Dock Street Theatre. "You could do one of those ghost-walk tours."

Jay opened his mouth, then seemed to think better of it as he pulled up to the curb and cut the engine. "We're here."

Leslie surveyed the tree-lined promenade across the street with a bit of confusion. "We're supposed to be at Emilie Fornier's house. This is a park."

Jay stepped out onto the sidewalk and fed a handful of quarters into the meter. "It's not *a* park—it's Battery Park. If you look out into the harbor, you can see Fort Sumter from here. And our meeting is just one street over. We can walk it from here. But first I want to talk to you."

Leslie pointed to his shirt pocket. "I think you're phone's going off."

Jay made no attempt to hide his annoyance as he fished the thing out and glanced at the display. His expression changed immediately.

"I'm sorry, Leslie. I have to take this." He turned his back to her as he answered, his tone all business. "Jay Davenport. Yes. Yes. Actually, I was hoping to speak with him personally, but if he's tied up I can give you the details until he can get back to me."

He switched ears then and stepped away, leaving Leslie to ponder a Civil War cannon with its dubious pyramid of shiny black cannon-balls. She had to admit he'd chosen a breathtaking spot to park. She eyed the palm-lined row of grand southern mansions across the street, still as proud and white as the southern belles who had once lived in them, then the broad green expanse of the battery itself, with its ancient, draping oaks, and thought of the belles who had almost certainly strolled there, prettily perched on the arms of beaus in Confederate gray.

From the corner of her eye she could see that Jay had ended his call, but instead of walking back to join her, he hiked a foot up on a nearby bench and placed another call, glancing back over his shoulder now and then, as if he feared she might wander off or slip up behind him.

It was a strange observation, yet it felt accurate somehow. He'd been tense since they left Peak this morning, barely speaking a word along the way, and then only in halting monosyllables. And there was the brooding frown that never seemed to leave his brow, as though he were a thousand miles away, or wished he were.

She was still searching her memory for anything she might have said or done to set him off, when she saw that he was finally heading in her direction.

"Everything all right?"

"Everything's fine," he said, dropping his phone back into his shirt pocket. "Just an old friend of my father's. We've been playing phone tag for a couple days."

"Oh, good. You looked so serious. Now, you were about to say something."

The tension had returned to his face. He hiked up his cuff and checked the time. "It'll have to wait. We drove six hours to meet this woman. Let's go get it over with. Before we head home we'll get some dinner. There'll be time to talk then."

Leslie squinted up at him. "Should I be worried?"

He seemed not to hear as he made his way back to the car and fetched the Rebecca from the trunk. Tucking it awkwardly beneath one arm, he steered her down the sidewalk toward the imposing iron gate that separated 26 Murray Boulevard from the riffraff. It was a massive house, two stories of pink brick with shiny shutters, half a dozen chimneys, and a soaring, half-round portico. The gate latch gave easily.

Leslie kept her eyes moving, half expecting a Rottweiler to dart from the manicured hedges as they moved up the walk. Jay gave the polished knocker two quick raps. After a few moments the door opened to reveal a sixtysomething beigy blonde in perfectly tailored St. John's knit. Her voice was slow and southern, finishing-school perfect.

"Ms. Nichols?"

"Yes, and this is Mr. Davenport. Thank you again for seeing me."

Emilie Fornier nodded crisply, stepping aside to let them enter. She said nothing as she led them through the foyer and into a room more reminiscent of a museum than a parlor. Leslie's mouth hung open as she gazed at the eclectic montage of jade carvings and paper-thin porcelains, religious artifacts and pre-Columbian pottery.

They were waved toward a long brocade sofa. As Leslie settled gingerly on the pristine cushions, she couldn't help feeling their hostess's silence was intended to give them time to be properly awed. There was something distinctly condescending in the cool blue gaze, a subtle reminder that while they had technically been invited, they should not confuse that invitation with being welcome.

"You have a lovely home, Mrs. Fornier," Jay said graciously.

"It's Ms. Fornier," she corrected. "I never married. And thank you. The house belonged to my grandfather, as I'm sure you already know." Her gaze shifted to Leslie, pointed and all business. "You said you had a piece you'd like me to authenticate. I suppose that would be what your friend is holding on his knees, wrapped in . . . a bedsheet . . . is it?"

A slow heat crept into Leslie's cheeks. "I'm afraid it is. As I said on the phone—"

Fornier spoke to Jay now, as if Leslie were no longer in the room. "Unwrap it, please."

Leslie bit her tongue. She was in no position to indulge her pride. Instead, she folded her hands in her lap, watching Emilie Fornier's expression as the Rebecca emerged; recognition, followed by a more critical assessment and a distaste that gave itself away in the slight flaring of her nostrils.

"Yes," the woman said finally, though what question she might be answering, Leslie had no idea. At the opposite end of the couch, Jay seemed equally baffled.

"Yes?" Leslie prodded, hoping for a more detailed response.

Ms. Fornier composed her face into something that might pass for a smile. "May I get you both some tea?"

Leslie opened her mouth to decline, but Jay cut her off, accepting the offer with a smile that was right off the cover of one of his novels. And just like that, a dozen years fell away from Emilie Fornier's well-powdered face. Her forced smile was visibly softer as she turned and left the room.

"She hates it," Leslie hissed when the slap of Emilie's soft leather mules faded from earshot.

Jay's brow furrowed. "Hates what?"

"The Rebecca—she hates it."

"All she said was *yes*. How do you know she hates it?"

Leslie rolled her eyes. "Didn't you see her face when you took the sheet off? You might as well have unwrapped a dead skunk."

Jay looked over his shoulder, then leaned in with a grin. "For a minute there I thought you were going to take a poke at her. She's certainly—"

Before he could finish the sentence Emilie appeared in the doorway. "We'll take the tea in my office. Bring the painting. I want to see it under proper light."

She hadn't framed it as a request, nor did she wait for a response, disappearing with her tray down a well-lit hallway and leaving them to follow. Leslie's eyes widened as they stepped inside Emilie Fornier's study. After the parlor's hectic opulence, the starkness of the room was jarring. This was no showplace, just a room filled with clean, naked surfaces, hues of beige and palest blue, like a beach in winter, swept of all traces of warmth and frivolity.

At Emilie's instruction, Jay set the painting on a wooden easel in the corner and took the chair beside Leslie. There were only two glasses of iced tea on Emilie's black lacquer tray. She handed them out, then moved to her desk, where she withdrew a pair of eyeglasses and a black velvet pouch containing a set of magnifying lenses.

Leslie sipped her tea, feigning patience while Emilie Fornier snapped on the light above the easel and turned her lens on the signature in the lower right corner of the canvas. After a few moments, she pushed her glasses to the end of her nose.

"I'll need to step out for a moment," she told them, heading for the door with her lenses. "Please wait here." She was gone less than ten minutes. When she returned she laid down her tools and fixed her gaze on Leslie. "The painting is what you think it is."

Leslie scooted to the edge of her chair. "So it *is* by this man, Tanner?"

"Yes."

"And did your grandfather ever own it?"

"At one time he owned them all. Or at least the ones anyone knows about."

Leslie opened her mouth but found no words. The questions that had formed over the last several days all tried to come out at once. "Do you know if this particular painting was sold before or after he came to the U.S.? And who he might have sold it to?"

Ms. Fornier pulled off her glasses and folded them carefully. "Might I ask, Ms. Nichols, why you're interested in the business dealings of a man dead almost thirty years?"

Jay spoke up. "Leslie's grandmother passed away recently, and she's handling the estate. She was curious how this painting might have come into her family's possession."

Emilie shifted her gaze to Leslie. "I'm not interested in buying it."

"Good," Leslie answered, bristling. "Because it's not for sale."

Jay seemed to sense that things were about to get out of hand. "Ms. Fornier, our intent isn't to sell the painting. We were only hoping you could provide a little history, since it passed through your grandfather's personal collection."

"Your last name is Davenport," she said, as if she hadn't heard a word he'd said. "Your face is familiar. What is your first name?"

"It's Jay—short for James. But you may know me as J. D. Hartwell."

"The writer, I thought so. Your last book—the one about the World War II pilot—was set here in Charleston. It was very popular with the locals. Even I read it. A little mushy for my taste, but you did the town justice. Every writer wants to set a story in Charleston these days but can't be bothered doing their homework. You and Conroy are the only ones who got it right."

Jay beamed at her. "I can't tell you how pleased I am to have the endorsement of a Charleston native, Ms. Fornier."

"Please, call me Emilie. Will you have more tea, or something stronger?" Then, as an afterthought, "Ms. Nichols?"

When they declined, Emilie settled back against the edge of her desk, slender legs crossed at the ankles. "Fine, then, North Carolina's a long way to come. What is it you want to know?"

Jay was the first to speak. "It would be helpful if you could tell us when your grandfather sold his collection, and if at all possible, who the buyers were. We know it's a long shot, but we were hoping maybe there were some old records."

"As a matter of fact, my grandfather was rather particular when it came to his records. Every piece he ever bought or sold was catalogued in a series of ledgers."

Leslie set her tea aside and scooted to the edge of her chair. "And you have these books?"

"I do."

"I don't suppose you'd let us see them?"

"No. But I may be able to tell you what you want to know. After you called, I did a little digging." Opening the desk drawer, she took out a sheet of paper and held it at arm's length as she read aloud. "Five oils by Jeremiah Tanner, sold in March of 1941 to Henry Gavin of Peak Plantation, North Carolina. It seems at one time your great-grandfather owned more than just the Rebecca, Ms. Nichols."

"And did the ledger say how much he might have paid?"

Emilie nodded coolly.

"You're not going to tell me, are you?"

"Suffice it to say that for the time, it was a considerable amount of money."

Leslie counted to ten. She was quickly losing patience. "Was there any information about how your grandfather happened to connect with the buyer? I ask because my great-grandfather was a tobacco famer who didn't know the first thing about art."

Emilie's lips pursed. "That would explain his taste."

Jay threw Leslie a sharp look of warning. "You're not a fan of Tanner's work, Emilie?"

"Let's just say he's not my cup of tea."

Leslie's eyes shifted briefly to the painting on the easel. "I don't understand. The way he captured her expression . . . it's so alive, so . . . sensual. That takes talent."

Emilie Fornier gave a delicate sniff. "Hardly fitting praise for what was supposed to be a religious study. But then, that was always Tanner's fatal flaw. He never approached his work with anything like reverence, choosing to exploit the corporeal instead."

Leslie spied the glint of metal at Emilie's throat and realized she was toying with a small crucifix. She blinked at it. Was it really as simple as that? Could this credentialed woman with her tidy hair and no-nonsense manner be so offended by the sensuality of Tanner's work that she refused to see his talent?

Suddenly, she couldn't help pointing out the obvious. "Your grandfather must have appreciated Tanner's work to go to the trouble of collecting every piece."

Emilie smiled, a mix of irritation and indulgence. "My grandfather may have been a connoisseur of fine art, Ms. Nichols, but he was also a man."

"You're saying his interest had more to do with the appreciation of women than with the merits of the artist?"

"Not women, Ms. Nichols—woman. The same woman. The same face over and over again, in every one of Tanner's paintings. I'm afraid she was something of an obsession for my grandfather."

Leslie found the idea vaguely unsettling. "That's odd, isn't it?

To be obsessed with an image Tanner might have conjured out of thin air."

"Ah, but he didn't. She's real—or was. She was Tanner's common-law wife. They met in the U.S. and she followed him to Paris. She returned alone several years later. He died in Montmartre, like so many French artists, an opium addict, I believe, heavily in debt, and rumored to have contracted syphilis."

Leslie said nothing, recalling similar words in the magazine articles.

Jay's eyes were still on the Rebecca. "How is that even possible when a man has this kind of talent?"

"You assume success in the art world is always about talent, Mr. Davenport. It's isn't. Tanner had two strikes against him. He was black, for one, which made finding a wealthy patron all but impossible. More damning, though, was his subject matter. A country famed for the cathedral at Notre Dame wasn't quite comfortable seeing history's most sacred women portrayed as sex objects. It's a conflict for a lot of people, myself included. It can be difficult to remain objective about art that offends your personal beliefs. My family never understood." Her eyes were bent on the carpet now, fingers working the crucifix. She glanced up with a wavering smile. "I don't know why I told you that. Forgive me."

"Ms. Fornier," Leslie said with newfound patience. "Emilie—I didn't come to dredge up old wounds. I just want to know more about my family. I've got all these questions, but there's no one left to ask. There are gaps, things I may never know, about my mother, and . . . other people. That's why I hoped you could help. But if this is uncomfortable we'll leave right now."

Emilie's expression softened. "That isn't necessary. I'll help however I can, though I can't imagine why anything I could tell you would be of any use. I believe you asked if I knew how the sale came about."

"Yes, I did. Aside from Tanner's work, there isn't another piece of art in the house of any consequence, and I can't imagine a tobacco farmer traveling in the same circles as an art dealer."

"It's my understanding that Mr. Gavin made the initial contact. It wasn't until things started coming apart that my grandfather finally agreed to the sale. When he lost most of his money, he had little choice. He liquidated nearly all of his personal collection, keeping only the things he couldn't bear to part with. Everything else went to keeping the gallery afloat."

"It had to be terrible parting with so many beautiful things, losing everything he'd worked for and loved."

"Come with me, Ms. Nichols. There's something I want to show you."

Leslie followed, jerking her head for Jay to come along. They stepped across the hall to the closed door opposite Emilie's office. The room was dark and masculine, not so very different from Henry's study with its requisite desk, leather chairs, and massive fireplace. An enormous portrait filled the space above the mantel.

Leslie's mouth sagged open.

"It's called *Eve and the Serpent*," Emilie said without fanfare. "Tanner's sixth and last known work."

It was magnificent, a life-size depiction of Claude Fornier's obsession, nude but for the snake writhing sinuously about the model's torso, poised to strike one ripe breast. Her dark head was thrown back, lips parted, as ripe as the fruit she had just plucked from the Tree of Knowledge.

"He kept one," Leslie breathed.

"Yes," Emilie said. "To my grandmother's everlasting shame."

"I take it she didn't approve?" Jay asked, craning his neck.

"According to family legend, the day my grandfather bought it, my grandmother threatened to move out of their bedroom. When he refused to sell it with the others, she finally did. 'Til the day she died, she refused to enter this room."

Jay had yet to look away from the painting. "Do we know the model's name?"

"It was Vivienne. I can't give you a last name. She usually went by Tanner, though they were never married. At one time my grandmother was convinced my grandfather had hired someone to find her when he learned she was back in the States."

Leslie dragged her eyes from the portrait. "Did he?"

Emilie shrugged. "I have no idea. For all the damage she did, he may as well have kept her in an apartment across town."

Jay finally dropped his eyes to Emilie. "I can't help wondering why, with such negative associations, you keep it. Why not sell it, or at least take it down?"

Emilie actually grinned. "Was that an offer?"

"No, I only meant—"

"I know what you meant. I was teasing. The truth is, I can't. Nothing in this house actually belongs to me. It's mine to enjoy as long as I live, but I can't sell it or move a single stick of furniture. When I die everything goes to the Charleston Historical Society. I'm an only child and never married, so there's no one left. And now, before I air any more family laundry, let's go fetch your painting from my office and get you two back on the road. It's a long drive back to North Carolina."

Chapter 34

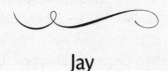

Jay

Jay said nothing on the short drive to the restaurant. Leslie seemed not to notice, too busy, he suspected, trying to forge some kind of link between Tanner's paintings and Adele Laveau to bother with small talk. Not that they'd heard anything that tied back to Adele. Maybe, when she realized she couldn't make it fit, she'd finally leave the whole subject alone.

Maybe.

Not that he was off the hook. Back at the Battery, before his cell phone had saved him, he'd been about to spill the whole thing, everything he knew or thought he knew—the journal full of notes, the fledgling manuscript in his desk, his meddling in her father's health issues—but by the time he hung up, there hadn't been time. Now he wasn't sure he had the nerve.

High Cotton sat at the corner of East Bay and Faber, its green canvas awning fluttering gently in the balmy breeze. Jay held the door, then followed Leslie into the dimly lit foyer. It was early, quiet except for a jazz trio tuning up in the lounge. Maybe they should start there, have a drink to take the edge off. But that would just prolong the inevitable. The hostess arrived, showing them to a cozy corner table, which she proudly informed them had been dubbed the most romantic table in Charleston by *Southern Living* magazine. Jay eyed the framed article mounted to the windowsill as he took his seat. Under other circumstances, perhaps, but he had the distinct feeling that tonight was going to end up being about as romantic as the siege on Fort Sumter.

Their waiter arrived, delivering an impeccable recitation of the evening's specials, then suggested they might like to start with a bottle of wine.

Jay waved away the wine list. "The lady's the expert. I'll leave the choice to her."

Leslie shot him daggers as she accepted the heavy leather folder. After a moment she closed it and handed it back. "I don't see Peak Cellars listed. I don't suppose you have a bottle of their Chardonnay by any chance?"

Jay stifled a laugh in his water glass.

"I'm afraid I'm not familiar with that label, ma'am."

Leslie feigned surprise, then cool disappointment. "That's too bad. I thought it might pair nicely with the scallops. Well, if you don't have Peak, the Sonoma-Cutrer will do."

"The Sonoma, then," he said, nodding crisply. "A very nice choice."

Jay waited until he was sure the waiter was out of earshot, then leaned close. "That was laying it on a bit, don't you think?"

"Twenty bucks says he's in the back right now, asking the wine steward if he's ever heard of us."

Jay shook his head, chuckling. "I've created a monster."

The Chardonnay wasn't long in coming. After placing their orders, they sipped their wine and nibbled warm bread, chatting easily about the weeks he'd spent in Charleston doing research. His thoughts never stopped churning, though. He never should have waited so long to come clean. He didn't know where to begin or how to explain why keeping the truth from her had seemed like the right thing to do.

"I can see why you like this place," Leslie said, interrupting his thoughts. "It's charming, very Charleston. But then, you know Charleston. You and Conroy, that is."

She was taunting him with Emilie Fornier's remarks and clearly enjoying herself in the process. "You can wipe that smirk off your face. Our hostess was merely expressing pride in her birthplace. They take it very seriously."

"She liked you."

"She liked my book."

"No, she called the book mushy. It was you she liked." She tore off another hunk of bread and began to butter it. "So . . . does that smile come natural?"

"What smile?"

"The one you turned on Emilie at precisely the right moment. I was just wondering if you had to work to perfect it."

Jay did his best to look wounded. "I don't think I like what I've just been accused of. Besides, what was I supposed to do? We were five minutes from getting tossed out on our ear. She really got under your skin."

"In the beginning," Leslie admitted. "Then I saw what an act it all was, to keep people from seeing how unhappy she is. I get that. You think being prickly will keep you safe, but all it ends up doing is keeping you alone."

She set down her glass then and laid a hand on his sleeve. "I wasn't very nice when I came back to Peak. I'm sorry for that, sorry for not seeing what Maggie meant to you, for suspecting you of— well, a lot of awful things. Growing up the way I did made me believe everyone had an angle, so you couldn't just be this nice guy who cared about my grandmother." She shrugged. "Life with Jimmy, I guess, but you didn't deserve it."

Jay squirmed uncomfortably in his chair, wishing he could bolt from the table or at least ask Leslie to stop talking. Maybe he hadn't come to Peak with an angle, but he sure as hell couldn't claim anything like innocence. Not when he was sitting on two hundred pages of unfinished Gavin family history and purposely keeping it from her. And now he'd added Jimmy to his list of transgressions.

He'd rather not contemplate the fallout when she learned he'd been meddling in the man's medical affairs, or that after six long years he'd picked up the phone and instructed his agent to pitch the manuscript so he could foot Jimmy's medical bills, and all to help a man Leslie despised. In retrospect, it seemed like a pretty bad idea, and one Leslie wasn't likely to forgive anytime soon. But it was too late for regrets, and much, much too late to examine his motives. The wheels were in motion. Maybe there was nothing to be done for the old bastard, but if there was, well then, he'd just have to let the pieces fall. It was time to face the music.

"Leslie, there are a few things—"

Before he could get the rest of the words out, their waiter appeared with an armful of appetizers, and he was forced to bide his time until the food was served and the glasses topped off. By the time they were finally alone again, Leslie had begun nibbling at one of the crab cakes and was portioning out paper-thin slices of tuna.

She paused, her fork halfway to his mouth. "What's wrong? Aren't you hungry?"

Jay accepted the bite, chewing mechanically. The dining room was beginning to fill. Strains of jazz filtered in from the lounge, piano and bass mingling with the low hum of conversation. Outside, the day was slipping away, the streetlights winking on. He was in his favorite city, his favorite restaurant, and he was with Leslie. Surely what he had to say could wait until after dinner.

"It's a shame we have to hurry right back," Leslie said, interrupting his thoughts. "It would be fun to do a little exploring. And after that meeting I could use a little fun."

Jay mustered a grin. "You don't classify sparring with Emilie Fornier as a good time?"

"No, I do not. And I'd be lying if I didn't say I'm disappointed. The only thing we know now that we didn't know when we left home is that Emilie's grandfather had a fetish for Tanner's so-called wife. We knew there was a good chance Henry bought the paintings from him. We just didn't know why. And we still don't. I mean, why go all the way to Charleston for them? And then there's the question of the money. It was 1941; the Depression was just ending. How would he have money to blow on art?"

"That's an easy one. Henry never trusted banks. Maggie said he would come home from the Smithfield market with his pockets full of cash. To her knowledge he never put a dime of it in the bank. It wasn't unusual back then, especially in the South, and it would explain his remaining afloat when so many had lost everything."

"That might explain *how* he bought them, but not why."

"Does the *why* really matter?"

Leslie pushed her plate back and folded her arms on the edge of the starched white tablecloth. "It's one more thing that doesn't fit, so yes—*why* does matter. I was really hoping Emilie would tell us something that tied those paintings to Adele."

"Such as?"

Leslie shrugged. "I have no idea. Something about her life, maybe. How she died—and why. Instead, I'm back to square one."

Jay was more than relieved to see the waiter arriving with their meals. She'd have her answers soon enough. For now, though, he wanted to savor the evening a little before whatever had started between them came crashing down around his ears.

"Do you realize," he said, raising his wineglass, "that we've been talking about dead people all day? Here's to changing the subject and to enjoying an outstanding meal together. By the way, they're very strict about dessert here. That praline soufflé you ordered won't leave the kitchen until you've cleaned your plate."

When dinner was over, the last vestiges of their shared soufflé scraped from its ramekin, they stepped out into the nighttime bustle of East Bay Street. Instead of heading back to the car, Jay took Leslie's arm and steered her across the street, toward the pier at Waterfront Park, silently rehearsing the opening lines of his confession. He had decided at some point during dessert not to wait for the drive back. He wanted to be able to say he had looked her in the eye when he finally told her the truth. She deserved at least that much.

He was conscious of the occasional brush of her body against his as they strolled to the end of the pier, their footsteps hollow on the weathered boards. As it was on most nights, the pavilion was filled with young lovers, huddled against the breeze around tables or in long slatted swings. The Gullah peddlers were about too, many of them children, selling woven sweetgrass roses to amorous tourists.

He was glad to find the end of the pier empty, the long, low benches deserted. He loved it here, especially at night when the air was sharp and fresh, thick with the brackish perfume of the marsh. Closing his eyes, he breathed it in, listening to the languid wash of the tide moving through reeds and shells, a queer and beautiful music.

When he opened his eyes again Leslie was at the railing beside him, face tipped toward the breeze, shivering visibly. "You're cold. We should head back to the car."

"Oh, no, it's beautiful here. Just get behind me and block the wind."

Jay stepped as close as he could without touching. He needed to keep a clear head.

"Mmmm," she murmured, nuzzling her head back against him. "That's better."

Instinctively, his arms crept around her waist, cinching her close, until her hips were warm and firm against him. Her hair smelled like lilies and rain.

"Thank you for today, Jay," she said quietly. "You were the one who finally broke the ice with Emilie. Then that delicious dinner, and now this."

"Leslie . . ."

"I know . . . ," she said softly. "We should be getting back."

But neither of them moved, and Jay couldn't seem to make his tongue work. Everything was perfect, too perfect to ruin with talk of her father or of surreptitiously written manuscripts.

He couldn't say how much time passed before he realized they were swaying almost imperceptibly, moving to the ebb and swell of the water below. Leslie must have realized it too. Turning in his arms, she found his mouth, tentative at first, then surer, hungrier. Before he could check himself, he was leaning into her, savoring the slight, sweet strokes of her tongue, breaths mingled, swaying still, with the quiet insistence of the sea.

Finally, through the rhythmic white noise, his senses returned. If he went through with this now, he'd be risking something he suddenly knew he wanted very badly, perhaps irrevocably. Sliding his hands to her shoulders, he pushed her away, holding her at arm's length.

"Leslie, we have to talk. There are things I need to tell you."

Her eyes were bright in the moonlight, heavy lidded and confused. She reached up to touch his face, her fingertips chilly against his cheek. "We've been talking all day. I don't want to talk anymore. I know what I want. I think it's what you want too. Let's not go back tonight. Let's stay."

When she tried to close the new distance between them, he kept his arm firm. "I don't mean small talk, Leslie. There are things you need to know before we take this any further."

Taking his hand, she folded it in on itself, kissing each knuckle with deliberate slowness. "I know how I feel, and that's enough. We're here now, and it's like a little piece of magic. Peak will still be there tomorrow. We can talk then. We'll compare scars, if that's what you want. You can tell me your secrets, and I'll tell you mine. But none of it will change what I feel now . . . what I want now."

"Leslie—" But the rest of what he meant to say died on his tongue as he gazed down at her, his blood thundering in two places at once.

"Please . . . ," she whispered against his neck. "Before the magic disappears, and it's just real life again."

Jay didn't know how to say no. She was so beautiful, her eyes luminous in the moonlight, an irresistible force. When she spoke again, the words came so softly they were lost on the breeze, but in the moonlight he could read her lips.

"Let's stay," they said again.

Chapter 35

Leslie

Leslie woke to sunlight knifing through unfamiliar blinds. There was a moment of disorientation, of trying to reconcile the deeply carved posts of an old plantation bed with the masculine leg pressed against her hip. And then last night began to flood back, the exquisite abandon of wills and limbs, breath to breath and skin to skin.

Beside her, Jay was still asleep, sheets tangled high about his hips, exposing one leg and a smooth expanse of belly and chest. She reached out, tempted to trace a finger down his midline, then changed her mind. The clock on the nightstand read just shy of eight; plenty of time to let him sleep, and for her to pull herself together.

In the bathroom she rummaged through the small satchel Jay had fished out of the trunk last night—an emergency bag he'd called it. She found a small tube of toothpaste, making do with her finger, then showered and scraped her wet hair into a ponytail with a scrunchie from the bottom of her purse.

When she emerged, Jay was already dressed, sitting on the edge of the bed, working his feet into his shoes.

"Good morning," Leslie said tentatively. "How did you sleep?" It was a trite question, she knew, but she was too anxious to be clever.

Dropping the satchel to the floor, she sank onto the arm of a striped silk wingback. "I tried to let you sleep. Did I wake you banging around in the bathroom?"

"Not at all," Jay said, standing to pocket his change and keys. "I'm surprised I slept this late. We've got a long drive ahead of us."

Leslie tried to ignore the alarms going off in her gut. "We're hurrying right back, then?"

Jay ignored the question. "There's a sweatshirt in there. You're welcome to it. It's probably chilly, and the heat in the Mustang takes a while to kick in."

"I thought we could get breakfast somewhere," Leslie suggested tentatively. "Maybe take a walk down by the harbor?"

"Actually, I was thinking drive-through. I'd like to get on the road. I'm expecting a call this afternoon, some business I need to handle."

A tight knot formed beneath her rib cage as she watched Jay disappear into the bathroom. He was so eager to get her back to Peak that he couldn't even look her in the eye. Under the moon's soft spell, she hadn't let herself think of consequences. But now, in the cool glare of morning, consequences were all she *could* think about. Last night had been a mistake, one that would sit between them like some grisly crime scene, to be roped off and carefully stepped around.

Jay finally emerged, clean-shaven and neatly combed. After a quick check of the nightstand, he zipped the satchel closed and slung it onto his shoulder.

"Ready to go?"

Leslie sat fixed to the arm of the chair. "I want— You can tell me the truth, Jay. Do you regret what we did last night?"

"Regret it?" For a moment he seemed astonished. "Did it seem like I was being taken against my will?"

Now it was Leslie's turn to avoid eye contact. "Not exactly, no. But it was my idea. And now you seem like maybe you wished we hadn't—"

He crossed the room, silencing her with a long, thorough kiss. "I don't regret anything that happened last night," he said, still holding her chin. "I just didn't want there to be any misunderstandings between us."

Leslie stood and sidled around him, pretending to search for her purse. "You mean you wanted to make sure I didn't get the wrong idea and start making rice bags."

"No, that's not what I mean. I wasn't sure last night was ever going to happen, but I know it was getting harder and harder to pretend I didn't want it to. And maybe I was trying to slow things down, but that's because there were things I needed to say . . . first . . . before."

"I'm a big girl, Jay, and I live in the real world. We both need to figure out where we go from here, and if we go together or separately. I get all that. Just please, please, don't say you regret last night."

Jay smiled, a quick, tight smile that didn't quite reach his eyes. "I won't if you won't."

The morning was spectacular, crisp and clear, with a chilly wind cutting in off the harbor. Leslie offered to drive, but Jay tossed the duffel in the back and slid into the driver's seat. After a few halting attempts at small talk, she gave up. He was clearly not in the mood for conversation, his attention fixed straight ahead with a kind of grim preoccupation she decided she would rather not question. For someone with no regrets, he certainly was having a hard time meeting her eyes.

When the Mustang finally crunched up the long gravel drive, Leslie shouldered her purse, ready to bolt the instant the car was in park. They both needed time alone, to digest what had happened and decide what, if anything, they wanted from each other.

"Thanks for coming with me," she told him over the roof of the car. "I guess I'll see you later?" It came out as a question, though she hadn't meant it to.

Jay looked at his watch. "I've got that call, but maybe later—"

"Oh, sure, maybe later—"

"Good, then. I guess I'll—"

"Yeah—me too."

In the kitchen, Leslie brewed a cup of tea, then let it go cold while she switched on her laptop and stared at the list of files. She had hoped to lose herself in work, but the muse just wasn't there. Instead, her mind kept wandering back to last night, to how right it felt to finally surrender to the feelings she'd been fighting for weeks. Had it been that way for Jay too?

It had certainly seemed so last night. But that was nearly twenty-four hours ago, when the wine from dinner had still been coursing through their veins, the moonlight still spilling through the shutters, playing pale and cool over tangled sheets and damply twined limbs. In the light of day he might feel very different, a prospect that didn't seem unlikely when she recalled that it was she who had pressed matters, while Jay had seemed uneasy from the moment their meeting with Emilie Fornier ended.

Weary of pondering the subject and needing something to divert her attention, Leslie considered popping by to visit Angie. But that would almost certainly involve a discussion about why the Mustang hadn't reappeared until this afternoon, and she wasn't at all ready to have that conversation. Instead, she phoned Mr. Randolph to fill him in on what they had learned from Emilie Fornier. It was only as she was ending the call that she remembered the Rebecca was still in Jay's trunk.

As she brushed out her hair, she tried to convince herself that retrieving the painting was a perfectly legitimate errand, not just a lame ploy to see Jay, but at the last minute she ended up changing her sweater and dabbing a bit of gloss onto her lips. No reason to show up looking like a frump.

The cottage door stood ajar. Leslie knocked tentatively, calling out as she stepped inside. The desk was littered with papers, but there was no sign of Jay or of Belle either. Maybe they were out for a walk. Suddenly, she wished she hadn't come. He was going to see right through this. He'd think she was desperate, or worse, some kind of stalker.

She was relieved when she finally caught the sound of running water from upstairs. It felt like a reprieve. She'd leave a note asking him to bring it by, then beat a hasty retreat. All she needed was a pen and something to write on. When the shower went quiet she grabbed the first scrap of paper she saw. It appeared to be a list of some sort:

Conference call—Simon & Schuster 9:30 a.m.
—Flesh out synopsis
—Negotiate advance ASAP
—Draft deadline
—Contact attorney re: royalty rights

He was writing again? Unconsciously, Leslie's eyes slid to the desktop. It was wrong, she knew, and certainly none of her business, and yet she found herself picking up a stack of neatly printed pages, scanning lines that wove the story of a married man and a forbidden love, the story of a woman named Adele.

Her chest squeezed painfully as she flicked through the pages, feeling the reality of them, and the betrayal, sink deep. All this time, behind her back, while he'd pretended—

"Leslie..."

She glanced up at the sound of her name, hanging in the air along with the scents of toothpaste and shampoo. Jay stood at the foot of the stairs, bare chested, his hair dripping wet.

"I've been trying to find a way to tell you—"

"All this time," she said, her voice a choked whisper. "All this time, you were writing about it... about her?"

"I wanted to tell you."

"When?" Leslie hurled back as she smacked the stack of pages back onto the desk. "When did you want to tell me? While you were pretending not to know anything about the photo Goddard gave me? Or while we were standing in front of her grave that day?"

"I wanted to tell you last night."

"Last night was a bit late, don't you think? Unless, of course, you dashed all this off after we came back from Charleston this afternoon." She paused, fixing him with scathing eyes. "You didn't, did you?"

Jay sighed. "Leslie, I swear this isn't what it looks like."

Leslie managed to laugh, a hollow, scraping sound in the small space. "Well, that's certainly a relief, because what it looks like is you using my family history to resurrect your writing career, and lying to me about it the whole time."

"But that's not what it is."

"How long have you been working on it?"

Jay sunk his hands deep into his pockets and rocked back on his bare heels. "I started jotting down notes after Maggie died, but they kind of took on a life of their own after you brought me to the ridge that day."

"Notes?"

"It's what I do when a story gets in my head. It was just notes at first, thoughts I couldn't seem to shake. Then, before I knew it, she was walking around in my head. The only way I knew to make it stop was to write it all down. That's how it works for me."

"I don't care how it works! I care that you went behind my back and deliberately kept all this from me—that you lied to me."

"I never meant for it to turn into a book."

"And yet, here it is. What changed your mind?"

"You did."

Leslie's mouth dropped open. "You think I wanted you to do this?"

"That isn't what I said. And for the record, this has nothing to do with my career. When you showed me the stone and began asking all your questions, it started the wheels turning again. Before I knew it, I had two hundred and thirty pages."

"And this?" Leslie held out the scribbled note. "Did I inspire this too? Maybe you'd like to explain how negotiating an advance has nothing to do with your career."

Jay looked away then, his eyes drifting beyond the narrow front windows. "Something came up," he answered flatly. "I needed to raise some money."

"How much will you make?"

"I don't know, or care really, beyond the advance. I didn't do it for the money. A family issue came up that needed to be dealt with, and I dealt with it."

"A family issue?" Leslie lifted one skeptical brow.

Jay's eyes flicked away again, roaming the room for someplace to light. "If you don't mind, I think it would be best if we stuck with one issue at a time. All I'll say is I did what I thought I had to, in the only way I knew how. Maybe that isn't the way it works in your world, but it's the way it works in mine. I don't expect you to understand, or to trust me, but I'm telling you the truth."

Leslie's eyes rounded. "You can stand there and talk to me about truth and trust? When I just found what I did? When until this minute there hasn't been a word about this so-called family issue? What a fool you must think me. And last night—"

Jay reached for her, then seemed to think better of it, folding his arms over his chest instead. "Yes, well, we've certainly come a long way from last night. What happened to nothing changing how you feel? That's what you said, isn't it?"

"I thought you were going to give me some crap about fear of commitment! I was willing to accept that. Hell, I was expecting it. But I never saw this coming. If I had, I would never have said what I did."

Jay dropped onto the corner of the desk and let his breath out slowly. "You weren't wrong, by the way. I did want last night to happen, but not while this thing was between us. That's why I wanted to talk first, because I was afraid of exactly this."

Leslie stared at him, blinking hard against the hot tears that threatened. "You were afraid? How hard would it have been to say *Leslie, I've been lying to you since the day I met you*? I'll bet if you tried you could've managed to fit it in while we were polishing off dessert. Never mind. It doesn't matter. None of it matters. I made a mistake. It won't happen again."

Jay slid off the desk and took a step toward her. "I was wrong to not be up-front with you. I should have told you that day on the ridge, but it was still just notes at that point. I had no idea it would ever go where it did. Then, when it started to become more, I knew I had to come clean. But by then the problem I told you about had reared its head, and I did what I had to."

"And went behind my back to do it," Leslie added stiffly.

"Yes."

The simple one-word admission stung more than anything else he could have said. For an instant, Leslie opened her mouth but realized there was nothing left to say. Turning on her heel, she headed for the door, then paused on the threshold.

"I guess I'll see you on the bookshelves."

Jay was beside her before she could get outside. "And where does that leave us?"

It took every ounce of strength in her to look him in the eye. "There isn't any *us*, Jay."

"So that's it. That's the end?"

She managed a smile then, a thin, cool curve that didn't reach her eyes. "Yes, that's the end. I should think you of all people would recognize one when you see it."

Chapter 36

Leslie pushed the curtains aside and peered out the kitchen window, at barren trees and piles of damp brown leaves stirring in the chilly breeze, and felt the familiar pang of restlessness, her constant companion of late. Maybe she should have taken Angie up on her dinner invitation after all, but after three weeks of gentle interrogation about what had happened between her and Jay, she couldn't bear the thought of yet another arm-twisting session. She wasn't looking to assign blame or get anyone to take sides; she just didn't want to talk about it anymore. Not to mention, there was always a chance Jay could pop in, which would be awkward, to say the least.

They hadn't spoken since the day at the cottage, probably because she'd taken care to avoid any chance meetings. It wasn't hard. Jay hadn't exactly been banging down her door, and she'd done her best to keep her head down, focusing manically on a handful of new marketing projects. Sooner or later, though, they were going to have to talk about what happened and decide how they were going to work together to open the winery.

Leslie let the curtain fall back with a sigh and shuffled back to her papers and laptop. Another reason she had buried herself in work was to keep from wondering what Jimmy might be up to and why she hadn't seen him since the night of the Splash. Maybe he'd gone and gotten himself nicked again. It certainly wasn't out of the realm of possibility. She didn't care, as long as he stayed far away from Peak. Emotionally, her plate was full.

Since stumbling onto Jay's manuscript, she found that she couldn't stop thinking of Adele and the questions surrounding her death. Maybe it was just another way to distract herself from thoughts she wasn't ready to handle, but a part of her was starting to understand what Jay meant when he spoke of Adele walking around in his head. Yesterday, she had wasted three hours digging around online, searching for the fates of the boys the police had questioned after the shed fire.

She had run a search for Samuel Porter of Level Grove and had finally isolated two possible matches, one long dead, buried beside his wife in Bristol, Tennessee, the other recently deceased somewhere in Maine, while Randy, and indeed most of the Porter clan, seemed to have dropped off the face of the earth not long after the fire. She hadn't bothered with Landis. After blowing three hours on the first two and coming up empty, she didn't see much point. Even on the off chance that he was still alive, the man would be in his eighties and not likely to be of much help.

And yet now, as she sat staring at the random bounce of screensaver bubbles on her laptop, she felt the pull to try once more. She was too restless to work. Maybe if she promised to limit herself to one hour. If she didn't have any luck by then, she would shut it down and force herself back to her work. It was a long shot, she knew, but it was only an hour.

Pulling up the people-finder site, she typed in Landis Porter's name, and then the town of Level Grove. When a single result popped up, she was so surprised she could only stare at it.

Landis Porter
DOB: 1/12/1925
121 Old Church Road
Level Grove, N.C.

Before she could second-guess herself, she had scribbled down the address and was out of her chair, dragging on her jacket as she hit the back door. She pretended not to notice Jay watching from the barn door as she slid into the car and backed down the drive. She wasn't sure what she planned to say when she got there, or what information, if any, she might be able to mine from the memory of an eighty-eight-year-old man, but the churning in her belly told her she had to at least try.

The day's chilly mist turned to rain as Leslie headed west toward the edge of town. It was the week of Thanksgiving, and the Christmas tree lots had already put up their signs. She hadn't celebrated the holidays since leaving Peak as a child, unless you counted the occasional turkey potpie with Jimmy. Now, as she passed by the neatly strung white lights, the thought of skipping them suddenly depressed the hell out of her. Angie had invited her for Thanksgiving, but Jay would almost certainly be there, which meant she wouldn't. Maybe there would be a time when she could sit across the table from him and share a meal like nothing had happened, but that time was still a long way off.

A battered wood sign with peeling paint alerted Leslie that she was about to enter the town of Level Grove. It was smaller than Gavin, rural and run-down, made drearier if possible by the low gray sky and steady drizzle. Following the directives of her GPS, she turned onto Old Church Road, a rutted strip of pavement clogged with overflowing trash cans, abandoned cars, and various articles of dilapidated furniture.

She felt conspicuous as she pulled the Beemer up in front of the mailbox carefully painted with the numbers 121. The house was small, a listing clapboard structure with a sagging porch and rusty tin roof. She was glad to see the column of white smoke chuffing from the crumbling brick chimney. Someone was home.

She moved quickly up the cracked walk, dodging a leaky gutter as she stepped up onto the porch. She still had no idea what she was going to say, or how she was going to convince whoever was inside that she wasn't crazy. She had just raised her fist to knock when a coarse voice startled her.

"Who you lookin' for?"

A man in an oversize camouflage jacket sat very still at the far end of the porch, his stringy white hair combed back from his forehead, a scruff of silver whiskers glistening along his jaw. Leslie moved down the porch, feeling the warped boards give with each step. Only when she was closer did she note the cigarette fuming in his right hand and the portable oxygen tank beside his rocker. A much-marked and well-thumbed Bible lay open in his lap.

"Would you be Landis Porter?"

"Might be." Cloudy blue eyes narrowed behind thick, wire-rimmed glasses. His voice was a strange combination of ragged and breathless, a smoker's voice. "Who wants to know?"

"I'm Leslie Nichols. Maggie Gavin was my grandmother."

"And?"

"And I've come to ask if you remember anything about a fire that occurred on Peak Plantation when you were a boy. There was an article in the *Gazette*—it mentioned your name."

Porter took a long pull on his cigarette, blowing the smoke out slowly. "Did it?"

Had she imagined it, or had his eyes actually shifted for the tiniest instant?

"There were three names, actually. Your brothers, I assume. I looked for them too, but you were the only one I could locate. I was hoping you might be able to tell me something about what happened that night."

"As I recall it, a shed burned down."

Leslie dropped into the rocker beside his without being asked. He clearly wasn't in the mood to make this easy. "Do you know how the fire started?"

"How would I know that?"

"The paper said the police suspected vandalism. It said you and the other two boys were questioned."

"Questioned ain't arrested," he shot back, flicking his cigarette out into the wet yard. A strand of hair flopped over his forehead. He pushed it back. "Why come around now, after all this time?"

"I just moved back this summer. My grandmother died and left Peak to me." For a moment she could have sworn she saw something like relief pass over his wizened face. "Did you know Maggie?"

"Used to do work for her mama way back when. She'd hang around sometimes."

The front windows were slightly open, and suddenly the strains of what Leslie was almost sure was the Temptations wafted out through the battered metal screens, followed moments later by the sound of running water and the clatter of pots and pans. She glanced at Porter's left hand but found no ring.

"You come here to talk about your grandmother?" he asked gruffly, steering Leslie back to the subject at hand. "If so, I'm afraid I can't help you."

"Actually, I came to ask about a woman who used to live at Peak at the time of the fire. Adele Laveau was her name."

Porter's face altered then, running through a flurry of emotions before hardening into a stoic blank. He closed his Bible and set it aside, then reached into the pocket of his jacket for a soft pack of Camels. His hands shook as he lit one and took a long pull.

"Can't help you there either."

Leslie played a hunch. "You can't, or you won't?"

He blinked at her from behind a scrim of smoke. "Does it matter? Doesn't seem much point speaking of a woman who's been dead more than seventy years."

Leslie folded her hands in her lap and looked him in the eye. "I never said she was dead. And yet you knew she was."

Porter began to rock, an agitated seesawing that gave away more than anything he might have said. "Everyone from those days is dead," he said hoarsely. "Just figured this Adele woman would be too."

"You know something, don't you? Something about that fire?"

The rocker went still. "I'm telling you to leave now," he said, his knobby knuckles white where they gripped the arms of his chair. "And I'm telling you not to come back."

Leslie was unmoved. "She died that night, didn't she? She was inside when the shed caught fire. And you were there—you and your brothers?"

Porter unfolded himself and stood, glaring down at Leslie over his glasses. "What happened to that woman has nothing to do with me."

Leslie stood too, and looked him in the eye. "They say the door was bolted from the outside."

"Leave me alone!" Porter bellowed hoarsely, before slumping back into his chair in a fit of dry coughing.

From inside the house came the hurried thump of heavy feet. A few seconds later the door opened a crack. "Landis Porter, what on earth—?"

The face that scowled through the narrow opening was female, stern and black as tar. "Who're you?" she asked, pulling the door back when she spotted Leslie.

"My name is Leslie Nichols."

But the woman wasn't listening. Instead, her wide white eyes were fixed on Porter, hunched over on the edge of his chair, still coughing.

With a huff of exasperation, she pushed through the door, squeezing past Leslie to jerk the cigarette from his fingers and toss it away.

"Fool man!" she hissed, reaching to untangle the coil of clear tubing wrapped around the base of the oxygen tank. "You know you ain't supposed to have those things, 'specially here next to this tank. One day you're going to blow us both to kingdom come, and this lady too."

Landis pushed her hands away. "Stop your fussing, Annie Mae. I'm fine, and Miss Nichols was just leaving."

Annie Mae stood with her fists planted on her ample hips, eyes hard on them both, as if trying to make sense of the tension she had just stumbled upon. And yet, somehow Leslie couldn't help feeling the woman knew exactly what was going on.

"Mr. Porter," Leslie said, taking another tack. "When I walked up on this porch you had a Bible in your lap. I believe somewhere in there, there's a passage about the truth setting you free."

Landis Porter stiffened as if he'd been struck. "I asked you to leave once, Miss Nichols. Don't make me ask again."

The look he gave her made it clear he was finished talking—about Adele, or anything else. Leslie turned on her heel, almost colliding with Annie Mae, whose smooth, dark face was now a mix of wariness and dread. Her mouth worked mutely for a moment, before she dropped her head and turned away.

Back in the car, Leslie sat shivering behind the wheel, staring straight ahead and waiting for the heat to thaw her fingers and toes. Eventually, when her circulation had returned, she pulled away from the curb, but as she turned to head back down Old Church Road, she had no doubt that Porter knew exactly what had happened the night the woodshed caught fire, and that whatever had happened was tied to Adele's death. She also knew nothing would ever make him admit it.

It was full dark and pouring buckets when Leslie finally pulled into the drive, and unfortunately, she hadn't planned for either, too distracted as she bolted out of the house with Landis Porter's address to grab an umbrella or turn on the porch light. Pulling her jacket up over her head, she darted for the front door and nearly tripped over the packet lying on the doormat.

Inside, she tossed her keys and purse on the stairs, flicked on a lamp, slipped out of her coat, and dropped into the nearest chair. Letting her head drop back, she closed her eyes, wishing now that she'd never gone to Level Grove. All the way home, and even now, all she could think about was the telling look on Annie Mae's face as she stood on Landis Porter's sagging front porch. She had no idea whether Annie Mae was Porter's wife or his housekeeper, but she was certain the woman knew something. Maybe if she went back to talk to her when Porter wasn't around, though when that might be she really had no idea. The man was almost ninety; he was hardly likely to schlep off to work every day.

God, she really didn't want to think about it right now. In fact, she wasn't even sure she still wanted to know what had really happened to Adele. It was all too dark and too sad. She was all stocked up on sadness these days; she didn't need any more, especially when it had nothing to do with her. Opening her eyes, she glanced down at the manila envelope resting heavily in her lap. With Christmas around the corner, she had just assumed it was junk mail, a catalog of some sort. Now she noticed the envelope was completely blank, no address of any kind.

Tearing open the back flap, she shook out the contents. Her breath caught as the stack of pages slid into her lap, astonished to find Jay's manuscript and a brief handwritten note.

Leslie,
    You've obviously made up your mind so I won't try to change it. I've enclosed Adele's story, or at least the part I know. It be-

longs to you. Burn it if you want, but I hope you'll read it first. Maggie never stopped trying to get me to write again. Part of me wonders if this wasn't what she had in mind all along. I can only say, again, how sorry I am about the way things turned out. None of this was what I wanted.—Jay

Leslie's belly churned as she read the note for the third time. A part of her wanted to believe what he said, that before Maggie died she had somehow set all this in motion, that what Leslie had initially taken as betrayal was all just part of some great cosmic plan. But the other part, the part that couldn't forget the look on Jay's face when he saw her holding the manuscript, wasn't ready to accept that.

And yet, the pages beckoned.

It seemed she wasn't as done with her fixation on Adele's death as she'd like to believe, or with Jay either.

Chapter 37

Adele

You never love a thing more than when you must leave it.

I am miles now from the green girl I was, that foolish girl who sat in Susanne Gavin's parlor with her eyes on the carpet. I have scars now, wounds that worked themselves so deep into these bones that they live with me still, oozing fresh beneath all this rocky soil.

Too late, I learned how tightly we hold to things, to the stuff and the lives we gather around us. When the time comes—when the smoke comes—letting go is impossible. We grasp and claw, unable to relinquish what has been our breath, our heart, perhaps even our ruin.

Henry is due back from Smithfield tonight. He's been gone three days, talking to some men he knows about a new way to cure tobacco. I have missed him keenly. We made up before he left, or rather, I decided to let the matter of the boys drop. When it comes down to it, Henry's right. I have no say in how Maggie is raised or who she's allowed to run with.

The cottage is quiet, the supper dishes put away, a plate warming on the stove. I've put up my hair the way he likes, and I'm wearing my best dress, the one he brought back from Raleigh for my birthday.

Jemmy is finally asleep, all arms and sun-browned legs sprawled over the settee, pajamas rucked up around his little belly. It startles me sometimes to see how he's grown, how his limbs have stretched and the baby fat has started to melt away. He's growing into such a solemn little man, his manner so like his daddy's that at times it takes my breath away to see it.

I scoop him up in my arms and carry him upstairs. He smells of baby shampoo, milk, and my molasses cookies. His mouth puckers at nothing as I tuck the covers up under his chin, a leftover from the thumb-sucking he seems suddenly to have outgrown. My heart swells as I finger springy bronze curls still damp from bath time, and I wonder if Mama ever felt like this. Like she might burst with all the love that seems to gush up from nowhere. He's mine—mine and Henry's—not an heir, but a son. Our son.

Henry.

After all the years—and all the hurt—my heart still turns over at the thought of him. When he is away I can almost believe I hate this place, its lies and charades and heart-tearing sacrifices. And then he comes home, and I know why I have stayed, why I'll always stay.

Back downstairs, I hunt for something to do. I pick up my sewing, then a book, but my nerves are too thin for sitting still. I decide to lay a fire, but the wood's run low. I tie an old scarf over my head and button on my coat, then cock an ear at the bottom of the stairs. If I hurry I can fetch the wood and get back before Jemmy wakes. Poor lamb, he's still so afraid of the dark.

I can see my breath as I make my way to the woodshed behind the cottage. Moonlight bounces off the old tin roof, thin and white. I shiver and pull up my collar, but not from the cold. There's a kind of prickle between my shoulders. Mama used to call it the third eye. I turn to see Susanne at her window. She has taken no pains for Henry's homecoming, I see. With the light behind her she looks like a ghost, her face pale as ash, her hair floating out around her head like a storm cloud.

She sees me, I know, in all this moonlight. We cannot make out each other's eyes, but the effect is the same, an instant of loathing so pure it feels like a live thing crackling across all that dark distance. It's me who looks away first, me who hurries off to the shed with my basket, pretending I've imagined it all.

The woodshed is ancient, windowless and so rickety it sags on its dry-stone foundation. Henry talks about knocking it down and putting up a new one, but there's always something else to do. For now it keeps the wood dry, but only just.

A plank of oak bars the door. I shove my basket into the crook of my arm and wrestle the thing out of its rusted iron brackets. I'm almost inside when I hear something, a sound that might be wind in the trees or might be voices. I slip around the side. There's no one there, just an old tin bucket and a pile of filthy rags. I leave them for now, too cold and too mindful of Jemmy to think of putting them away.

But my legs won't move. I can't shake the feeling that someone has been there, is still there. I listen to the quiet beneath the wind, an uneasy kind of quiet, the sound of bodies gone still, breaths being held. The hair on my neck bristles. More silliness, I tell myself as I turn back to the shed and step inside.

The moon spilling through the open door is all the light I have as I make my way to the pile of seasoned firewood Henry has put by for the winter. I have just picked up the first log when the wind slams the door and darkness swallows me. Before I can move, I hear the plank drop into its brackets, a telling thud that makes my blood run cold. I grope my way back to the door, already knowing I will find it bolted from the outside. I call out but there's no answer, just the fading scrape of feet, and then silence.

It's several minutes before I catch the first whiff of smoke, before my heart leaps into my throat and I realize what's happening. I grope at the door, but there is no handle, nothing at all to grab hold of. I throw my weight against the wood, screaming in a voice that isn't mine, a voice made wild by rage and panic. No one comes.

I will myself to go still, to get my bearings. Moonlight leaks through the chinks in the walls, turning the air gray in places. For the first time, I see the fingers of smoke curling between the bone-dry boards and remember the pail and the rags, and I know sickeningly why they were there. I wonder if Susanne is still watching from her window. And I wonder where Maggie is.

It's a hideous thought, but there's no time to complete it. There is the sudden, oily stench of kerosene, then a roaring rush of wind as the back wall goes up. The flames spread like liquid, lapping up the tinder-dry walls and a winter's worth of firewood. The air boils around me, hot and thick as tar. When the coughing starts, it nearly drives me to my knees. I try again to call for help, but I realize, very soon, that I must choose. Breathe or scream. The smoke is too thick now to do both.

Behind me, I hear the pop of wood knots as they catch and explode, spewing sparks into the searing air. There is a peculiar kind of wind in the tiny space, a storm of smoke and ash, and my mind flashes back to fist-thumping sermons about fire and brimstone and the wages of sin.

My eyes are streaming now, my face running with tears and sweat and mucous. There is a hideous rasp in my ears. It takes a moment to realize it's the sound of my own breath, a wet grinding that fills me with terror. I drag my scarf down over my mouth and nose, but it does no good. I can see a little, but only because the flames are raging on three sides now, splashing my shadow against the door in a grotesque sort of dance. I hurl myself at it, clawing at the wood until I feel splinters drive beneath my nails. The door holds. There is nowhere to go.

When my legs buckle, I go down like a sack of corn. I don't get up again. There's no reason to get up. How long, I wonder? How much will I feel—and for how long?

I need to pray. But I can't pray. I can't think. There's something I need to remember, something I need to do. I reach for the thought, but it slips away, lost in the ashy air. I've stopped coughing, or if I haven't, I can no longer hear it. The sounds around me begin to grow faint, the smoke like a blanket, curling tighter and tighter. There isn't much time now, I know. I think of Henry and Maggie and Mama. Pray, I tell myself. Pray now, before it's too late. Instead, I wonder who will comfort my poor boy when he wakes up alone in the dark.

Chapter 38

The smoke has already taken me by the time Henry arrives.

I feel no pain, only a queer sense of detachment from my arms and legs, as Henry yanks me out into the cold, clear night. His hands are on me, on my face, in my hair, his lips moving silently, prayerfully, urging me back to him. But I am gone, capable now only of watching his misery, as if I am caught in a dream from which I cannot seem to wake.

Finally, he seems to understand. It is a terrible moment. I long to touch his shoulder, his face, to comfort him, but that is no longer possible. He is as out of reach for me as I am for him. How cruel it seems to me in that instant, that when the body dies, the heart must live on, that in that quick and quiet snuffing of our flesh, love turns to loss, and joy to ache, unfinished things we must carry through our separate eternities.

Henry's cheeks are soot streaked and shiny with tears as he carries me to the barn and locks me inside. His clothes are scorched, his hands and face already blistered. By the time the police arrive, the fire has begun to burn itself out; only a heap of smoldering wood remains, coughing occasional showers of spark up into the breeze. He's numb as he answers their questions, his eyes hollow as they continually shift back to the barn, where he has left me cocooned in an old wool blanket.

When they leave he goes to the cottage to check on Jemmy, asleep like an angel in the narrow bed we used to share. He tucks the poor little thing up in a blanket and scoops him onto his shoulder, then carries him downstairs and across the lawn. Everything in me rails when I see what he means to do. I don't want my boy in that house, or anywhere near that woman, but he cannot hear me, and so up the stairs he goes. Maggie doesn't stir when he pulls back the covers and slips him in beside her. I wonder what she will think when she wakes to find Jemmy beside her—and what Susanne will think.

He comes back to the barn then and locks himself in with me. He wipes the soot from my face and touches his lips to mine, whispering all the while that he is sorry, so very, very sorry. I almost believe I can smell the smoke clinging to his clothes as he draws up a chair and drops down beside me. I cannot, of course; I am beyond such things, but there is some small measure of comfort in feeling connected, even by this tenuous thread.

He's still at my side when the sun comes up.

He has watched over me through the night, while I have watched over him. I have never put much stock in the idea of messages from the beyond, but now I find myself praying that there was at least some tiny shred of truth in all the charlatans back home, with their candles and their crystal balls. In the only way I know how, I beg him, and the angels, too, to watch over my boy, to keep him safe from whoever bolted that shed and struck the match, to please, please, send him to Mama.

Chapter 39

Bad news always did travel fast in Gavin.

There's an article in the paper the next morning, but I am not mentioned. No one knows I was inside, and Henry does not tell. I am glad he doesn't. No good can come from the questions that would arise. I am gone, and nothing will change it.

Hollis Snipes has already seen the paper when Henry walks into his hardware store to buy a load of pine. Hollis guesses he means to put up a new shed, and Henry doesn't tell him any different as they load the boards into the back of the old truck. He waits 'til the sun is down and the hands have all gone home for the day before locking himself in with me again and setting to work.

He measures and saws and hammers all night, sanding and fussing over the join work like he's building a bed instead of a box to bury me in. His hands are bandaged now, but he seems not to feel his burns as he works. When he's finished, he lines the inside with the quilt from our bed and shuts me up inside.

He sleeps for an hour or two then, until the sun comes up, his backside on a stack of old wood crates, his head on the lid of my box. It's the first sleep he's had in two days. He looks awful when he finally wakes up. His face is ashen, his eyes red rimmed with smoke and sorrow, smudged with the blue-gray shadows only grief leaves behind. At the cottage he changes clothes and downs a cup of coffee. Maggie doesn't ask any questions, just gulps noisily and blinks two big fat tears when he asks her to look after Jemmy a while longer. She knows all too well what has happened and what her father has been about.

He drives me to the top of the ridge then—to our place. It takes every ounce of strength he has left to dig that hole and get me in it. He's on his third shovelful of dirt when he begins to sob in earnest, the reality of the deed striking full force as the top of the box begins to vanish into the earth. It's a terrible sound, like a wounded animal, or a very young child, and I'd give anything then to touch his face once more, to say I'm sorry for leaving him.

He stays there on his knees until he's all cried out and his lips are blue with cold, one hand clutching his book of poems, the other resting on the fresh mound of earth that covers me. I can feel the warmth of his fingers leeching through the soil, way down into my bones, but I want him to go now. He needs warmth and food and sleep. There's nothing more to be done for me.

Chapter 40

Leslie

Leslie flipped over the last page and closed her eyes, her throat scorched with unshed tears. She had no idea what time it was; she hadn't been out of the house in two days, unable to step away from the pages Jay had left on her doorstep.

She saw now why he'd earned the moniker Master of Heartbreak. He had done an amazing thing, capturing both the joy and the sorrow of Henry and Adele's love, page after page of emotions so raw they stung, spun out in a voice that felt like memory. She had devoured it all greedily: the grief of a girl longing for home, the awakening of a young woman's heart, the joy and shame of a love that should not be, and finally, a life cut tragically short.

Leslie shivered as she recalled the fire chapter. A young mother deliberately murdered, and in such a hideous way—it was inconceivable. But fires didn't start out of nowhere, and doors didn't bolt themselves. Her mind and stomach were churning again. In her mind she could feel the splinters wedging beneath her own nails, taste the smoke at the back of her throat.

And yet he'd never so much as hinted that he thought Adele's death might have been anything other than an accident. In fact, he'd gone to great lengths to dissuade her from that notion. When had he changed his mind? He'd mentioned once that Maggie had a secret that tormented her in her last days. He also said he was glad she'd never told him what it was. She had asked him why but hadn't given his response much thought. Now, suddenly, it made her uneasy.

Sometimes when you love a person there are things you'd rather not know.

Like it or not, she needed to put her personal feelings aside and talk to Jay, tell him about her visit with Porter and try to enlist his help. If they went back together maybe Jay could persuade him to talk, or maybe he could just turn one of his charming smiles on Annie Mae, like he'd done in Charleston with Emilie Fornier.

Leslie was halfway across the lawn when she realized what she must look like—her baggiest sweats, zero makeup, hair scraped up in a messy bun—but then it really didn't matter anymore what he thought of her looks.

She was glad to see the cottage lights on as she broke free of the trees. She knocked briskly, then, on a whim, pulled the pins from her hair and shook it loose. Her belly clenched when she heard the deadbolt unlatch.

"It's me," she said ridiculously when he opened the door.

There was a long pause, then finally, "What can I do for you, Leslie?"

She swallowed hard, struck by the chill in his tone. "What you wrote—it's good."

There was a stretch of quiet, the harsh silence of things not said. Finally he pulled the door open and turned back to the parlor, leaving her to follow.

"In fact, it's wonderful. But I need to know more."

"There isn't any more."

"Of course there is. Fires don't start by themselves."

Jay glanced up, then looked away, saying nothing.

"You have to finish it, Jay."

"As far as I'm concerned, it is finished."

"Then why put me through this? Why give it to me if you mean to just leave it hanging?"

"Because Adele Laveau is part of your family's history. Her story belongs to you."

"But I've only got part of it."

Jay shoved his fists into his pockets, his face unreadable. "I gave you what I had, Leslie, everything I know. I'm not inventing an ending so you can feel better."

Leslie fiddled with her jacket zipper, wondering just how far she was willing to take the conversation. "In your note you said you were starting to wonder if Maggie hadn't meant for you to write Adele's story all along. If that's true, don't you think she'd want you to finish what you started?"

A tick appeared along his jaw, his eyes suddenly hard. "If she wanted me to finish, she would have told me the rest. She didn't, so there's an end to it."

"No, it isn't. Adele was murdered. We both know it, and until now I didn't think we'd ever know—"

Before she could bring up Landis Porter, he was heading for the kitchen. Again, she followed, watching with folded arms as he poured himself a mug of coffee. He didn't offer her one.

"I guess I'm confused, Leslie. Is this about me, Maggie, or Adele?"

"Why can't it be about all three?"

"Because a few weeks ago you stood here and made me into some kind of bastard for writing it. Now you want me to finish it? Forgive me for being surprised that you now want to give me your blessing—or to suppose that I'd need it."

"I need to know how it ends."

"You know how it ends. She died. Isn't that enough?"

"I have to know who would do such a hideous thing and why."

Jay set down his untouched mug. "I can't help you."

"But you can. I found Landis Porter. He's one of the boys who—"

"Leslie, I'm leaving Peak."

Leslie felt the air go out of her as the words penetrated. "Leaving?"

"It's time for me to move on."

"What about the winery?" she blurted, fighting an annoying sting of tears. "We were supposed to open in the spring."

"I've had a change of plans."

Leslie's fists curled at her sides; anger was safer than tears. "What happened to all the sermons about Maggie and her dreams for Peak? Was it all just bullshit?"

"Leslie, let's not do this."

A thought suddenly struck her. "You said you had taken an advance on the book, but you gave the manuscript to me. I assume that means you're running out on that too?"

"That's my problem." Moving past her, he opened the back door, a clear invitation for her to leave, then scooped an envelope off the table and handed it to her. "This is for you."

Leslie's stomach went queasy when she saw the logo for Goddard and Goddard. Tearing back the flap, she shook out several carefully folded pages marked with tiny Post-it flags. She scanned them, frowning at the words *Grantor . . . Grantee . . . free and clear.*

Finally, she looked up. "What is this?"

"What should have been yours from the beginning. Good-bye, Leslie."

Chapter 41

Leslie was too dazed to know what she was feeling as she marched back from the cottage, dry brown leaves crunching noisily underfoot, Jay's quitclaim deed half-folded, half-crumpled in her hand. How could he just leave, turn his back on everything they'd accomplished, and just move on, as he put it? He was the one who'd done the betraying, not her, and instead of trying to figure out how to get past all that and find a way to make what was left work, he was running.

But it was her fault really.

She had known from the beginning that giving in to her feelings for Jay meant risking more than her heart. She just hadn't expected it to hurt so much. She hadn't had a chance to tell him about Landis Porter, she realized, as the lights from the house became visible through the trees. It didn't matter now, she supposed. He'd made up his mind.

The wind kicked up as she reached the back porch, sharp and icy, whistling through the bare branches. She eyed the sky, low and flat and pewter gray, hinting at the possibility of an early snow.

Fabulous.

"Leslie . . ."

For a moment she didn't recognize him, hovered blue lipped and shivering against one of the porch columns. Then, when she did, she was too stunned to move. From the time she was old enough to re-member, Jimmy Nichols had been a bull of a man, square built and as hard as nails. Now he seemed little more than a scarecrow, his skin the color of putty, his thick head of near-black hair grizzled and threadbare, his clothes hanging on him like rags.

"I thought I told you not to come back." She could feel the old panic creeping in, her pulse thundering in her ears and at her temples. "I also told you there isn't any money. That hasn't changed."

"That ain't why I'm here, Baby Girl."

Leslie raised both hands as if to shield herself. "Stop calling me that!"

Jimmy blinked at her uncomprehendingly. "I've always called you that."

"And I have always hated it."

Their gazes locked then, old wounds oozing open. It was Jimmy who looked away first. He swayed slightly, grabbing tighter to the porch post.

Leslie stepped closer, testing the air for bourbon fumes. "How much have you had?"

His head swung heavily from side to side. "None . . . I . . . haven't had any."

She studied him through lowered lashes, noting for the first time his sunken cheeks and deeply shadowed eyes, his bone-white knuck-les wrapped for dear life around the porch column. My God, how had she not seen it before? He wasn't drunk; he was sick.

"Do you think you can make it into the house?"

Jimmy managed to nod. Taking his arm, Leslie led him inside, through the mudroom and the kitchen. By the time they reached the parlor, his lips were an unpleasant shade of lavender. Leslie pulled off his coat and sat him down.

"I can make you some tea," she offered lamely.

She took the weak nod of his head as a sign of agreement and disappeared into the kitchen, relieved to have a moment to collect her wits. While the water heated she opened two bags of Earl Grey with shaking hands and tried to remember how her father liked his tea. She honestly couldn't say. She only remembered how he liked his bourbon.

He was slumped forward when she returned, head resting in his hands. She set his tea before him and backed away, perching warily on the arm of a nearby chair.

He glanced from her to the tea, then back again. "Thank you."

Leslie nodded and took a sip from her mug. "There's honey in it. I didn't know how you took it."

"That's fine," he said, making no move to lift the mug.

"How did you wind up tracking me down, Jimmy?" she asked, when the silence became excruciating.

"I always do, don't I?"

"Yes, and you always want something when you do." It was a terrible thing to say, she knew, but their history was hard to deny.

Jimmy's mouth curled, half smile, half grimace. "If that wasn't the truth, I'd be hurt. As it is, I don't have a leg to stand on. I do want something from you."

Leslie barely digested the words, still shaken by the sight of him, his hollowed-out cheeks laboring like an old squeeze-box in an effort to fill his lungs, each spongy rasp sounding as if it were being squeezed through a straw.

"You're sick," she said softly. "Is it . . . bad?"

"Yes."

"How bad?"

"It's *that* bad, Baby Girl."

Leslie let the nickname go. "Have you . . . seen someone?"

Jimmy picked up his mug with shaking hands. "I'm taking . . . treatments."

"And your doctors are okay with you traipsing up and down the eastern seaboard?"

"I'm a grown man. I don't need permission to visit my daughter."

For an instant she caught a glimpse of the old Jimmy, sullen and spoiling for a fight with the world. It vanished as quickly as it came.

"I'm sorry you're sick," she said, startled to realize it was true.

"Don't be. We all get what we earn in this life."

Leslie squirmed, trying not to contemplate what that might mean. "Drink your tea before it gets cold," she said, to change the subject. God, he was so thin, his muscles wasted, his skin sallow and loose on his bones. "I could fix you something to eat—eggs and toast, maybe, or soup?"

At the mention of food Jimmy grew visibly paler. "The treatments don't leave me with much of an appetite."

"Do they know . . . ?"

"How long I've got? No. That's still up for grabs. I go back for tests in six weeks."

"Back where?"

"Connecticut. That's where the doctors are."

"But how did you . . ."

"One story at a time," he answered wearily. "Right now we're going to talk about something else."

"You said you wanted something from me. I'd like to know what it is."

Jimmy pulled himself up straight and met her eyes. "I want you to make up with Jay Davenport."

Leslie couldn't have been more stunned if he'd asked her to jump off the roof. "What do you—? How do you know about Jay Davenport?"

"What I know, and how I know it, isn't important."

"Jimmy—"

"I'm your father," Jimmy barked suddenly. "Do you think maybe you could stop calling me Jimmy, like I'm the guy who walks your dog?"

"I don't have a dog," Leslie fired back drily. "And why now, after all these years, do you give a damn what I call you?"

"Because *now* is what I've got." His voice lost its sharpness as he went on. "It's amazing what you find yourself giving a damn about when it's all you *do* have. Leslie, I've made enough mistakes in my life to know there are some things you can't walk back, and walking away from that man *is* a mistake."

Leslie stiffened. She didn't want to have this conversation with anyone, let alone Jimmy.

"I can take care of myself."

"Can you tell me you're happy? If you can look me in the eye and tell me you are, I'll leave right now."

The question made her throat ache. Not just the words, but the way he said them. "Why are you saying this? What do you want from me?"

"I want you to listen. There are things you don't know." He winced and briefly closed his eyes. "Who do you think arranged for me to have my own private team of doctors? Paid for me to stay up north all this time? Did you think I won the lottery, or put in a call to a couple buddies from prison? Think about it."

Leslie stood but dropped back into the chair when the room began to tilt. "Are you telling me that Jay—? Why would he do that?"

"Well, he didn't do it for me. That's for damn sure."

"I don't understand," she said, shaking her head. "How did he know you were sick?"

"The day after your shindig we had a little talk, with him doing most of the talking. He threatened to bury me out in the grape fields if I didn't keep away from you. Then I told him I was sick, that I had come to make things right with you. He must have believed me because he offered me a deal."

Leslie's eyes narrowed warily. "What kind of deal?"

"If I promised to leave you alone for a while and clean up my act, he'd send me to a doctor friend of his daddy's."

Leslie took a deep breath, then let it out in one long hiss. It simply wasn't possible, and yet the pieces were beginning to fall together; the sudden need for cash and the decision to sell Adele's story, the mysterious phone call from a friend of his father's. Jay had told her there was a family issue. She'd just assumed he meant his family.

"So the night you showed up with Rachel, you hadn't been drinking?"

"I had a couple snorts before I showed up, to help with the pain. At least that's what I told myself. The truth is I was trying to get up the nerve to face you. I didn't come to ruin your party, by the way, or to ask for money."

"Then why?" She hated the distrust that had crept into her tone, but old habits died hard.

"You're my daughter, Leslie, and I haven't seen you in almost seven years. I am human, no matter what you think." His voice was thin, his eyes bent on the carpet. "I know what you think happened the day your mother died."

Leslie shot to her feet, crossing the room to put as much distance between them as possible. "Don't say any more."

"We've never talked about that day."

"And we're not going to talk about it now."

"You think it was on purpose, that I wanted it to happen. That I . . . made it happen."

Leslie's palms were suddenly slick. "Please, don't do this."

Jimmy wasn't listening. His eyes were fixed and blank, lost somewhere in the past. "It was an accident. She grabbed my arm, probably to shake some sense into me, and I fell into her. She went down before I knew what was happening . . . with the scissors in her hand."

His face was the color of parchment as he continued, propped like a mummy against the sofa cushions. "For a long time I wasn't sure. I was pretty well lit. And after . . . well, I just stayed that way, relieved not to remember. Then a man looks you in the eye and tells you you're about to meet your maker. You get real clear when your hourglass is almost empty."

He glanced up, waiting. Leslie met his gaze without expression, her silence clearly wounding him more than anything she could have said.

"I didn't do it," he said finally, the words rushing out as if a levee had suddenly broken. "I've made myself remember it a million times, and I know now. I was lit and I was mad, but the fall was an accident. That's what I came to Gavin to say—that and nothing else. I don't expect you to forgive me. I can't forgive myself. What happened on those stairs was still my fault, just as sure as if I'd pushed her, and I have to live with that for as long as I have left."

Leslie sat down heavily. She was shaking, her clenched hands bone white in her lap. "Why are you bringing this up now?"

"Why do you think?" His voice broke then, shuddering with all the guilt and pain he'd been trying to outrun for so long. He dropped his head into his hands, his wasted shoulders hunched and shaking. "You're all I've got left, Baby Girl. I've ruined so much, for me and for you. I can't just . . . leave it like that."

She had never seen him like this, vulnerable and emptied out, devoid of excuses. Once she had been skilled at reading him, at spotting every lie and ruse, but years of separation had dulled that skill, and she found herself unarmed, forced to choose between blind trust and self-preservation.

"Well, you've said what you came to say. Now what?"

Jimmy looked as if he'd been shaken awake in the middle of a dream. "I don't know. I never expected you to listen."

"You didn't give me much choice."

"You have every right to hate me. I never gave you a damn thing, but before you kick me out, there's one thing I am going to give you, and that's a piece of advice. Fix this thing between you and Jay."

"How do you even know about . . . this thing?"

"He called up there to check on me, to make sure I was living up to my end, probably." He paused, turned his head, and coughed harshly. When he finally got his breath back, he went on. "When I asked how you were he said you two had fallen out. He wouldn't tell me what it was all about, but I got the feeling it wasn't his idea."

"Maybe not, but he certainly set it in motion."

Jimmy looked at her for a long moment, as if gathering his words carefully. "Fix it. Whatever it is, fix it. Don't be so stubborn that you miss a chance at happiness."

"It's a bit late to start offering fatherly advice, don't you think?"

Jimmy ducked his head in acknowledgment. "It is at that." Something soft and wistful touched the corners of his mouth as he regarded her. "You always were a tough little thing—nothing but breath and britches. And in all my life the only thing I ever saw you run from was me—until now."

Leslie squared her shoulders. "I didn't run. I chose to end a relationship with a man who didn't know how to be honest."

Jimmy scrubbed a hand through what was left of his hair. "I don't know what that means, and I don't expect you're going to tell me, but Leslie, honey, a man doesn't put himself out like he has for me for no damn reason."

Leslie shrugged.

"Do you love him?"

"No . . . maybe . . . I don't know. It doesn't matter. He's leaving."

Jimmy's dull eyes went suddenly sharp. "What do you mean, he's leaving?

"He's deeded his half of Peak over to me. He gave me the papers a few minutes ago."

"Why the hell would he go and do that?"

"He has other plans. And they don't include me."

He looked her square in the eye then. "Was that his choice or yours?"

"What difference does it make? It's done. Look, I know you're grateful for what he's done, but there are things you don't know, things that might change your opinion of him."

Jimmy lowered his head as another spasm of coughs racked him. When he finally looked up, his face was sheened with sweat and as pale as chalk. "I don't know anything about the man, except that he obviously feels something for you. He doesn't give a good goddamn about me, but he did what he did, and that's because of you."

Leslie's head was swimming. "You look tired," she said, to change the subject. "You should rest."

"I'm fine."

"I'm going to make us some soup. Will you at least try to eat some of it?"

He nodded. "There are some pills in my coat pocket. They help with the nausea."

Leslie stood and went to retrieve the pills. There were three bottles in the right pocket.

"It's the smallest one," he said, when he saw her holding all three. "The others are for the cancer. One's supposed to slow down the tumor. The other's supposed to slow down the pain."

She padded back to the couch, handing him the pills. "Are you . . . in pain now?"

"Not much."

She stood there, watching him fumble with the lid, hands trembling as he shook two pills into his palm and reached for the mug of cold tea. A wave of sadness washed over her at the sight of him, unsteady and spent, like a candle whose wick had burned down. He blurred for a moment, becoming a watery smear of browns and grays. She blinked and cleared her throat, then stepped to the window to peer out.

"Do you have a place to stay?"

"I've got a few bucks left. I'll find a place."

"It's starting to snow," she said thickly, as she watched the first lazy flakes drifting past the chilly panes. "You'll stay here tonight."

Chapter 42

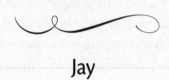

Jay

Jay glanced around at the piles of papers and books littering the floor of the tiny living room, marveling that a single man could collect so much junk in just five short years. Except those years didn't feel short; they felt like a lifetime, one that for better or worse, he was leaving behind. He'd kept his distance the last few weeks, from the Shivelys and from Leslie. It wasn't hard to keep busy. There was plenty to do before he pulled up stakes.

He tried not to think about where he was going or what he was going to do, mostly because he didn't have a clue. And sooner or later he was going to have to break it to his publisher that he wasn't finishing the book and that the advance money was gone. There'd be hell to pay, though just what kind he couldn't say. He'd never run out on an advance before.

Go ahead . . . Run . . . It's what you do.

Angie's words—thrown back at him when he told her he was leaving—had been playing in his head for days. And why not? They were true. He had run from his marriage, then from a wildly success-ful career; now he was running again, because it was somehow better to cut the cord himself than risk being hurt again. But maybe this time there was a twisted rightness to it all, a messy way of bringing things full circle. Leslie was back where she belonged. In that, at least, Maggie had gotten her way.

A knock at the door brought those thoughts up short. No one ever knocked on his door but Leslie. Picking his way around half-packed cartons, he opened the door, already bracing for an awkward scene. He nearly fell over when he saw Jimmy Nichols propped against the frame, face gray and glistening with sweat, despite the ground being patched with melting snow.

"What the hell are you doing here?"

Jimmy mopped his brow on his sleeve. "You gonna ask me in, or are we going to have this out on the doorstep?"

Jay looked him up and down once more before stepping aside. "You've got five minutes."

He watched in disbelief as Jimmy wheezed across the threshold and into the living room. Beneath a few lonely wisps of hair, his face was the color of modeling clay, his body all awkward angles, bones visible through his loose-fitting clothes. What the hell had the doctors been doing up there?

Jimmy braced himself with a hand on the back of the couch and took another swipe at his damp forehead. "You look almost as surprised as Leslie."

"We had a deal, Nichols. You were supposed to stay in Connecticut."

"My treatment's finished for now," he pushed out between breaths. "I needed to see my daughter. And you."

"What did you tell her?"

Jimmy smiled—or grimaced. Jay wasn't sure which. "Everything, including how you threatened to kill me if I bothered her."

"And you have bothered her."

Jimmy shrugged, clearly unfazed. "I figured the worst you could do was make good on your threat. And what with already dying, well . . ."

Jay's fists curled instinctively. "You think this is a joke?"

"Easy, Rambo. I'm here by invitation this time. Leslie and I struck a truce, and I plan to make good on it. There'll be plenty of things to regret when I die. Leaving things a mess with my little girl isn't going to be one of them. It's too bad you can't say the same."

Perhaps for the first time in his life, Jay understood what it meant to *see red*.

"Where do you get off waltzing in here like father of the year? Because you managed to stay sober for two whole months?"

Jimmy's smirk vanished. "I'll never be able to repay you for what you did, Davenport, though I'm guessing right about now you wish you hadn't bothered. But since you did, I'm going to set you straight about some things. When I'm done you can knock my teeth down my throat if you still want to."

Jay was only half listening, distracted by the way Jimmy had begun to waver on his feet. He didn't give a damn what happened later, but he wasn't about to let the old man keel over in his living room.

"Sit," he ordered gruffly. "You don't look so hot."

Jimmy sagged down onto the couch and briefly closed his eyes. When he opened them again he seemed to notice the mess for the first time.

"You going somewhere?"

"Leslie didn't tell you?"

"I wanted to hear it from you. You're walking away from a good thing, son—a sure thing."

"I assume you mean Leslie?"

"You tell me. All I know is, you started something, and now you want to bail."

Jay shoved his hands in his pockets, glaring. "Are you done playing Yoda?"

"I'm not playing anything. I'm trying to figure out what the hell you two are doing. You were no help on the phone, and my daughter won't tell me anything."

Jay was beginning to regret ever letting him in. "Look, I get that you feel the need to swoop in here and make up for all the shit you've done in your life, but it's more complicated than that."

"I'm guessing it was your fault."

"Why would you guess that?"

"Because if it was her fault you wouldn't be packing up everything you own right now and hightailing it out of town. And because you won't look me in the eye."

Jay tried to force his eyes to Jimmy's. It was no good. The bastard had read him like a book. What the hell was he supposed to say? *I can't stay because your daughter hates my guts? It kills me to know I've lost her and I've got no one to blame but myself*? He wasn't saying that, not to this man.

"I lied to her," he blurted instead. "When she found out, she blew up."

"Told you where to head in, did she? You married?"

Jay shook his head. "No, nothing like that. I thought I was protecting her."

"Protection isn't what she needs, son. She's tougher than you think."

"I'm finding that out. I tried to explain, but she wouldn't listen."

Something like a smile flitted across Jimmy's ashen features. "Girl always was stubborn, probably a little light in the trust department, too. You can thank me for that."

"So what am I supposed to do?"

"Say you're sorry."

"I have."

"Then say it again."

"And if she doesn't want to hear it?"

Jimmy thought about that for a moment, fingers scraping at the gray stubble on his chin. "Well," he said finally, leveling his gaze on Jay. "That falls directly under the heading of your business, but if it were me—I'd stick around 'til she did."

Leslie was nowhere in sight when Jay walked into the tasting barn, despite Angie's assertions that he would find her there. Circling a large stack of boxes labeled FRAGILE—the tasting glasses, he guessed—he eyed the walls, admiring photos Leslie had taken of the old mule exchange and fire station. She really did have an eye.

"Well, well, I certainly didn't expect to see you here."

Leslie's voice came from behind him, cool and more than a little distant. He turned to find her in the doorway of the storage room, a hammer in one hand, a box of nails in the other.

"I figured it was time we talk."

"Is there anything to talk about?"

"That's what I came to ask you. The photos are a nice touch, by the way. The locals are going to eat it up."

"That's the plan. So?"

Jay stood staring, surprised at how much he'd missed seeing her face. "So?"

"You said we should talk," Leslie prompted tersely. "So talk."

"You're not going to make this easy, are you?"

"I'm not inclined to, no." She took a stool at the bar and laid down her tools. "But I will listen, as long as it has to do with you staying."

"You don't need me. The tough stuff's behind you." He scanned the beamed ceiling a moment before bringing his gaze back to hers. "Why don't you sign the papers, Leslie? I don't want to sell to a stranger."

"Then don't."

"You sounded like your father just then."

"He told me he went to see you a few days ago. I'm sorry about that. He shouldn't have bothered you."

"Is he bothering you?"

Leslie shook her head, and for a moment her mask slipped. "He's too sick to bother anyone."

"That's not entirely true," Jay shot back, wanting to lighten the moment. Her scorn was so much easier to take than her sadness.

"He was sick the night of the party," she said, ignoring his attempt at humor. "But then, I guess you know that. I suppose I should thank you for what you did. I'm just still trying to figure out why you did it."

"Let's not do that now. The man needed help and I knew a doctor. Frankly, I'm surprised you don't want to wring my neck."

Leslie lifted vacant eyes to him. "No, I . . . needed this time . . . before he's too sick to say what he needs to."

"Is he . . ."

Leslie cut him off. "He goes back in six weeks. We'll know more then. In the meantime, he's staying with me."

Jay studied her face a moment, half-hidden behind a curtain of dark hair. There were shadows beneath her eyes that he hadn't seen since she first arrived. "Your plate's pretty full. Are you going to be able to handle it all?"

She shrugged and pushed back her hair. "I have to. This is my life now. I own a winery, and my father has cancer. I wasn't here for Maggie—I can't not be here for him too."

They sat quietly for a time, each seemingly fascinated by the grain in the varnished oak bar top. It was Jay who finally broke the silence.

"Your father thinks I should hang around until you forgive me."

"I'll bet," she answered curtly. "He's big on forgiveness these days."

"What do you think?"

"I think you should stay whether I forgive you or not. You started something here long before you met me, and I don't just mean the winery."

Jay's spine stiffened. "If that's a reference to the book, I'd prefer to change the subject."

"You took the advance. Why would you take the money if you never meant to finish it?"

"Why do you think?"

She looked away then, folding her arms on the edge of the bar. "You're going to wind up in court over this."

"Quite possibly. It won't be the first time I've ended up on the wrong side of a judge."

Leslie shot him an incredulous look. "You think this is a joke?"

"Far from it, but it is what it is. I did what I thought was right, and I'm okay with that."

She didn't answer right away, just stared at him in the bar mirror, as if working out her words very carefully. Finally, she spoke, her eyes probing places he didn't want her to go. "If you did know the truth— if there was a way to find out what really happened that night— would you finish it?"

"No."

His answer was immediate, too sharp, perhaps, but she needed to understand that for him it was over. He'd gone as far as he was willing to go. He'd been there the day they put Maggie in the ground, burying her ghosts along with her, and that's how he wanted it to stay.

"Besides," he added. "We both know there's no way for that to happen."

Leslie swiveled her barstool around to face him, green eyes bright with suppressed excitement. "What if I told you I could help you?"

"Help me?" Jay fixed her with a look of astonishment. "Leslie, your plate is full. Your father's sick. You've got a winery to open in ten weeks. You don't have time to save me from debtor's prison."

"I can promise you, the last thing on my mind is saving you from anything. This is about finding answers to a bunch of eighty-year-old questions. And I don't believe it's as impossible as you think it is. In fact, I'm pretty sure I've already found the man who can help us."

Jay stared at her uncomprehendingly. "What man? What are you talking about?"

"His name is Landis Porter. He was one of the boys the police picked up the night of the fire."

"Who, if memory serves, they wound up letting go. Leslie, if he couldn't tell the police anything that night, what makes you think he'll be of any help now?"

"Because I saw his face when I told him why I had tracked him down. He knows something, Jay. I'm sure of it. He just won't say what it is. He all but threw me off his porch."

"And this is the man you think is going to answer all your questions?"

"Maybe, if you went back with me. We could—"

Jay held up a hand, cutting her off. "I'm not getting dragged into this."

"But you are in it! You've got three-quarters of a novel written. All you need to know is how it ends. Instead of leaving, you should stay and find out."

"Leslie, I don't know how to make this any clearer. I don't want to know how it ends. I don't care."

She drew a deep breath and let it out forcefully. "Fine. Then stay to help me open the winery. I'm not helpless, but it would sure be easier to do this with a partner."

"A partner," he repeated tightly. "And where does that leave us?"

She was hiding behind her hair again, hands knotted tightly between her knees. "I haven't changed my mind about us; I can't. But I don't think that should matter. We're adults. We can work together without it having to be messy. There was no *us* when I agreed to stay, and we did all right. It was only when we got . . . silly, that things went wrong. It doesn't have to be about us. It can just be about the wine."

Silly.

The word landed in his belly like a fist, brutal and without pity.

Was that what she thought, that they were just being silly? Jesus, he'd been a fool; the worst kind of fool, in fact, since this was hardly his first time getting punched in the gut. Still, Maggie would want him to see his commitment through. It was the least he could do after all she'd done for him.

"Six months," he said finally. "That gets the doors open. At the end of that time you sign the quitclaim deed and we go our separate ways—clean break, no arguments."

The proposal seemed to satisfy, though some small part of him had held out hope that she might protest the leaving part. Instead, after a curt nod, she gathered her hammer and nails and slid off her stool, leaving him to watch her retreat.

Chapter 43

Leslie

Angie set a mug of hot chocolate in front of Leslie, then slid into her own chair. "Okay, out with it," she said, after venturing a cautious first sip.

"Out with what?"

"With whatever's going on. You pop over here in the middle of the day, but you're a million miles away. Something's up, so let's have it."

Leslie stared into her mug, watching her marshmallows dissolve into a slick of pale froth. "I talked to Jay yesterday," she said, without looking up. "He promised to stay six months, to get us through the opening."

Angie nodded. "He told me this morning. He also told me your father was back and that he's pretty sick."

Her head came up then, her hands squeezed tight around her mug. "He's been paying for Jimmy's treatment all this time. Did he tell you that? With the money he got for the manuscript."

Angie's mug came down abruptly. "He sold the book?"

Leslie made a face. "Not exactly. He took the advance but never finished the book."

Two weeks ago, in a moment of weakness, Leslie had finally broken down and told Angie about the manuscript. She'd wanted only to be left alone to lick her wounds in private, and hoped spilling the whole ordeal would put an end to all the sidelong glances and not-so-subtle questions. Instead, Angie had doubled down on her attempts at reconciliation.

Angie looked alarmed now. "But he's *going* to finish it, right?"

"No. But the money's gone and he can't pay it back."

Angie scowled as she reached into the nearby bag of marshmallows and dropped a few more in her mug. "That doesn't sound like Jay. Why doesn't he just finish it?"

"That's what I keep saying, but it isn't that simple. Adele—that's the woman buried up on the ridge—has been dead almost eighty years. We think—or at least I do—that she died in a fire, but we don't know how or why."

"But you don't think it was an accident."

"No, I don't. And I don't think Jay does either. There was some kind of secret, something Maggie wanted to tell him before she died, only she never got around to it. He thinks it had to do with Adele's death."

"Has he said what he thinks it might have been?"

Leslie shook her head as she took another sip of cocoa. "He won't talk about it. It's like he gets squeamish every time I bring it up. He cuts me off or changes the subject. I just don't understand it."

"Maybe he's frustrated. Maybe he wants to finish the book but can't."

"But he could. I managed to track down a man I think could help us, but he won't talk to me. When I asked Jay if he'd go back with me to try again, he turned me down flat."

Angie was quiet for a time, running the ball of her thumb around the rim of her mug. "It sounds like Jay might not be the only one frustrated about this book not getting finished. That's a pretty big change of heart for you."

Leslie nodded sheepishly. Somewhere along the way she had simply stopped being angry, somewhere around chapter three, she guessed.

"You'd understand if you'd ever read those pages."

Angie popped a trio of tiny marshmallows in her mouth and stood to gather the mugs. "I don't have to. I was a fan long before I ever met him."

"I guess I'm a late bloomer."

"Do you love him?"

Leslie closed her eyes, shook her head. Why was everyone asking her that? "I can't."

Angie threw her head back and laughed, a throaty peal somewhere between amusement and disbelief. "You're not one of them, are you?"

Leslie felt vaguely annoyed. "One of who?"

"One of those women who think if they talk fast enough and long enough, they'll eventually drown out what their heart's telling them. You can't, honey. The heart wants what it wants. If you're in love with Jay Davenport, you may as well just look in the mirror and say so."

"And then what?"

"And then you make damn sure he stays."

Jay stood cool and expressionless on the back porch when Leslie opened the mudroom door a few hours later. He was holding what appeared to be a heavy carton of books.

"I'm bringing these back," he said in lieu of a greeting. "I found them mixed in with mine."

Leslie stared at the neatly packed carton, wondering why he was bringing it now. There was something final in the way he set it down just inside the door, a sense of loose ends being wrapped up, that made her look up at him questioningly.

"I also need to ask a favor," he said gruffly.

Leslie nodded, not trusting herself to speak.

"I've got some boxes over at the cottage that I brought down from the crawl space. It's junk, mostly, but I was hoping you'd come over and see if there's anything you want to keep before I haul it away."

A hot lump formed in her throat. She tried to swallow it, but it remained. "Been doing a little early spring cleaning?"

"Something like that. Can you come? I'd really like to get rid of them." He surprised her by smiling. "I'll feed you, if that sweetens the deal."

Leslie tried to ignore the little giddyup in her belly, warning herself just how fickle that smile could be. "Um . . . sure. Let me check on Jimmy and grab my coat, and I'll be over."

He was standing in the doorway when she reached the cottage, waiting for Belle to finish investigating a pile of soggy brown leaves. "Watch yourself," he warned as she stepped past him. "The place is a disaster."

She felt a sickening pang of dread as she looked around the tiny parlor. Everything the man owned seemed to have been yanked from its closet, shelf, or drawer: battered textbooks, laceless shoes, and other household wreckage, all ready for packing into the large empty cartons stacked by the front door.

"You've been busy," she said stiffly. "I thought you said you were staying."

"For six months, yes." He kept his back to her while he spoke, rummaging through a carton of old sweaters. "I figured it might be a good time to sort through some of this stuff while I've got a little downtime. Come spring there'll be lots to do for the opening, and then plenty of loose ends to tie up. The boxes I told you about are in that corner."

Leslie hurled a scowl at his back. She had hoped he'd have second thoughts about leaving. Instead, it seemed he was counting the days. She thought of Angie's advice—*make damn sure he stays*—and wondered how she was supposed to do that when he clearly already had one foot out the door. Wishing now that she hadn't come, she eyed the trio of boxes Jay had indicated, bulging with an assortment of lampshades, cookware, vases, and shoe trees. It was hard to imagine finding anything worth keeping in the tangle of castoffs. Still, she rolled up her sleeves and bent to the task, leaving Jay to his own boxes.

An hour and a half later she had finally neared the bottom of the last box. She lifted out the last two items, a dented teakettle and a small, flattish box. The teakettle she cast aside, only slightly more interested in the box. Its weight told her it wasn't empty, but years of heat and grit had glued the lid fast. Using the heel of her hand, she wiped away layers of dust until the words LA PALINA DE LUX appeared.

"Hey, is this yours?" she asked over her shoulder, giving the box a rattle.

Jay left a stack of old magazines to join her in the corner. "What've you got?" He took the box, wiping a bit more dust from the lid. "It's an old cigar box. And no, it isn't mine." Prying the lid loose, he peered inside. "Looks like an old sewing box."

After a brief, disinterested pick through its contents, he handed it back. Leslie poked at a tangle of spools, a cloth doll riddled with tarnished straight pins, a measuring tape and thimble.

"It isn't just a sewing box," she said softly, her eyes fixed on its contents. "It's *her* sewing box."

Jay heaved an impatient sigh, then turned on his heel and headed for the kitchen.

Leslie trailed after him with the box. "But this could be something."

"It is. It's a sewing box."

Leslie groaned. "You know what I mean."

She waited while he foraged for a Milk-Bone and tossed it to Belle, then waited again while he washed his hands, and tried again.

"I don't understand you at all. The day I found the manuscript you told me you were so haunted by Adele's story that the only way to get it out of your head was to write it all down. Now you don't give a damn about how it ends? That doesn't make sense."

"You think the answer's in that box?" he shot back, the familiar pulse ticking angrily at his jaw.

"I never said that. But every time I come anywhere near the subject, you bite my head off, walk away, or both, and I don't know why. I care about how Adele's story ends because of what you wrote. How can you not care at all?"

"You think I don't?" His eyes flashed briefly before he turned away, hands fisted on the edge of the counter. "The difference is I've had time to think it all through, to think about where those questions might lead. I was here, Leslie. I saw Maggie's face when she tried to talk about it."

But Leslie was barely listening, her attention fixed on the contents of the box: an old cloth tape measure, a small tin of buttons, a packet of needles, a hopeless tangle of spools. Then, near the bottom, a square of calico tied with a faded grosgrain ribbon.

"Jay . . . look at this."

His expression was dark when he turned, annoyed. She held up the neatly tied parcel, then laid it in her lap, setting to work on the ribbon with unsteady hands. When the knot finally gave way and the folds of cloth were peeled back, she stared down at a plain white envelope and a case of deep green velvet.

"What is it?" His voice had lost some of its edge as he came to stand beside her.

Leslie lifted the case, small enough to fit into her palm, fitted with a tiny metal hasp. Her heart thrummed as she flicked it open and lifted the lid.

"It's a necklace," she breathed, holding the pendant up, a tiny book of tarnished silver.

Jay took the necklace and laid it in his palm to examine it.

"It's a book locket," he said finally. "My grandmother had one. See that little notch? You just get your thumb in there, and pop." The clasp released with a neat metallic snick. He handed it back, letting the chain puddle in her palm. "Open it."

Her hands were clammy as she teased the wings of the locket apart. Her breath left her softly as a pair of faces appeared, the first a girl with dark hair and a mouth like a rosebud, the other a chubby-cheeked boy in a sailor suit, his head a mass of shiny-bright ringlets.

Leslie's eyes met Jay's, wide and full of questions. When it was clear he would say nothing, she teased the girl's photo from its tiny frame. She was hoping for some sort of identification but found a lock of hair instead. It was darker than ink as it spilled into her palm, as soft and fine as silk. Behind the second photo was another scrap of hair, a single copper ringlet.

"Two babies," she breathed, staring down at the mismatched locks of hair. "And we don't know what happened to either one."

Jay cleared his throat, a dry, uncomfortable rasp that got Leslie's attention. He had opened the envelope and was reading the yellowed but carefully folded pages, his eyes moving rapidly from line to line. Finally, he looked up, his face an astonished blank.

"I think we know what happened to one of them," Jay said, handing over the papers.

Leslie slumped against the back of the chair as she read the first line.

Contract to Secure Legal Adoption.

Horror took the place of confusion as she read on, her hands growing unsteady as she reached the document's end. The signatures at the bottom swam dizzyingly, but there was no mistaking what the paper meant. Slowly, methodically, she folded the single sheet back along its creases and laid it in her lap. Her head came up, eyes wide as they met Jay's.

"Maggie . . . was Adele's," she said softly.

"Yes."

"That was the secret, then, the thing Maggie never told you."

Jay's eyes shifted to the floor. "I don't think so. It was something else, something . . . worse."

"What's worse than learning your mother isn't really your mother, that the woman who gave birth to you gave you up to her rival?"

"The fire."

Leslie could only gape at him, trying to make sense of his response, of the uncanny stillness in his body as he stood looking back at her. And then, suddenly, she understood.

"You think it was her," she said quietly, rocked by the words even as they left her mouth. "All the times you wouldn't talk about it, that's what you were thinking, that Maggie set the fire, that she killed Adele?"

"She was a child, Leslie. Her father had a new family. Jealous children sometimes do desperate things. I don't want to believe it. God knows I've spent a year trying not to, but I saw her face, and I can't forget it."

Leslie stared at the locket, all apart now on the tiny kitchen table, and tried to imagine how Maggie must have felt about her father's new family—a family that could never really include her since legally, she belonged to Susanne. She tried to envision an eight-year-old girl bolting the shed door and striking the match, but it was impossible. Wasn't it? Or was it the story Landis Porter refused to tell?

"I guess I get why you didn't want to know. And why you won't finish the book."

"I'm sorry." Jay dropped his arms to his sides, then quickly recrossed them. "It's also why I tried to steer you away from the whole thing and why I didn't show you the manuscript. I hated the idea of you thinking what I did."

Leslie stood abruptly. "I need to get home," she said woodenly. She fumbled briefly with the locket, trying to get it back together, then backed away, leaving it where it was. "I need to feed Jimmy. And I need time to digest all this."

Chapter 44

Adele

Henry is sending our boy away.

I am relieved, mostly, though I know full well the toll his leaving will take on poor Henry. He waited so long for a son and now must give him up. Still, it is the wise thing to do, and the safe thing.

The morning he is to leave, Henry brings Maggie to the cottage to say good-bye. She's as pale as milk, and thinner than I remember, with a kind of frailty about her that is new and so very hard for me to see. Her lashes are wet with tears, clumped like dark stars about her smoky eyes as she stares up at her daddy, her mouth working in a soundless plea.

It breaks my heart to see her so tortured—even after all that has happened. She is too young to carry such grief, or such remorse, a child come face-to-face with passions she is too young to understand, but whose consequences she must now live with. I only hope and pray that one day she will learn to forgive.

Jemmy has no idea what is happening. He giggles gleefully when Maggie throws her arms around his neck, hanging on to him for dear life. When her daddy finally peels them apart, Maggie wails pitifully that it isn't fair. She doesn't understand why he must go, why she must lose someone else. She has lost too much already.

Henry is nearly out the door when Maggie rushes forward to press her beloved Violet into Jemmy's chubby hands. He gurgles happily, planting a noisy kiss on the doll's smooth porcelain cheek. Until today, Violet has been off-limits, but now, as I look at the doll's shiny dark ringlets and wide, unblinking eyes, at her rosy pout of a mouth, I suddenly understand the gesture. For Maggie, the doll is no longer Violet, but a tender keepsake, the only part of her that can go with him.

At the train station, Mama is already waiting.

Henry spots her instantly. But then, he would; folks always said I was the spitting image of her. Her eyes lock on Jemmy the minute she spies him, perched high on Henry's shoulders, his head of copper curls bobbing brightly above the rest. Her dark eyes suddenly swim with tears, but she manages to keep them from spilling. Mama always did know how to hold in a good cry. Lord knows, life's given her plenty enough practice. She looks tired; not old, but worn down, her once lovely face creased now and weary, a map of all her sorrows. And now I have given her another. I only hope Jemmy will atone.

He is wriggling like a fish in Henry's arms, clutching the already bedraggled Violet tight to his chest, suddenly shy in front of this woman who is staring at him so intently, a woman who looks somehow like his mother but is not. Mama reaches out a finger to brush back one of his curls, and he quiets, breaking into a broad, toothy grin. I'm startled to see how much he looks like Mama just then and sad that I have never noticed it until now.

When Mama's gaze finally shifts to Henry, there is blood in her eye, as if she believes he killed me with his own two hands. Henry says nothing, just stands there clutching the boy, his head bent low, as if he believes it too. Her eyes drag over him, glittering and slow, wanting to hate, to blame, but I see she cannot. She sees his sadness instead, the black grief he carries in his bones now, like a virus, and in that instant they are kindred spirits, allies in loss. She knows that he loved me. For Mama, that is enough.

The conductor is standing at the edge of the platform, periodically checking the large silver watch chained at his ample waist. Henry's spine stiffens at the sight of him. It's time to hand Jemmy over to Mama, and it's tearing him to pieces. Jemmy resists, clutching wildly at his father's suspenders, back arched stiffly in protest, eyes wide and uncomprehending.

"Go on now, son," Henry says gruffly, the first words he has uttered since leaving the house. "Go with your gran, and be a big boy."

But the words mean nothing to Jemmy. He keeps on with his struggling, then sets up a whine that echoes down the platform, catching the eye of several passersby. Henry tries again. This time Mama's arms wrap him up tight, cradling him against her brown wool coat, and for a moment I sting with jealousy, though I am not sure if this is because I am afraid my son will forget me, or because I wish it were me wrapped up in Mama's arms.

The conductor hollers, "All aboard!" through cupped hands. Henry stiffens, bracing himself against the words and what must come next.

"You'll look after the girl?" Mama asks, her voice harsh with pent-up tears.

Henry only nods, his eyes hidden by the battered brim of his hat.

"She can come to me, you know," Mama adds. "If you change your mind."

"I can't," he tells her, tugging the hat lower. "I have already explained why. Besides, she is all I have left now."

Mama bobs her head, her eyes full again. This time the tears spill unchecked, rolling fat and shiny down her cold cheeks. She blots them tenderly against Jemmy's curls, then sucks in a jagged breath as she reaches for the satchel Henry has packed with Jemmy's clothes. Her shoulders hunch miserably as she turns and takes a few shuffling steps. Then, at the last instant she turns and hurries back. It's a fleeting touch, Mama's lips to Henry's cheek, and then she is gone, hurrying away down the platform, my little boy perched stoically on her hip as she vanishes into the last car.

Henry watches, dry-eyed and broken, as the train grinds away from the emptied platform in a cloud of thick fumes, taking his son away forever. My heart wrenches beneath my ribs as I recall another day, another station, and the look on Mama's face the day she put me on that bus and sent me away, and suddenly I realize how very weary I am of good-byes—the ones I have been forced to say, and the ones I have been cheated of.

Chapter 45

Sending Jemmy away has finished Henry.

When he returns from the station he goes to his study and fills a glass with bourbon, and he just keeps right on filling it, day after day, year after year, until there is little left of the Henry I once knew. For a while I think the grief will kill him, but it doesn't. Instead, he has become a shadow, a man who wears his sadness like a skin, whose eyes are so vacant it's as if he moved out of his body the day I moved out of mine.

The years that follow are not kind.

With every day that passes he recedes further into his bottle, living in a blurry kind of dream, until it seems all that is left is the dying. He spends his days on the ridge, reading from his book of sonnets and staring at the gravestone he went half a state away to order in secret. Most nights, he takes his supper in the study, then sits nursing his bourbon, mooning over that silly wall of paintings until the last of the light is gone. He doesn't turn on the lamps then, just lights up one of those pipes of his and sits there smoking in the dark.

It's a pity to see him make such a waste of his life, a pity perhaps, though not quite a surprise. I see clearly now what I could not, or would not, back then, that Henry has always shrunk from the uncomfortable bits of life, retreating into his books or his tobacco—or into the arms of a woman who would love him blindly.

It would be a lie to say I suffer any remorse when Susanne is buried a handful of years later. Henry barely seems to notice. He is dry-eyed and stoic at the funeral, dutiful in his starched collar and good Sunday suit. He bows his head at all the right times, throws a handful of dirt when the preacher tells him to, mumbles thank you when friends file past with condolences. Maggie stands at his side, somber in her black dress and hat.

From that day forward she takes care of everything, hiring a woman to look after that great big house, and another to handle the cooking when Lottie's rheumatism finally gets too bad to stay on, all so she can spend every spare minute with her nose in her father's ledgers. Through all of it, she has been his rock, the glue that holds Peak together.

Henry can no longer be bothered. He pretends to take an interest, but it's Maggie running the show these days, Maggie doing the hiring and firing, Maggie holding the purse strings, and Maggie still giving her daddy all the credit. When Henry's drinking starts to take its toll, when he quits overseeing the fields, shows up late to market, loses half a year's crop to soft rot, it's Maggie who picks up the pieces, putting herself where grown men don't think she belongs, and besting them too, more often than not.

By the time she's eighteen she knows the business almost as well as her daddy, though whether that's to do with her love of Peak or with her sobering realization that without her it would all crumble, I cannot say. I only know it saddens me to see that so much has been heaped upon her strong young shoulders, and to see how quietly she bears it all. But then she has never had much choice.

Chapter 46

Leslie

Leslie stifled a yawn as she watched Jimmy scoop the last forkful of eggs from his plate. It was good to see him eat, good to see a little flesh finally beginning to stick to his bones. She pushed his untouched glass of orange juice toward him.

"You working out in the barn again today?"

"Yep." He paused to drain his coffee cup, then tossed his crumpled napkin onto his plate. "We finished the rest of the patio tables yesterday. Today we start on the benches."

"Buck says you've been a big help."

"Just trying to earn my keep, Baby Girl."

Covering her mouth, she swallowed another yawn. She hadn't been sleeping much these last few days. She had Jay to thank for that. The revelation that Adele had given birth to Maggie and then given her to Susanne to raise would have been enough to keep her awake, but then he'd tossed in his suspicions that her grandmother had purposely set the fire that killed her father's mistress. Now, every time she closed her eyes, she saw an eight-year-old Maggie carrying a bucket of kerosene.

"You finished with that plate?" Jimmy was on his feet, pointing to her half-eaten breakfast. "I need to get out there."

Leslie handed him her plate, watching as he moved to the sink and began to fill it. In all the years she had lived with Jimmy, she'd never seen him wash a dish. But then, so much about him was different now.

"Daddy . . ." She paused to clear her throat, reluctant to broach the subject she'd been putting off for weeks. "You need to remember that you're supposed to go back to Connecticut right after New Year's. You said six weeks, remember?"

Jimmy blinked at her as if he'd been roused from a dream. "I guess that is coming up," he said, tracing a finger around the rim of a juice glass. "Time flies—that's what they say, isn't it?"

"Daddy . . ."

Turning away, he slid the plates, one at a time, into the sink of soapy water. "Looks like we'll have to forget that new bottle rack. I'll call up and get the particulars on the appointments. Might need your help with the plane reservation, though. I don't know who to call. Jay took care of all that last time."

Leslie heard the hitch in his voice and suddenly it dawned. *He thinks I'm sending him away.* She stood and brought the mugs over, then turned off the tap. Her father's hands went quiet in the dishwater.

"I'll make the reservations, Daddy. Two of them."

Jimmy raised uncertain eyes to hers.

"Whatever the doctors find—whatever they tell you—I want to be there with you when you hear it. And then you're coming back here, and we'll deal with it together."

He broke then, his craggy face fracturing into a million miserable shards. She didn't know what to say. She had no idea if he was grateful, or relieved, or afraid. Probably he was all those things. At that moment, though, it only mattered that he was her father and he needed her. Wordlessly, she folded him into her arms, feeling the sharp bones beneath his skin, and simply let him cry.

Leslie had no idea how long they stood there holding on to each other, how many hoarse thank-yous Jimmy murmured against her cheek, or who was crying harder before it was all over. Five weeks ago she couldn't have imagined sitting in the same room with him, let alone living beneath the same roof. Now, for reasons she was only just beginning to understand, the thought of losing him filled her with a sense of loss that was hard to fathom.

She had blamed him for so much, some of it warranted, some not, and all the while he'd been blaming himself, torturing himself for his mistakes with even larger mistakes. Then, when it all finally unraveled, he had tracked her down one last time, not for the customary handout, but for a chance at redemption. He'd been willing to subject himself to her loathing, to risk rejection, because he needed to make amends, to make peace. What she had first considered a show of weakness had in fact been an incredible act of bravery.

After lunch, Leslie fired up the laptop. She had just settled in at the kitchen table, hoping to find a pair of cheap flights, when she heard the front door knocker. In the parlor she peered out the window, frowning when she saw the lime green Cadillac sitting empty in the drive. They never got solicitors out here. Turning the bolt, she eased the door open a crack, startled to find Jay standing on the front porch and to see that he wasn't alone.

"I found these two sitting in the driveway." Jay hiked a thumb toward the Caddy. "They said they're here to see you."

Leslie pulled the door full open, too stunned to manage a smile, let alone a greeting for Landis and Annie Mae. The old man was bundled in his same camouflage coat, a rust-colored scarf wound several times around his stringy throat. Beside him, Annie Mae stood with wide, watchful eyes, the gloved hand she kept on his arm at once protective and possessive.

"I been thinking about what you said the day you come up on my porch," Landis wheezed through lips that were chapped and slightly blue.

Leslie ignored Jay's frown, keeping her focus on Landis. "About the fire?"

"About the truth."

Annie Mae jerked her chin in mute acknowledgment.

"Well then," Leslie said. "I guess you'd better come in. I'll make some coffee."

In the foyer, Jay shot Leslie a dark look. "What's this about?" he hissed when they were out of earshot.

Leslie smiled grimly. "You heard the man. It's about the truth."

"Was this arranged for my benefit?"

"Yes, Jay, it was. Because I knew you'd be the one to find them sitting in the driveway and bring them to my door. But since you are here, why don't you give me a hand and make us all some coffee."

He said nothing more as he followed them to the kitchen. Landis moved slowly, unsteady on his feet. Annie Mae held fast to his arm, matching him step for halting step, as if she were an extension of him.

"Jay, this is Landis Porter, and Annie Mae—" She broke off briefly. "I'm sorry, I'm afraid I don't know your last name."

"Speights," Porter supplied gruffly. "Her name is Annie Mae Speights."

"Mr. Porter, Ms. Speights, this is my . . . my business partner, Jay Davenport."

Jay merely scowled, a scoop of coffee poised over the fresh paper filter.

Porter cleared a phlegmy throat, and weaving slightly as he made his way to the nearest chair, sagged into it. "Shall we get on with this, then, young lady?"

Leslie moved her laptop off the table and took the chair beside him. "Mr. Porter, I'd like to know what made you change your mind.

The last time we spoke, you chased me off your porch and told me never to come back. Today you're in a hurry. Why are you willing to help me now?"

"Not," he grunted. "But what you said—about the truth setting you free—it stuck with me. And it damn near burned a hole in Annie Mae. She wouldn't let it out of her teeth. Said it was time to come clean—time for both of us."

Annie jerked her chin again but said nothing.

"So you *do* know what happened—both of you?"

Landis and Annie Mae shared a furtive glance. Before either could reply, Jay arrived with a tray. The silence thickened while he poured out four mugs, then set out the cream and sugar. When he was finished he stood behind Leslie's chair, arms folded, waiting.

Annie Mae stirred two spoonfuls of sugar into one of the mugs and passed it to Landis, who cupped it unsteadily and sipped. His glasses steamed briefly. When they cleared, his eyes were fixed on Leslie.

"We was all just boys."

"Randall and Samuel were your brothers," Leslie supplied to bring Jay up to speed. "The other boys the police picked up that night."

Landis barely nodded. "We used to do odd jobs for Mrs. Gavin, chopping wood and such. It wasn't much money, but back then it was more than a lot of folks could get their hands on. Then one day she paid us each a little extra to bother that woman."

Leslie abandoned her own mug and sat up straighter. "You mean Adele?"

"I didn't know her name then, but yeah, the woman who lived in the cottage. We'd mess up her garden, or yank her clothes off the line and stomp 'em in the mud. She knew it was us, of course. She didn't like us much. Didn't like your granny running with us, either. One day she caught us all out behind the barn and gave us what for. Me and Annie Mae lit out, but my brothers, they never got past it, especially Randy. The way he saw it, a woman like that didn't have no place telling him what to do. Even if she was grown and taking care of old man Gavin on the quiet."

Annie Mae was staring down at her lap, fidgeting with the frayed finger of one of her gloves while her coffee went cold.

Leslie didn't bother to hide her surprise. "You knew Adele was Henry's mistress?"

Porter nodded, shaking loose an oily lock of hair so that it fell into his eyes. "Everyone knew. Only people liked the old man too much to talk about it. It was all pretty quiet until she had that boy."

"Jemmy," Annie Mae supplied, the first words she had uttered since her arrival. "His name was Jemmy."

"That's when the real talk started," Landis continued. "Didn't look nothing like his daddy, but we knew it for sure."

Leslie glanced between them. "How?"

Annie Mae pushed away her mug and folded her hands on the scarred oak tabletop. "Because I was there the day he was born. Mr. Henry was too, proud as any new daddy I ever saw." She swallowed hard and let her eyes slide to the window. "That's how they knew for sure—'cause I told."

Landis picked up the thread as if Annie Mae hadn't spoken. "Didn't take long for word to get back to the old man's wife. After that I guess she lost her mind. One day she called Randy up to the house and put a proposal to him."

It was Jay's turn to join the conversation. "What kind of proposal?"

"She offered to pay him fifty dollars."

Leslie blinked at Porter, uncomprehending. "Fifty dollars . . . to do what?"

Behind the thick glasses the old man's eyes fluttered closed. He dragged in a deep, wet breath. "To burn her."

Leslie was aware of the blood slowly ebbing from her limbs, of

Jay's hand closing hard on her shoulder, of the slow, heavy tick of the kitchen clock, but there were no words in her head, nothing that could convey the horror of what she'd just heard. If Porter noticed her distress, he gave no sign. He went on talking, as if having begun, he found himself unable to stop until he'd told it all.

"Randy offered to split the money three ways if we'd help him. We said we would. Fifty dollars was a fortune back then. It took five nights of waiting before she finally come out to the shed. Randy had the kerosene, and Sam brought a bunch of old rags. We waited 'til she was inside; then Randy counted to three and we all lit out—only I ran the other way. Reckon all those nights of waiting turned me chicken. I tore all the way to Annie Mae's and told her everything. She made me call the police. I didn't give my name or rat on anybody, just said there was a fire at the Gavin place. Then me and Annie Mae lit out on my bike to go back and wait for the engine."

For a moment Leslie thought she was going to be sick. "You let them do it," she whispered hoarsely. "You knew they were going to murder a woman, and you just let them do it."

Porter's narrow shoulders sagged. "They may've been my brothers, but one time I saw Randy beat a kid so bad he lost an eye, and he'd have done worse to me if I told. So yes, I let them do it. Been living with it ever since, too. That's why I'm here today, because I'm sick to death of living with it."

Leslie had gone from being physically unable to speak to simply having no idea what to say. Was she supposed to commend him for coming forward—now, when it was too late to help anyone? Comfort him for his years of guilty suffering? But no, Annie Mae was taking care of that. Her hand closed tight over the old man's blue-white knuckles, her eyes soft and full of feeling.

"Miss Nichols, I know what you think, but I been living with this man ever since my Minnie Maw died. I wasn't but sixteen when my pa kicked me out, couldn't cook or wash or nothing, but he took me in, took care of me. He's a good man who got caught up in a bad thing when he was young. He's done a lot of good since then. None of it can bring back that lady, but he would if he could, I swear it."

Jay's face was strangely pale as he stepped from behind Leslie's chair. "And where was Maggie when they started the fire?"

Porter raised damp eyes, clearly confused. "The girl?"

"Henry's daughter," Jay barked. "Where was she?"

"I guess she was in the house with her mama. How should I know?"

"You're telling us she didn't have anything to do with the fire?"

Porter's eyes shot wide. "Where in hell would you get a fool idea like that?"

Leslie took a breath so deep it left her dizzy. "It doesn't matter. What matters is that we finally know what happened that night, and why."

"Lots of folks wouldn't care to know," Annie Mae answered softly, her lower lip jutting thoughtfully. "Most folks just be happy to leave it all stay buried, couldn't bother themselves to learn what happened to a woman like that."

Leslie felt her protective hackles rise. "And what kind of woman would that be?"

Annie looked momentarily startled, then shook her head. "Oh no, ma'am, I didn't mean that. I helped Minnie Maw bring enough babies on the quiet to know that happens pretty regular. No, I mean not white."

Leslie's mouth hung open a moment. "I don't . . . I'm sorry . . . not white?"

Porter had been wiping his glasses on the hem of his shirt. He looked up now. "Sweet God in heaven, Annie Mae. The girl has no idea what you're talking about."

"He's right, Annie Mae, I don't."

Annie Mae squirmed uncomfortably, her eyes back on the gloves in her lap. "I mean, not white, Miss Nichols, just like I said."

Leslie blinked several times, then swiveled her head in Jay's direction. He looked almost as dazed as she felt. Not white? How was that even possible? She thought of the portrait over the fireplace, her grandmother's skin so smooth and pale, her features fine as porcelain. If Adele was Maggie's mother—and they had a document proving that she was—how could she have been anything but white? Unfortunately, it wasn't a question suitable for sharing with Landis and Annie Mae.

"But I've seen her picture," Leslie said instead. "She was—"

"The prettiest woman I ever saw when she grow'd up. Yes, ma'am, I'll give you that. Had that creamy skin and all that shiny hair. If it wasn't for that little boy coming along, she might have gotten by. Plenty of folks did back then, so they could get work, or schooling. Hard life, though, breaking off from your family, and scared to death all the time that you'll slip up and give yourself away. Passing, they called it. Fitting, I suppose, since it really was a kind of dying."

Leslie shook her head as the truth of it sunk deep. Adele Laveau had been of mixed race. By the standards of the day, that made her black, which meant, fair skin or no, Maggie would have been counted black as well, since the one-drop rule still applied in those days. And in the South, had it ever really stopped applying? Her head came up slowly as a new thought occurred.

"Did Henry know?"

Annie Mae nodded. "Oh, he knew all right. No way not to when the boy came. All curly headed and brown, he was. But Mr. Gavin wasn't one bit surprised when Minnie Maw put that child in his arms. He loved him right off. There wasn't no missing that."

A sickening possibility struck Leslie. "The night of the fire, was Jemmy—" She let her voice trail off, the words too awful to say aloud.

"No." It was Porter who chimed in, his voice thinner than before but emphatic. "The boy wasn't with her. She was alone."

"Mr. Gavin sent the boy away not long after," Annie Mae went on.

"To live with his grandmama, I expect. My uncle, he was a porter back in those days, said it had to be Adele's mama who carried him onto the train, because she favored the boy's mother so much. Said Mr. Gavin looked like he was about to break in two when he handed the child over. After, when the story went around about Adele's mama taking the boy back home, no one who knew better said different. And that was the end of it."

No one said anything for a long time. Annie Mae snuck a glance at Landis, who continued to study the floor, his slender shoulders heaving with the effort to breathe. Jay stood with his arms folded, clearly too numb to speak.

"Tell whoever you want," Porter wheezed at last. "I'm long past caring."

His lips were a deeper blue now, his skin waxy and gray. He needed to get home to his oxygen, and truth be told, Leslie was ready to be rid of him. Her head was already pounding, and she desperately needed time to digest the news and to contemplate this startling new branch on her family tree.

"Mr. Porter," she said, standing more abruptly than she intended. "I know you said you didn't come to help me. I'm also sure you can't understand why this was so important. Just know that it was, and that I'm very grateful to you both."

Annie Mae took her cue gracefully, lurching to her feet. Wedging a thick arm beneath Porter's, she helped him up from his chair. When she attempted to rewrap his scarf, he swatted her hands away and shuffled toward the door.

Chapter 47

Leslie glanced up when she heard the front door close. Jay flipped on a lamp and stood looking down at her on the sofa.

"Have you been crying?"

Leslie dabbed at her eyes. "No . . . maybe. Did they get off all right?"

Jay nodded grimly. "Annie Mae's driving, thank God. He looked awful."

"I'm sure that wasn't easy for him. Hell, it wasn't easy for me, and all I had to do was listen."

Jay squatted down before her, curling her chilly fingers in his. His hair was damp with melting sleet, the scent of winter still clinging to his jacket. "Do you want to talk about it?"

Leslie shook her head. "Honestly, I'm not sure I can. I have no idea what to think, let alone say. It's all so awful."

"Not all of it."

Jay's relief was palpable. While she'd been horrified by the grisly details of that awful night, Jay had been relieved to learn once and for all that his suspicions about Maggie had been unfounded.

"You're relieved," she said, a simple statement of fact.

"I'd be lying if I said I wasn't." He dropped down beside her on the sofa. "I've been grappling with those thoughts for more than a year, hating myself for having them, and yet never quite able to shake them. Now I get why your grandmother couldn't bring herself to tell me the rest. All that time I thought she was involved. Turns out just knowing what happened was enough."

"You think she knew it wasn't an accident, then?"

"She knew something. Maybe she overheard the boys talking or saw something the night of the fire. We'll never know."

"And the part about Adele being her mother and not being white—do you think she knew about that too?"

"Again, we'll never know. Does it . . . bother you?"

Leslie turned to look at him, mildly surprised. "You mean that I . . ." Her voice trailed away as she inventoried her jumbled emotions, trying to locate some shred of shame or outrage simmering just beneath the surface, but there was nothing. "No, I don't think it does. I'm still me. Adele Laveau was my great-grandmother. The rest is just ancient history. Maybe that's why I've been feeling so drawn to her, because some part of me knew. Do you think that's possible?"

Jay squeezed her hand but gave no answer.

"'When I gave you up to a new and better life,'" Leslie said softly. "The letter I found in the attic—the one from Adele's mother—spoke of giving Adele up to a better life. She meant a white life. But it wasn't a better life. It was just a different life, one that forced her to hide who and what she was. And then Maggie had to lie."

"It was a different time, Leslie. And it was the South. The scandal would have ruined Henry and taken Peak down with it. In those days if you crossed racial lines they'd burn a cross on your lawn."

Leslie turned her eyes up to him. "Or burn down your shed?"

"Or burn down your shed, yes."

Leslie closed her eyes and let her head fall back against the sofa cushions.

"It's hard to imagine, isn't it? Living a lie all those years, trying to fit into a world that wasn't hers, loving a man that wasn't hers, giving birth to a child, a daughter, that was never really hers. And then to die like that, alone and trapped. It's . . . incomprehensible."

The final word was little more than a choked whisper. A pair of drops squeezed between her lashes. Embarrassed, she brushed them away and turned her head. Part of her wished she'd never stumbled across the grave, never heard the name Adele Laveau. But even as the thought entered her head she knew it was a lie. Adele was as much a part of Peak as Maggie. Her heart and bones were buried in its soil, her echo trapped in its walls, and nothing would ever change that.

"You've had quite an afternoon," Jay said gently. "What do you say you go soak in a nice hot tub, then lie down for a bit? I need to go out to the barn and take care of a few things. When I come back I'll throw something together for dinner." When she started to protest he cut her off. "Go—you'll feel better."

Jay had been at least partly right. The bath did make her feel better, but lying down had produced no rest at all, only the churning and rechurning of the day's revelations. After half an hour she had given up, venturing down to the study instead. It seemed right somehow to be among Henry's things when his losses felt so fresh, to roam his sanctuary, touch the things that had both comforted and tortured him in his grief.

Pausing before the small cloth-draped table that showcased the old phonograph, she reached for the handle with its polished oak knob. It wobbled as she touched it, making the large metal horn lurch dizzily from its crane. Steadying it, she lifted the cloth to peer at the table beneath, only to find herself looking not at a table but at a battered old trunk turned on its side.

It seemed an odd use for such a thing, especially when the table near the window was much better suited for displaying a delicate antique. Curious, she lifted the cloth further, noting badly scarred corners and a plain brass latch, suggesting the trunk's original purpose had been functional rather than decorative. Kneeling, she squinted to make out the tarnished brass plate riveted to one corner. PARSON'S HARDWARE, NEW ORLEANS, LOUISIANA. EST. 1914.

New Orleans.

Was it possible she was looking at the trunk Adele had brought with her to Peak? After carefully moving the phonograph to the floor, she dragged off the cloth and wrestled the trunk over so that the lid faced up. It landed with a promising thud, clearly not empty.

She held her breath as she tried the latch, cursing under her breath when she found it locked. Moving to Henry's desk, she searched the drawers for a key, then for a letter opener or anything else that might be used to pick a lock, but found nothing. Not that she had the slightest idea how to perform such a task.

It took a moment to remember the ring of keys Goddard had given her all those months ago, and several more to finally remember where she'd put them. There had to be twenty keys on the ring, but only one that had any shot of fitting. To her surprise it slid home easily, turning with a rusty click. The smell of mothballs wafted out as she lifted the lid. Her heart thrummed in her ears as she pushed aside several yellowed sheets of the *Gazette*.

Beneath the newsprint, the trunk was crammed with plain, everyday things: dresses of softly worn calico, flattened hats and serviceable shoes, bedclothes and kitchen linens—and a weathered leather pouch.

Her hands trembled as she unwound the leather thong that fastened it, then reached inside to extract its contents. Letters. She recognized the faded stationery at once, and the cramped, scratchy hand. There were eight in all, tied up with plain brown twine. They were addressed to Henry. Leslie held her breath again as she tugged the knot free and fanned the letters out in her lap. They were in order by date and spanned more than a decade.

She lost track of time as she began to read, savoring the small details of a young boy's coming-of-age, of schooldays and spelling bees, bike riding and bandaged knees, of learning to dance and drive and play the saxophone. But perhaps more compelling than the letters themselves were the photographs included in every one, a progression that ran from a round-cheeked boy with tawny skin and a mop of bright curls to a man full grown, strikingly handsome in his United States Army uniform.

But what then?

Leslie studied the face of the young soldier, trying not to think about why the letters had suddenly stopped. Had he died? Had Vivienne? They would never know. A realization struck Leslie as she stared at the date in the right-hand corner of the page—*October 4, 1957*. The letter in her hand had been written a full ten years after Henry's death. In fact, several of them had. And yet here they all were, carefully stored together.

Maggie.

It made sense, of course, but the thought of it left her heartsick. Closing her eyes, she imagined Maggie opening letters still addressed to her father, reading, again and again, news of the brother who had been torn from her life. When she was finished she would have folded them tenderly and slid them back into their envelopes before tucking them away with the others. She had obviously never bothered to write to Vivienne of Henry's death, but why? Was she afraid the letters would stop? Or was she simply too proud to acknowledge a socially inconvenient brother, however loved? It was one more thing they would never know. Sighing, she refolded the final letter and placed it with the stack in her lap. They were making her sad, and she was tired of feeling sad.

The smell of coffee and bacon wafting through the study door was a welcome diversion. After retying the string of twine, Leslie slid the packet of letters back into the leather pouch and tucked it beneath her arm.

In the parlor she found two trays set up in front of the sofa and a fire crackling in the grate. She slipped the pouch between the cushions, on her way to the kitchen to lend a hand, when Jay appeared carrying plates heaped with pancakes and bacon.

"I'd think with your father here you'd have more in the house than eggs and soup. He's already eaten, by the way. Angie brought sandwiches out to the barn so they could keep on working." He handed her a plate, then the bottle of syrup beneath his arm. "I thought you were trying to fatten him up."

"I am, but all I can get him to eat are eggs and soup, so there's no point in anything else. I got ambitious last week and made a meatloaf. He barely touched it."

Jay grinned as he slid in behind his tray. "Sure it wasn't your cooking?"

"It was good!" Leslie shot back as she tore a strip of bacon in two and crumpled half into her mouth. "I did potatoes and everything."

"You seem to be feeling better. I'm glad you got some rest."

Leslie pulled the leather pouch from between the cushions and placed it in her lap. "I didn't, actually. After you left this afternoon, I went into the study and I found something. Turns out the table that's been holding up that old Victrola all these years isn't a table at all. It's an old trunk, and I'm pretty sure it was Adele's. I found this inside." She paused to hand him the pouch. "It's full of letters."

Jay eyed the pouch almost warily. "What kind of letters?"

"From Adele's mother to Henry. They're all about Jemmy, about him growing up. There are pictures too."

"Did you read them?"

"Of course I read them. They're wonderful—and they're sad."

Jay reached for the fastening, but Leslie stopped him. "Would you mind not opening that right now? I'm sort of on overload. I'd really like to just sit here and eat."

"Sure." Jay grabbed his jacket off the arm of the sofa and slid the pouch into an inside pocket. "They'll keep 'til later."

They ate their pancakes in silence, content to savor the fire and the quiet, but Leslie still felt on edge. After dinner she was going to break the news to Jay about her upcoming trip to Connecticut. The timing was incredibly bad, but it wasn't something that was negotiable. She also planned to ask him about finishing the book. With Landis and Annie Mae tying up the loose ends, there was no reason she could think of for him not to.

Jay drained his mug and set it on his tray, then shifted so that he was facing her. "So have you forgiven me?"

After the long stretch of silence the question was startling. "Forgiven you for what?"

"For believing Maggie could have set that fire."

Leslie sat back, sipping her coffee thoughtfully. Eventually, she met his gaze over the rim. "There isn't really anything to forgive. I wanted to be mad at you. I really did. But I couldn't. The more I saw things through your eyes, the more your suspicions made sense. It was too horrible to think about, but no matter how hard I tried, I couldn't think about anything else."

"Then why dredge it all up again with Porter?"

"Because I needed you to be wrong and because I was almost certain Porter could tell me you were. Still, I'm glad there's no more to know. It's all so unreal and so terrible. Think of it, giving up your child to the wife of your lover."

"We never really talked about that. Does it make you think less of Adele?"

The logs shifted noisily in the grate, sending up a fan of orange sparks. Leslie stared at the flames, tongues of orange and amber licking up behind the screen. It was a valid question, and one she'd been asking herself since they'd found the adoption papers. How did a woman give up her firstborn? But then, circumstance had left Adele little choice.

"I think a lot of things," she answered finally. "Mostly, how incredibly hard it must've been. But I don't think less of her. I can't. She was broke, and miles from her family at the height of the Depression. She must've been terrified."

"It doesn't bother you that she took the easy way out by giving Maggie up?"

Leslie blinked at him, startled by the absurdity of the question. "You think she took the easy way out? Jay, watching Susanne raise Maggie had to have been the worst possible torture, far worse than anything she might have endured as a single mother, even back then. She gave Maggie up because she knew she couldn't take care of her on her own, and because she loved Henry too much to leave Peak."

Jay tilted his head, studying her. "How is it possible you know so much about a woman you've never met?"

A small smile lifted the corners of her mouth. "It isn't hard to fill in the blanks. Under the skin we're not so very different—women, I mean. The heart wants what it wants. A friend told me that."

"And you believe it?" Jay's eyes were warm in the firelight, lingering softly on her face.

"I'm starting to, yes."

It was true, she realized. The heart did want what it wanted. And her heart wanted Jay Davenport. She'd known it since Charleston, perhaps even before that. But was she ready to open that door again, to risk her heart when everything in her life felt so completely upside down? She honestly didn't know.

The opening and closing of the mudroom door prevented any further musing on the subject. Jimmy had finally come in from the barn. She waited a moment for him to call out or join them in the parlor. Instead, she heard the heavy scuff of his boots moving up the back stairs. It was a slow, weary sound, and her heart squeezed at the thought of what might lie ahead for him, for them both.

"Can we take a walk?" she asked Jay, when she heard Jimmy's bedroom door close.

Jay looked at her as if she had suddenly sprouted horns and a tail. "Leslie, it's been sleeting on and off all day. It's freezing out."

"Please." She raised her eyes pointedly to the ceiling. "I need to talk to you, and I don't want to do it where Jimmy might hear."

Outside, all was glistening and frozen. The clouds that had been dumping sleet all day had finally begun to break up, shredding and sailing on an icy wind that stung Leslie's cheeks and made her eyes water. They said nothing for a time, shoulders brushing now and then as their steps crackled over the icy lawn. Finally, the lake slid into view, shimmering and iridescent in the cold moonlight.

Leslie took the lead, heading for the dock, her boots clomping noisily on the weathered boards. It seemed colder out over the water, the breeze stiffer, and she found herself wishing she'd grabbed something heavier than a sweater. Yanking her sleeves down over her hands, she stared up at the three-quarter moon, trying not to think of another moonlit walk, another dock, and wondering if Jay was thinking of it too. It seemed like a hundred years ago now. She turned, expecting to find him behind her. Instead, he was standing several yards back.

"Come in from there, Leslie. It may be icy, and I don't relish having to go in after you if you go skidding into the drink."

Leslie shot him a grin, but it faded as she walked back to where he was standing. "I need to tell you something. I know my timing stinks, with the opening getting close, but Jimmy's due to go back for his tests after New Year's, and this morning I told him I'd go with him."

Jay nodded, blowing on his cupped hands to warm them. "I think it's a good idea. He shouldn't be alone if the news isn't good."

"I also told him no matter what the doctors say I want him to come back with me."

If Jay was surprised, he gave no sign. "Did you think I wouldn't approve?

"I don't know. I'm not even sure I approve. All I know is he's scared, and I can't let him go through this alone."

A strand of hair blew into her eyes. Jay brushed it aside. "You never banked on any of this when you came back here, did you?"

Leslie shook her head. "Avoiding Jimmy was a big part of why I came back, so him living with me now is a little unexpected, yes."

"Maggie always said things happen for a reason."

"Maybe they do," she answered softly.

For years, she'd kept her childhood memories buried, content to leave them in the dark, untouched. In coming to Peak she had hoped to rid herself of them once and for all. Instead, Jimmy's illness had forced her to face them head-on, to look at them in the light, and ultimately, to lay them to rest. And in the process, she had stumbled onto fresh secrets, unwittingly exhumed memories that belonged to another woman and another time, secrets that after eighty years had finally found their way into the light.

A fresh blast of wind sent a shiver down her back. Jay noticed and took hold of her arms, rubbing vigorously.

"You're freezing. We should get back."

Leslie pushed his hands away. It was hard to think clearly with him touching her, and there were still a few points of business that needed tending.

"This afternoon, while I was in the study, I started thinking. Now that we know the whole story, if you wanted to finish the novel, you could. And you'd have the study all to yourself while I'm gone."

Jay threw his head back and laughed. "I wondered how long it would take you to get around to that. You made it all the way through your pancakes. I'm impressed."

"Don't j-joke." Her teeth had begun to chatter. "You can't tell me you haven't at least thought about f-finishing it."

Instead of answering, Jay unzipped his jacket and slipped it around her shoulders, then marched her back toward the shore. "Come on, you're freezing."

The jacket nearly swallowed her, but the corduroy lining was warm with his body heat. She pulled the collar tight.

"You're changing the subject."

"And you're turning blue."

Over her shoulder, she saw the lights of the Big House receding. "Why aren't we going back to the house?"

"Because the cottage is closer. And because I have brandy."

Leslie couldn't argue with that, content for the moment to let the subject drop until she could get her teeth under control. The close warmth of the cottage felt wonderful after the biting wind. Belle danced about Jay's legs as he bent to adjust the flue and touch a match to the wood in the grate.

"I'll pour us each a snifter in a minute," he called, heading to the kitchen with Belle at his heels. "I'm just going to let her out back for a minute."

Leslie slipped out of Jay's jacket and moved to the hearth, holding frozen hands out to the flames. She didn't realize Jay was back until Belle's tags jangled in the quiet. She turned to find him holding out a snifter.

"Thawing out?"

"Starting to, thanks." She sipped slowly, savoring the burn as it snaked toward her belly. "Can we talk about the book now?"

Jay reached for the poker and gave the logs a prod. "I don't want to talk about the book right now, Leslie. I want to talk about something else." He took her glass and set it beside his on the mantel, then took her by the shoulders, turning her to face him. "You said earlier that the heart wants what it wants."

"Yes." Leslie swallowed past the sudden thickness in her throat. "We were talking about Adele."

"What about you? What does your heart want?"

Leslie let her eyes slide to the fire, staring at the wavering amber flames. She could feel him staring, waiting for an answer. He was close now, his breath soft on her cheek, warm and brandy scented, leaving her faintly dizzy.

"I don't know," she said finally, softly.

"Yes, you do. We both do. And I need to hear you say it."

Leslie closed her eyes. "What if I can't?"

But even as she formed the words she was leaning into him, reveling in the thud of his heart against her ribs, the feel of his mouth closing soft and insistent over hers, driving away her last shreds of denial. Maggie was right. Things did happen for a reason, and Jay and this moment were part of that.

"Say it," he murmured again, his lips still warm on hers.

Leslie pulled back, feeling slightly off balance as she looked up into those warm amber eyes. "All right, I'll say it. I want you in my life. I want you to stay—with me. Is that what you wanted to hear?"

"It is."

The smile he gave her set little wings fluttering in her belly. She placed her hands on his chest, fingers spread. "I warned you once that I'm not any good at this."

"And I seem to recall telling you the same thing. I've heard, though, that practice makes perfect. What do you say we give it a whirl?"

Leslie nodded, feeling absurdly giddy as she pressed her forehead to his. "I still don't know how this happened. I certainly never wanted it to."

Jay pulled back, scowling. "Gee, thanks. Should I stop kissing you?"

Leslie slid an arm around his neck and drew him close. "Promise you'll never stop kissing me."

Chapter 48

The sun was well up when Leslie opened her eyes, splashing the pale blue walls of Jay's bedroom with late-morning light. The smell of coffee tickled her nose. Sitting up, she pushed the hair out of her eyes to find Jay grinning down at her.

"Morning, Sunshine."

Leslie propped herself on one elbow and reached for the coffee. "You really are too good to be true," she said, eyeing him over the rim. He was still in his pajamas, shirtless, hair standing on end in a way that would have looked messy on most men.

He reached out, pushing a strand of hair off her cheek. "Bed hair agrees with you."

A pleasant warmth surged into her cheeks. "I've got you to thank for that."

"It was my pleasure. Now, scoot over so we can eat." He pointed to a tray at the foot of the bed, then stretched out beside her, handing her a plate of toast and bacon. "How'd you sleep?"

"Like the dead," she said, crunching a piece of bacon. "I didn't hog the bed, did I?"

"Not unless you call a pair of knees in my back hogging the bed. Though I might just miss those knees while you're in Connecticut."

"You could always come with us."

"I wish I could, but it's bottling time. I can't leave Buck now. You could stay with my parents if you want, while Jimmy's in the hospital. It's a quick train ride into the city."

Leslie's brows lifted. "Without you?"

"My mother will love you. She'll be thrilled to know her son isn't destined to die bitter and alone."

A flutter of invisible wings tickled her insides at the implications of Jay's remark but she was too happy to risk breaking the spell with a lot of questions. For now she'd let it pass. "And your father?"

Jay's eyes slid to her breasts, lingering on the rise of pale flesh just visible above the sheets. "Well, if you show up dressed like you are now, he'll probably chase you around the kitchen. Seriously, though, if you're interested, I'll call and make the arrangements."

Leslie wet her lips nervously. "Speaking of fathers and arrangements, I was thinking . . ."

Jay's toast hovered halfway to his mouth, his eyes suddenly wary. "Yes?"

"I was thinking that if the doctors say it's okay, maybe Jimmy could move in here."

Jay put down his toast and brushed the crumbs from his fingers. "Nothing against your father, Leslie, but there's barely enough room for Belle and me."

"No, I thought—" She looked down at her hands, wadding and unwadding the sheets in her lap. "I thought maybe the two of you could switch places."

"Switch . . . as in I move into the Big House, and Jimmy moves in here?"

She still couldn't look at him. "If it's too soon, just say so. I know it's moving awfully fast, but I thought—"

"It's not too soon for me, but it might be for your father. Just playing devil's advocate here, but how do you think he's going to take getting kicked out so I can move into his daughter's bedroom?"

"Honestly?" Her eyes came up from her lap. "I think he'll jump at the chance. He reminds me ten times a day that he can take care of himself. And it's not like I'd be far away."

"You haven't answered me about the other part. He's not going to have a problem with me moving in on his daughter?"

Leslie rolled her eyes. "You wouldn't be moving in *on* me—you'd be moving in *with* me. And to tell you the truth, I think he's wondering what took us so long."

"I'm not the one you have to sell." He took her plate and set it aside, then pulled her to him. "Talk to your father. If he's okay with it, I'll tell Belle to pack her Milk-Bones."

Leslie spent the rest of the morning at the house, working through the packet of paperwork outlining Jimmy's follow-up appointments. When she had a handle on the dates and times, she booked two round-trip flights and hotel accommodations a block from the medical center. She was grateful for Jay's offer, but under the circumstances, she thought it best to stay close to the hospital, particularly if the news wasn't good.

She felt a little better with the arrangements made, more prepared for whatever might come. So did Jimmy. When she finally folded the papers and slid them back into their envelope, he gave her fingers a squeeze, his Adam's apple bobbing tellingly.

Leslie squeezed back. "Will you need help packing?"

He cocked an eye at her, the way he used to when she was little. "You know, I did manage to get there and back all by myself the last time. I think I can throw my skivvies in a bag." He pushed back from the table then, but before he could stand she stopped him.

"There's something else I want to talk to you about, Daddy. I was wondering if after we get back from Connecticut you might not want a place of your own. I was thinking you might like to move into the cottage."

Jimmy aimed one narrowed eye at her. "You're talking about Jay's cottage?"

"You wouldn't be moving in with Jay, of course. He'd be moving out . . . and moving in here with me."

"So, it's like that?" He pursed his lips. "The two of you?"

Leslie nodded. "He says he won't move in unless you agree. He's coming over to cook tonight, but I wanted to talk to you first."

"He's cooking?"

"He's a great cook, Daddy."

"Well, I guess one of you has to be." He broke into a crooked grin, wagging the eyebrows that were just beginning to grow back. "When you're young you think you can live on love, but sooner or later somebody's got to make the biscuits."

"Then you don't mind?"

"How could I? I knew he was the one for you the minute he threatened to kill me. So yeah, tell your boyfriend I'm okay with moving out to the cottage. Now, I'm going to scoot out to the barn to see if my varnish is dry. I'll be back in time for dinner."

Dinner was a pleasant and surprisingly comfortable affair, with conversation revolving around future improvements to the tasting barn. After dessert, Jimmy hung around just long enough to help with the dishes, then excused himself, saying he was tired and wanted to turn in early.

"He's leaving us alone," Leslie whispered as his footsteps faded up the back stairs. "Not that an early night is a bad idea. He needs to rest up before this trip. I'm worried about him at the airport. Our connection's pretty tight, and he still gets tired pretty easily."

"You could get him a wheelchair."

"A wheelchair? He won't even let me help him pack."

Jay flipped off the light and dropped an arm around her shoulders as they left the kitchen. "I wish I could go with you, but Buck needs me here. And I suppose I've got a novel to finish."

Leslie's head swiveled, her eyes wide. "You've decided to write the end?"

"I think it was the letters that finally convinced me."

"You read them, then?"

"After you left this morning. It's pretty amazing when you think about it. The woman had every reason to hate Henry for what happened to her daughter, and yet she made sure he knew his son was doing well. I left the pouch of letters on Henry's desk, by the way. I wasn't sure what you planned to do with them."

"I haven't decided yet. It doesn't seem right to shut them up somehow."

They had come to the door of the study. Leslie opened it and led Jay inside. "I was thinking that maybe you could write in here. Maggie would like it, I think, and it seems fitting to write the end of Adele and Henry's story here, where they spent so much time."

Jay ran a thoughtful eye about the room. "I don't know. Walking into this room has always felt like stepping back in time. I'm not sure how I feel about dragging a bunch of electronics in here." He crossed the room then, to the trunk that until yesterday had doubled as a display table for the old Victrola. He reached for the lid, then pulled back. "Mind if I have a look?"

Leslie shook her head. "It's household stuff mostly, tablecloths and curtains and things. Henry must have packed it all after she died."

As Leslie had done the previous afternoon, Jay pushed aside sheets of old newspaper, wrinkling his nose as he explored musty layers of sheets and blankets, old clothes, and even old shoes. Finally, he held up a yellowed square of lace-edged linen.

"He kept it all—even her handkerchiefs."

Leslie took the hanky from him, tracing the fragile lace with one finger. "I suppose her things were all he had left."

"Hello—what's this?"

Something in his tone caught Leslie's attention. By the time her head came up, Jay was already down on one knee, probing a tear in the trunk's cloth lining.

"What are you doing?"

He said nothing at first, his lips thin with concentration as he continued to probe the opening. After several minutes he teased out what appeared to be several sheets of folded brown paper and handed them to Leslie.

"I noticed a rip in the lining. When I slid my hand in, I felt these."

They weren't paper, Leslie realized as she began to unfold them. They were too stiff, oily smelling and musty. Instead, she found herself holding three unfinished paintings. In each, the face was the same.

"It's her," Leslie breathed, staring at the ripe mouth and honey-colored limbs, younger and more crudely rendered, but unmistakable. "It's Vivienne—the woman who posed for the Rebecca. My God, how could I have missed it?"

"I barely saw the tear myself."

"Not that," she said, rolling her eyes as she handed him the paintings. "Look closely, and think of Jemmy in his uniform. She's the spitting image of him."

Jay studied them carefully, shuffling the canvases and holding them to the light. "You're right," he pronounced at last. "The likeness really is uncanny."

"The first letter, the one I found in the attic, spoke of a legacy from Adele's father. Those canvases had to be what she meant. Which means—"

"Tanner was Adele's father, and the woman who posed for all these was her mother."

"Vivienne," Leslie said, her voice hushed with astonishment. "Her name was Vivienne." Her gaze settled on the Rebecca then, ripe and lovely above the mantel. "Henry bought the paintings because they looked like Adele, because having them on the wall made him feel like she was still here. At some point she must have told him about Tanner." Her eyes went wide suddenly. "Of course she did. They named their son after him."

"Jeremiah," Jay supplied. "Jemmy, for short."

"Yes."

Leslie dropped into the nearest wingback, letting this fresh insight settle into place. "The story really has come full circle, then. I could never understand Henry's fascination with those paintings. Now it makes perfect sense. It wasn't Tanner's work he admired, but what, in his mind, they represented. It's sad in a way, but beautiful too."

Jay was carefully folding the canvases along their creases, preparing to return them to the trunk. "We went all the way to Charleston and put Emilie Fornier through her paces, and all the time the answers were right here under our noses."

Leslie looked up at him, trapping his hand a moment in hers. "I'll never be sorry we went to Charleston."

Jay dropped a kiss on the top of her head, then pulled her to her feet. "No, me either. Now, what do you say we leave all this for the night. There's a perfectly good fireplace going to waste in the parlor, and I think I spotted a bottle of Merlot in the kitchen."

Leslie nodded, standing back while Jay closed the lid on all that remained of Adele Laveau's brief life. They knew it all now. And yet, somehow it wasn't quite finished.

"What do you think happened to Jemmy, Jay? Do you think he ever came back?"

"You mean to Peak? I don't know. It doesn't seem likely. If he had any memories of this place at all, they couldn't have been very happy ones."

"It would be an interesting story—don't you think?—to know what happened to him after he left Peak, to know if he was . . . happy."

"Leslie—"

"I was just thinking it might make a perfect—"

"The answer is no. I know where you're going, and I can assure you, you're wasting your time. I have the ending I was looking for."

"For this one," Leslie said softly.

Jay's expression was one of astonishment. "I haven't even finished this one, and you're already plotting a sequel?"

She shrugged, pouting prettily. "Never mind. It was just a thought." Turning off the desk lamp, she beckoned from the doorway. "Are you coming? Someone said something about a fireplace and a bottle of wine."

Chapter 49

Adele

I't's time at last to tell the truth.

Maggie is mine—or was—relinquished a week after she left my body. I do not think often of that terrible day, but I must think of it now. It is an awful thing to have to tell, and yet I find I must tell it. There will be no rest for me until I do. I made a devil's pact all those years ago, and the misery of it lives with me still, so fresh and raw it feels like yesterday.

To this day I cannot believe Henry could ask such a thing of me, to deny the mother's heart already beating in my breast, to surrender my flesh and blood to the very woman who stands between us. It is her way of getting back at me, I know, of getting her hands on Henry's child at last, and punishing me with the taking. I can think of no other life but the one I have here with Henry, however, and do what he asks.

Two days later I am summoned back to the study. Henry is there, but it is Susanne who sits in the large chair behind his desk. Her eyes gleam sharply as I step into the room, lingering greedily on my belly. She does not ask me to sit down, only slides two neatly typed sheets of paper across the desk and holds out a pen.

"Your name at the bottom," is all she says, and for a moment I think of running from the room. I think about it, but my legs won't move.

The pages are identical, I see, and I wonder as I take the pen from her thin, cold fingers, who typed them out. Who else knows I do this vile thing? A voice in my head, perhaps Mama's, warns me to be on my guard, not to trust a woman who could propose such a bargain, or a man who could stand by while it is done.

I force myself to read the words. They blur and swim before my eyes. *Contract to Secure Legal Adoption*. It is more terrible on the page, more wrenching because it has become more real now that the pen is in my hand. When I have signed both copies, she ends the meeting, warning me not to mistake this offer as anything but an attempt to protect the Gavin name. She will not have "her child" born under a blanket of suspicion. I only nod my head, too miserable to speak.

Maggie is a week old when Henry comes for her, soft and pink and unimaginably perfect. I wonder, as he takes her from my arms, if one day she will see me and know—somehow down in her bones— that I gave her life. His eyes are shadowed as they slide away from mine, his voice gritty as he vows that nothing between us will change. He could not see, even then, that all had changed already.

He is nearly to the door when I reach for my scissors. He says nothing, only watches as I snip a tiny wisp of dark hair from her head—all I am meant to have of her. And then she is gone.

After a while I make myself get up. I turn on the lamp and reread the horrid paper with my smudged signature at the bottom, then fold it into an envelope. I hide it in the bottom of my sewing box, where no one ever goes. I'm hiding it from myself because I cannot bear to see it. And because there is a part of me that does not trust Henry to stand strong in a storm.

Chapter 50

Leslie

The wind at the top of the ridge was stiff, and so cold it made Leslie's eyes water. It had snowed again during the night, not heavily but enough to cling to the scrubby weeds and bits of grass still dotting the rocky ground. Her boots crunched over the frozen earth as she walked the last few yards to the low gate and pushed it open.

Behind her, Jay cleared his throat. "Leslie, what are we doing up here? You need to leave for the airport in less than an hour."

Leslie clutched the nylon tote dangling from her shoulder. "You'll think I'm silly, but I woke up knowing there was something I had to do before I left."

"And whatever it is . . . is in that bag?"

"Yes."

Turning back to the grave, she went down on one knee, brushing a dusting of snow from the face of the stone. She didn't bother trying to read the words. She knew them as well as she knew her own name, knew them so well they almost echoed in her bones—words meant to bridge death and distance. And somehow, they had. That she was kneeling here now was proof of that.

Sliding the tote from her shoulder, she withdrew a rusty trowel she'd found in the tractor barn.

"Leslie?"

"It's all right," she said, stabbing at the frozen ground.

"Honey . . . what are you doing?"

"I'm making things right."

"Can I help you, at least, with whatever you're trying to do?"

Leslie shook her head. "This is my part."

She could feel Jay's frown aimed at her back, could sense his apprehension that she'd gone round the bend and was trying to exhume a long-dead relative with nothing but a trowel. To his credit he said nothing more, just hunched deeper into his jacket and shoved his hands in his pockets.

She should try to explain, she knew, but she wasn't sure how to even put into words what she was trying to do, and so she kept silent and kept digging. When she was satisfied she set the trowel aside. It had taken nearly twenty minutes to dig a hole less than one foot deep.

The wind rose suddenly, humming through the bare branches and sending her hair swirling about her face. She pushed it back, dimly aware of the gate creaking open and shut behind her, of Jay's boots scraping closer. She heard his breath catch as she slid the cigar box from the tote and opened it.

Jemmy's photos and Henry's book of sonnets lay inside, along with the green velvet locket case. She had intended to open the locket, to look one last time at Adele with her children, but somehow it felt intrusive now. Instead, she closed the box and laid it gently at the bottom of the freshly dug hole.

"Leslie . . . honey, what are you doing?"

He was only a silhouette when she glanced over her shoulder. "I'm going to bury it, the locket, Jemmy's pictures, the sonnets, all of it."

"Why?"

There were tears in her eyes when she met his gaze. "Because she's alone up here, and has been for eighty years. This box is her family: Henry in the book, her children in the locket. Nothing will ever make things right for her, but I can do this. I can give her this."

Jay intercepted a tear as it slid down her cheek. "What did you mean when you said this was your part?"

"You're telling her story. This is what I can do. I know it won't change how things ended. It won't erase all the terrible things that happened. But I need to do it." She reached into her pocket and held out a photo. "It's the shot I took for the label."

She lifted the lid and placed the photo in the box, aware of Jay's hand on her shoulder as she began to scrape the mound of earth back into place. When she finished she stood and wiped her hands on the front of her jacket.

"It's done."

Jay caught her wrists and pulled her close, planting a kiss on her forehead. She leaned into him, content to let his warmth seep into her bones and to share the rightness of the moment.

"Thank you for coming with me," she said into the collar of his jacket. "And for not thinking I'm crazy."

"Can I ask you something?" His chest hummed as he spoke. "Why include your photo? With the exception of that picture, everything in the box belonged to the past."

She stepped back but kept hold of his hands. "I've never been very sentimental, but I wanted there to be something of mine. I'm here because of her—all of this is. It was Adele who gave Henry his children, Adele who's responsible for Peak still being in my family. I didn't want this to just be about the past. I wanted it to be about the future too. I wanted her to know that something good finally came from all that love and pain."

Jay smiled and wiped a streak of dirt from her cheek. "For someone who's never been very sentimental, you're certainly making up for lost time."

"I know you're teasing, but I've been thinking. Most of my family's problems occur because we never stop trying to run away from home. Maybe we don't all pack knapsacks and hitch a ride out of town, but we find ways to do it. Adele left an entire race behind. Maggie spent years pretending to be someone she wasn't. Jimmy drank himself into a stupor trying to drown the voice of his conscience. And I ran off to the big city, hoping I'd forget I was ever here at all."

Jay lifted a strand of hair out of her eyes. "And yet, here you are, back for good."

She kissed him then, a warm, brief graze along his lower lip. "That's the thing. That's what I finally figured out. The past never dies. And no matter how hard you try, you can never really run away from home."

Epilogue

The Poison Moon was standing room only, the air humming with idle chatter. It seemed half the town had turned out. Leslie's stomach knotted. She'd expected twenty, maybe even thirty, but nothing like this. As she scanned the sea of familiar faces, the bell on the front door jangled and another string of guests filed in.

She took a deep breath and tried to focus on the strains of Celtic holiday music drifting through the shop. The place looked amazing, a wonderland of twinkle lights and evergreens and gold and silver ribbon. Deanna had gone all out, but then she wasn't likely to skimp when it came to a reading by Gavin's own Master of Heartbreak.

Young Buck had already found the refreshment table and was filling a pair of plastic cups with something pink and frothy, a star-shaped cookie stuffed into his mouth. Beside him, Angie looked vaguely frazzled, shooing Sammi Lee from the cookie tray with one hand, holding her rounded belly with the other. Sammi Lee's baby brother was due at the end of February and, if Young Buck had his way, would likely end up being called Baby Buck, despite his mother's strenuous objections.

The front door jangled open again. Leslie checked her watch. They'd be starting soon. Heading back to her seat in the front row, she dropped down beside Jimmy, grateful when she felt him give her shoulder a squeeze.

If Jay was nervous, he gave no sign, standing in the small clearing amid the sea of folding chairs, chatting with Deanna, resting one hand on a table groaning with copies of *The Secrets She Carried* waiting to be autographed. He must have felt her eyes because he turned and shot her a wink. Deanna snuck a look at the clock behind the checkout counter, then leaned in to whisper something in his ear. When he nodded, she stepped away, moving to stand beside the stool.

"Everybody," she called over the low drone of guests. "If you'll take your seats I think we're ready to start."

After several moments of rustling coats and clanking metal chairs, a hush fell over the room. Deanna smiled her bright pink smile and cleared her throat.

"First, I'd like to thank everyone for coming out tonight. I'm sorry about not having enough chairs, but we've never had this kind of turnout before. I hope we're not breaking any fire codes, but if we are, I'm counting on Sandra Toomey to smooth things out with her hubby, who is on shift as we speak."

She paused until the chuckles subsided. "As most of you know, we've had a bona fide celebrity living right here in our little town. Seven years ago, Jay Davenport—sometimes known as J. D. Hartwell—honored us by choosing Gavin as his home. I doubt anyone missed the recent notice in the *Gazette* announcing his engagement to Maggie Gavin's granddaughter, Leslie, who finally came home to us last summer. But what most of us didn't know is that for quite a while now, he's been working on his eighth novel, called *The Secrets She Carried*, and now, after years of silence from one of the country's most beloved authors, it's finally here—hot off the presses and sure to sell like hotcakes."

There was a premature smattering of applause. Jay smiled tightly, tugging at his collar as if it had suddenly grown too tight.

Deanna gushed on. "The best part is we have him here tonight to read an excerpt from that new book." She held out an arm, beckoning him forward. "So now, without further ado, please welcome our own...Jay Davenport."

Jay took a seat on the stool, nodding graciously while he waited for the applause to die down. When it did, he opened the book to the last page and began to read...

It's a soul-wrenching thing to live a lie.

God knows I've lived more than my share—but not with Henry. From the beginning he knew who I was, and what I was. There are lots of names for what I was. Quadroon, high yellow, colored—and lots more polite folks don't say in company. Henry knew them all. He knew what loving me might mean, but loved me anyway. If the good people of our little town ever guessed the truth about me—about us—it would have finished him. Not the breach of his wedding vows; plenty of folks overlooked that transgression. It's the other they would never forgive.

Forgiveness is a pretty word, flung down into pews on Sunday mornings, but in the backs of small-town shops and in the parlors of neat white houses, it is not so freely tendered, and harder still to find when it is ourselves we must forgive. And yet that's all that's left to us, really, when our fires burn down and our embers are all out, to own the choices our hearts have made, and not pretend we could have done different.

We are each of us dealt our little measure of time, set down on a road, and made to find our way home. But every man's road is different, every woman's, too, and the right way comes clear only when we're looking at it from over our shoulder, when for better or worse we have chosen at the forked places and must live with what we chose. I suspect, for those who never had to stand at such a fork, the way must seem very clear indeed.

It's a mean thing for the heart, straddling the fence between the known and the new, walking between worlds and belonging to none. Sooner or later the heart must choose. Mine was no different. I know now that when I got on that bus all those years ago, I was really just making my way home, to Henry and this place he loved with his whole heart. Peak is where I belong, where, thanks to Henry, my blood will always flow in the veins of its women, and my bones will always lie in its soil.

You've heard my story now—my sin and all its wages. I am weary from the telling but sorry for none of it. I made my choices and I have answered for them. Do I have regrets? Once perhaps . . . but no more. The heart wants what it wants, you see, and eternity is much too long for regrets.

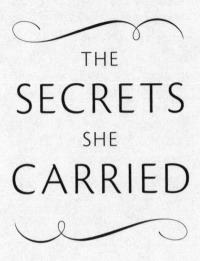

THE
SECRETS
SHE
CARRIED

BARBARA DAVIS

This Conversation Guide is intended to enrich the
individual reading experience, as well as encourage us
to explore these topics together—because books,
and life, are meant for sharing.

QUESTIONS
FOR DISCUSSION

1. Running away rather than confronting uncomfortable situations is one of the themes of the book. What situations, past or present, is Leslie fleeing? Are the potential consequences she fears emotional, physical, or both?

2. What other characters in the book are seeking to run away from something, and how does that avoidance express itself? What pitfalls do they encounter as a result?

3. In the early part of the book, the relationship between Leslie and Jay is tense and wary. What events eventually lead them to realize they may have misjudged each other?

4. How does Adele's voice (first person, present tense) contribute to the overall flavor of the book? How did you feel about her story being told from beyond the grave?

5. Do you have a favorite passage or scene from the book, and if so, what about it speaks to you?

6. The book includes two women who evolve deeply as a result of story events. Discuss how Leslie and Adele change, learn, and grow over the course of the book. What specific events lead to this growth?

7. Discuss Henry's strengths and weaknesses. Though Adele never stops loving him, how does her perception of him change as the book progresses? How did you feel about his decision to send Jemmy away?

8. How does Leslie's sense of family evolve over the course of the novel, and what events or discoveries specifically influence that evolution?

9. Discuss the concepts of forgiveness and redemption and how they are addressed in the book. Which characters require redemption and why? Which characters bestow forgiveness, and how is it shown?

10. *The heart wants what it wants* is repeated several times throughout the book. Do you see Adele relinquishing Maggie to Susanne as an act of strength or weakness? Does love justify any action?

11. At the end of the book, we discover that Adele is part African American and has been passing as white. How do you think southern society in the 1930s would have responded to someone like Adele, especially in light of her relationship with Henry?

12. The book closes with Adele speaking of the choices she has made over her life, as well as the wages of her sins. How does her assertion that we can only choose in the moment and then live with what we have chosen stand up to your own beliefs about life choices and regret?

About the Author

After spending more than a decade in the jewelry business, **Barbara Davis** decided to leave the corporate world to pursue her lifelong passion for writing. *The Secrets She Carried* is her first novel. She currently lives near Raleigh, North Carolina, with the love of her life, Tom Kelley, and their beloved ginger cat, Simon.